The Celebration Husband

A Novel

Maya Alexandri

TSL Publications

First published in Great Britain in 2015
By TSL Publications

Copyright © 2015 Maya Alexandri

ISBN / 978-1-911070-00-9

The right of Maya Alexandri to be identified as author of this work has been asserted by the author in accordance with the UK Copyright, Designs and Patents Act 1988.

All characters and events in this publication, other than those clearly in the public domain, are fictitious and any resemblance to actual persons, living or dead, is purely coincidental.

All rights reserved. No part of this publication may be reproduced, stored in a retrieval system or transmitted, in any form or by any means without the prior written permission of the publisher, nor be otherwise circulated in any form of binding or cover other than that in which it is published and without a similar condition being imposed on the subsequent buyer.

For those whose contributions to the

East Africa Campaign

have been unacknowledged or forgotten

*This palpable-gross play hath well-beguiled
the heavy gait of night.*

– William Shakespeare,
A Midsummer Night's Dream, v.i.

Prologue

How the manuscript came to be in my possession is another novel. The novel that I've written is not that story, but the story that (I think) the manuscript told. Inevitably, this novel is also the story of why rewriting the manuscript was an undertaking I accepted.

The problem was that the manuscript wasn't, shall we say, reader-ready. Technically, I suppose, it was in English. But it was an odd kind of English. If the manuscript was a record of a pidgin English, then the people who spoke it were likely bedeviled by chronic communications failures. If I was the first person to have persevered through the entire manuscript, I wouldn't be surprised; and I can't say I understood all of it.

Or maybe the problem was that, despite the inaccessibility of the text, I couldn't put it down. The manuscript loosed rare powers of evocation: the events described were manifest to me, as if they were my own past. As if my own past had come to claim me. The more I read, the more committed I became. The sense of honorable obligation to the people and events in the story grew in strength, until it found expression in my act of remaking the manuscript into this novel.

The mechanism by which I was captured by an antique manuscript and made to refashion it for readers of a century after its origin remains opaque. Sometimes, I fancy that opening the manuscript freed a djinn, not the wish-granting sort, but the more strident variety that thinks you're there to do its bidding. And, I suppose, if we gave the djinn the name, "Love," then we can all admit acquaintance with forces of the kind that lured and buoyed me along through these many years of labor in the service of a very elusive master.

— *Maya Alexandri, 5 August 2014*

ONE

The fifth of August, 1914, was the day that Tanya Rungsted's husband, Baron Isak von Brantberg, avalanched into the drawing room with the heart-stopper that England and Germany were at war.

"Whatever for?" Tanya asked, once she regained her breath.

"You have me there," Isak shrugged.

Isak's response made Tanya wonder if she'd overreacted to the news of the war. "The colonies won't fight," she hazarded.

"Kenya is fighting," he corrected her. And without further discussion, he rumbled off to a meeting of the Swedish settlers, convened to decide whether they should volunteer their services to the leanly-staffed and ill-prepared British Army.

They did.

The Swedish settlers' farms, their families, their investments (both of finances and of passions) – all were embedded in British East Africa, which had welcomed European settlers of all nationalities under the auspices of the Empire. Now that its German neighbor to the south, Tanganyika, menaced Kenya, the Swedish settlers stoked their fighting instincts and rushed to her defense.

Isak joined an *ad hoc*, "irregular" military unit. His commander was Lord Delamere, the leading nobleman of the British colonists. The unit's mission was to defend the border. As the border was more than 750 kilometers long, and the unit had twenty-four men, Lord Delamere hoped to enlist the aid of native Masai warriors as scouts and guards.

About the eruption that, within thirty-six hours, took her newlywed husband from her and to a situation of deadly risk, Tanya knew nothing more.

* * *

THE CELEBRATION HUSBAND

A week after Isak departed, he sent Tanya a telegram:

> MUST SEE YOU AND YOUR SUPERB PARTS, WRISTS, ETC. GO TO KIJABE RAILWAY STATION. TELEGRAPH BABU AN IDIOT, HIS JOB IS YOURS. IT WILL BE FUN.

Reading the telegram, Tanya flushed with contradictory emotions. She was elated at Isak's ardor and simultaneously mortified at his references to the carnal. But however much she cringed, picturing the numerous eyes that must have been privy to this telegram, she was also proud to be identified (almost publicly) as a compelling beauty.

Her pride, however, was quickly offset by her despondent suspicion that Isak had sent the telegram from the Kijabe railway station. Whoever the poor Indian telegraph operator was – in (racist) colonial parlance, "Babu" – he was not going to be her champion. Never mind that she knew nothing about telegraph machines.

Nevertheless, the most important fact was that Isak wanted to see her. Eventually, that imperative emerged implacable through the emotional uproar, and Tanya bolted from her chair. She waved the telegram, rushed around the house, and – between many confusing and astonishing remarks – ordered Hassan to pack their effects.

"Memsahib?" Hassan blinked, uncharacteristically baffled.

"Yes Hassan?"

"You are joining the army?"

"Volunteering. Like Bwana Isak."

"You are a Baroness," he objected, arms folded over his chest.

"Bwana Isak is a Baron."

"You are a lady."

"Who owes obedience to her husband. Bwana Isak told me to go."

"Sunstroke?"

"We all have a duty to the cause."

"What cause?"

Tanya almost said, "You have me there," but her impulse to educate and civilize overrode her urge for flippancy. "The cause of Western culture, Hassan, of Lord Byron, Beethoven, pre-Raphaelites —"

"— This Beethoven is German."

Hassan had her there. Tanya groped for a response amid a crowd of self-reprimands: she herself had been the Prometheus who'd brought Beethoven to Hassan; she'd regularly played the Fifth, Seventh and Ninth Symphonies for him on her gramophone; she'd even cited Beethoven's awe-inducing ability to compose while deaf as an inspirational anecdote. Now she had a sharp insight into her English neighbors who opposed education for the blacks.

"You speak German," Hassan added ominously.

If their conversation had been a chess game, Hassan would have check-mated Tanya with this point. His remark, though an accurate statement of fact, invoked the menace of British gossips in Nairobi who fingered Tanya as a German spy.

Tanya tossed her head and straightened her shoulders in an effort to maintain her composure, but she had a lump in her throat. She resented being bested by Hassan, and she was furious at the British and their ignorance. Hadn't the English looked at a map? Didn't they know that Denmark and Germany were neighbors? Didn't they appreciate that speaking the language of a neighboring country is not suspicious? Didn't many British speak French? (Well, she conceded, probably not.) Besides which, were the British totally unaware of history? Had the two Schleswig-Holstein wars between Denmark and Germany in the 19th century made no impression on the British? (Well, she conceded, probably not.)

Among the Danish victims of German military aggression had been her father, who'd fought and been injured in the second Schleswig-Holstein war, and who eventually died of complications from his wounds when Tanya was ten. But Tanya doubted that even her father's sacrifice would be sufficient to exonerate her from British suspicion of treachery. "Hassan," Tanya finally managed, "why can women be shot as traitors, but not as soldiers?"

"You are not a traitor."

"Tell it to the bloody bitches in Nairobi. They'd see me hang! That may be all they can do to contribute to the cause, but we can do better. Pack up."

"You are," Hassan paused, "mad."

"Didn't you tell me that Allah loves the mad?"

"We must hope so, Memsahib."

* * *

Reporting for duty on 14 August, our heroine and her entourage were an odd group:

Commanding the procession was Tanya, small and shapely, mounted on her mare, Scarlet, a temperamental reddish-brown horse. Tanya wore her beige cotton safari suit and her knee-high, black leather boots with flat heels. Wisps of her light brown hair sprang from under her safari hat. She'd had the outfit tailored when she'd gone on safari with Isak in March, and it was among the few items in her wardrobe suitable for war service. For Isak's sake, she would have taken out of storage her silk stockings, feather boas, petticoats, and bejeweled heels, and carted them to Kijabe, but Hassan had thwarted this romantic whim.

Although Tanya had dressed for the job, and not for Isak, her motivations were entirely opposite. She was the British Empire's first telegraph station manager who served for love, not of King and country (England wasn't her country, after all), but of her husband. This love, she'd discovered, was an instrument of transformation. It had remade her from a daughter of the bourgeoisie into a Baroness; from a resident of Denmark into a colonist in Africa; from a girl who'd been to a Parisian art school into the Memsahib of a coffee plantation. That it should now recast her as a military telegraph operator was a development that Tanya, like Hassan, might have been inclined to question; but with Isak's word to bolster her confidence, she averted her gaze from her misgivings and saw herself transformed by Isak's desires.

Hassan, the second-in-command of Tanya's little war party, held Scarlet's bridle and stood taller than the horse's head. Even without his crimson turban (which added an inch or two), Hassan exceeded six feet, and he appeared taller still because he was extraordinarily thin. Above his camel-hide sandals, he wore a gold-brocaded white cotton shirt and trousers (notably unsullied by the day's exertion in punishing sun). A

Somali, Hassan prided himself on his handsome, refined features: the elegant eyebrows offsetting his magnetic eyes; his generous endowment of lashes; his broad jaw, sharp chin and straight teeth.

Unlike Tanya, Hassan was not a Romantic; he was a businessman, like his father. Growing up in Mogadishu, Hassan had assimilated as background noise his father's constant stream of complaints about the damage clan feuds were inflicting on his business. Always on the cusp of the trade that would make him wealthy, Hassan's father was perennially undermined by an inopportune murder, culminating in his own. Hassan was second to none in his appreciation of Somali tradition and the imperative of slaughtering the members of one's rival clan; but he wanted to make money. Events, moreover, had aligned to confirm Hassan's belief that his enrichment was the will of Allah: as majordomo in the von Brantberg household, Hassan had the security, stability and opportunity to make his fortune.

Rounding out Tanya's warriors was Kamau, the cook. Taller than Tanya, but shorter than Hassan, Kamau was a Kikuyu tribesman, the single member of their party who'd been born in Kenya. Slender and young, Kamau had alert eyes and plump cheeks. He wore canvas trousers of a drab green and a yellowish muslin work shirt. Both his feet and his shaved head were bare. He was holding a rope to which was attached a disgruntled mule carrying a trunk, several boxes, Tanya's rifle and various cooking utensils.

Kamau served neither for love nor money, but for the spirit of adventurousness. He'd adopted a Kikuyu proverb as his motto: travelling opens one's eyes. Astonishing upheavals had occurred since the arrival of the British twenty years earlier, and Kamau was driven to journey through this remade world. Raised on the slopes of Mount Kenya to worship a god who lived at the mountain's peak, to be a warrior and defend his village from the cattle-raiding Masai, Kamau had shaken off the confines of his communal upbringing shortly after he and all the boys in his age-grade had been circumcised. To protect him on his journey outside Kikuyuland, he'd purchased a powerful (and expensive) charm from a witch-doctor; by force of this charm, he'd become the cook in the von Brantberg kitchen. Although cooking was woman's work, Kamau recognized the magic's effect: he was an independent individual, the first in his family, among the first such persons in his tribe.

The final member of Tanya's eclectic band had no motivation beyond canine loyalty. Dionysus, Tanya's cherished Scotch deerhound, followed Tanya, although he allowed himself leeway to deviate from her path to chase small animals. A tall, rangy dog with a wiry, brown-and-white coat, Dionysus was now engaged in annoying the already ill-tempered mule. Though the party had stopped, Dionysus was agitating at the mule's heels, until a spasmodic kick that nearly collided with its target convinced Dionysus to have a seat and pant a bit.

Gokal (the "Babu" of Isak's telegram), having rushed out of the station at their arrival, halted and examined his new colleagues curiously. An imperial servant of some many years, Gokal was accustomed to a certain degree of order in the world. He understood that the British Army would, of necessity, deploy "irregular" units in this war: August 5, 1914 had caught the military in British East Africa prepared for a native uprising, but totally unready for the challenge of a foreign war. The British Army lacked commanders, rank-and-file soldiers and logistical support – which is to say, everything. Without "irregulars," the Protectorate would be overrun with Germans.

But this assembly of wayfarers seemed especially irregular. Gokal had seen old men and young boys, British and foreigners, nobility and their servants, as well as men in all manner of dress – and states of undress – composing (and disorganizing) the irregular units; but the salient point is that they'd all been men. He'd never seen a woman "irregular," much less one as young looking as the female before him. (That Tanya was twenty-seven would not have assuaged Gokal; he was forty-five.)

Nor did her entourage balance out the deficiency of her sex. Somalis were notoriously unreceptive to discipline. And Somalis in Kenya were typically the cowards and rejects of their clans, who'd fled Somalia in the (usually vain) hope of escaping the blood feuds and tyrannical rule of their elders. As for Kikuyus, they were ranked low among the tribes of Kenya for military prowess – the British usually tapped them to carry cargo.

Nonetheless, Gokal was an optimistic man who had seen everyone from Jews to untouchables contribute to the cause of the Empire, and he saw no reason to prevent these three from offering their contributions. Indeed, their manifest unsuitability for war evoked a sense of protective indulgence in Gokal. To deny them the opportunity to serve – however they could – would disrespect their dignity. (Of course, Gokal's generous view was reliant on the fact that he'd been sick with dysentery the day Isak had sent the telegram summoning Tanya.)

Tanya (ignorant, naturally, of Gokal's convenient illness) met Gokal's gaze and then, uncertain, looked away and eyed her surroundings. The station was a squat wooden structure surrounded by corrugated iron shacks, sheds, piles of railway ties, wood and debris. Though bordered by thick underbrush that shaded into forest of pencil cedar and juniper, the land cleared for the station had been utterly stripped. It looked like a corpse, stiff and shriveled, disintegrating into red dust – though Tanya knew that, with rainfall and human neglect, the ground would resurrect the forest with fearful speed.

Looking beyond the station, Tanya absorbed the sumptuous Eastern Rift Valley: game-rich forest and fertile farmland punctuated by the voluptuous protrusion of the extinct volcano, Mount Longonot, to the west. Verdant green after the rains and dusty yellow during the dry season, Mount Longonot hid from Tanya's view Lake Naivasha, a vast stretch of fresh water so well integrated into the landscape that it often deceived observers into thinking it was part of the sky. Augmenting the Valley's grandeur were the clouds, transformed by moody and variable weather into actors in an epic drama, involving much darkening and glowing, rearing up, rolling about, thunder-and-lightning sound effects, and honey-cognac lighting.

Pitched midway on the escarpment that descends into the Valley, Kijabe afforded Tanya a prime vantage point for this spectacle. As her eye roamed the scene, grey and gold clouds floated at eye level, so that the capacious sky seemed to arch overhead and then drop below her into the Valley. Tanya had never before known the sensation of sky beneath her. Kijabe elevated her; Tanya felt that the scenery demanded that she present a better, more loving, more noble self.

Turning back to Gokal, Tanya asked shyly, "Who is in charge here?" She hoped to evade any awkwardness with Gokal by reporting directly to his superior.

Gokal furrowed his brow. He was a stationmaster, not a soldier. His boss was in Nairobi and, although Gokal had to defer to the military, no military was posted at the station. Captain Isak had meant to upend that situation. Incapacitated as Gokal had been during the Captain's last visit,

Gokal was definite about the instructions: military reinforcements were to take charge of the telegraph machine. However much this detachment could only qualify as "military" in a lunatic's army, Gokal supposed that Captain Isak could make anyone a soldier if he chose. Besides which, Gokal had had enough experience with colonial memsahibs to know that questioning one's authority was a mistake. "You are, Memsahib," he answered.

* * *

"It will be fun." Tanya studied the telegram intently, as if concentrated examination might coax a coded message to reveal itself. Less than two weeks into her Kijabe assignment, Tanya was already befuddled, disoriented and struggling for the Romantic gloss and noble approach to her experiences. Deprived of Isak's company and seeking guidance, she turned to a paltry substitute: his words.

Repeatedly she scrutinized the telegram, now ragged from having been too many times handled by her sweaty hands, refolded and shoved into her dusty pockets. But the telegram continually failed to satisfy. What could Isak possibly have meant by, "It will be fun"?

Tanya couldn't make Kijabe fun. Hunger bedeviled her. Game was the most reliable food, and it was typically too lean to sate hunger pains for long. Deprivation became a constant, and Tanya's hunger pangs expanded their scope, demanding fresh fruit, seafood from Mombasa, soft bread and sweet cake, wine, bathing in her own bathtub with lavender oil, talcum powder, clean hair, her gramophone, her books, bed linens, a restorative night's sleep, romance, her husband, Isak's company, his jokes, his body.

Discomfort dominated her existence. The conditions at the station were better than in the field, but only marginally. The outhouse was too foul to use. Living quarters were primitive.

Tanya's accommodation was a tent behind the wood pile. The tent was a simple contraption – a piece of canvas stretched over the crossbar of a metal "T" and tacked down at its four corners. The ground she covered with a blanket. Dust churned by trains invariably penetrated the interior. Shivering through the cold nights, Tanya was deprived of sleep by an oppressive number of bugs: spiders, beetles, mosquitoes, moths, ticks, flies and millipedes all demanded their share of her space.

Day and night the trains passed, and with each train came work. The offloading soldiers always needed assistance: return this cargo to Nairobi, post this letter to England, find these last-minute supplies for the field. And telegraph this message.

Tanya didn't know how to operate the telegraph machine, but Gokal had persuaded her to supervise his use of it, rather than to learn Morse code herself. Supervise she did: she sorted the habitual crush of soldiers clamoring to send messages, corrected Gokal's English on outgoing telegrams, rustled up replacement parts when the machine broke, and kept Gokal company.

She also handled the runners from the field; these native men bore information for conveyance to Nairobi and carried back to their camps whatever intelligence had accumulated at the station. The runners from Lord Delamere's unit assured Tanya that Isak would make the trek himself. But Isak had not yet appeared.

His absence provoked a riot of unpleasant emotions for Tanya. When she'd first begun relying on Isak's telegram for solace, she'd focused on its first sentence: "Must see you." But the contradiction between Isak's urgency in the telegram and the time he was taking to materialize in Kijabe caused Tanya terrible stress. Why didn't he come? Was he being worked day-and-night by Lord Delamere? Was Isak injured? Wouldn't the native runners have told her if Isak had been hurt (or worse)? Or had they been ordered to lie to "protect" her? To avoid these painful and (for the moment) unanswerable questions, Tanya had shifted her attention to the last sentence of the telegram: "It will be fun."

And although Tanya spent many hours attempting to discern what Isak had intended her to do in order to make that sentence true, she knew that Isak – automatically, as naturally as he breathed – could have made Kijabe fun. A mountain among men, he was a man around whom celebration coalesced, like clouds clinging to a peak. Isak was impossible not to love. Tanya's great impetus to marry him was her intuition – correct if the first nine months were any indication – that he could transform even a dour bourgeoisie institution like marriage into good time. Kijabe wouldn't even be a challenge for him. Dirt? He would lick it off her. Exhaustion? He didn't know what it was, and his ignorance was infectious. Wine? The man was so ingenious at maintaining a steady supply of the lubricant that Bacchus himself could have studied Isak's methods.

Tanya refolded Isak's telegram before stashing it in a hidden pocket inside her shirt. Ah, Isak, but that you were here, thought Tanya, closing her eyes.

"Memsabu," came a breathless voice.

Tanya opened her eyes to face Kinuthia, a barefoot, compact Kikuyu man, who was struggling to regain his breath. He was a runner with Lord Delamere's unit, and Tanya was startled to see that he was wearing Isak's hand-me-downs: blue canvas trousers and a cotton shirt, both too large and much soiled.

Tanya hadn't seen Kinuthia's approach. Rolling cloud cover on the escarpment had blocked her view of the Eastern Rift Valley; besides which Kinuthia's path was hidden in the foliage. Preferring her excitement (at a messenger from Lord Delamere's unit) to her disappointment (that Isak had once again sent a runner in his place), she greeted Kinuthia enthusiastically: "What's the news? Is it from Isak?"

Kinuthia nodded.

"Gokal!" Tanya called inside the railway station, where the telegraph machine was housed in a backroom. "What did Isak say?" Tanya turned back to Kinuthia expectantly.

"No telegraph, Memsabu," said Kinuthia, recovering his voice and straightening up.

"No?"

Kinuthia shook his head. "No, nothing for Nairobi. For you."

"For me?" Tanya asked and immediately blushed, thinking how indiscreetly Isak had summoned her to Kijabe. Now she braced herself for another embarrassing breach of privacy. How could Isak send a love message via native runner?

"Gather supplies and get a man to take them to Narosera River," Kinuthia recited from memory.

"Supplies? What kind of supplies?" Tanya asked, surprised – as well as relieved, and then disappointed – at the impersonal nature of the message.

Kinuthia retrieved a list from his trousers pocket and handed it to her. It was soggy with sweat.

Accepting the list gingerly, Tanya read, "Petrol, tins of bully beef, biscuits, sugar, wheat flour, corn flour, paraffin –" She broke off with a frown. "They want wagons and wagons of supplies. Who's going to take the supply train to them?"

"Isak said get a man," Kinuthia repeated.

"What man? They're all enlisted," Tanya worried. "The only men who aren't fighting the war are German sympathizers and prisoners." Tanya looked searchingly at Kinuthia.

He wanted to respond, "I'm a man." Instead, he adopted a blank facial expression. Kinuthia knew that, when Isak said "man," he didn't mean "man," but "white man."

Tanya seemed like she might be more progressive in these matters than her husband, but Kinuthia dismissed the possibility that anyone in the East African theatre of war – even a misfit like Tanya – would put a black man in charge of a supply train. The colonials didn't trust the natives. Even as a military enlistee, Kinuthia was forbidden to carry a gun – despite his long run across disputed territory – because the British feared a native uprising as much (probably more) than they feared the Germans.

Kinuthia's mask was possibly less vacant than he'd intended because Tanya's next remark was, "I wish I could send the supplies with you, Kinuthia, but I could never forgive myself if you were caught."

Kinuthia was taken aback and a little confused by her statement. Perhaps she didn't know, he thought, that he was wearing a magic totem to combat this evil. "To the Germans, I am invisible," he offered.

"Not the Germans, the British. You know the regulations. No one would believe that you weren't stealing."

Kinuthia looked away. Colonial mandate reserved rations of sugar and other supplies for white people; natives were forbidden to possess them. Kinuthia nodded. "They would think that, Memsabu."

Tanya sighed and then resolved herself, "I'll have to find someone. Where do the supplies need to go?"

"Narosera River," Kinuthia reiterated.

"Where's that?"

"Masailand." Kinuthia uttered the word with a combination of disgust and gloating: disgust because the Masai were historic enemies of the Kikuyu; gloating because "Masailand" now referred to the reserve onto which the British had confined them.

No less than for Kinuthia, the word "Masailand" conjured a complex response from Tanya. She'd heard much about Masailand from other settlers and, if what those settlers told her wasn't as nuanced and objective as might be necessary to term their intelligence "accurate," it was in any event the only intelligence Tanya had on the topic. And based on those settlers' reports, she was sure she could more readily find a volunteer to lead a supply train to hell. It would be cleaner.

The Masai lived in huts plastered with dung that were – unsurprisingly – always covered in flies. Their primary food was sour milk mixed with ox blood and urine, a culinary concoction that Tanya could not fathom being consumed by any creature with a sense of taste. Somehow the Masai had developed the notion that goat fat was good for the skin, and they slathered it all over themselves, with the consequence that they stank like rancid incense.

Amazingly, these hygiene practices did nothing to curb the tribe's decidedly non-Christian (and disturbingly frequent) sexual practices, which themselves were incomprehensible in light of the Masai circumcision customs. The Masai circumcised both sexes and left, in the female's case, almost nothing with which to work.

Despite (or perhaps because of) this deprivation of certain aspects of female company, the Masai warriors had – until the advent of colonialism – slaughtered all intruders into their immense territory, which included substantial stretches on both sides of the border that Britain and Germany had drawn. They had also demonstrated redoubtable skill at slaughtering the tribes in any territory beyond the areas they claimed. Their resulting reputation for fighting prowess endowed the typical Masai male with a stunningly arrogant attitude.

It had also inspired effusive admiration from certain of the male settlers. Lord Delamere, for instance, lavished unstinting affection on the Masai. It was Lord Delamere's opinion – much urged upon Tanya – that the Masai were now safely caged on their reservation, and that the necessity of foreswearing their warring ways had been impressed up on them . . . but Tanya didn't believe him.

Even if she could assemble the supplies, and find a man foolhardy enough to lead the ox wagons, Tanya doubted it would ever reach Lord Delamere. If the Masai simply stole the goods and didn't butcher the supply train staff, she'd consider it a victory for the British cause.

"Where in Masailand?" Tanya asked weakly.

"Far south. Near the border."

Tanya raised her eyebrows hopefully at the possibility that the supply train would be ambushed by the Germans and plundered honorably, instead of being barbarically destroyed by the Masai. "No map?"

"No map, Memsabu," Kinuthia confirmed. "I shall draw one?" he suggested helpfully.

"Never mind," Tanya shook her head, familiar (as she was) with Kinuthia's maps and the sorrow that inevitably followed any attempt to use one. A yearning for Isak gripped Tanya like a cramp. Isak: now there was a man who could draw a map.

* * *

"Hassan!" Tanya raced up to him, flushed. "Organize a supply train – this is the list of the supplies – do we have wagons?"

"Yes, Memsahib."

"How many?"

"Four."

"That should suffice. We'll need porters – take workers from the coffee plantation. We'll need about twenty, I expect, for four wagons. And find oxen." Tanya frowned thoughtfully; four wagons would need at least forty oxen – eighty would be better, though, if they were available – and the coffee plantation was already short of livestock. "Get as many oxen from neighboring farms as you can, tell them it's for the cause."

"What cause, Memsahib?"

"Not again, Hassan, please. We're upholding civilization against . . . well —"

"Against German civilization, Memsahib?"

"They're very brutal to their natives, Hassan. Anyway, the settlers won't ask, just tell them it's for the cause, and they'll understand. Oh, and we need a man."

"A man, Memsahib?"

"Yes, a man, Hassan. Someone who can lead the supply train through Masailand to Lord Delamere's camp on the Narosera River. Ask the natives if any *mzungu* men are left on the farms. If there are, they're cowards or German sympathizers, but ask anyway. I don't know of anyone, but you know how the natives always know everything."

Her generalizations about the "natives" did not discomfit Hassan because he did not consider himself a "native," a perspective with which Tanya agreed: Hassan, like herself and Isak, was an expatriate taking advantage of economic opportunity offered by the Empire.

Hassan also didn't consider himself black, although here he and Tanya parted ways. Hassan, like most Somalis, identified himself as a descendant of the Prophet's relative, Abu Talib, whose seafaring progeny had marooned themselves on Africa's Eastern Coast some time after the Prophet's death. The visibly apparent admixture of Bantu genes that had occurred in the intervening twelve or so hundred years did nothing to persuade Hassan of his relation with the natives of British East Africa. His obviously black appearance, on the other hand, did nothing to convince the British that his entitlements should be equivalent to theirs.

"Who is that, Hassan?"

Tanya, now that she had conveyed her orders, relaxed enough to notice that she had interrupted Hassan in the middle of a business transaction. She'd seen money change hands – not a lot – but she hadn't seen any goods, and now the man was walking away along the denuded land around the railway tracks. Like Hassan, the man wore a turban.

"My brother," explained Hassan.

"Which brother? That's not Aden. Has more of your family come to Nairobi since the war started?"

"My brother-cousin," elaborated Hassan.

"Brother-cousin? What's that?" Then, remembering that Hassan himself had three wives in Mogadishu, Tanya hazarded, "One of your father's sons by another of his wives?"

"Not in this case, Memsahib."

A motor started behind Tanya. The sound was significant because the Kijabe railway station had only one motor lorry, and it belonged to the British Army. Tanya turned to watch Hassan's brother-cousin driving away in the British Army's lorry. Gawking helplessly at the lorry rumbling down the rudimentary road descending the escarpment, she reflected that, in addition to forbidding blacks from carrying guns, the colonial administration might do well to prevent them from driving.

Whipping around to face Hassan, Tanya narrowed her eyes, flared her nostrils and thrust out her lower lip. "Hassan, you have just sold a lorry that isn't yours."

"Not sold, Memsahib. Rented."

"Renting is just as bad!"

"Not bad, Memsahib. Destined. We Somalis say: a dog that doesn't eat meat laid before it is not alive."

Tanya dismissed Hassan's proverbial argument with a wave of her hand and an exasperated cry: "That brother-cousin of yours is never going to return that lorry!"

"No, no, Memsahib. Bwana von Otter is building a greenhouse, and my brother-cousin takes charge of the construction. These preparations," Hassan added purposefully, "are for growing food for the British cause. My brother-cousin will return with the lorry tomorrow."

Tanya considered Hassan's story. Lief von Otter, like Isak, had volunteered for the war effort. His farm was at the base of the escarpment, just below Kijabe; and, like herself, Lief von Otter had a Somali manservant. (Indeed, many settlers with aristocratic pretensions had Somali manservants, a trend fueled by the Somalis' own view that they themselves were noble and superior to the Bantu "slave races.")

But even if Hassan's "brother-cousin" would return the lorry tomorrow, Hassan was still profiteering off British government property. Tanya felt sure that she would be held responsible for Hassan's wrongdoing, were it discovered. She imagined the gossip in Nairobi: "She was *pretending* to help the cause, but in reality she was *stealing* from the Army," with the knowing supplement, "She diverted the money through her *servant*." Seizing her brow with both hands, Tanya inhaled sharply and rasped, "Hassan, go back to the coffee plantation."

"Memsahib?"

"The coffee plantation. Get on the next train. Go home. You can't stay here."

"But the supplies?"

"I'll do it myself. Somehow. Go. Really." And then catching sight of the conflicted expression on his face – should he be insulted? Or should he summon a doctor to treat Memsahib's nervous exhaustion? – she snapped, "Oh stop it. I'd like nothing better than to get on the next train myself. I need a bath! I'm jealous of you getting to take one."

Tanya turned sharply and crossed the railway tracks with emotional strides. She was about to enter the stationhouse when Gokal hurried out of the corrugated iron shed that served as his quarters and stopped her with a question: "Memsahib, you are thinking of telegraphing?"

Tanya turned to Gokal with snort of frustration. Gokal, she knew, was well intentioned, but she was tired of his constant questions. What she was thinking of doing was none of his business.

Sizing up the kindly Goan, however, Tanya relented. Gokal was very thin, but he had a wobbly tummy that protruded from his abdomen and reminded Tanya of a soft-boiled egg. Although he was clean-shaven, unlike many of the Indians she had seen in British East Africa, his hair was in need of trimming. With his stiff mane sticking out in all directions and his expression of wild neediness to please, Gokal struck Tanya as a toy imbecile, a kind of village idiot for children. (She never would have conceived that he was an amazing catch in India – that women's families had feuded over him – and that his well-fed wife and educated children enjoyed considerable status among their peers because of Gokal's earnings and cosmopolitan residency on another continent.)

"I am thinking," Tanya said, articulating her words for emphasis, "of going back to my coffee plantation and taking a bath."

"Now is a good time for such thinking because the telegraph is not working," Gokal said approvingly.

Tanya glared at Gokal, but he didn't seem to be mocking her. Her sigh betrayed fatigued resignation. "Why isn't the telegraph working Gokal?"

"It is the usual giraffe gallivanting, Memsahib."

In constructing a telegraph line to traverse British East Africa, from Mombasa on the Indian Ocean to Kisumu on Lake Victoria, the British had failed to consider the low esteem with which the African fauna would hold their handiwork. If the telegraph poles weren't being eaten by termites or knocked down by rhinoceroses, the lines themselves were constantly being snapped by baboon acrobatics or giraffe migrations.

"Why couldn't the British have strung the wires higher than the giraffes?" Tanya groused. "Gokal, why didn't the British measure the giraffes and build the telegraph poles higher than them?"

Gokal gave the question the grave consideration of one who, in the Imperial scheme, would have been tasked with measuring the giraffe. "Memsahib," he answered finally, "by what method are you proposing to measure the giraffe? I am not feeling confident that a giraffe is easily measured even in death, on account of the stiffness and the decay stench and the hyena and the jackals and the vultures, and in life, a giraffe —"

"Gokal, send a *fundi* to fix the telegraph line!" Tanya burst out.

"Memsahib, it is impossible."

"Why?"

"With what am I fixing the telegraph line? Copper wire we have not."

Recalling the duty incumbent on Baronesses to maintain an aristocratic mien, Tanya composed her face in what she hoped was an expression of noble suffering, rather than mere hysteria. She straightened her spine, adjusted her shoulders and, in a sharply confined movement, tossed her head. "Gokal, I will find the copper wire."

* * *

"Hassan, get some copper wire," Tanya instructed. She'd found him in the Kijabe station storehouse, sorting tins of bully beef. After he didn't respond promptly, she added unnecessarily, "The telegraph line is down again."

As Tanya had a habit of banishing him, only to seek his assistance within the half hour, Hassan had learned that the best way to serve Memsahib was to disobey her exile orders. Of course, her banishments typically involved restriction to another part of the coffee plantation; never before had she commanded him to ride a train. But that extreme injunction seemed strictly a side-effect of their situation in wartime; and, as they both knew, that same situation made his presence all the more necessary.

Beyond being indispensible, however, Hassan was irreplaceable: as their service at the Kijabe railway station made too clear, human resources in wartime were even scarcer than baths. Nonetheless, Hassan's security in his position did little to reduce his inclination to show dudgeon.

"Where should I get copper wire, Memsahib?" he protested dully, still concentrating on his tins of bully beef.

"I know you can get copper wire, Hassan. You have to get it. For the cause."

"What cause, Memsahib?"

"Not again, Hassan! You know that the British stopped the tribal fighting. They brought peace. And to maintain that peace, we need copper wire, so you have to get it."

"Peace, Memsahib?" Hassan sat back on his heels and looked innocently at Tanya. "What peace are we enjoying with this European tribal war?"

"This is a great war, Hassan, not a tribal war!" Tanya bristled. "We're not fighting over goats and camels!"

"This fact is curious, Memsahib," Hassan conceded, evincing genuine interest. "A Somali wars for camels; a Masai for bulls; a Kikuyu for goats. What do the English war for?"

"Principles."

"What principles?"

"Peace. Ending tribal warfare." Then, realizing the ridiculousness of fighting a war over the principle of peace, Tanya blustered, "England and Germany aren't tribes! They're nations. Like Denmark."

"Like Somaliland."

"No, Somalis are a tribe."

"What's the difference between a tribe and a nation?"

As sincerely as Tanya wanted to extricate herself from Hassan's end-run around her orders, she found herself trapped. Hassan expertly played on her conviction that educating her lessers was a noble duty. "Nations have governments . . . and culture . . . and land boundaries —"

"And armies."

"And armies."

"Armies that cross oceans and conquer foreign lands," Hassan suggested.

"That need supplies," Tanya corrected him. "And communications. Which is why we need copper wire. Hassan, please. Getting copper wire is another opportunity for you to profiteer, so please just do it and get rich and go back to Mogadishu to your wives and your camels. All I want is a bath, and I'm stuck here like a prisoner."

"Memsahib, you must not stay here," Hassan agreed.

"Hassan, do you think I can return to the coffee plantation, bathe, and get back here by evening? If I catch the next train —"

"Memsahib, you must go to Malena Holmberg's farm."

"Why? Even if I take a bath there, I won't have a change of clothes, and this outfit is too dirty —"

"Because the man is at Malena Holmberg's farm."

"The man, Hassan?"

"The man, Memsahib."

"The man for the supply train," Tanya muttered, and her face crumpled. The morning's events had frayed her completely; and it was only mid-day. Biting her lip, Tanya internally cataloged: another day without Isak, another day without hygiene, another day without any recognizable pleasure – another day in which the war took precedence to everything beautiful and worthwhile in life. She felt herself teetering between a bath, on one side, and going berserk, on the other. The satisfactions and pleasures of cleanliness and the scent of soap – and maybe some powder and perfume – were all the restorative she needed. But she needed it. Or she could get on a horse and ride for an hour and half each way in an insane attempt to commandeer some farm overseer – who was no doubt a coward or a German sympathizer – for the war effort. For the cause. For her love of Isak. Tanya had to make her choice.

"He is the only man in Kijabe," Hassan added, not entirely suppressing an amused smile.

Gamely brushing the hair off her forehead and coaxing her face into an expression that she hoped passed for *noblesse oblige*, Tanya proclaimed, "Hassan, I am going to get the only man in Kijabe."

TWO

Malena Holmberg's farm sprawled along the floor of the Eastern Rift Valley for six thousand acres that stretched from the edge of Lake Naivasha out towards the escarpment. It occupied geography formed by a tectonic tear, a cleaving of rock that produced the dramatic scene of cliffs presiding over an undulating landscape of volcanic craters and flamingo-studded lakes. Left unmolested, the terrain boasted a magnificence of plant and animal life appropriate to an area that would come to be hailed as the actual Garden of Eden. (When, almost fifty years later, Tanya heard about the fossilized remains of ancestral humans that Louis and Mary Leakey were excavating from Olduvai Gorge, Tanya understood immediately that the resplendence of the Rift Valley had been the catalyst for those transitional monkeys to develop the brain capacity for aesthetic appreciation.)

Candelabra euphorbia – a satyr-like plant: half-cactus, half-tree – along with the ubiquitous flat-top acacia, provided Tanya with dominant images for her memory, along with the wild coffee bushes blossoming in the shade of the cedar and juniper forests. The shrubby whistling thorn tree and its bulbous, black, ant-filled galls was an abiding warning of the deprivation and hostility that could characterize the landscape if insufficient rain withered the softening cover of gangly leleshwa, skinny stemmed wild marigold, and purple-flowered Sodom apple.

The antelope in their many varieties – impala, Thomson's gazelle, dik dik, water buck – seduced Tanya with their combination of coquettish prancing and powerful leaping. She had less fondness for baboons and warthogs, both of which seemed almost cute as babies, but which degenerated into massive, ugly beasts as they aged. Tanya was also disappointed that the appealing smile of the hippopotamus was paired with a rude – potentially fatal – temperament. And leopards terrified her because they ate dogs.

Dionysus, who ran beside Tanya as she cantered through the Valley, was not allowed outside after dark because Tanya wished to avoid grieving her companion's fate as a leopard's dinner. Had he possessed the communication skills to convey his opinions about Tanya's curfew policy, Dionysus would have expressed relish at the opportunity to chase and fight leopard and would have shrugged off the risk of death as one honorable for a creature of his station. Precisely because Tanya intuited Dionysus' stupidity without being told, she kept him indoors at night.

Lions, in contrast to leopards, struck Tanya as lordly and (importantly) manageable because, on safari with Isak back in March, she had killed two. That safari – memories of which always surfaced when she immersed herself in the Valley's scenery – had been the most complete celebration of life that Tanya had experienced to date. Stalking game in the lush grassland, Tanya had near swooned from the vibrant engagement of all her senses. She'd struggled – happily, excitedly – fully to absorb the melodies of troubadour birds in the surrounding bush, the feel of moths purring beside her ears at dusk, the dwarfing sight of the expansive geography, the smell of warm dung when they were close on the trail of their prey, the taste of Isak's salty sweat on her lips after he kissed away her fear of the deadly animal she would eventually shoot.

The safari had shown Isak at his most glamorous. His unerring sense of direction, along with his ability to map the ground they covered in his head, prevented them from losing their way in the bush; and his impressive speed and accuracy with his rifle protected them from any animal dangers. Even his colossal form seemed proportionate in the immensity of a landscape that accommodated volcanoes, elephants and lakes that might be mistaken for seas; beside Isak in the wild, Tanya felt herself the "freeborn soul, which" – in Byron's account – "loves the mountain's craggy side." Accepting Isak's attentive lessons on proper rifle usage, listening to his ribald and intimate stories over the campfire, allowing him to sponge her off with the hot water that legions of porters had carried in buckets for her pleasure, Tanya thrived on the strengthening, health-giving effects of the undivided, loving attention of her husband.

When Tanya reached the Holmberg's property, civilization – or at least, an outpost of it – intruded on Tanya's recollected idyll. The approach to the Holmbergs' modest farmhouse betrayed some of the extent to which Malena and her husband, Erik, had not left the Eastern Rift Valley to its own devices. The diverse and chaotic conglomeration of plants had been cleared, and the floor of the Rift Valley itself appeared to have been trammeled into polite presentation.

Visible in the distance were rows of potatoes and maize – this year's crop. Last year, Erik and Malena had planted wheat and lost everything. Unlike the wheat, the potatoes and maize were at least surviving, but their market value was too paltry to save the farm from a second year of debt. Erik and Malena had been considering experimenting with grapes or apples the following year, but the war had halted all their planning for the future.

Tanya rode past a small pond, the byproduct of a dammed stream, which had been stocked with trout, courtesy of the colonial administration's permissive attitude towards invasive foreign species. What few of the Holmbergs' Hereford cattle remained, after the most recent rinderpest outbreak, milled (along with the occasional zebra) in an adjacent pasture. Goats and sheep grazed on the short grasses around the house, while scrappy chickens and lean turkeys pecked at crickets and stray specks of grain. A kitchen garden on one side boasted tomatoes, carrots, cucumbers, aubergines, cabbages, sweet peas and fennel. Potted geraniums lined the steps up to the veranda around the simple stone and wood house.

Malena and Erik were among the small group of Scandinavian settlers who, like Tanya and Isak, had taken advantage of the British Empire's hospitality. And because British hospitality can be variable, Tanya was grateful for Malena's presence. The population of British East Africa boasted some five thousand or so colonial administrators and settlers, and some untold million plus people from other groups – social and economic refugees like Boers, Indians and Somalis, as well as the innumerable tribes of natives like the Kikuyu, Masai, Swahili, Kavirondo and Ndorobo. In this polyglot and pluralism, the other Scandinavian settlers offered Tanya the pleasures of home.

Since her sojourn in Kijabe had begun, Tanya had frequented the Holmbergs' farm, and she'd managed to establish friendly relations with Ibrahim, the Holmbergs' Somali manservant, to whom she now handed Scarlet's reins. Tanya's cordial relationship with Ibrahim was an accomplishment, given the unhappy coincidence of Ibrahim's and Hassan's clans being enemies committed to the obliteration of each other's members. Tanya at first tried to broker an "immigrant's peace" that would leave blood feuds in the homeland. When it became apparent that the most likely outcome of Tanya's efforts would be the knifing death of one or the other of Hassan or Ibrahim, Tanya elided the problem by leaving Hassan at Kijabe.

A more devout Muslim than Hassan, Ibrahim shunned dogs, and he paired his greeting of Tanya with a vigorous hiss that sent Dionysus scampering after a long-legged, orange-faced secretary bird that was hunting snakes in the kitchen garden. Notwithstanding his rebuff of Dionysus, Ibrahim greeted Tanya with the respect due to the sister of the Memsahib of the house – or sister-cousin, as Ibrahim thought of Tanya, since she and Malena were of the same Scandinavian tribe.

For tribe mates, Tanya and Malena couldn't have contrasted more sharply in their physical appearances. Where Tanya was short, Malena had height; Tanya's hair was an undistinguished color offset with a limp wave, while Malena's was a fine-stranded blonde; and Tanya's brown eyes rested on Malena's light complexion: blue eyes, near non-existent eyebrows and pale thin lips.

Despite the physical differences in coloring and build, the friends were able to share clothes, thanks to Tanya's impatience with her weight. The moment a waistline buttoned with less than total compliance, the instant a bust was filled a smidgeon too completely, the offending garment was bequeathed to Malena. For her part, Malena was happy for novel attire and, since she rarely left the farm, she didn't mind shirt sleeves and trouser legs ending above her wrists and ankles respectively. When Tanya's weight dipped again, and she regretted her hastiness (shopping not being an activity that Nairobi supported with any vim), she sheepishly requested the return of her clothes. At first taken aback, Malena nonetheless complied and eventually came to view Tanya's wardrobe as a kind of rotating supplement to her own.

Now, as Malena greeted Tanya in an embrace, Tanya pouted, "I could use those twill slacks. The ones I'm wearing are filthy."

"You shall have them then," Malena smiled. Holding her friend at arm's length and appraising Tanya like she was a wayward sheep home from a night dodging hyenas, Malena concluded, "The good Lord is keeping you fine."

"Under His ministrations, I've lost enough weight. Anytime I complain about the war, please remind me that it's starving me thin."

"Surely not, dearest," Malena clucked, concerned. She guided Tanya from the wooden veranda into the white washed, sparsely-furnished sitting room.

"I'm not thin?"

"Yes, of course," Malena murmured soothingly. "But not starving, I pray."

"Game, game, game . . . and I have to shoot it —"

While Tanya talked, Malena signaled to her servant, Mugo, to bring tea. From a sideboard, Malena took a brightly patterned Swahili kanga – a textile she'd purchased when she'd arrived at the Port of Mombasa – and spread it on the handmade wooden table.

"— I ran out of bullets around Eid and wasn't resupplied until yesterday, so Hassan had to break his Ramadan fast with wimbi porridge. Thank heavens his imam gave him dispensation to eat game. It's not *halal*, you know."

Malena didn't know. Indeed, the significance of breaking a Ramadan fast with wimbi porridge eluded Malena – who had no awareness of the goat with which Ibrahim and his family had broken their fast – but the idea of starving for lack of bullets impressed her. "I've been remiss," she apologized. "I'll send vegetables to Kijabe for you. I'd send dairy, but we're giving what little we have to the soldiers. Between the rinderpest, foot-and-mouth disease, and East Coast fever," Malena passed a hand across her brow as if to wipe away memories, "I can only pray that the vultures will help the cause since they've been eating all the carcasses of our poor cattle that were supposed to feed the troops."

Tanya had drifted to a bookshelf on the opposite wall and was examining Erik's books, the only nonfunctional items in the room. *Diary of a Seducer*, *A Midsummer's Night Dream*, *Don Juan*, *Our Mutual Friend*, *Anna Karenina*. Tanya winced. She'd long ago memorized the titles of Erik's few books; she didn't know why she insisted on rattling the past with the titles on their spines. Desperate as she was for reading material at Kijabe, she couldn't read these books. Again. She'd had the misfortune to have read them all during her sojourn at art school in Paris, and Erik's books were consequently evocative of circumstances she needed to forget.

Mugo thankfully steered her away from any further thoughts of Paris by entering with the tea tray.

"Bread!" Tanya swooped, snatching a slice of toast off the tray.

"My most sincere apologies," Malena said, as Mugo placed the tray on the table. "We haven't had fresh bread since the war started, so it's," Malena counted, "three weeks old."

"Mold!" Tanya grimaced. She covered her mouth with her hand.

"Here dearest," Malena handed her a cloth napkin. "I am so sorry. Try another slice."

"Ugh," Tanya grumbled, balling up the napkin in which she'd deposited her mouthful. "Tea?"

"Again, my apologies," Malena frowned, pouring the tea. "It's a bit light. I'm afraid that, with tea in short supply —"

Tanya gulped the cup down before Malena could finish. "Bliss," she pronounced.

"— We sent our stores of tea, and sugar and flour and everything else to the troops —"

"— Now it's my turn to apologize, Malena." At the tone of Tanya's voice, Malena glanced up anxiously. Tanya plunged on, "That's why I've come, too."

"Kijabe needs tea?"

"No, Kijabe needs a man." Tanya jumped up and walked over to the curtainless window. She peered out at the assortment of thatched-roof mud huts belonging to the squatters – natives whose land the farm had been before Malena and Erik had bought it from the British government; natives who now tended the potato and maize fields in exchange for the right to continue living on (what they considered to be) their own property. Despite the latent potential for hostility about territory claims – a potential that was to lose its latent character in the coming decades – in 1914 Malena and Erik, like most colonial settlers, welcomed the squatters as a guaranteed source of farm workers in an otherwise tight labor market.

In the shoe-less, shrieking children of the squatter families, Dionysus had found friends. He was earnestly engaged in a vigorous game of chasing the children, while the children jubilantly pulled at the gentle dog's ears and fur. A crooked but formidable grandma interrupted the festivities to order the children back to work, tending goats. Tongue lolling and panting, Dionysus watched the children disperse, after which he reluctantly resigned himself to lying in the sun and scratching numerous itches.

Tanya was hoping to catch sight of the last man in Kijabe; but, if he was on the Holmberg farm, he was not within sight of the sitting room window. Turning back to Malena, Tanya explained the ox wagon predicament. "The natives betrayed your secret: you've managed to keep an able-bodied man unenlisted up until now, but – alas, I'm sorry – no longer."

"Ah, Mr. Baden," Malena nodded. "He's just arrived from South Africa, since you visited last. A poor Boer come here looking for work. He's not stupid that one. Mr. MacKinnon, our farm manager, joined our troops, just like Erik, and the good Lord knows we need the help. No, Mr. Baden is not stupid . . ." Malena's voice trailed off and her eyes adopted a far-away, transfixed gaze that indicated her unwillingness to speak of unpleasant topics.

"I'm sorry Malena," Tanya commiserated. "I don't know how you'll run the farm without a man, but I have to have him for this supply train. I'm barely managing without having to organize these ox wagons, and —"

"— I quite understand, Tanya," Malena assured her.

"I don't know how to do anything —"

"— Surely not, precious, you're very competent —"

"— I'm utterly helpless! Isak didn't tell me what to do, or how I'm supposed to run the telegraph machine if I don't know Morse code, and I don't know where Isak is or why he doesn't come, and I can't get the things Gokal or Kamau need. I have to rely on Hassan, and I don't know how he seems to solve all problems! That is, when he's not creating them. Did you know he was 'renting' – well, never mind. I can't even *talk* to Hassan, he has an answer for everything – I feel like an idiot —"

"— We never see ourselves as the good Lord makes us —"

"— and if you don't give me Mr. Baden, I have no idea what I'll do, Isak told me to 'get a man,' but he didn't tell me how, and if I don't have Mr. Baden, I have no recourse, no second-best —"

"— The Holmberg farm will soldier on, Tanya, don't waste worry on us. The good Lord has already seen fit to test us," Malena lowered her eyes, "with the assurance of financial loss for this year. I just wonder . . . Mr. Baden, as I said, is not stupid, but he's not . . ."

Malena's murmuring evasion piqued Tanya's interest. "Loyal to the cause?" Tanya hazarded. "He's a German sympathizer."

"Oh no!" Malena protested. "I don't think Mr. Baden takes sides. Not that I know him at all. But I'm not confident that you want Mr. Baden's assistance."

"Why?" The more Malena equivocated, the more curious Tanya became. "He's a coward?"

"I have no reason to believe that," Malena replied quickly.

"What then?" Tanya exclaimed. "If you harbor some objection to the man, do say so!"

"Oh Tanya, please forgive me," Malena burst out, rushing over to Tanya and enfolding both her hands in Malena's own. "Of course, take Mr. Baden. I pray that he'll be of more use to the cause than he's been to me."

"What do you mean?" Tanya asked charily.

"I've not had the impression that Mr. Baden is reliable," said Malena quietly.

"How so?" Tanya pressed.

"Have you seen him today?" Malena asked.

"No."

"Neither have I," Malena admitted.

Tanya raised her eyebrows. "Drink?"

"I dare not say," Malena shook her head and closed her eyes. "I don't know. But," Malena opened her eyes, "now the good Lord has seen fit to prescribe a path and a purpose for Mr. Baden, and we can only pray that he will find within himself the strength to maintain the course —"

"Nonsense, Malena," Tanya interrupted. "Hassan told me about Baden, and I've never known Hassan to be an instrument of the good Lord's prescriptions. More likely that Baden will be paying Hassan a percentage of whatever money Baden can make or steal off this supply train. But it doesn't matter. Whatever his drawbacks, so long as Mr. Baden leads the supply train, all will be well enough: our men will have their supplies."

"You are definite?" Malena confirmed. "You want Mr. Baden for this job?"

"Yes."

"Then I shall find him and send him to you."

"Saint Malena," Tanya thanked her and kissed her cheek. Then, grabbing a stale (but refreshingly mold-free) slice of toast, Tanya donned her hat.

As Tanya mounted Scarlet and whistled for Dionysus, who came bounding around the corner, Malena gathered her courage to ask the question she'd been deferring since Tanya had arrived. "Tanya darling," Malena called, running from the veranda to where Tanya was poised to ride away, "I know you would have said something if there was any news, but forgive my poor heart, I can't help myself. Have you heard from Erik?"

Meeting her friend's eye, Tanya felt immediately callow for not having given Erik any but the most passing thought since her arrival on the farm; but the topic of beloved relations was a sore one for Tanya. She tried to swallow back the lump that had just sprung to her throat; she missed Isak. Tanya touched Malena's hand where it clutched at the saddle. "No, Malena, I'm sorry," she answered softly. She feared that if she spoke any more loudly, she would begin to cry.

"I miss him so," Malena murmured, covering her mouth with her hand as if she'd betrayed a sinful thought.

"I'm sure he's safe," Tanya pursed her lips with determination. She took a breath. "I'm sure they're all safe."

Malena nodded and turned her face away to hide her tear-filled eyes.

"We'll both be with our husbands soon," Tanya said with labored optimism. "We must sacrifice for the cause."

Malena nodded again and sniffled. "Of course, you're right." Then, as Tanya tugged Scarlet's reins to go, Malena burst out, "Wait!"

Tanya pulled Scarlet to a standstill. From the corner of her eye, Tanya could see Malena fumbling. "Your trousers," Malena exclaimed, sliding off the article and thrusting it into Tanya's hands.

Her incredulous laughter almost pitched Tanya out of the saddle. "Malena! What if Ibrahim sees you?"

Eyes daring nervously, Malena whispered, "The good Lord will protect me from all peepers."

"Better run before He turns His attention back to the war."

THREE

"Memsabu, the Cumberland sauce."

"Yes, Kamau?" Tanya looked up and shaded her eyes. The afternoon sun, blazing directly behind where Kamau stood in the doorway, rendered him in silhouette.

"For the wild pig, Memsabu. I will cook the sauce."

Pulling off the telegraph machine headphones, Tanya was detained by the necessity of detangling them from her hair. She was seated in the closet-like telegraph room in the back of the Kijabe railway station. Stray railway ties leaned in the corners.

As soon as she'd returned from Malena's farm and stabled Scarlet, Tanya had ducked in to check on the telegraph machine. She was stunned to discover that it appeared to be working. Morse code was definitely pinging through the line, though she couldn't decipher it. Since Gokal wasn't in the vicinity, the message from Nairobi would have to be resent.

Although Tanya had agreed to Gokal's proposed division of labor with respect to the telegraph machine – he to operate, she to manage – she was increasingly frustrated by the arrangement. In it, she detected the implication that a woman wasn't smart enough to learn Morse code.

Such an attitude pressed painfully on the emotional bruises she still carried from her struggle to receive an education on par with that of her brothers. Surely, she reasoned, Morse code cannot be so difficult – Gokal learned it!

Gokal, for his part, had much respect for Tanya's intelligence. Her conversation consistently challenged and interested him, and she had obviously read many learned books. But Gokal didn't associate knowing Morse code with being smart; Gokal agreed with Tanya's fundamental opinion that any dolt could learn it. Tanya was not a dolt. Nor did Tanya, a white woman and a Baroness, strike Gokal as a logical recruit for semi-skilled labor. Typically, memsahibs oversaw the laborers. (Of course, Gokal knew of exceptions. He'd seen memsahibs cook and garden, milk cows and pick crops; he'd seen them shoot guns, drive trucks and manage money. But Gokal had never seen a white woman – much less a white noblewoman – labor on a task that she'd been trained to do by an Indian.) The idea of being replaced as telegraph operator by a Baroness was deeply perplexing to Gokal, and he wasn't quite confident that the whole scheme wasn't a trap. And so both Tanya and Gokal remained ignorant.

"Kamau, the telegraph is working," Tanya stated, baffled.

"Yes, Memsabu," Kamau replied impatiently.

"I have only been away for four-and-a-half hours," Tanya murmured. "I've never known them to work this quickly. Have they forgotten that we're in Africa?"

"No, Memsabu." Kamau hopped lightly from one foot to another.

"Where's Gokal?" Tanya asked. "Nairobi is trying to tell us something."

"Test message after telegraph line repair, Memsabu," Kamau replied.

Tanya narrowed her eyes in annoyance at this display of her apparent superfluousness. "Did you need something, Kamau?"

"Memsabu, the Cumberland sauce," he repeated triumphantly.

"Cumberland sauce." Tanya registered what Kamau had been saying. Just after dawn, she'd shot a wild pig at a nearby watering hole, and Kamau knew that Tanya like nothing better with pork than Cumberland sauce. His gesture to please was touching and, in light of war time shortages, near sorcery. "But how? Where did you find the port for the sauce?" Tanya asked.

"I traded Hassan for it, Memsabu," Kamau announced proudly.

"Hassan is a Mohammedan," Tanya frowned, although she didn't know for certain that Muslims were prohibited from trading in alcohol, as opposed merely to drinking it. She doubted such refinements of Islamic law would mean much to Hassan anyway. "Where did *he* get the port?" Tanya wondered. A rarity since the war's outbreak, alcohol had been beyond Tanya's reach for weeks.

"Memsabu, he got it."

This statement, Tanya knew, was as elaborate an explanation as she would receive. Tanya couldn't decide whether language barriers sabotaged her investigatory efforts, or whether obstinacy was the cause, but she had already learned from experience that no amount of repetition or rephrasing of the question would produce a more meaningful answer. Changing tactics, she parried, "What did you trade him for the port?"

"Copper wire, Memsabu," Kamau answered promptly.

His narrow focus on the Cumberland sauce had blinded Kamau to the explosive potential of this revelation. If she'd been confused by the speed of the telegraph line repair, and surprised by the prospect of the Cumberland sauce, Tanya was absolutely shocked that Kamau had been in casual possession of a commodity as valuable as copper wire. Had Kamau had some inkling of Tanya's response, he would have drawn out the moment of epiphany for even greater dramatic effect. Nonetheless, as the situation stood, Tanya's response was fairly gratifying:

"Where —" she sputtered and had to stop for a breath. "Where did you get copper wire, Kamau?"

"Memsabu, I got it."

* * *

As she approached the wood pile by her tent, Tanya braced herself against the air blast from the incoming train, and she raised her arm to shield her face from the flying particles. When she lowered her arm, she saw a bloated, round-faced sausage of a man standing by her tent. Tanya guessed that he was probably middle-aged, but sun exposure had ravaged his features beyond age identification. His greasy blond hair hung over his eyes, and scabs on his knuckles suggested punching-related activities.

Dionysus, who immediately upon their return to Kijabe had bolted into the surrounding underbrush in pursuit of a genet cat, suddenly materialized by Tanya's tent and growled. "Hush, Dionysus," Tanya chided, and then turning to the man, she asked, "Are you lost? May I help you?"

"Miss Tanya is it?" the man grunted, flexing and unflexing his hands.

"Yes, I am Baroness von Brantberg," Tanya answered, standing as tall as she could – a useless effort, she realized, as she measured her full height at the man's sternum.

"Miss Malena sent me." The man looked sideways guiltily, as if the fact of having been told to do something by Miss Malena was a shameful admission.

"Oh, Mr. Baden!" Tanya exclaimed, having forgotten in her recent conversation with Kamau the pressing urgency of the supply train. At Tanya's exclamation, Dionysus growled anew, this time escalating his throaty expression of displeasure to a bark. "Hush Dionysus!" Tanya scolded.

Unwilling to be dressed down in public, Dionysus bounded away, but not before lavishing on Tanya his most large-eyed wounded look.

Focusing her attention on the last man in Kijabe, Tanya smiled in an attempt to dispel the vaguely threatening atmosphere that Baden's presence, lurking around her tent – and Dionysus' negative reaction – had imparted. When Baden remained indifferent to her smile, Tanya inquired, "Are you ready for an adventure through Masailand, Mr. Baden?"

"Miss?" Baden grunted.

Even allowing that English was probably not Baden's first language, his persistence in addressing her as anything other than "Baroness" irked Tanya. "Mr. Baden," Tanya adopted an authoritative tone, "you are to set out before dawn tomorrow, from here, in charge of supplies to be delivered to Lord Delamere. I understand that he is camped on the Narosera River. In Masailand."

"A safari?" Baden grunted, apparently his habitual mode of communication.

"Yes a safari. But it won't be a pleasure trip, I'm afraid. The challenges of a safari through Masailand are, no doubt you aware, very serious. Water, for example – there isn't any. No roads, either. If you break a wagon wheel, you'll be stuck. Obviously, you will not be able to provision spare parts in Masailand. Then there are the lions. They like oxen for dinner and just try to move an ox wagon without oxen. And if the lions don't eat the oxen, they'll eat you. And if they don't kill you, there's elephant, buffalo, rhino, leopard, cheetah and wild dog. And, of course, the Masai themselves are a disgusting and dangerous people. Did you know they drink blood? But the risks are in some sense irrelevant because the journey must be undertaken. For the cause."

"For money, Miss."

Baden's quip reflected a facility with the English language that was more advanced than Tanya had expected. "Money?" she repeated, so taken aback that she forgot to be annoyed about his term of address.

"If Shaka Zulu didn't finish me in the Anglo-Zulu war, and the British didn't send me to my Maker in the Boer War, I am not expecting any skinny Masai is going to do me in," he pronounced, "and lions don't cause me no pause, either."

"Well, that's very encouraging," Tanya said, nodding agreeably with this confidence.

"But."

"But?" Tanya prompted him to continue, despite an intuition that she was not going to like what was to follow.

"I didn't do battle with Shaka Zulu for free —"

"No —"

"And I didn't take up arms in the Boer War for free —"

"No, I expect not —"

"And I'm not going to run a supply train in this war for free."

"No, why should you?" Tanya sympathized. "But you have to," she immediately corrected herself.

"Why's that?" Baden grunted, folding his arms over his chest.

"For the cause," Tanya explained.

"What cause?"

"Don't you start, too!" Tanya wailed. "You've been talking to Hassan, of course."

"Hassan? Who's that?" Baden grunted with, what Tanya thought to be, questionable credibility.

"We're all volunteers," Tanya explained, struggling to maintain control of her voice.

"Plenty of volunteer work for me to do in South Africa. I came here for pay."

"There's no money to pay you!"

"*Au weiderschein*, Kraut sympathizer," Baden grunted and pushed against Tanya.

"Wait!" Tanya shrieked, ignoring the insult and desperately grabbing Baden's arm. "Mr. Baden, please wait. How much money do you need?"

Baden didn't shake off Tanya's hold, but he stared down at her with an expression of contempt that a baboon might cast on a termite. "Four thousand rupees should do," he grunted.

Tanya gaped. "That's more money than Malena pays you in a year!"

"No Masai on Miss Malena's farm, is there?"

"But you said that you weren't scared of the Masai!" Tanya protested.

"That's why the price is only four thousand," he grunted, roughly extricating himself from her grasp.

"It's impossible," Tanya cried, scarcely concealing the tremor in her voice.

"*Au weiderschei—*"

"Wait! Wait!" Tanya yelped, throwing herself in his path and holding her arms out to block his passage. "You have to do it Mr. Baden. You *must*."

"Why?"

"Because you're the last man in Kijabe."

"Then there's something more important for me to do than transport supplies," he grunted and lunged at Tanya, slamming her into the corner of the train station.

The sharp blow of the building against Tanya's spine knocked her near unconscious, and Tanya staggered around disjointedly for several steps before she realized that Baden's body was no longer imprisoning her own. Attempting to focus her eyes, she eventually assembled a picture of her surroundings that, though unblurred, was nonetheless inexplicable. She identified Baden, but he seemed to be horizontal, prostrate on his back, although how he came to be in this unexpected position she could not explain. A foot on Baden's throat offered some clue, but allowing her gaze to roam from the foot, up the leg, over the hip, to the waist, chest, shoulders, and finally to rest on the handsome countenance of her rescuer revealed what could only be ghost or vision. Tanya shook her head in wonder as she goggled at the apparition of Hilary Gordon, youngest son of the Earl of Chillon.

But events were proceeding at a pace more rapid than Tanya could fathom. She heard the sound of a pistol cocking and realized that the apparition of Hilary Gordon was wielding the weapon. Then the apparition did something well beyond the scope of capacities that apparitions typically possessed (at least in Tanya's understanding of such matters): it yelled.

"I will murder you," came the impassioned cry – and Tanya was amazed at the apparition's ability to mimic Hilary's voice (so lifelike!), "if your pestilent hide remains in British territory by dawn."

Tanya wracked her memory of Coleridge's *The Rime of the Ancient Mariner* – her main source of information about apparitions, wraiths and the like – for an explanation of why this ghost was able to yell. Had not the Ancient Mariner's apparitions been silent?

> This seraph-band, each waved his hand,
> No voice did they impart —
> No voice; but oh! The silence sank
> Like music on my heart.

Hilary had read the poem to her, taught her to love it, taught her to know it by heart – and so she was sure that apparitions, whether singly or in bands, didn't yell; they waved their hands silently.

But no silence sank like music on Tanya's heart. Instead two shots – expertly placed to shear the cartilage off the tops of each of Baden's ears – wrung a scream out of Tanya. Then, with the yelling and shots that followed – Hilary admonishing Baden to run, and then shooting at the ground around Baden's heels – Tanya concluded that she was mistaken in thinking she'd been seeing the apparition of Hilary Gordon. She'd been visited by the man in the flesh.

And then his lips were on her forehead, and his arm was around her waist. "Titania," he murmured, twinning Tanya with the Queen of the Fairies in *A Midsummer's Night Dream* – a nickname he'd last uttered ten years earlier. Brushing her hair off her forehead, he continued, "You're all right?" he asked, pulling away to examine her face.

Far from all right, Tanya was quaking with emotions too intense to be pleasant. "I thought I'd never see you after I left Paris," she forced out of her throat as she willed herself not to tremble.

Hilary grinned impishly and clapped his hands around her upper arms. A lock of curly brown hair flopped onto his brow. "Never see me again? After all the Shelley that passed between us?" And then he passed some more:

> Nothing in the world is single;
> All things by a law divine
> In one spirit meet and mingle.
> Why not I with thine?—

Tanya blinked, scandalized by his implication. "I'm not single. I married a Baron."

"I heard," he replied dispiritedly.

"What are you doing in British East Africa?" Tanya asked roughly.

"Fighting a war, sad to say. Thomas, my brother, in Europe, and me here, we're both soldiering. Boring as public school, but I can't play hooky because I'm second-in-command of Cole's Scouts. Number one after Cole, you know. Thankless job, commanding Somalis. But they're the 'scouts,' poor devils, so my job would be even more useless without them. We just arrived on the train." Then, seeing her increasingly shattered expression, he urged, "Let me be of aid. You're shaking."

"I'm fine!" Tanya snapped. "Tell me," she said, taking a deep breath and steadying herself against the side of the train station, "why you chased off the only man who can lead the supply train that is departing tomorrow to provision Lord Delamere's unit in Masailand?"

"Because he thought rape was part of the job, Titania," Hilary retorted amusedly.

"Stop calling me 'Titania!'" Tanya ordered. "I'm Baroness von Brantberg!"

"Baroness," Hilary bowed his head and stepped backwards, "I beg your pardon. Arriving in Kijabe, the nice stationmaster mentioned the presence of a woman who I once had the pleasure of knowing, and I sought her out to pay my respects. If I can be of any service, please do not hesitate to say so."

"You can take the ox wagons to Lord Delamere," Tanya suggested.

Hilary weighed the proposition. "Our orders are to report to the Besil River fort immediately," he said apologetically. "Obviously I couldn't leave my company, much as I'd like to, and we cannot divert the entire company to deliver the supplies. I am truly sorry."

"Don't be," Tanya replied, raising her chin defiantly. "I don't need any help from you, Hilary Gordon. I never did, and I don't now."

"I understand," he said quietly.

"No, you don't," Tanya insisted. "You can't. You're not a serious person. You're just a troublesome dilettante with a talent for walking in on embarrassing situations. So – I beg you – save your trouble for the Germans and walk out."

"As you wish, Baroness."

Hilary vanished so quickly and silently that, alone in the dusk, watching the engorged sun yield to the allure of the mountainous horizon, Tanya began to wonder again if she'd seen a ghost. With the incoming night, Tanya felt the thick tangle of creepers, weeds and thorns encroaching from the boundary around the railway. The towering escarpment, which on some evenings had made her feel safely nested in the bosom of a tender giant, struck her now as a personal humiliation, reducing her as it did not merely to meager height and disfavored gender, but to total insignificance. Tanya shivered with a sensation that seemed like fear. Imagine meeting Hilary Gordon in Kijabe! After all these years . . .

. . . Paris still possessed a claim on her passions that she hated to acknowledge. After her juvenile delinquencies in Paris, she had trusted the good doctor, time. Time was supposed to have weakened the power of her past connections until the chains that had bound her to Hilary snapped or rusted apart; but time seemed to have been neglecting its duties.

Of course, time might be lazy, but Tanya knew that she bore a teeny bit of the blame, too. She'd been so mulishly adamant about being educated. She'd carped and complained about the unfairness of leaving her mind fallow until her mother had sent her to art school in Paris – a compromise. If only Tanya hadn't accepted! Art school was a stupid compromise: she hadn't learned anything, not even to draw properly, since all the women students were banned from the classes that used live models (who were female!).

And if she hadn't compromised on art school, she wouldn't have gone to Paris, and then she wouldn't have met Hilary, on his European tour, fresh from Oxford and eager for a pupil of his own. Tanya was such a hungry pupil and, as Byron had foretold, "glances beget ogles, ogles sighs," and so on.

But, as Byron's verse ends with "broken vows and hearts and heads," far better for Tanya's hunger to have gone unattended, unnamed and unsated than for her to have feasted with Hilary Gordon. If she hadn't gone to art school, at least she wouldn't have learned how uneducated she really was; nor would she have learned the little she did know of literature, poetry, music, painting, sculpture, geography, history, classics, sports and the tactile arts – topics about which Hilary seemed to know everything.

And, if she hadn't gone to art school, she wouldn't have met Grigory.

Grigory. Prince Grigory Kropotkin-Oblomov. A verse-inclined crocodile would be easier to find than a man less poetic than Prince Grigory, but how tempting was the notion of being a princess! What greater culmination of Tanya's romantic sensibility than to lead a life devoted to art, the welfare of peasants, and a temperamental, heavy-drinking *prince*? Most importantly, how jealous Hilary was of Grigory!

Of course, the role that Tanya's provocation of Hilary played in the ultimate rupture of their relations wasn't a matter about which Tanya showed particular interest. As far as she was concerned, the problem was Hilary's non-serious nature, which had caused him to fail to grasp the gravity of his offense, walking in on the intimate scene between Tanya and Prince Grigory.

Dionysus nosed his way out from the dusky undergrowth and trotted up to Tanya. Thorn apple burs were stuck in his wiry coat, and a wayward vine of creeping groundsel made an improvised wreath around his ears. Licking her hand, Dionysus presented himself for curfew. The warm, textured tongue against her palm coaxed Tanya back to Kijabe and, slowly, to the reality of her circumstances: she'd spent the entire day wheedling, ordering and begging, but she still didn't have a man to lead the supply train.

* * *

"Memsabu, it is very good you come," Kamau greeted Malena, as Malena dismounted from her horse, Pancake, tied his reins, and gave him a pat on the nose.

"I hate to ride after dark," Malena said, walking with Kamau towards Tanya's tent, "but thankfully the good Lord saw fit to give me half a moon on a cloudless night. I was worried when Mr. Baden did not send word or return to the farm, but then I thought I would come find him and ask him to convey a message to Bwana Erik when he sees him."

Kamau, who had been cooking during the entirety of Baden's misadventure at the Kijabe railway station – and who consequently neither understood nor cared what Malena was talking about – repeated himself: "Memsabu, it is very good you come."

A melodramatic resonance in his voice caused Malena to stop and face him. "Nothing is wrong, Kamau, is it?" she asked anxiously.

"Memsabu is not eating her wild pig with Cumberland sauce," Kamau replied gravely.

Malena repressed a smile. These native servants were adorable! Like little children, they so strenuously needed one's approval of their efforts. Poor Kamau had no doubt toiled mightily over his pig and sauce, and Malena pitied him: he would never comprehend the rationale of a woman obsessed with her waistline, for whom the most favored and beloved dishes were often the most damaging.

Having had experience with the vagaries of Tanya's appetite, Malena saw no cause for anxiety in Kamau's report. Looking at a hippopotamus could provoke Tanya to skip meals for a week, and Tanya had fasted almost to the point of fainting after Isak had made a drunken – but fond – reference to his wife's "full bottom" when they'd been on their hunting safari in March.

While the news that Tanya was now apparently fasting did not suggest a happy disposition, Malena had no curiosity about the cause of Tanya's unhappiness, attributing it to Tanya's regular neurosis about her womanly shape. Because Malena also did not ascribe to Kamau the capability of making astute observations about Tanya's psychological state by reference to her eating patterns, Malena was caught off guard by the shriveled figure collapsed against a log by the campfire, a plate of untouched food at her side.

"Tanya darling," Malena called, kneeling next to her friend. "What ever is the matter?"

"Oh Malena," Tanya moaned, almost falling into Malena's arms.

Malena embraced her and then seated herself so Tanya could rest her head on Malena's shoulder. "Tell me anything but that the pig and Cumberland sauce is inedible," Malena murmured and then, lowering her voice even further, "I don't think our kind Savior has given Kamau the strength to receive a bad review of his cooking."

"What are you talking about," Tanya muttered. "Kamau has been very sweet today. The food is delicious. He's a culinary genius. Have you eaten?"

"No, I set out in the late afternoon because I hoped to arrive here before dark."

"Then you must eat, Malena, don't let it go to waste please. Waste in war time disserves the cause."

Accepting the plate gratefully – Malena was, in fact, famished, a state heightened to the point of discomfort by the food's rich smells – Malena asked, "But why aren't you eating Tanya?"

Choking back her urge to confide in Malena about Hilary, Tanya opted instead for an explanation both true and evasive: "This supply train is grieving me endlessly."

Malena took the opportunity of chewing and swallowing to hide her relief. Her first thought upon seeing Tanya had been that Isak had fallen on the battlefield. She was pleased to learn that Tanya was merely overreacting to the regular obstacles with which the good Lord assists us in maintaining our resilience. "But why, Tanya? Surely the supplies are Mr. Baden's concern."

"Your Mr. Baden will be halfway back to Cape Town by now," Tanya snorted. "As you said, he's not stupid."

Malena put down her fork. "Tanya, what happened? Tell me instantly."

"Oh don't worry, Malena. It's not your fault. No, Mr. Baden encountered a deranged soldier, who shot off Mr. Baden's ears."

"Oh how terrible!" Malena exclaimed, covering her mouth with her hand. But, as she listened to the sound of wood crackling in the fire, Malena found that she could not repress her growing smile. Removing her hand from her mouth, she confessed, "Tanya, I am a sinner. This is horrible of me, but . . ."

Tanya glanced at Malena inquisitively. "What is it Malena?"

"I can't help thinking that Mr. Baden now looks like one of those Masai with holes in his ears!"

Tanya and Malena stared at each other for a moment before they succumbed to simultaneous giggles. The Masai *moran* – young warriors – widened circles in their ear lobes, so that in extreme cases the lobes hung down to their shoulders. Staring at the empty space between the now-stringy lobe and the remaining ear was always a flinch-worthy and scary experience, which made the opportunity for laughter even more gratifying.

Covering her eyes with her hands, Tanya corrected Malena on the particulars, "No, no, not like the Masai, Malena. Mr. Baden's ear lobes are intact. It's the tops of his ears that are gone."

"My goodness, fancy shooting!" Malena marveled.

"A waste of bullets," Tanya sniffed. "I have not witnessed a greater misuse of ammunition. Why you'd think that soldier thought ammunition supplies were at their pre-war abundance! A real disservice to the cause he is."

Malena was taken aback by Tanya's outburst, so she concentrated on eating. The food really was expertly prepared. The wild pig had been dressed with garlic and wild herbs and roasted in a pot that Kamau had buried over a bed of hot coals until the meat was tender enough to eat with a spoon. As for the much-vaunted Cumberland sauce, the dried currants, apricots and sultanas, plumped with the rich reduction of wild pork drippings and port, combined to produce a concoction that, Malena felt, could induce even a Mohammedan during Ramadan – even Buddha under the banyan tree! – to break his fast with relish. "These sultanas are delicious! Tanya," gushed Malena, trying for a fresh conversational direction, "where did Kamau get the dry fruit?"

"The last of our stores at the plantation," Tanya mumbled.

"And the port?"

The groan that Tanya emitted reverberated with such misery that Malena's hands shook. The source, Malena concluded, must be profound suffering. In a gentle tone, she urged, "Confide in me, Tanya darling, what is it?"

Tanya's refusal to name the cause was not, ultimately, a function of distrust of Malena. In truth, Tanya was simply incapable of admitting, even to herself, that the reappearance of Hilary Gordon had undone the knot of her life. She realized that she was unusually despondent, but – to the extent that she found any cause for her melancholia – she assumed it was the guilt of having to delay the supply wagons until she accomplished the impossible: finding another man. "Our husbands are going to starve before I enlist a man to take those supply wagons to Lord Delamere, Malena, and their suffering is my fault."

"Oh no, Tanya." Malena stopped chewing and shook her head. "No dearest."

"Who else's fault is it? Isak told me to find a man, and I've failed." Tanya sighed heavily and leaned her head against her hands. "I don't know what I'm going to do. Mr. Baden was the last man in Kijabe."

Malena watched Tanya struggle against tears. Then, putting her plate aside, Malena said, "Thank you for that meal, Tanya. It was so generous of you to share your food with me, and those truly were the most delicious victuals I have tasted in British East Africa."

Tanya shrugged. "You have certainly fed me when food was dear."

"And because I now know of Kamau's impressive skills and therefore have no desire to be too far from him, I have an idea." Malena paused to gather the courage to speak her audacious proposal: "Why don't we both go on the safari?"

"What safari?" Tanya asked, too tired and confused by Malena's roundabout approach.

"Let's go together to Lord Delamere. Oh let's do it, Tanya. Two women have to be near as good as one man, and we can keep each other company. And then I can see Erik!"

Taken aback by Malena's bold proposal, Tanya raised her eyebrows. "We can't do that."

"Why not?"

"Isak told me to get a man."

"There isn't one."

"But we can't go – there are lions."

"You'll shoot them."

"I can't shoot lions!"

"You've done it before."

"Yes, with Isak next to me."

"We'll avoid the lions."

"We can't avoid the Masai."

"The Masai are on excellent terms with Lord Delamere."

"We're not Lord Delamere!"

"But we're going to meet him."

"We could get caught in fighting between the British and the Germans."

"A hardship I'll happily endure for Erik. Oh, I know you'll do the same for Isak!"

"I can't lead a supply train."

"Of course you can!"

"No, I can't, Malena. I'm not good enough. No one listens to me. I don't know what to do."

"Ridiculous, Tanya. Look what an admirable job you're doing in Kijabe!"

"Unwarranted praise, and that's another problem: I can't leave Kijabe."

"What are you doing here that's more important than delivering food to our husbands? Oh let's do it, Tanya. Let's bring succor to our husbands!"

Tanya considered the expression of ecstatic enthusiasm on Malena's face. Love was driving Malena into this rapture. Tanya recognized the symptoms. For Isak, Tanya had thus far gone anywhere, done anything, changed herself in any way. Love had already molded her into a wife bearing little resemblance to her unmarried incarnation.

Guided by Malena's example, Tanya relaxed her grip on her fears enough so that she could capitulate to love; and if love had made her manager of a military telegraph station, why shouldn't it recast her, again, as a supply train leader? "All right, Malena."

"Truly?"

"Truly. It will be fun."

"Oh Tanya!" Malena clapped her hands together as if about to engage in fervent prayer. Envisioning Erik enfolding her in his arms, Malena smiled up at the night sky, a diamond-crowded canopy of black velvet that reflected back in her joyous eyes.

More earthbound in her outlook, Tanya looked away and sighed. She'd said, "It will be fun," impulsively – as a way to invoke Isak and his blessing for their journey – but she didn't believe it. Far from anticipating an enjoyable adventure, Tanya felt that she was heading off a map into an unknown – which would be scary enough, but Tanya also intuited that acquaintance with this unknown was not going to be a happy event.

Well, at least, she consoled herself, if I die on this supply mission I'll never again see Hilary Gordon.

FOUR

Tanya spent a sleepless night worrying about Isak. She feared that he was becoming emaciated from hunger. Knowing how cold the Eastern Rift Valley was at night, Tanya hoped that Isak had enough warm clothing and blankets. The thought that he'd been wounded startled her eyes open.

Tanya dimly perceived Malena beside her and felt covetous of the rapturous relaxation that characterized Malena's sleeping form. Tanya rolled over and closed her eyes again.

Fresh anxieties greeted her: was there any quinine available if Isak had contracted malaria? What if Isak couldn't endure the physical rigors of military operations in the bush? Who would reassemble Isak's limbs if he'd been torn apart by a lion? But even Tanya, as self-deceiving as she sometimes was, couldn't wholly avoid the knowledge that these various fears were surrogates for a single underlying concern: what would Isak do if his wife loved another man?

Four a.m. therefore found Tanya grateful for the opportunity to wake Malena, dress and make final preparations for their departure. Kamau brewed tea for his Memsabus over a fire he'd built outside their tent, after which he dismantled the tent and gave it to the porters to stow in the ox wagons. Hassan gave Tanya an inventory of the ox wagons to compare with the list of requested supplies. At Tanya's request, Gokal requisitioned two mules for Tanya and Malena to ride. (As eager as she was to serve the cause, Tanya did not want to risk having the British Army – which was desperately short of horses – confiscate Scarlet and Pancake.)

Sipping her tea, Malena discerned bats flitting above her. Shivering – Malena loathed bats – she finished her tea in a gulp. Then she jumped up and crossed the railway tracks to offer her assistance to Kamau and the twenty porters, who were readying the supply train for its imminent safari. Upon her arrival, the porters ceased their conversation in Swahili, but Malena nonetheless sensed its gist.

"You are all very brave to be venturing into Masailand," she marveled brightly.

Kamau retorted with a Kikuyu adage, "Death is not something you meet by appointment." All the same, as he worked, he was alert for birdcalls. Notwithstanding his distance from Kikuyuland, Kamau couldn't reject the Kikuyu belief that a journey must be aborted if a bird cry is heard at its outset. Death might not keep a date book, but Kamau saw little point in ignoring the bird's warning of death's proximity.

One of the porters, a recent convert to Christianity, placed less stock in received Kikuyu wisdom: "We rely on the protection of Jesus," he said.

Malena agreed readily: "And He shall not fail us."

"Masai *moran* slaughtered my aunt like a sheep," another of the porters informed Malena.

Malena stared dumbly, unable to read the porter's expression. She knew that the Masai were the historic enemies of all the surrounding tribes, from whose ranks Tanya had drawn her farm workers and porters. But for Malena, "historic enemies" were like Sweden and Russia; and she'd never seen a relative murdered by a Russian. She was so stunned that she fumbled for the consoling word. "The blessings of the good Lord upon you and yours," she murmured eventually.

The man turned away, and the crowd of porters resumed discussing in Swahili the madness of trekking through Masailand with a pair of *mzungu* women.

Across the railway tracks, Hassan crouched beside Tanya who was reviewing the supply list and the inventory by the campfire light. When she turned to glance at him, he whispered, "Memsahib, you must keep this on your person. Secretly!" He widened his eyes for emphasis.

Into Tanya's hands, Hassan thrust a small velvet bag with a drawstring closure. Putting aside the lists, Tanya opened the bag.

Inside was an oval picture frame containing the sepia-toned visage of Lieutenant-Colonel Paul Emil von Lettow-Vorbeck, the high commander of the German East African forces. The photo was inscribed and signed. Hassan didn't speak German, but he guessed with fair accuracy at the meaning of the writing, which was (as he'd hoped and feared) evidence of a connection distinguished by reciprocal affection and esteem: "Dearest Tanya, Your charm, wit, intelligence and social graces have rescued me from many a restless hour, and for that noble service I remain, Your faithful servant, Paul."

"Where did you find this?" Tanya demanded. Despite the sharp cold, Tanya felt suddenly hot; she hoped that the blush that was spreading up her neck and across her cheeks wasn't visible in the pre-dawn darkness.

"Quietly, Memsahib," Hassan cautioned, gesturing to their compatriots across the railway track. "It was in your boudoir."

"Yes, I know it *was* in my boudoir. What is it doing here?" Tanya stood and stared angrily down at Hassan.

Her power play lasted less than a second because Hassan rose also and, tall as he was, standing was a position from which he could only look down on Tanya. He did so with none of her hostility, however. "Memsahib," he explained in muted, but intense, voice, "for your safety. I took it to Kijabe in case of German attack on the train station."

This impressive display of Hassan's foresight silenced Tanya. German troops were unlikely to harm a woman (and a German speaker) carrying an inscribed photograph of their leader. Tanya wished she'd thought to bring the picture herself.

It had lain among her silk dress stockings – articles of clothing that she'd brought from Denmark under an upbeat misimpression that opportunities to wear such fineries would abound.

The photograph of von Lettow-Vorbeck had been mixed among Tanya's underclothes, not because of a mutual association with intimacy, but because both the stockings and the picture were items that she had scarcely touched since disembarking from the *S.S. Annus Mirabilis* in Mombasa. Von Lettow-Vorbeck had been a fellow passenger on her maiden journey to Africa and, as they had been the only German speakers on board, he had naturally gravitated to her company. (From the perspective of linguistic compatibility, Tanya, of course, had had many other potential partners for socializing, but none was as cultured – or as fully possessed of the skills appropriate to a consort of a noblewoman – as the dignified German military leader.)

Despite having allowed his picture to remain sequestered and neglected in a rarely-opened drawer, however, Tanya had not in any sense forgotten the man. In fact, she'd maintained a lively, if sporadic, correspondence with him over the nine months since they'd last seen one another. The outbreak of war and the consequent cessation of mail service between the British and German East African territories had left unresolved their debate as to whether Beethoven was "vulgar and formulaic" (von Lettow-Vorbeck) or "evocative of passions not typically responsive to restraint" (Tanya).

Tanya had felt herself at a loss when, for reasons both pragmatic and, she guessed, habitual – her father *had*, after all, fought the Germans – she found it necessary to take a political (and military) stance directly opposed to a man for whom she felt so great a personal affinity. Her position in the war made her mildly embarrassed; Denmark was neutral, but she had chosen sides. She was almost inclined to apologize to von Lettow-Vorbeck – although when she gave the matter any sustained thought, she concluded (hoped... fervently) that he would not think that any apology from her was necessary.

Perhaps because of her ambivalence, and (obviously) because of the eagerness of her British neighbors to tar her as a German sympathizer, Tanya had – since the outbreak of the war – conveniently forgotten that she had a picture of the enemy chief. Hassan, apparently, had not. (Although why and how he'd come to be aware of the photograph's presence among Tanya's underclothes was a matter Tanya would have to explore with him at a more opportune moment.)

"You should have asked me," Tanya frowned.

"I acted for your wellbeing, Memsahib."

"For your own wellbeing, too," she countered, defensive. "You've taken a liberty with my personal items for your own safety."

"I rely on Allah alone for my wellbeing," Hassan corrected her. "Your infidel photograph is as nothing to my safety."

The confidence Hassan derived from his fatalism annoyed Tanya; it made any expression of fear on her part impossible. Yet she was frightened. "The Masai are a murderous tribe," she warned him. "You swagger foolishly. It could be your death."

"If it is the will of Allah, God is great. I fear no death. If death descends to wrestle with me, my contempt will be like a knife in his ribs." The freight of his righteousness caused Hassan's voice to crescendo, and his eyes commanded Tanya's gaze: they were pulsing.

"You are mad."

"Allah loves a madman."

"We must hope so, Hassan." Tanya slipped the photograph into her inside shirt pocket. Whatever Hassan claimed, his welfare – and the welfare of their entire supply train – depended on Tanya's ability to navigate their caravan past the Germans; she could not refuse any instrument that might help her do so.

The photograph safely hidden, Tanya held out her hand, and Hassan assisted her to rise. "Hassan," she said, as they made their way across the railway tracks to where the ox wagons awaited them, "I have a request."

"Yes, Memsahib."

"If death comes for me, loan me your contempt."

* * *

Dawn in the Eastern Rift Valley is an event not easily described without invocation of the holy. The cradle of the Valley is a favorite resting place for weary clouds. They pile together, each the pillow for the one atop. When the sun rises, it reveals a scene of heaven descended to earth. Over this cherubim bed, rays of the sun roam in ever-greater profusion, tickling the clouds into a softly rolling golden-tinged froth.

Bearing witness to this splendor, Tanya felt a kinship with Malena, who stopped to cross herself at (what she took to be) the miracle unfolding before her. But Tanya's sense of kinship extended also to Hassan, who was already shading his eyes; and to Kamau, for whom the sunrise represented release from the cold that had caged him since he'd awakened; and to the porters, none of whom dared stop to enjoy the sunrise for fear of rebuke; and to Dionysus, who was oblivious to the sunrise as his attention was focused on a hare in the underbrush; and to the nocturnal animals of the Rift Valley (yes, even the leopards) who were just now dozing off, and to the diurnal animals (yes, even the baboons) who were just now venturing forth, and to the birds – the birds whose song was the symphonic accompaniment of their safari. Indeed, experiencing her nearest equivalent to the missionary urge to share the good news, Tanya swelled with an encompassing sense of kinship that extended literally to every other living thing in the Rift Valley over whom the sun was unfurling its grace.

And, in the throes of this goodwill, Tanya wondered how anyone (or, more to the point, any country) could put a flag under this sun, and under these clouds, on this land, and on that basis claim ownership to such an extent that they would kill other people for it. Was not the gloriousness of the sunrise its own self-evident proof that it belonged to all and was owned by none? Was not heaven's use of the Rift Valley as a bed an indictment of the false distinction between the law of the Kingdom of Heaven and the rule of the province of humankind? That thought was the nearest Tanya had yet come to questioning the colonial endeavor.

* * *

By mid-day, the supply train had reached an open plain. The ground was patchily covered in low green scrub and punctuated by acacia trees. Herds of zebra, eland and wildebeest grazed placidly in the distance. In closer vicinity, rhinoceros, interrupted mid-mastication, blinked at the supply train before undertaking to place themselves several steps further away. Giraffes, catching the scent and scuffle of the caravan, loped away, their sentimental eyes averted, their uneven gait keyed to a rhythm secret to their species. Female impala skipped to safety, urged on by the strident snorts of their dominant male. Warthogs, startled while mating, scooted through the brush, tails vertical and manes ruffling.

Surrounding the plain in a curvaceous sweep were escarpments and mountain ranges, over which the sky was cupped like the palm of God. The effect infused in Tanya a heady sensation of being dwarfed within a globe composed of the cradle of the Rift Valley and the vault of the overarching sky.

Her wonder was a mild (and much needed) restorative; even wearing a hat and riding a mule (in contrast, say, to the porters, who were bare-headed and walking), she was already – only halfway into her day – fatigued, sweaty and feeling drained by the sun. Tanya was not too tired, however, to be grateful for the recent rains, without which traversing the plain would have been an unpleasantly dusty experience.

A grouping of low mud huts became visible in the distance. The architectural feature soon revealed itself to be a Masai *manyatta*. Tanya weighed the positive and negative aspects of this development. On the one hand, their safari was making good time: they were out of the "white highlands" and in the Masai reserve. On the other hand, they were in the Masai reserve.

Possibly the most anthropologically-examined of any tribe in Africa, the Masai have attracted extensive and studious attention from many a mind inclined to organize, classify and categorize. Tanya's was not such a mind. She neither knew nor cared about the difference between a *manyatta* and an *enkang*, although the distinction would have been relevant. An *enkang* is an encampment of homes for the Masai elders, their wives, children and livestock.

A *manyatta*, on the other hand, is a village occupied by the *moran*, the fearsome Masai warriors of the late-adolescent and extended-post-adolescent age group. Because the *moran* excel at activities like killing, cattle-raiding and lion-hunting, as well as dancing, flirting, grooming and love-making, but tend to show less expertise in the areas of house-building, cleaning, cooking and livestock-milking, the *moran* in the *manyatta* require the company of their mothers, sisters and uncircumcised brothers (who herd the cattle, goats and sheep). The presence of these non-combatants in the *manyatta* did not, however, ameliorate in any way the fevered state of the *moran* who were running in a battle line, spears in hand, shields at their front, towards the supply train.

Catching sight of the rapid onslaught, Tanya wished Hilary were beside her. Gasping at the impropriety of her thoughts, Tanya swapped a mental image of Isak for the one of Hilary. Her thoughts appropriately purified, she turned to a man who was actually beside her: "Hassan, you don't have another picture with you? One of Lord Delamere perhaps?"

"No, Memsahib."

"Tanya, what should we —" Malena began, but Tanya cut her off:

"The oxen!" Tanya yelled, turning in her saddle to gesture to the porters to do . . . she didn't know what, but *something*. Tanya had heard of the two-pronged Masai precept that (1) god had bequeathed them all the world's cattle, and that (2) possession of cattle by non-Masai was a cosmic mistake in need of rectification. At a minimum, the Masai were apt to steal the oxen.

The porters were, understandably, without a clear idea of their directive. Nonetheless, each hailed from a tribe that had long fought the

Masai. Each had been taught to meet the Masai assault with a lethal counterstrike, had quickened his pulse with a boyhood fantasy of victory over a Masai warrior. And each had lived through a Masai cattle raid. Every one of the porters knew of the risk that a swooping platoon of *moran* posed to the oxen. The twenty porters fell in to protect and calm the forty-eight oxen, while Kamau grabbed – Tanya thought she must be dreaming – copper wire out of one of the ox wagons and raced suicidally out to greet the attackers.

Kamau's response was reflexive. He had been raised for this moment: to confront the Masai without fear. Only ten years earlier, he would have rushed with similar bravado into the enemy assault, but he would have carried a spear. Now, however, he recognized himself as a different kind of warrior, engaged in a battle with entirely different stakes: this was culture war. "*Hongo!*" Kamau shouted, as he waved the copper wire in the air. "*Hongo!*"

Hassan snorted with exasperation. Somalis being braver than Kikuyu (a slave race, after all), Hassan had wanted to be the first into the fray.

"What's he saying?" Tanya called to Hassan, but he had taken off at a run after Kamau. "What's *hongo*?" Tanya repeated, turning to Malena.

"I don't know," Malena murmured, her face a mask of some Italian church's *pieta*.

The *moran* had not stopped running with the approach of Kamau and Hassan, but the line of warriors had slowed its advance. Pursing her lips determinedly, Tanya resolved, "I can't let Kamau sacrifice himself. He's too good a cook to let him die." Tanya looked over at Malena with a pained expression. "He hasn't even made lunch yet!" And she spurred her mule after Kamau and Hassan. Dionysus eagerly tore after her.

Though terrified, Malena murmured a prayer and then urged her mule to follow.

Arriving at the scene of the confrontation between the *moran*, on the one hand, and Tanya's staff, on the other, Tanya was – forgivably – disoriented. Gone was any whiff of threat or notion of violence. The atmosphere seemed like a market, not like a battlefield. Standing on the open plain, the fifteen or so *moran* were milling in a circle around Kamau and Hassan, admiring the copper wire and chatting amiably in Swahili and Maa, the Masai language.

Uniformly, the *moran* were elongated men with lean musculature. Mostly naked, their nudity was not immediately apparent through all their adornment. In addition to their spears and shields, their accoutrements included brightly-colored beaded earrings, necklaces and belts, into which sheathed knives had been stuck. Their headwear were so fantastic that, in Tanya's opinion, the *moran* put even Marie-Antoinette and her bird-cage-bedecked pouf to shame: on the *morans'* heads, thread extensions and beads ornamented long plaits, over which the warriors had fitted headbands exploding with black ostrich plumes. Finishing off their military dress, they had daubed their skin with a mixture of goat fat and ochre. Under the mid-day sun, they fairly fluoresced red.

Tanya's arrival on mule-back, followed by Malena's moments later, stirred a chorus of commentary from the *moran*, a number of whom began to gesture at the women with their spears. One of the *moran* pointed at himself and then opened his mouth to emit a sound that Tanya identified, with trepidation, as an uncanny imitation of a lion's roar. He wants to eat me, Tanya thought. "Hassan," Tanya called nervously, "are the Masai cannibals?"

Hassan gave Tanya a look of thinly-veiled pity. "No, Memsahib."

Tanya yanked her mule away from the reach of one of the curious *moran*. Then, seeing another *moran* extending a hand to Dionysus, Tanya yelped, "Hassan! Do the Masai eat dogs?" Without waiting for an answer, Tanya ordered Dionysus back to the ox wagons.

Silently thanking Allah that the Masai could not understand English, Hassan assured Tanya that dog was not on the Masai menu.

"What are they saying? Why's he roaring?" Tanya demanded.

Hassan and Kamau began speaking Swahili to one of the *moran*, who translated their communiqués into Maa. Much conversation and laughter bubbled up in response to the translator, and additional lion roars were offered as well. Unable to catch either Kamau's or Hassan's eye, Tanya exchanged a withering glance with Malena.

"At least the good Lord has seen fit to allow us to witness another of his sunrises," Malena whispered hopefully.

"The *moran* want to know," Kamau called, "whether you are married."

"Who?" Tanya asked.

"Both of you Memsabus."

"Of course we are, Kamau." Tanya made an exasperated expression, but then called, "Wait! Tell them our husbands are great warriors, that they're fighting in the war."

Her answer provoked a torrent of vocalizing from the *moran* and more roaring.

"What is the meaning of this roaring?" Tanya cried. By now she'd decided that, if the Masai were not going to kill them or steal the oxen, then she was not going to stand around in the noonday sun listening to them make animal noises. She had a supply train to lead; Lord Delamere was waiting.

"Memsahib, the *moran* have been waiting many years for the return of joy to their lives, and they are very eager to fight in this tribal war," Hassan explained. "They wish by their resemblance to the lion to demonstrate for you their excellence, so that you may send your husbands to fetch them for battle."

Ridiculous as the *morans'* behavior was, Tanya recognized in their request a thorny diplomatic issue, as well as her own inadequacy to the occasion. From Lord Delamere, Tanya had learned that, within the last ten years, the Masai had been corralled onto a reserve and prohibited from making war on their neighbors. To Tanya's mind, such an abrupt revocation of the *moran*'s social function and *raison d'etre* was as dramatic a reversal as any in history, and she was not without sympathy. But Tanya also knew that colonial settlers were agitated about the risk of a native uprising creating a "second front" in the war. Encouraging the *moran* in their warrior vocation seemed at odds with any policy of containment of the natives. At a loss for the elegant sidestep, Tanya defaulted to scolding Hassan, "It's not a tribal war. It's a great war, and we have supplies to deliver."

After more relaying of messages between English, Swahili and Maa (during which Hassan assured the Masai that Memsahib's husband would be coming to recruit them for war), Hassan signaled to one of the porters to bring more copper wire from the ox wagon.

Struggling to control her mule, who had become skittish with the repeated and assorted proddings by the *moran*, Tanya asked, in a voice that concealed little of her frustration and confusion, "What are you doing?"

"We are giving them more *hongo*, Memsabu," Kamau explained.

"Oh do tell us," Malena broke in, "what's *hongo*?"

"A gift," Hassan said gruffly. "For protection. They will send runners now to inform about our presence, and we will have water and shelter at the Masai villages we pass."

This diplomatic achievement seemed so incredible that Tanya and Malena gaped, astounded. "It's a trick, they mean to steal our oxen," Tanya cautioned.

"No, Memsahib, the Masai offer their hospitality. They are a noble people, not a slave race." This much Hassan believed to be true; he did not add, "They are a trustworthy people," because, in his experience, the Masai were not. Hassan had no doubt that additional negotiations and proffers of *hongo* would be necessary the deeper they pressed into Masai territory, but in his judgment *hongo* for hospitality was a fair exchange.

Malena was impressed: "How wonderful, Hassan, safe passage for a bit of copper wire."

"Copper wire that we could be using for the telegraph!" Tanya objected.

"The copper wire is very valuable," Hassan affirmed. "The *moran* will give it to his girlfriend, and she will wrap it around her arms and legs and her beauty will be thricefold."

"With the added attraction that she'll conduct Morse code signals," Tanya griped.

"Have you any children?" Kamau called, translating another query from the *moran*.

"Who?" Tanya asked.

"Both of you Memsabus."

"I dearly want children!" Malena answered. "And soon."

"No," Tanya answered sullenly. "You know we don't, Kamau. Why are they asking these personal questions?"

"The *moran* are trying to decide proper term of address," Hassan clarified. "You are not mothers. You are married, but you lead a caravan.

You have the look of women, but you do not have the status or conduct of women."

"Are you circumcised?" Kamau blurted, in a wrong-headed attempt to elucidate. Hassan smacked Kamau's chest with the back of his hand. Coughing, and observing the greenish hues that crept into Malena's coloring, Kamau let the question drop.

Sweating under the midday sun, a porter ran up with two more coils of copper wire, and Hassan busied himself with its distribution among the *moran*. Thus placated, the war party began to drift back towards the *manyatta*.

Before his platoon-mates departed entirely, a warrior signaled to Kamau and nodded at Malena. Nervous, but unwilling to refuse the warrior's bidding, Kamau apologetically translated the *moran*'s request to Malena: "Memsabu, the *moran* asks that you lift your trouser leg."

"Pardon me?" Malena asked, waxing from green- to red-faced and glancing nervously at the warrior from whom the request had come.

"What idiocy is this Kamau?" Tanya blustered.

"He wants to see if the hair like the beard of maize is also on her leg," Kamau whined, miffed.

Malena met this request for exposure with further covering up: she twisted her yellow hair into a pile and secured it under her hat. The gesture engendered uproarious laughter among the remaining *moran*. Embarrassed, Malena fled, slapping her mule and galloping back to the ox wagons.

Catching up with her, Tanya offered the soothing word: "They're savages."

Malena rode on without reply.

Tanya elaborated: "They don't know any better. They think you're an animal, and they want to see the color of the fur on your hind leg."

Malena continued riding onwards until, glancing backwards, breathing audibly, Malena confessed, "That warrior reminded me of Erik."

FIVE

"I wonder where we are now," Malena murmured as she pulled the hairbrush through Tanya's tangle. They were seated on the floor of the canvas tent, Malena behind Tanya, and Dionysus – as large and dusty as he was – snoring contentedly in Tanya's lap.

"We're in the *manyatta*," Tanya answered flatly, still oblivious to the *enkang-manyatta* distinction. (Actually, they were at a Masai *enkang*, the living quarters of the Masai elders and their families.)

"I know, silly," Malena chided gently. "I mean on the map. Where's that place we need to go, where Lord Delamere is —"

"Ow!" Tanya exclaimed, and then she waved away Malena's apology, saying, "We're south and a bit west of Kijabe, Malena. That's what those *moran* told Hassan, that to find Lord Delamere, we have to go south and a bit west."

"I just wonder," Malena said, working the hairbrush gingerly around a knot, "if we can trust the *moran*."

"What choice do we have? You know there's no map. There's never been a reliable map of this country, not even for the railway. Ow!"

This time Malena's apology was overshadowed by the shy intrusion into the tent of a Masai woman, who was craning her head through the flap. Her eyes widened at finding two *mzungu* women grooming one another like baboons.

Dionysus woke, lifted his head and peered inquiringly at the Masai woman.

Whether from surprise, or from concern about Dionysus, or from general second thoughts about inviting an exchange with these foreign creatures, the Masai woman froze midway into the tent, until Malena gestured welcomingly and cooed, "Come in, precious."

The Masai woman didn't understand English, but Malena's beckoning gesture was universally comprehended vocabulary. With hesitation, the woman mincingly entered the tent and began a careful visual cataloging of the paraffin lamps, quilt, rifle, pairs of women's boots, folded nightdresses, washbasin, bar of soap, hand mirror and empty tea cups.

Stroking Dionysus' ears to calm him and keep him quiet, Tanya observed the Masai woman observing. She was a thin, bare-breasted woman with a shaved head offset by elaborate beaded earrings. She wore numerous necklaces, an embroidered leather skirt and a multi-colored beaded belt. Off her belt hung a tan calabash ornamented with cowrie shells. The woman's oval face was anchored by her expressive eyes, which revealed a conflict between her fear and her curiosity.

Behind this woman, another woman now entered the tent, followed by another and another, until Tanya and Malena sat staring open-mouthed at eight Masai beauties and a gaggle of their extremely shy children, who gripped the women's legs or quaked in their arms. The sight of Dionysus, silent as he was, provoked a flutter of frightened exclamations from the children, and their mothers laughed indulgently as they comforted their little ones.

The women were all attired in some variation of the outfit displayed by the first woman into the tent. Some of the women wore stunning, three-tiered beaded collars that stood out from their necks like fantastic versions of Dutch Renaissance ruffs. A few of the women displayed the offending (to Tanya's eyes) copper wire coils around their arms and lower legs. Calabashes of various sizes and shapes dangled from the women's belts. The children were mostly naked, covered or wrapped in *shukas*, distinctive Masai fabrics. One of the women was much older than the others, and she wore over her shoulders a leather cloak with beaded decoration.

And then there was the smell. Goat fat. Tanya had sniffed it on the *moran* warriors earlier in the day. They had been slathered in the grease, but the open plain had facilitated dissipation of the olfactory consequences of that fashion choice. The tent, on the other hand, compounded them. At first overwhelming, the odor brought Tanya near to the point of swooning, and she resisted covering her nose and mouth with her hands. After gritting her teeth and resigning herself to the noble course of ignoring the smell, Tanya found that she could accommodate herself to it. It wasn't *per se* unpleasant, just unusual. It had hints both of sweetness and musk, not dissimilar from patchouli, with additional earthy, gamey and – unavoidably – goat-y components. Tanya wondered if an effort to persuade the Masai to switch from goat fat to shea butter could work.

Scrutinizing this crowd, Tanya imagined that the women, whose hospitality she was accepting, had come to extract some reciprocation for their kindness, perhaps only in the form of ogling their *mzungu* guests. She was wrong. The women had come on a mission.

The first Masai woman into the tent pointed in the direction of the washbasin and said something in Maa. Before Tanya or Malena could decipher her request, a commotion among the women drew everyone's attention to the tent flap, where Hassan was attempting simultaneously to clear the Masai women from his Memsahibs' abode, and to avoid having to interfere with his Memsahibs' privacy. The resulting compromise involved Hassan closing his eyes, plunging his arms into the tent and wrestling the Masai women out. The Masai women weren't acceding quietly to Hassan's strong-arm tactics, nor could Hassan resist responding in kind to their verbal castigation.

Dionysus leapt to his feet and would have joined the fray, but Tanya held him back. "Hassan, stop that!" she ordered. However much the Masai women had been an unexpected addition to the evening's company, they were no more unwelcome than a phoenix – and phoenixes were what Tanya had decided these women were most like.

"Oh Hassan," Malena called, jumping up, "they are our gracious hosts." She tried to infiltrate the crowd of Masai women and children by the tent flap, but she became ensnared in a torrent of darting hands, eager to run fingers through her hair and caress her skin. Also, Malena was vaguely aware that someone's jewelry was snagged on her clothing. "Hassan?" Malena called, wriggling slightly to disentangle herself.

"Memsahib?" Hassan's frustrated, but dutiful, face appeared at the tent flap.

"I must thank these women for their hospitality. Would you be kind enough to interpret? Do these women speak Swahili?"

Hassan looked morose at this postponement of the Masai women's eviction. But he was a professional: "Just a moment, Memsahib," he replied, disappearing from the tent's entrance.

The first woman again pointed to the washbasin.

"What does she want, Tanya?"

"I think she wants the washbasin," Tanya guessed, grabbing it and extending the bowl to the Masai woman.

The Masai woman shook her head and pointed again towards where the washbasin had been.

"Oh she wants the mirror!" Malena exclaimed. Holding her hand in front of her face, Malena mimed admiring herself in the hand mirror, and the Masai women conveyed their assent with smiles, bobbing heads and various communications in Maa. Malena nodded her permission.

Moments later, Tanya found herself surrounded by Masai women and children clamoring to use the mirror. Whether from the smell of goat fat or an overwhelming submissiveness to females, Dionysus had retreated to the safety of the blanket area behind Tanya, and she had to contend with the flailing limbs on her own.

The first woman into the tent had won the scramble for vanity and was intensely baring her teeth before the looking glass. Examining the result in the mirror's reflection with wide-eyed satisfaction, the mirror-holder deflected the open hands and overlapping pleas of her peers.

Seeking to extricate herself from the crowd, Tanya brushed against one of the babies who had been staring stupefied at her. The jostle seemed to have assisted the baby in arriving at a decision: her face puckering, she turned to her mamma and unleashed a terrified wail. The mother obliged her baby with her breast, and Tanya cringed at the spectacle.

Outside the tent, Hassan coughed. Then he called, "Memsahib, I have brought an elder who speaks Swahili and Maa. He and I will translate."

Malena pulled aside the tent flap to reveal Hassan and, lurking behind him, a middle-aged Masai man with a shaved head. He was clothed in a red cloak. "Oh do bring him in, Hassan," Malena encouraged.

"A bit crowded, Memsahib," Hassan demurred, inwardly astonished at Malena's lack of decorum.

"Quite so," Malena agreed. "Please have him tell the women —"

Though Tanya would have sworn that the Masai women were absorbed by the mirror, which was now being passed from hand to hand and subjected to a full range of pouts, smiles, snarls and other facial expressions which Tanya failed to recognize as seductive, the women were, in fact, sensible to the presence of the elder in the shadow of the tent's entryway. Many of the utterances that had constituted mere background noise to Tanya and Malena had been communications from the women to this elder, and he began translating the women's queries into Swahili, while at the same time Malena verbalized her gratitude in flowery English. Hearing the questions in Swahili, Hassan realized he would have to edit them; hearing Malena's monologue in English, Hassan knew he would have to shorten it. Faced with the dilemma of which to translate first – Swahili into English or English into Swahili – Hassan's brain, somewhat overstrained at this point, short-circuited, with the result that he spouted, "Are your lovers from your husband's age-grade?"

"What?" Malena asked, breathless.

Tanya's tongue was paralyzed. At the mention of "lovers," guilt muted her. She knew her notion was hysterical, but she wondered if the Masai woman had used the word to embarrass her, to expose the indecency of Tanya having spent the previous night sleepless and tormented by the reappearance of her past lover.

Signaling to the elder for silence, Hassan apologized. "Forgive me, Memsahib, the Masai questions temporarily confused me, and I spoke by accident. Be braced please."

"But what did that question mean, Hassan?" Malena asked, her voice full with wonder.

"It's not suitable," Hassan objected.

"We must not offend, Hassan," Malena chided him. "They may be heathens, but they are our hosts, and we must endeavor to accommodate their customs as far as Christian modesty permits."

"They ask," Hassan relented reluctantly, "if you share their married women's custom of taking lovers from the group of men who were circumcised with their husbands."

"But our husbands aren't circumcised, Hassan," Malena protested.

"I know, Memsahib," Hassan said gravely.

"Lovers?" Tanya croaked, finally regaining some capacity for speech. But before Tanya could elaborate, the Masai woman next to her squeezed her breast, and Tanya screamed.

The Masai women recoiled as a group and then immediately began giggling and chattering.

"Ha-Hassan?" Tanya asked weakly.

"My most sincere apologies, Memsahib," Hassan expressed, listening simultaneously to the elder's explanation of the odd gesture. "As you may recall, I was telling the women to leave you exactly from fear of such indignity. The woman is curious why you do not have milk."

Tanya and Malena reddened. Malena unconsciously crossed her arms over her chest; Tanya consciously did so.

Thinking that avoidance of breast milk as a topic of conversation was a wise policy, Malena opted for a missionary approach: "Hassan, you must tell these women that taking lovers is adultery, outside the covenant with their husbands that Jesus has blessed. Whatever the age of the lovers, adultery is a grievous sin."

"I will tell them, Memsahib," Hassan lied.

"But Ha-Hassan," Tanya called, struggling to control the tremor in her voice, "are these women saying that taking lovers is *normal*? I mean," Tanya placed a hand on her chest to steady her breathing, "the women are willing to talk about it even through that *man*," Tanya pointed at the elder still standing behind Hassan.

Hassan turned to the accused elder and conversed in Swahili for several minutes. Nodding in conclusion, Hassan provided a succinct translation, "He says: of course."

"Of course?" Tanya blustered. "Of course what? Are you telling me that he spent the last five minutes saying 'of course' repeatedly? What did he say?"

While Hassan and Tanya parried, the elder said something in Maa to the women, in response to which the women laughed exuberantly. Then the oldest woman in the group clapped her hands several times, after which she issued a pronouncement, with which much agreement was expressed.

"Now what did she say?" Tanya asked.

The message was duly relayed from older woman to elder man to Hassan and then to Tanya and Malena. In the course of this passage, the message changed languages twice and was undoubtedly subject to modifications deemed necessary by the translators, both of whom were males dealing with females. The accuracy with which the message was transmitted may therefore be questioned. Indeed, that the message was stripped of some of its potency can safely be assumed. Nonetheless, Tanya might have wished that the message had been even more diluted before it reached her ears.

"She says," Hassan related, "that marriage without lovers is impossible."

* * *

"*Effendi*, do you think," Kamau asked Hassan, as they bedded down next to the embers of that evening's campfire, "that Memsabu is truly a woman?"

The night was cold, and the temperature was to descend even further – to hover just above freezing – before it would ascend again. Through this clear, cold air the sky revealed itself a vacuum black, a color that seemed, to Kamau, capable of sucking him into itself. The profusion of stars stood out against this force as defiant rebels, beacons of the possibility of resistance. They inspired in Kamau the confidence to ask Hassan this long-standing question.

Of course, Kamau knew that Tanya looked like a woman and, further, that Tanya – and Bwana Isak, and the other colonists – were human, like himself. Still, these colonists distinguished themselves in ways other than in the physical oddity of their light skin, and the matter of their females was one that Kamau found especially vexing.

The colonist men were identifiably male. Their appearance was masculine, and additionally their actions accorded with the man's role: they hunted and made war, drank alcohol, commanded men and meted out justice.

But the women presented troubling issues. They also hunted, drank alcohol and commanded men – usually native men, but even colonist males were sometimes seen acceding to the orders of their females.

Most disturbingly, the colonists definitely expected the natives to accept and adopt their practices. The colonists, for example, hired men as porters, even though carrying cargo was women's work. Cooking, too, was women's work that the colonists assigned to men.

This last point was one on which Kamau cultivated a sophisticated rationalization, an extrapolation from the fact that Kikuyu men, to avoid the risk of being poisoned, ate food cooked only by their wives. Taking similar precautions, *mzungus* ate food cooked only by men, women being too untrustworthy for such an important post. (Kamau discounted the fact that most Kikuyu men preferred their womenfolk to remain in their villages, rather than working in the colonial economy.)

Having eliminated the theory that Tanya was a witch – she was openly derisive of magic and, besides, his close scrutiny of her personal effects and conduct confirmed that she engaged in no ritual spell-casting – Kamau was now examining the possibility that these colonists organized themselves into groups of men, women and a third, as-yet-unnamed category to which someone like Tanya might belong.

Hassan had been on the brink of sleep, when Kamau's question – dimly perceived – distracted him. "Hmm?" he inquired.

"The trousers," Kamau explained. "Bwanas wear trousers. What woman wears the clothing of men? Do Kikuyu women wear skirts that expose the legs like the Kikuyu warriors? Do Masai women wear the belt of the *moran*? Do Somali women wear a turban?"

At the mention of his tribe's females, Hassan was jolted into responding: "Somali women are pious before Allah, modest before men and reflect the blessings of wealth bestowed upon their husbands."

"Exactly." This litany impressed Kamau, and he mulled it while listening to the oxen making night-time noises within the *boma*, a cattle enclosure constructed from thorn tree branches and situated in the middle of the *enkang*. "A woman in man's clothing is without sense," Kamau elaborated. "She does not show her allegiance with the females of her age-grade. She does not reflect her husband's wealth. She imitates his penis." In the dark, Kamau's outsized facial expression conveyed his distaste for the vulgarity of such conduct. "Unless," and here Kamau paused for dramatic effect, "she is not truly a woman."

"Memsahib is a woman," Hassan grumbled, rolling away from Kamau.

"Consider her actions," Kamau continued. "Not since Wangu Makeri have women ruled men in Kikuyuland. Masai women do not give orders to the *moran*. Somali men do not go to war under the command of their womenfolk."

"Somali women," Hassan's voice wafted over from where he lay, "are at home or in the grave. Somali women are obedient to their parents and in-laws, generous to their children, and at the service of their husbands' desires."

"Exactly." Kamau pulled the blanket up to his neck and wiggled a stone out from under his back. A nearby porter interrupted his snoring to cough out a beetle that had crawled into his open mouth. When his coughs subsided, Kamau carried on, "A woman who commands men is not unnatural. She is the worst of nature. She is a hyena: a pain for the eyes, a burden for the ears, a scavenger of the dead." Had Kamau sought another example of matriarchal animals – meerkats, say, or lemurs, or even elephants – his analysis would necessarily have required revision, but such details did not detain him. Nor did he stop to consider the question of what a man commanded by a woman was – surely, also a hyena? "Such a woman has no place in the home or family. Unless," Kamau paused again for emphasis, "she is not truly a woman."

"Memsahib is a woman," Hassan replied dismissively, adding: "Go to sleep."

"But women everywhere are the same," Kamau said, ignoring Hassan's obvious preference for ending the conversation. "The man is an irresistible temptation. I have heard that these Masai women become ill from having too many lovers. A Kikuyu woman is so needful that a Kikuyu warrior finds relief when his age-mate helps him with his wife from time to time. Somali women —"

"— Somali women," Hassan interrupted to prevent Kamau from uttering an offense that would require violence to rectify, "see their husbands, brothers and sons only. A woman may never be in the presence of her husband's age-mate without her husband's protection. A woman's faithfulness is best guaranteed when never tested."

"Exactly." Proud as he was of his Kikuyu heritage, Kamau was not a little awed by Hassan's depiction of Somali gender relations. Polygamy being the norm in Kikuyu society, Kamau now entertained the fantasy (non-traditional as it would be) of taking a Somali wife – perhaps when he was very old and very rich. Indeed, the idea prompted his next comment: "A woman, whatever her tribe, who does not desire the men around her is old, sick, barren or possessed. She has rejected nature and banished herself to the realm of demons. Unless," and here Kamau paused triumphantly, feeling that he had brought his case to an inarguable conclusion, "she is not truly a woman."

As tiresome as Hassan found this conversation, he did not – as he previously had – dismiss Kamau's assertion with the abrupt counter-assertion of Memsahib's womanhood. Mostly, he worried that Kamau would think that Hassan's confidence derived from an intimacy that Hassan had neither experienced nor would welcome. Tanya was so far beyond the parameters of an appropriate wife for Hassan that he endeavored to identify her simply as a sexless wielder-of-power in his life, an opportunity for him to exploit, as well as a pitfall for him to avoid. She was an accepted fact of his employment, and he side-stepped the kind of inquiries into which Kamau was wading.

Nonetheless, Hassan did occasionally wonder at the inhumanity of Christianity. Condemning men to a single sexual partner for life seemed the kind of punishment that would make hell a welcome release. Similarly, Christian women seemed deprived of the entitlements that are the glory of Somali women. Christian women received, for example, no bride-price – in fact, Hassan had heard (though he wasn't sure that he should believe) that the families of Christian women actually paid a husband-price, a custom (if it was a custom) so barbarically insulting and demeaning to the women that Hassan ultimately decided that it couldn't be true: Christian women would all die of shame. Hassan had also discreetly noticed that Christian women did not seem to have the sexual rights in respect of their husbands that Somali women enjoyed. On the contrary, the Christian women seemed to view celibacy as a variety of exalted state, rather than (as it obviously was) a condition of humiliating social ostracism. But these matters were not ones on which Hassan wished to dwell. Beyond wondering occasionally how Christianity obtained any converts at all, Hassan got on with his work and left the philosophizing to Kamau.

"Memsahib is a Baroness and Christian," Hassan sighed. "To be Memsahib is to be like obsidian. You can make from that stone a knife or a necklace, but the qualities of the stone remain unchanged. Whether she acts the part of the knife or the necklace, Memsahib remains a Christian Baroness. Only a madman questions a stone. Only an idiot seeks understanding of a noblewoman."

Having thus spoken, Hassan felt the matter resolved and dropped immediately into sleep. For Kamau, however, sleep took much longer to claim him, as he was savoring his victory.

She is not truly a woman, Kamau gloated to himself, I knew it: she is a *noble* woman.

* * *

Contrary to Masai custom, and to the invitation that had been extended, the supply train party slept outside the huts of the *enkang*. Inside each of these huts was two beds – one of which was for guests – and the Masai were stunned at their guests' refusal of it. But none of the Kikuyu porters was willing to sleep in a Masai bed. Whether they distrusted the offer of hospitality and anticipated murder in their sleep, or whether they feared being joined by a Masai woman in the bed, is not known. What is known is that the porters chose to sleep on the ground by the campfire.

Hassan chose the same bedding in order to maintain close proximity to the supply wagons. He associated Masai hospitality with neither murder nor seduction, but (rightly or wrongly) he was quite confident of theft – friendly larceny – in the absence of adequate preventative measures.

As for Tanya and Malena, wishing to give no offense to their hosts, they steeled themselves for the ordeal of sleeping in a dung-plastered hut, until they realized that, at night, while the Masai oxen go into the *boma*, the Masai goats go into . . . the hut. Tanya and Malena opted for their tent.

Thus, 2:30 in the morning found one of the porters shooing an insect off his face, exposed as it was to the elements and all within them. The insect, however, was persistent. It was also a bit wet, a sensation that the porter found disgusting. In consequence, the porter began swatting vigorously at the insect, his hand colliding at one point with a very non-insect-like fur-covered cheek. Annoyed at the curious giraffe-antelope-whatever-it-was that was sniffing him, the porter sat up and clapped his hands angrily into the face of a lioness.

She was laconic. Notwithstanding the porter's rudeness, she wasn't terribly provoked. Her tail twitched a bit at the end, and her ears adjusted themselves to accommodate the sounds of the night. Other than that, she stood still, eyes shining, and continued to take in her surroundings.

For the porter, such reservation of judgment was unwarranted. Although he had never before come face-to-face with a lioness, his lack of prior experience did not deprive him of an understanding that the occasion required immediate defensive measures. As quietly as he could, and with movements as measured as he could make them, he woke the porter beside him, who – upon appraising the situation – woke the porter beside him, and so on, until Hassan was roused to fetch Memsahib with the gun.

Eyes transfixed by the leonine threat, minds raced: each of the twenty porters wondered (in various formulations of the question) how the colonial administration could justify denying them firearms. They were the people most likely to confront lions. Memsahib, on the other hand, was inexplicably allowed to possess guns, even though she was not only more likely to be at a safe remove, but was also unable to inspire confidence in her ability to shoot true.

Hassan, unlike the porters (and unlike Tanya herself), had no doubt that Memsahib could shoot the lioness; he had seen her do it before, on the hunting safari in March, and he was satisfied that Isak's current absence would not impair Memsahib's ability to do it again.

Nonetheless, Hassan also had occasion to question the wisdom of the British Empire. Knowing, as he did, that Somalis served as invaluable soldiers in the colonial military, Hassan did not see the logic in denying Somalis the privilege of shooting guns in private life. Natives, of course, were different; slave races should be kept away from weapons. But if Somalis could be trusted to shoot guns in military operations on behalf of the Empire, they should likewise be trusted to shoot lions on behalf of colonial Memsahibs . . . instead of having to advance, unarmed, past a lioness in order to alert Memsahib to the danger.

Rolling over very deliberately, making as little noise as he could muster, Hassan lit the paraffin lamp beside him. The light, he prayed, would allow him safe passage under the lioness' nose. At a minimum, he could throw the fire at the beast if it attacked.

Their visibility thus enhanced by the glow of the little lamp, the porters began emitting muffled cries. Surveying their surroundings with dilated eyes, they spied not one, but seven, lionesses and a lone male, sniffing around the encampment and congregating around the *boma* – within which, of course, the lions had detected the inviting scent of oxen.

Confronted with this bounty of lions, Hassan held his breath and willed himself to keep his eyes open. (While the Angel of Death merited nothing but Hassan's contempt, lions were another matter: he respected them.)

The lioness who had been sniffing the porter seemed to lose interest in the row of men lying before her, and she meandered lazily forward to investigate the soot of the campfire. By the *boma*, the scent of lions was creating a disturbance among the livestock, but the lions did not appear to share the excitement. A couple of fat females were rubbing against each other, and a third was urinating. Oblivious to the skittishness of the cattle, the male stretched out beside the *boma* and imbibed the pleasing aromas.

Hassan resumed breathing – quietly – and signaled for the porters to remain still. From the calm manner of the pride, as well as from the lions' protruding bellies, Hassan concluded that they'd just eaten. Far from looking for another meal or spoiling for a fight, these lions were simply making a pit stop before slumberland. With this thought emboldening him – and sending thanks to Allah for making it so – Hassan crept past the lions.

"Memsahibs! Memsahibs!"

The sound was a desperate hiss. Immediately upon opening her eyes, Tanya saw the paraffin lamp glowing through the canvas. Cautiously peering out and trying not to expose her nightdress, Tanya found Hassan crouching by the tent, holding the lamp like Aladdin preparing to conjure the *djinn*.

"What is it?" Tanya whispered.

In response, Hassan's arm made a wide sweep with the lamp.

Tanya's eyes followed the movement and beheld the magic it revealed. She gasped. "'(God shield us!) a lion among ladies is a most dreadful thing," she heard Hilary laugh, as if, by some invisible force, he'd been instantly transported beside her.

"What is it?" Malena whispered, she – and not Hilary – suddenly at Tanya's side.

"Careful!" Tanya warned, losing the dream of Hilary in the reality of danger. "Don't let Dionysus out!" When Tanya had assured herself that she and Malena were adequately blocking Dionysus from exiting the tent, Tanya gestured with her head in the direction of the *boma*.

Hassan accommodated Malena by pointing out the multiple sets of flashing lion eyes. Four of the females had congregated near where the male lay, and their yawning and paw-licking gave ample opportunity to observe the apparatus with which they would kill, dismember and consume their prey.

"Oh fetch the gun, Tanya!" Malena urged in a near-hysterical whisper. "Shoot them before they eat all our poor porters! Only one has had a Christian baptism!"

"Hush Malena!" Tanya soothed, grabbing her hand. Tanya had wrapped the rifle in her blanket – the gun had been discomforting her sleep all night – but she shied from shooting these lions. Scanning the scene, Tanya, like Hassan, gathered from the lions' easygoing conduct that they were simply padding through the *enkang* on their way to a post-meal nap. Tanya was relieved; she didn't want to have to try to shoot a lion without Isak. Besides which, wasting bullets on animals that were neither food nor threat disserved the cause.

Watching the porters, Tanya was convinced that her intervention was unnecessary for their safety. Their physical postures were transitioning from rigid to relaxed. The porter who had clapped his hands in the lioness' face was now leaning forward, resting his chin in his palms, watching the goddess who had awakened him roll in soot. Other porters were lighting additional paraffin lamps that blinked into the night like giant fireflies.

But ultimately honor decided the issue for Tanya. These lions moved her with their regal bearing and powerful grace. Tanya felt the same awe she'd experienced the first time she'd seen a wild animal – a giraffe, passing by the railway track, while Tanya had been riding the train from Mombasa to her new home in Nairobi. At the sight of that giraffe – as with these lions now – Tanya surrendered to a profound humility with which she'd had no experience in Denmark: an understanding that the world and the creatures in it was vastly and inevitably beyond her grasp, regardless of her years of study and experience. Her comprehension –

indeed, her destiny – was always to be insignificant in relation to the whole, and yet that knowledge filled her with a sense of rightness, proportion and beauty.

"The lionesses salute the Baroness," Hassan whispered.

"I salute them in return," Tanya replied.

Pulling Malena's hand, Tanya opened the tent flap wider and felt Malena resist behind her. "Don't be scared," Tanya assured her, and then turning around, saw the real problem. Malena, crouching in her neck-to-ankle nightdress, was holding the garment's collar up to her ears. "Blast modesty for one night, Malena," Tanya urged. "We may never get to see lions like this again. Besides, Erik won't care if lions see you in your nightdress."

Then, looping one arm through Hassan's, and insistently holding Malena with the other, Tanya prodded their threesome forward for a better view.

SIX

A hallmark of nobility is the power to disarrange schedules and, especially, to precipitate delay at one's whim. In this respect, the lions lived up to their aristocratic reputation. Everybody in the supply train party – even Hassan – slept passed his or her intended 4 a.m. wake-up. Although the lions ultimately didn't stay within the *enkang* more than twenty minutes, their presence had been so stimulating that the hour was past three before anyone fell asleep again, and once asleep the group remained thus for a whole REM cycle.

By the time Tanya and Malena were ready to set forth, therefore, the sun had long-ago sent emissaries to herald its arrival on the horizon, and Tanya struggled to control the frenzy that would seize her if they did not *depart immediately*.

"Hassan!" Tanya called. Immediate departure remained aspirational because she could not locate Hassan. The twenty porters were at attention by their assigned wagons, Malena had already mounted her mule,

Dionysus was pacing beside Tanya's mule, Kamau was stowing the tea kettle onto one of the wagons – but Hassan had disappeared.

"Hassan!" Tanya rounded the back of the third ox wagon and almost crashed into Hassan, who was deep in discussion with the Masai elder who'd served as translator the previous evening. "Hassan!" Tanya exclaimed, equal parts annoyed and relieved.

Then her mood shifted as she caught sight of several other Masai elders hurrying away from the supply wagons. "What did you sell them?" Tanya demanded, eyes narrowing.

Hassan stared blankly at Tanya. The translator elder gave Tanya a curious look, as if she were a mechanical device, the operation of which eluded him. Suppressing a growl of frustration, Tanya motioned to follow the departing Masai elders, but Hassan stopped her with his hand on her shoulder. "Memsahib, do not misunderstand the situation. I have sold the Masai nothing."

"These supplies are for Lord Delamere's troops!"

"Yes, Memsahib."

"Bwana Isak is with Lord Delamere!"

"Yes, Memsahib."

"You cannot sell these supplies!"

"I never would, Memsahib."

"I don't believe you!"

"Yes, Memsahib."

"What does *he* want?" Tanya turned to the Masai elder whose facial expression was fast evolving from one of curiosity to one of amusement, a response that incensed Tanya.

"We are discussing guides, Memsahib."

"Guides?" Tanya spat the word as if it were nonsensical in the context – as if Hassan had confessed that the subject of their conversation was *lederhosen* or confectioner's sugar. "We have to go, Hassan! The sun is already rising! We were supposed to have left two hours ago!"

Hassan remained calm until Tanya ran out of exclamations. Then he offered, gently, "We have no map."

"Don't waste the cool moments of the day telling me what I know!" Tanya snapped.

"A Masai guide will —"

"— We need to go south and west!"

Recognizing the twin imperatives of challenging Tanya, and ensuring that she didn't feel that she was being challenged, Hassan played to her prejudices: "But can we trust those *moran*?"

Hassan's echoing of Malena's question troubled Tanya. Of course, Tanya herself didn't trust the Masai, but she sincerely wished to extend them the benefit of the doubt when doing so was convenient. "Why does every one think that the *moran* gave wrong directions? If we can't trust the *moran*, why can we trust a Masai guide?" she asked, triumphantly identifying the flaw in Hassan's logic.

"The *moran* return to their *manyatta*, and our fate is of no concern to them. A guide stays by our side and suffers our fate with us," Hassan replied.

Tanya felt a constriction in her throat, and she appreciated the irony that here, in the widest expanse of earth on which she'd ever tread, she was feeling trapped. She did not want any Masai accompaniment to the ox wagons. The years were too few since the presence of Masai meant death to caravans. Tanya worried that a woman-led supply train might prove an irresistible target, that the Masai might well risk Imperial ire for the spoils of such easy prey. Anxiety-approaching-paranoia seemed to her a healthy attitude on this point. A Masai guide could lead them directly into an ambush, an attack that *hongo* couldn't buy them out of, a battle in which her only hope would be rescue by Hilary – Isak! Isak!

Tanya gritted her teeth. The Masai and their environs seemed repeatedly to be conjuring Hilary, summoning and provoking reminders of his existence. Tanya desired nothing more than freedom from these people, their filthy sexual morals and the scourges they unleashed. Distance! Several impassable mountain ranges, and perhaps an ocean, between herself and the Masai was what Tanya craved.

On the other hand, Tanya had no idea where the Narosera River was, and she was not so stubborn as to fail to recognize that "south and west," taken to its logical conclusion, would land them in Lake Victoria.

"We are departing now," Tanya ordered. "Without a guide."

* * *

Another defining characteristic of nobility is *noblesse oblige*, the generous gesture that makes less intolerable the gross imbalance in benefits that otherwise prevails between aristocrat and plebian. Tanya preferred to demonstrate *noblesse oblige* in instances when it required some self-sacrifice, so she had to maneuver to make her halting of the supply train at mid-day appear to be an action against her own interests.

"Hassan," Tanya croaked, her dry tongue swollen in her mouth, "the men look exhausted."

Hassan looked over his shoulder. To his eye, the porters looked well-rested. They were moving at a good pace and with a sprightly gait. Rhythmic switching of the oxen provided an almost-musical undertone to the procession. A lively conversation in Kikuyu pitted the porters manning the second ox wagon against the porters assigned to the first. Because Hassan didn't speak Kikuyu, he couldn't understand the badinage; but Hassan guessed that the conversation involved mocking those porters who had exhibited particularly cowardly responses to the lion visitation.

"Memsahib, it is okay," he assured her. "We can walk through the day because of the late start."

Tanya frowned. Beneath her shirt, her shoulders were aflame, and the coarse fabric rubbing against them was excruciating. "Malena," Tanya called behind her to where Malena was ambling on her mule, "I'm worried about you." Tanya twisted in her saddle and sized up Malena. Sun exposure had bronzed her friend, and Malena looked vital enough to satisfy a virile Viking. "You look pale," Tanya pronounced.

"Oh don't stop on my account," Malena protested. "Whenever I feel that I'll die if I go any farther, I think of Erik. Knowing that each step takes me closer to him gives me the strength to persevere."

Malena's speech depressed Tanya. She felt that she was entitled to Malena's unquestioning support, and Malena's siding with the porters was (in Tanya's view) a fickle abandonment. Malena's defection was so disappointing, indeed, that Tanya couldn't summon the energy to persuade her friend otherwise.

Feeling that she would tumble off her mule if she didn't dismount momentarily, Tanya looked around for someone who wouldn't argue with her. The sight of loyal Dionysus walking beside her mule, panting, filled Tanya with gratitude.

"We better stop, Hassan," Tanya announced, halting her mule. "Poor Dionysus is going to collapse, and you know that he endures the heat much better than the porters."

Staring at Dionysus' glossy coat, Hassan initially thought to reassure Tanya that panting was not merely normal, but healthy, for Dionysus, when Hassan finally realized that he was misconstruing his job duties. "Memsahib," he said, offering his hand to assist Tanya dismounting, "seeing how you place their needs above your own, the porters will follow you to the corners of the earth."

Struggling to stand after hours in the saddle, Tanya replied, "Following me to Narosera River will be sufficient. I don't have the stamina for the corners of the earth."

Only after the supply train party had refreshed itself with tea and dates and a nap under the ox wagons did its members chance to see how travelers whose leader did not yield to the noonday sun fared.

The line moving in the middle distance, heading south, did not at first appear to be composed of humans. The individual elements were variable in both their shape and the speed at which they moved, characteristics which seemed to eliminate the two groups of humans most likely to be traversing the territory: the British military and the Masai. Further complicating the problem of identification was the dust rising from the uneven landscape.

"Wildebeest," Kamau hazarded. He based his guess more on his knowledge that wildebeest migrated than on his sense that the shapes before him corresponded to wildebeest.

Hassan thought that the moving objects were wild dogs, and Tanya suggested that they might be swarming bees. While Kamau ran to retrieve field glasses from the ox wagons, Malena commented that the shapes looked like our Lord and Savior carrying his crucifix through the

Stations of the Cross, and her remark prompted the realization that the shapes in question were variable – as was the speed at which they advanced – because they were, in fact, humans carrying items of different shapes and sizes.

Peering through the field glasses, Tanya confirmed that the line was comprised of porters traveling on foot, carrying loads – mostly what appeared to be sacks of grain, mechanical components and weaponry. She was appalled to see that the men were largely bare-chested and bare-footed; such attire did not seem adequate to a day-long trek over land strewn with thorns and writhing with insects adapted to attacking the bottoms of feet. Even from a distance, she could see that many of the carriers were suffering, stumbling under crippling loads and from what must have been innumerable, painful assaults on their soles. Searching at the front of the line, Tanya found what she expected: a white man. He was walking, like the porters, but he wasn't carrying a load – and he wore a uniform and boots.

At this point, Tanya became aware of the surrounding hum. It was the buzz of the porters speaking Kikuyu, but no understanding of the language was necessary to comprehend the nervousness being expressed. A single word punctuated the buzz; the word emerged repeatedly from the background noise, articulated by different voices, in varying tones and pitches, but always with a trembling intensity. It was a Swahili word, and Tanya had heard it before, but she had never meditated on its meaning or implications. Now it reverberated around her: *kariakor.*

The Carrier Corps, Tanya knew, was the British Army's solution to the massive logistics problems posed by the territory of the East African Protectorate. In the absence of roads and refilling stations for lorries, and given the presence of tsetse fly, which eliminated the utility of pack animals, the British Army demanded that human muscles, backs and legs form the supply chain linking the depot in Nairobi to the frontlines on the border with German East Africa. (The Germans, as well, dealing with roughly equivalent geographic challenges, had devised an identical solution.)

In one respect, organization of the British Army's Carrier Corps began with the declaration of war; in another respect, however, the Carrier Corps was never organized. The basic problem of supplying the suppliers – of feeding the carriers – was never to be solved. Officially, the carriers were required to haul fifty pounds of supplies, plus all their food for the journey (and the pots in which to cook it). In practice, the carriers were perpetually malnourished or starved, when they weren't dying of dysentery, malaria or fatigue. For obvious reasons, recruitment of carriers was always to be a struggle, and the British Army eventually resorted to forced labor.

Already, only a month into the war, the Carrier Corps had such a dismal reputation that Tanya's porters couldn't speak of it without expressing a degree of hysteria that would have impressed Dr. Charcot. Nor were potential carriers the only ones concerned by the reputation of the Corps: potential supply recipients were also reluctant to rely on decrepit slave labor for their necessaries; hence Isak had simply circumvented the Carrier Corps and gone directly to Tanya for provisions.

Still, notwithstanding her awareness of the fear *kariakor* inspired in natives, Tanya was confounded when, turning away from the carriers in the distance, she found all twenty of her porters, along with Kamau and – in what must have been sympathetic pain – Dionysus, huddled under the four ox wagons.

They reminded Tanya of children hiding under the bed during a thunderstorm. For the first time, Tanya looked at her workers without having to defend herself against their certain ridicule or subversion of her authority. There was no question, in this moment, of their mocking her, and Tanya was aware of that same human neediness that, when expressed (as it often was) by herself, inspired Hassan and Kamau to their most thoughtful services on her behalf.

"What are you doing?" Tanya crawled under the ox wagon, next to where Kamau squatted. "The carriers can't see you at this distance," she assured him. "Anyway, *kariakor* can't grab you off this supply train,"

Kamau and the porters seated beside him looked hollowly at Tanya. "It cannot, Memsabu," Kamau intoned, "only if you say it cannot."

Tanya blinked a few times until she grasped Kamau's meaning: employment with a *mzungu* was the only way to escape conscription into *kariakor*, a condition that vested extraordinary powers in ordinary mortals. Kamau and the porters felt this power acutely: at Tanya's word, *kariakor* would be held at bay . . . or take them away. Tanya had assumed that the thunderstorm from which her staff was hiding was *kariakor*. Now she realized that the thunderstorm might also be her.

"Kamau," Tanya said, putting her hand on his shoulder and meeting his gaze, "no one on this supply train will be taken by *kariakor*. I will be a carrier before any of you are."

"Memsabu," replied Kamau, "your word is like Cumberland sauce to the pig: it sweetens a hard service."

Kamau, of course, had intended his statement as one of gratitude, but in its confession that working for Tanya was difficult, the remark contained an unpleasant truth; and in Tanya's acceptance of Kamau's perspective – in allowing him to tell her that an important benefit of working for her was that it preempted working for somebody worse – Tanya committed her first genuine, uncalculated act of *noblesse oblige*.

* * *

The prerogative of the noble-born is to represent not merely him or herself as an individual, but also something larger – a fiefdom or polity or concept, like Schleswig-Holstein or the people of England or profligacy. And however grand it may be to puff the identity out beyond the normal limits of self, this characteristic of nobility also has its dark side, as French aristocrats being carted to the guillotine had the opportunity (though insufficient time) to ponder.

Lions, too, have suffered for their symbolism. Representing, as they do, the untameable power of the uncivilized, the horrendous destruction implicit in that state of nature and, additionally – as Tanya experienced – the tempting beauty of the world unfettered by the law of humanity, lions found themselves as out of favor with the colonial administration as Marie-Antoinette did with the Jacobins.

Tanya decried this wanton slaughter of lions for sport (although she'd been guilty of same), but she also believed in the noble conflict: as the two Schleswig-Holstein wars between the kingdoms of Denmark and Germany had proved, deployment of fatal force by nobles against nobles was sometimes necessary. With this understanding, Tanya shot the lioness that appeared in their encampment that night.

Unlike the near-silent lion visitation the previous night, this encounter was distinguished by gut-wrenching noise. Having failed to find an *enkang*, the supply train party had broken for the night on the open plain.

The porters had assembled a rudimentary *boma* around their encampment, using thorn tree branches that they'd gathered from the surrounding scrub. But lions are no strangers to acacia trees, and their motivation for tip-toeing between the thorns is never greater than when oxen wait dumbly on the other side. Thus, the sleeping porters were awakened not by the gentle tickle of lioness whiskers and the wet smudge of lioness nose, but by the death-wail of an ox, thrashing to throw the lioness from his back.

Immediately joining the cries of the participants in this battle were the shouts of the porters, the howls of Dionysus and the clang of pots being vigorously smashed into each other by Kamau, who was charging towards the slaughter. Knowing that the visibility was too poor for decent aim, Hassan was attempting to light multiple paraffin lamps as he chased Kamau. Malena – foreswearing modesty – tore out of the tent in her nightdress, grabbed a whip off one of the wagons and raced after Kamau and Hassan.

"Malena, no!" Tanya screamed. After the previous night's lions, Tanya had slept in her clothes, gripping her gun. But now, rifle in hand, she had no chance of getting a clear shot in the mêlée. And she was far from confident that, even with a clear shot, she could kill this lioness: the lions she'd shot previously had been eating a zebra carcass, not thrashing around furiously. Fleetingly, Tanya wished she'd never let Malena persuade her to take the supply wagons. "Blasted good intentions," Tanya muttered, running after Kamau, Hassan and Malena.

Heedless of safety and seemingly possessed by whatever spirit compels the Masai *moran* to confront lions in spear-to-paw combat, Malena landed a punishing lash on the lioness' face, which so discombobulated the creature that she fell from the ox's back. Immediately, however, she turned to Malena, with a snarl and a crouch.

Knowing well that the lioness' pose meant an imminent spring that would result in Malena's death, all witnesses to the lioness' posture took action. Malena let loose another lash of the whip from which the lioness flinched, turning her head directly into the pot that Kamau had heaved with stunning accuracy at her eyes. Roaring violently, the lioness then suffered the crash of the paraffin lamp that Hassan had hurled at her shoulder blades. Understandably, the sensation of her fur flambé-ing behind her ears incensed the lioness, and she threw herself at Malena in an enraged lunge.

The bullet pierced the lioness' heart and lungs when she was airborne, but for many reasons – the games adrenaline plays with perception, the dilatory nature of sound waves, the elastic properties of time during emergencies – parsing the exact sequence of events was impossible: the explosion of the gun, Malena's collapse under the dead cat, and Hassan's and Kamau's jaws dropping all seemed to happen simultaneously.

In the aftermath of the shooting, Tanya was temporarily deaf. The rifle was of a larger caliber than she liked to use, and the force of the shot had sent quake tremors through her skeleton. She dropped the gun. Eventually, however, cognizance of the smell of burning gunpowder, along with the odor of bloody ox entrails, prevailed upon her to hear the mournful screams of the dying ox, lying in shreds several steps away.

Taking a deep breath, and begging her bones to quit their quivering, Tanya willed herself to retrieve the gun. Then, holding her breath and squeezing shut her eyes, Tanya shot the ox.

Turning around, feeling well and truly like a tuning fork, Tanya saw Hassan and Kamau rolling the lioness' carcass off Malena's body. Kamau called to one of the porters to bring a knife so that he could skin the lioness and, in the next breath, cursed in Swahili that the charred part of the lioness' fur had ruined the skin as a trophy.

Ignoring Kamau's criticism, Hassan helped Malena to sit up. The task was not easy. The lioness weighed some four hundred pounds, and even with the weight lifted, Malena felt herself compressed into two dimensions. Hassan eventually, however, succeeded in peeling Malena off the ground, and she wobbled in a semi-upright position. Then, wide-eyed with astonishment, Malena suddenly burst into hysterical laughter.

"Malena!" Tanya strode to her, concerned. "Malena!"

Malena's laughter continued, chest-shaking and convulsive. Tears streamed from her eyes.

Tanya exchanged a worried look with Hassan, who was holding Malena's hand and propping her body upright with his other arm. "Malena!" Tanya took Malena's other hand. "Are you well?"

"Tanya!" Malena finally spluttered through her laughter. "Tanya, the good Lord has seen fit to throw a lion at me."

Tanya looked confusedly at Malena, who was still laughing. "Yes, Malena," Tanya said finally, "even Daniel just sat with them."

"It is the will of Allah that the lion is defeated," Hassan remarked. "God is great."

"Oh Hassan, you are right," Malena bolted straight, suddenly serious. Facing Tanya, Malena said, "You have truly been an instrument of the good Lord's work, Tanya. No man could have timed that shot better or aimed with greater accuracy."

"Luck," Tanya muttered shyly. "I was a fool to let the oxen be lion bait." She frowned, thinking about the difficulties that a team of eleven – rather than twelve – oxen pulling a heavy wagon was going to encounter. "But you're not hurt, Malena?" Tanya asked, laying a hand on her leg.

It was wet.

Only then did anyone notice that Malena's lap was covered with blood. "Oh my," Malena squeaked, staring at the clotting puddles on her nightdress.

"It's the lioness' blood," Hassan suggested.

"Where do you feel pain?" Tanya asked.

"Nowhere," Malena shook her head, and then her facial expression changed from confusion to fear: "My legs."

Hassan immediately hoisted Malena into his arms and carried her to the tent, where Dionysus was having a fit from having been shut inside during the lion adventure. "Hush, Dionysus!" Tanya commanded, as Hassan lay Malena down on the blanket.

"Wait outside," Tanya ordered Hassan. Once they were safely alone, Tanya lit a paraffin lamp and rolled up Malena's nightdress. Malena's thighs were a bloody mess of scratches and punctures, some of them deep. As a parting gesture, the lioness had sunk her claws into Malena's legs.

As if commiserating across whatever unknown distance separated them, Hilary materialized in Tanya's mind, *le quote juste* (as always) on his lips: "Devouring Time, blunt thou the lion's paws," he murmured.

"Am I going to die?" Malena asked, looking away from the wound.

"No, silly, you have some surface scratches," Tanya chided her, while thinking that Devouring Time would – must – cause the inevitable scars to fade. "But we'd better clean and bandage these wounds. Hassan!" Tanya called. "Bring the medicine box!"

"Memsahib?" came Hassan's voice from without.

"The medicine box," Tanya repeated, turning to the tent flap. "Bring it."

Hassan's pause annoyed Tanya, so she charged out of the tent. "I'll get it myself," she declared. "Where is it?"

"With the Masai elders," Hassan admitted.

Tanya stared, uncomprehending, at Hassan. "Where?"

"At the *enkang* where we stayed last night." Hassan's face wore, not a guilty look exactly, but an expression of disappointment that he had disappointed Memsahib. "I am truly sorry, Memsahib."

"The medicine box," Tanya repeated a final time, hoping that she was experiencing a mere linguistic malfunction. "With the tincture of iodine."

"Yes, Memsahib."

"And the bandages?"

"Yes, Memsahib."

"And the quinine tablets?"

"Yes, Memsahib."

"At the *enkang* where we stayed last night?"

"Yes, Memsahib."

"I told you not to sell anything to the Masai!" Tanya exploded.

"Not sold, Memsahib," Hassan clarified quickly. "Traded."

"Traded! Traded for what?"

"For a guide, Memsahib."

"A guide?" Tanya could have slapped Hassan. But she restrained herself by biting her knuckles vigorously. "What guide? Where is this guide?"

"A Masai guide, Memsahib. He has been following us all day at a distance, waiting for the moment of introduction."

"Send him back! Tell them we need the medicine box returned!"

"Impossible, Memsahib."

Tanya was on the verge of ordering Hassan back to the coffee plantation when he averted her useless gesture by suggesting, "Perhaps the guide could be of some assistance to Memsahib Malena."

"Do you imagine that allowing a *moran* to rape and murder Malena will be of assistance right now?" Tanya snapped.

"The guide is familiar with Masai medicine, Memsahib."

"Masai medicine?" Tanya snorted. "And you think people who live in dung huts practice a useful variety of medicine, do you? You think this guide will know a cure well-praised for its hygiene and effectiveness, perhaps? More likely their familiarity with Masai medicine was the reason they wanted our medicine box!"

"The Masai are a warrior people, Memsahib. They are accustomed to killing lions. They know how to treat open wounds."

"As do I!" Tanya retorted. "You wash the wound, disinfect it and bandage it!" Tanya was so frustrated that she was choking back tears and gulping repeatedly to clear her throat.

Impulsively, she yearned for her mother; Tanya had never seen Bess Rungsted flustered by a physical injury – not even during Tanya's father's long decline resulting from his war wounds. In an attempt to calm herself and think reasonably about the situation, Tanya imagined she was her mother. Bess Rungsted in this situation would find a doctor, and Tanya needed to do the same.

The nearest doctor – or, at least, the closest medicine box – would be with Lord Delamere. Tanya hoped they weren't too far from the Narosera River, but even another two or three days (and Tanya knew she couldn't guess how far they truly were) would be a long time to let an infection fester. Leaving a wound without antiseptic in East Africa was courting disaster. Chiggers, ticks and all manner of insect eggs could find their way into it. Bacteria, moreover, were tenacious, emboldened by the climate. (Tanya recalled the scar on Gokal's arm, from a cut that had healed on the surface, but was a roiling bag of puss beneath the skin; Gokal eventually had had to slice open the wound to drain it.) Nor was Tanya comforted by the knowledge (too terrifying to dwell upon) that death from infections was common in East Africa.

The best solution, Tanya concluded, was to treat and dress the wound as comprehensively as possible now. The supply train had both soap and water with which to clean the wound, and Tanya could rip up Malena's nightdress for bandages. Then they'd have to drive the wagons as fast as feasible to Narosera River, where Malena hopefully would find proper medical treatment.

Having taken this decision, Tanya did not waste ego on the realization that optimal implementation of both prongs of this plan required the assistance of the Masai guide. In the circumstances, refusing the guide would have been petty, and the price for such childishness would have been paid with stubborn scars on Malena's thighs – or worse. Tanya was too much of a noblewoman to allow any such outcome.

"Hassan," she ordered, "bring the guide."

"Memsahib," he replied, relieved, "he is come." Hassan pointed to the campfire area, where the porters were bedding down again after the night's excitement. There, among the trousered Kikuyu porters, was a lanky man clad only in a *shuka* thrown over his shoulder. Tanya realized that, after she and Malena had retired into their tent, this *moran* must have joined their party, as the dangers of the East African bush foreclosed any possibility of a man sleeping alone under the stars.

Seeing that the moment for introductions had arrived, the *moran* approached Tanya with a confident strut. Frowning, she examined him, from his shaved head and dangling ear lobes to his long, knuckled toes. When her eyes returned to his face, his smile seemed to convey that he didn't have cause to look her over in the same manner. He pointed at his chest and said, "Lekishon."

SEVEN

Lekishon drove their supply train so hard that Tanya thought him an ideal recruit for the Carrier Corps: if getting goods from Nairobi to the frontlines in record time was the goal, Lekishon ought immediately to be pressed into service. His pace had the oxen on the verge of foaming at the mouth, and even Hassan groaned periodically.

But Tanya dared not complain. Although she was confident that her Kikuyu porters would have wanted her to put the Masai *moran* in his place and slow down their caravan, Tanya refused to give Lekishon the satisfaction of knowing that he was wearing them out. Indeed, Tanya resisted giving Lekishon the satisfaction of having his presence acknowledged.

Tanya's grudge was more deeply rooted than her initial resistance to a Masai guide. Rather, she was embarrassed. When he'd reappeared, Tanya hadn't recalled Lekishon. But Malena had. Shorn of his warrior headdress and clothed in a simple *shuka*, Lekishon had looked like a fungible Masai *moran* to Tanya, but Malena had recognized the warrior who'd asked to see if her leg hair was yellow.

By then, however, Tanya was powerless to send him away. Lekishon had already gathered the roots of the droopy-flowered terere plant and crushed them to make a poultice; and he'd already skimmed the sap from the pale bark of the mbebe tree as a sealant for the open wound. These he was applying to Malena's ravaged thighs when Malena said, "Hassan, please ask him if he sent the lioness to attack me, so he could see if the hair of the beard of the maize is also on my legs."

Hassan almost certainly did not translate the question verbatim. Nonetheless, in response to what Hassan did say, Lekishon looked up with a smile that featured so many nuanced implications – of hedonism, of heroism, of seduction, of self-satisfaction – that Douglas Fairbanks would have gladly amputated his leg (below the knee) for the ability to flash such a smile. Then Lekishon replied with a sentence that Hassan translated as, "The lioness has initiated you into a bond."

Lekishon leaned back from where he'd been kneeling next to Malena, and he began rolling up his *shuka*, which he'd tied around his waist (at Hassan's insistence) before entering Tanya's and Malena's tent. Dionysus, who had been lying supportively by Malena's side, emitted an anxious growl. Malena and Tanya caught their breath (although they'd already seen anything he could have shown them when they'd first encountered him). But Lekishon stopped unveiling before exposing the ladies to any unseemly flesh.

Malena and Tanya convulsed again, but this time for different reasons. Malena was disappointed. Tanya was amazed: there, on Lekishon's thighs, was a mass of scars. They were subtle – light and thin. Neither

Malena nor Tanya would have noticed them without Lekishon pointing to them. But once examining them, neither Tanya nor Malena could fail to notice that the formation looked similar to the gouges on Malena's thighs.

"He says a lion also mauled him. Long ago," explained Hassan.

Gesturing to Malena and then to himself, Lekishon made a pronouncement. "You and he are now like brother and sister, Memsahib," Hassan translated.

Malena, suspecting that the tenor had been different in the original, blushed. Tanya, likewise suspicious of Hassan's interpretation, changed the subject: "Did he put the same plant treatments on his lion scratches?"

Hassan confirmed with Lekishon and then replied in the affirmative. Tanya felt relieved. She was still too frightened of the possibility to utter the word "infection," but she opined hopefully: "Real medicine is soon within reach anyway."

Lekishon said that they were two or three days away from Narosera River, but in Tanya's experience natives were incapable of accurately estimating travel times or distances. In addition, Lekishon seemed to be ignoring the fact that ox wagons couldn't travel as fast as Masai *moran* could run.

Still, Tanya was determined that the supply train would match Lekishon's speed to whatever extent possible. Getting Malena to reputable medical treatment justified any hardship in Tanya's view. Despite Lekishon's ministrations, Malena was too weak, and in too much pain, to ride her mule. Hassan was riding the animal, while Malena lay (with Dionysus curled against her) in the first ox wagon, drifting fitfully in and out of sleep – a condition that terrified Tanya. The prospect of entrusting Malena to the care of a doctor, and simultaneously of divesting herself of responsibility for her friend's health, provided so much relief to Tanya that she willingly charged after Lekishon and demanded that the rest of the supply train follow suit.

Besides, the faster they reached Narosera River, the faster they'd be free of Lekishon, whose rapidity was (in Tanya's opinion) an antic demonstration of prowess. That he was attempting to impress a woman like Malena, whose Christian morals and genuine devotion to her husband could have set the benchmark for those qualities, suggested that

Lekishon had a penchant for blondes that went well beyond the normal scope of that failing. Tanya vaguely worried that Lekishon might be a greater danger to Malena than blood-loss, bacteria or any other injury-related complication. Given this nagging concern, as well as her realization that Lekishon's haste was a form of unintended cooperation with her own plan to rid the supply train of his presence, Tanya was not inclined to slow him down.

As tea-time approached, however, Tanya began to hallucinate that a skeleton wearing a Masai cloak – the Indigenous Reaper – was riding behind her on her mule, wrapping the sun-baked bones of its arms ever tighter about her waist. A chorus of angels behind it sang:

> *Shosholoza!*
> *Kulezontaba*
> *Stimela si phume*
> *Kenya*

The song had an uplifting lilt to it, and Tanya turned in her saddle out of curiosity to see what kind of angelic choir could accompany death with such a jaunty bounce. The skeleton then spoke in a familiar voice: "Memsahib," it said, "you must drink water now."

The water was hot from having been kept in a calabash in the ox wagon, but the temperature was no obstacle to its rehydration properties. And with her first sip, Tanya's heat delusion faded. She was nominally in the saddle, but Hassan had brought his mule directly beside hers and was preventing Tanya from falling with his arm about her waist. He was practically forcing her to drink. She pushed him away weakly. "I can do it myself Hassan," she murmured.

Hassan steered his mule away respectfully, and Tanya steadied herself. Gulping from the calabash, Tanya began to feel restored. She could feel her blood draining downward from her head, as if it had coagulated in the heat and had just now been thinned by her intake of water. But as Tanya was about to return the calabash to Hassan, she realized that her hallucination was ongoing. The angel choir was still singing:

> *Wenuyabaleka*
> *Kulezontaba*
> *Stimela si phuma*
> *Kenya*

Tanya jerked around, causing Hassan to lurch towards her, ready to catch her should she plummet from the mule. But she stayed on her mount as her eyes struggled to comprehend the scene behind her. "Hassan?"

"Yes, Memsahib?"

"Are the porters singing?"

"Yes, Memsahib."

"Why?"

"The weariness, Memsahib, is relieved by singing."

And, indeed, the porters were on the verge of the kind of cake-walk marching that appears only in military parades staged in musical comedies. "But what are they singing?"

"A South African song, Memsahib. One of the porters worked for a Boer whose servant taught it to him."

Swallowing thickly, Tanya turned to face forward. She didn't understand the words of the song or the powers at work that had inspired the porters collectively to seek strength in music. But the song was like the monsoon winds that push dhows across the Indian Ocean, between the Eastern coast of Africa and the Western coast of India. The song at her back was thrusting their entire supply train forward, over the earthen undulations of Masailand to the replenishing currents of the Narosera River, and Tanya gratefully surrendered as it carried her along.

"Go forward!" the porters sang in Ndebele (although they didn't know what language they were singing). "Hurry over the mountains/the train is coming from/Kenya." Composed by miners as an anthem to empower work gangs with the strength for sustained toil, along with the hope that they would live through the day, the song represented the transformation of body-destroying labor into art. It was a distillation of the most regenerative aspects of human capacity, preserved in music to outlast the black lungs that first powered the sound with their expansions and contractions. Without knowing the song's history, the porters, Hassan, Malena, Tanya – even Lekishon, who was pretending to ignore the singing – could sense the tremendous triumph pent up in its measures. Buoyed by that victory, the supply train went forward, hurrying over the harsh and rich ground of Kenya.

THE CELEBRATION HUSBAND

* * *

A week later, they reached Lord Delamere's camp on the Narosera River.

The delay was not the fault of Lekishon, who true to his promise had led the supply train along the most direct route; nor was it the fault of Tanya, whose determination to maintain a swift pace never flagged. Nor were the porters to blame – they excelled themselves in their feats of physical endurance on the safari. Malena, also, had not been a drag on the supply train's pace: with continued application of the herbal poultices (a job that Tanya took over from Lekishon), Malena was making an impressive, infection-free recovery, so much so that she was able to sit at the front of the first ox wagon and read Bible stories to the porters, who wished she was still sick enough to lie quietly and allow them to chat amongst themselves.

Rather, the long travel time was the result of the rate at which oxen plod: even whipping oxen mercilessly – even singing "Shosholoza" to oxen – doesn't produce a top rate of much more than two miles per hour. And Lord Delamere's camp was some hundreds of miles from Kijabe. (Their supply train would have made faster time if the porters, like those enlisted in the Carrier Corps, had carried the goods.)

Compounding the oxen's sluggishness were the challenges of the geography. Before reaching the camp, the caravan had to pick its way along the Narosera River, which twisted beneath a canopy of dense botanicals. Fat baobab, yellow-fever acacia, and shiny-leafed mango trees shaded the river and hosted handsome colobus monkeys, their black fur augmented with white strands streaming down their backs and culminating in impressive white pom-poms at the end of their tails. Gnarled networks of exposed tree roots demarcated the crowded river banks, on which papyrus, purple amaranth and the poisonous datura thrived. Strangler fig snaked around trees; orchids augmented the lower trunks; wild pumpkin drooped over the river, eventually casting its round fruit adrift.

Alert for lurking hippopotamus and crocodile, the caravan had to detour for elephants, unexpectedly soft-footed and, despite their heft, capable of much more flexible navigation of the terrain than the caravan.

Both the oxen and the wagon wheels were maladapted to this jungle, and at one point the party had to stop to dislodge the wagon pulled by only eleven oxen.

When they finally arrived at Lord Delamere's camp, Tanya mistook it for a *manyatta*. Her error was not reasonable. The previous day, the supply train had encountered one of Lord Delamere's native runners, who had advised that they would reach the camp within a day. But though she knew the camp was nearby, Tanya could not reconcile the human gathering before her with her idea of a camp that might house Lord Delamere. Tanya's confusion was no doubt augmented by her selective perception: she was blind to the canvas tents and the white soldiers; she didn't notice the British flag hanging limply in the breezeless heat; she didn't register the snippets of English-language conversation.

All she saw was Masai men. They were standing in groups around tent entrances and lolling on crates of military supplies; they were drinking milk out of shared calabashes and arguing with each other on topics incomprehensible to Tanya. Platoons of *moran* were briskly striding into and marching out of the camp in what appeared to be a perpetual cycle of activity.

"Hassan," Tanya snapped, "tell Lekishon that I don't care if his brother or whoever lives at this *manyatta*. We're not going to break before we reach Lord Delamere."

But Lekishon had already disappeared into the crowd of Masai men, a blur of *shukas*, walking sticks and hanging earlobes from which Tanya couldn't distinguish him.

"Memsahib," Hassan explained apologetically, "we are arrived."

Tanya looked quizzically at Hassan; but, before she could seek clarification, Malena, who was experiencing none of Tanya's disorientation, hobbled beside her and clasped her shoulder. "I knew we would make it," she gushed. "Oh Tanya, you are so magnificent. I don't know another woman who could have taken us across Masailand. Even a man couldn't have done better than you. The blessings of the Lord upon you!" Malena fairly crushed Tanya in a hug of unexpected strength. Then Malena released Tanya and sang, "I'm going to find Erik!"

"Erik? You're not even supposed to be walking. You need to see the camp doctor!" Tanya started after Malena, who was moving with terrific agility for a woman with two scratched-up thighs, but Tanya's plunge into the camp's hubbub abruptly halted at a sight that elated her: navigating the milling Masai, threading his way towards her on a little bicycle, was an enormous Swede.

Big and broad, generous in spirit and smile, the Swede was overjoyed at seeing his wife at the camp. "Tanya!" Isak boomed, dropping the bicycle out from under him as he rushed to her on foot. "My *prinsesstårta!*" he cried, lapsing immediately into his habit of referring to Tanya as a Swedish cake. He enfolded Tanya in a crushing hug for the second time in as many minutes. Giggling, Tanya surrendered to his affectionate onslaught of kisses. The scent of his body – sweat and dirt and tobacco and *Isak* – flooded her with a joyous warmth. Wagging his tail with a vigor that threatened to propel him airborne, Dionysus was yelping and jumping at the couple's lower regions, begging for inclusion.

"Look at what you've done!" Isak exclaimed, lifting Tanya into the air and swinging her around. As he set her down, he regarded the ox wagons. "Let the Germans look on the bravery of our wives and tremble!" Feeling a wet tongue coating his hand, Isak cried, "Dionysus!" and bent to kiss the nose of his ecstatic pet. "The dust of Masailand has added sheen to your coat!" he proclaimed. "Hassan!"

As Isak delightedly clapped Hassan's hands between his own, Tanya flushed with embarrassment at her sudden awareness that her reunion with Isak was public – and observed. A variety of soldiers in various states of dishevelment had gathered around the ox wagons; some had already begun to examine the supplies, but others were simply staring at the peculiar sight of a white woman on the banks of the Narosera River.

Tanya shushed Dionysus, who was barking himself hoarse with happiness at seeing Isak. She then hurriedly removed the supply inventory from her inside shirt pocket and handed it to Isak, who – engrossed in pleasantries with Hassan – passed the list automatically to another white man.

"Hassan, take the porters to that tent," Isak gestured to the mess, "and eat. You've earned this meal thrice over. Tanya, my *prinsesstårta*," Isak said, cupping her jaw with his two hands, "May I offer you honey mead from my own goblet and feed you Turkish delight with my own hand?"

"Oh yes please, Isak," Tanya giggled, and then she blushed again, angry at the ease with which Isak could charm her into forgetting the greedy eyes surveilling them. "Perhaps in your tent? And, oh, Malena needs a doctor. We must first attend —"

"Doktor!" Isak yelled in greeting to a passing white man, "See this *mzungu* flower?" Isak swept Tanya into his arms, and the doctor swallowed his bemused smile. "There's another one running around the camp, though not as lovely to behold as this one —"

"— Her name is Malena —"

"— Find her and fix her. Something is wrong with her —"

"— She was mauled by a lion!" Tanya called after the doctor, but Isak was already charging to his tent, with Dionysus in excited pursuit. Isak barreled into the cool, dark space and deposited Tanya beneath him on his blanket with a tad less gentleness than her mule-sore body would have chosen. Exercising more discretion than his master, Dionysus stopped outside the tent and, after panting and looking about for several minutes, lay down to guard the entrance.

Pushing himself up and hovering over Tanya, Isak tickled her face with his shaggy hair and asked, "Was she really mauled by a lion?"

"Horrifying, Isak, yes," Tanya answered, closing her eyes miserably at the memory. "She was bloody like my father must have been after the Germans shot him open."

Isak rolled onto his side and traced Tanya's facial features with his fingers. His own face then clouded in an atypical expression of anguish. "You have come through hell, I can see it. You are gaunt. But that I could have been by your side!"

Isak pulled Tanya to him, and she thought to protest that, in light of their dramatic and well-marked decampment into his tent, modesty demanded that they forebear engaging in any act that gossips would attribute to them; in any event, she wanted to bathe, she suspected that a tick was boring into her leg, and – like the porters – she could do with food and drink. (She felt that she'd earned a meal since Isak had just recognized that she was, blessedly, thin). But wrapped in Isak's arms, her face pressed to his chest, with his breath around her head and the thump of his heart reverberating in her cheek, she realized that her most immediate desire was to tell him everything: about the paralyzing frustrations at Kijabe, the profiteering of Hassan, the insolent violence of Mr. Baden – and the more insolent behavior of Hilary Gordon – the anthropological scrutiny to which Kamau subjected her; the heat, dehydration and exhaustion of the safari; the cruelty of the *kariakor*, the stress of not knowing how to find their way to Narosera River, her fear both of the Germans and of being thought a German sympathizer, the cultural assault of the Masai, the physical assault of the lioness, her terror that Malena would die; her constant sense of humiliation, inadequacy and dislocation; and her struggle to maintain, throughout, the dignified bearing of a Baroness.

Opening her mouth to confide in him, however, she discovered herself beyond words, shaking and sobbing, Isak's hot tongue licking the tears off her face.

* * *

Tanya needn't have worried about nosey minds calculating the time she and Isak were in his tent and speculating about their activities within. The ox wagons were so spectacular a development that they eclipsed anything as pedantic as a fellow soldier's relations with his own wife. Cheers greeted each fresh item unloaded from the wagons. Ammunition and rope, dried fruit and tea – whatever it was received a reception fit for a pony on Christmas morning.

Howls of ecstasy, however, greeted the emergence of a crate of rum. "Finally, I can have breakfast!" one soldier delighted.

Feeling hungry, Isak and Tanya left their tent and wandered, hand-in-hand, Dionysus trotting beside them, towards the mess, pausing along their way by the crowd around the supply train. Isak nudged through the throng until he stood beside the man holding the supply train inventory. "My wife is amazing, isn't it?" Isak inquired jovially.

"A damned fine piece of work," the man agreed. "Only a couple of items missing."

"Missing?" Tanya balked. She'd checked and rechecked the inventory list before their departure from Kijabe; all items on the inventory had been on the ox wagons. "Hassan," Tanya growled under her breath and strode toward the mess tent, leaving Isak joshing with his colleagues.

In the mess, Tanya found rows of unstable-looking wooden tables, accompanied by crates instead of benches. At the back of the tent, several black soldiers were stirring large cauldrons. An odor – equal parts grease, porridge and wood-smoke – thickened the air inside the tent, and dark smudges adorned the tent's sides.

Tanya's supply train staff was grouped around a single table, where they ate with the mechanical dutifulness of starved men consuming tasteless grub. Tanya scanned the raft of porters for Hassan.

A white officer stepped into her line of vision. "You're the supply train saint?" he asked.

"I'm Baron Isak von Brantberg's wife," Tanya deflected, shy of praise.

But the officer savaged her expectations with his next comment: "Just now your porters have eaten the equivalent of all the food you brought on those wagons."

"I'm certain it can't be that – I'm sorry," Tanya stammered, confused. "They've worked very hard for many days."

"Bloody waste: feeding natives," the officer scoffed and stalked off.

Shocked at the exchange, Tanya stood immobile and distracted for several moments. By the time she regained her bearing, however, she was again diverted, this time by Lord Delamere. "Baroness, kindly accompany me," he said as he scooped her along with a tsunami motion of his arm that carried her all the way into his tent.

The tent was teeming with Masai elders, drinking, smoking and conversing. They perched on chairs and on the table, and they lounged on blankets and pillows on the floor. The mixture of alcohol, tobacco and goat fat stenches made Tanya gag, and she froze inside the tent at its entryway, prepared – indeed hoping – to flee.

Utterly unfazed by the conversion of his tent into a pub for Masai elders, Lord Delamere stomped into the center of his tent where, without any preliminaries, he began shouting furiously in Maa. Similarly unimpressed with Lord Delamere's display of rabid temper, the Masai elders agreeably sauntered out of the tent. Wholly astonished by the responses on both sides, Tanya fought to hide her trembling as the elders filed past her.

When the tent had belched out the last Masai man, Lord Delamere sighed and collapsed into a chair next to the table. He rubbed his bald scalp. A short man, Lord Delamere married in his person the will of Ivan the Terrible and the body of Marcel Proust. His head was overlarge, his muscles stringy and his facial features tended towards comparisons with geese. Often, he was sick; at this moment, he was between bouts of dysentery and heading for a serious case of malaria. Nonetheless, Lord Delamere commanded more authority and respect than the entirety of the colonial administration. His word determined, to large extent: what crops the colonists grew; what employment opportunities were available to natives and on what terms; and what governance policies the colonial administration adopted. No man's influence in British East Africa was greater in times of peace and, with his gambit on the Narosera River, Lord Delamere hoped to extend his contribution into the sphere of war.

"Baroness," Lord Delamere sighed, "my hospitality is sadly impaired at present. Brandy?"

"Yes, thank you," Tanya replied meekly. Tanya wouldn't normally have accepted a brandy at noon and on an empty stomach, but she was frightened. She had met Lord Delamere before, and she was on familiar enough terms with him to call him by his preferred nickname – D. – but she could see no reason for him to seek a private conference with her. He was a powerful and busy man and, if he'd wanted to thank her for bringing the ox wagons, he could have done so in the mess. His demeanor only enhanced her sense of foreboding.

"Bloody good shooting, I hear," he commented, as he poured generous doses into two tin cups. "Sit," he gestured to the other chair by the table.

"I'm sorry?" Tanya replied, obeying by sitting primly on the chair's edge.

"Killed a lion, saved that woman's life. Unusual bravery for anyone," he said, handing the tin cup to Tanya.

"Oh, I don't know," Tanya lowered her eyes.

Lord Delamere clinked cups with Tanya. "Cheers," he said and bolted the brandy. Taking a moderate sip from her own cup, Tanya immediately felt the physical confirmation of her hunch that drinking before lunch would be injudicious. Lord Delamere, for his part, refilled. "This war has been hell on my brandy reserves," he grimaced. "I pray every night that the brandy will hold out until we beat the Germans." He gulped from his cup. "Not that it makes a damned difference."

"Well it's nice brandy," Tanya said, feeling that compliments were never out of place with powerful men, "though I suppose you could drink gin —"

"— Not that. Beating the Germans in East Africa isn't going to end the war, Baroness. This war will be settled in Europe."

"Then why are we fighting here?" The question escaped – softly, but impossible to ignore – before she could squelch it, and she looked down, nervous to be challenging Lord Delamere.

Lord Delamere shrugged his shoulders. Then he snorted derisively. "Von Lettow-Vorbeck's trigger finger is faster than a torpedo blasting off a U-boat. We no sooner heard about the war than he was blowing up the railway."

"But I thought the British navy attacked Dar-es-Salaam in early August?" Tanya asked, now genuinely confused. "Wasn't that the first battle of the war?"

Lord Delamere looked annoyed. "The navy doesn't count. It didn't get us into this war. Von Lettow-Vorbeck was mobilizing, so those incompetent sea cretins shelled Dar-es-Salaam." Lord Delamere scowled. "As if von Lettow-Vorbeck needed Dar! He invaded British East Africa and occupied Taveta a week later. He was within fifty miles of the railroad – a perfect staging ground for raids. We can't very well let him cut our crops off from the market, can we?"

"So this front is about the economic welfare of the settlers," Tanya began, and then hastened to rephrase her question to clarify that her interests were aligned with those of the British, "That is to say, we're fighting for our finances?"

"Land, too, of course – the German farms are all bunched up on the slopes of Kilimanjaro. They'd love to stretch out in the Rift Valley. But we can't have German soldiers running amok here – they'd rape and loot, and we have our values to uphold."

"We're fighting them because they're fighting us, D. That's what you're saying isn't it?"

He sighed and smiled, "That's not what *I* said." Then he changed the subject. "How did you find this camp?"

Tanya didn't know whether to be more perplexed by the apparent lack of cause for the fighting in East Africa, or by the readiness of people like Lord Delamere to dismiss this troubling void. She didn't understand how men could fight for no reason (though she wouldn't have admitted her disquiet to Hassan). But Lord Delamere seemed obviously unwilling to continue the conversation, so she answered his question: "We followed the Ewaso Nyiro River until we came to the Narosera River tributary."

"How did you know to do that?"

"A guide, a Masai, led us that way."

"Good, aren't they? The Masai scouts," Lord Delamere nodded.

"I don't trust them."

"Good woman," Lord Delamere smiled. Then his smile evaporated. "You're not British, Baroness."

"No."

"But are you trustworthy?" He sat forward and scratched his forehead. "Mind you, I'm an ass to ask you that question."

"D., you know I'm trustworthy," Tanya insisted, hoping her voice didn't betray her desperation. If being thought a German sympathizer by the Nairobi busybodies irked her, the idea of Lord Delamere distrusting her was unbearable. Tanya groped for the right argument that would persuade him. "We grew coffee on your advice. My husband is volunteering with your men. I just risked my life and the lives of my farm staff to bring you supplies. I would never betray the English cause. I am a noblewoman, a woman of honor, a Baroness."

Lord Delamere studied her with a thoughtful, if depressed, expression – as if deploring the pandemonium of the British Army that left him reliant on a foreign woman, but steeling himself to make the best of the situation. "Do you know why I'm here in Masailand?" he asked finally.

"You're recruiting scouts?"

"Baroness, at all costs, secrecy must be maintained about my next statement."

"I understand," Tanya nodded and placed her drink on the table to signal her seriousness.

"You cannot confide our conversation even to your husband."

"I understand."

"Nothing short of absolute secrecy can be tolerated —"

"— D., I would die by my own hand before I would betray your trust."

"I hope so."

"I would!"

Lord Delamere scrutinized her set jaw and trembling eyes. "I believe," he said softly, "that you believe that you would."

Tanya quivered with confusion, not knowing if he was mocking or crediting her.

"I will tell you," he said, making a calming gesture with his hand. "'Recruiting scouts' is a convenient cover for the more important – and secret – part of our mission: we're making maps." He paused for Tanya to digest the information. "Have you seen a precise, detailed, accurate map of British East Africa?" he continued. Tanya shook her head slowly. "That is because none exists," he declared. "Correction: none existed until today." He reached below the table and rummaged in his leather boot, eventually producing a folded piece of parchment. He held it out to her. Tanya hesitated, but Lord Delamere waved the map until she reluctantly accepted it. "Open it." As Tanya complied, he finished his brandy and poured himself another, topping off Tanya's cup in the process.

The map had been drawn with a firm, confident hand. It depicted the portion of British East Africa extending from the Magadi branch line of the railway (east of Lord Delamere's camp) south into German East Africa. Tanya absorbed the stretch of land shown on the map, including the Eight Mile River, the Besil River, Lake Magadi, Lake Natron, the Ingito Hills and Mount Longido, just over the border. The map identified paths carved by frequent foot traffic, watering holes, *manyattas* and *enkangs* available for shelter and food, and points at which Germans had been spotted or where skirmishes with the enemy had occurred.

"The Germans are enjoying a fine time on Longido," Lord Delamere complained gruffly. "They're sending raiding parties out from the mountain to blow up the Magadi branch line."

"I heard over the telegraph at Kijabe that they're doing the same thing out in Tsavo."

"Using Kilimanjaro as a base," Lord Delamere affirmed. "We'll get there. Tsavo is our next mission, although I don't know what we'll do without the Masai – Tsavo's out of their range. We started here because these Masai know every thorn tree and creek bed in this area. Nomads and marauders, yes, but damned useful if you want to make a map," Lord Delamere chuckled. "Damned necessary, in fact, because it's bloody difficult to do a proper survey here and, without a map, where are you?" he demanded, either ignorant of the pun or taking it very seriously. "We can't secure our borders, we can't protect our railway, we can't route the Germans out of their bases. This map," Lord Delamere pointed emphatically at the parchment in Tanya's hands, "will change all that."

"Why are you telling me all this?" Tanya swallowed uncomfortably. She refolded the map and placed it carefully between them on the table.

"Baroness, intoxicated women make me nervous, but I have noticed that you stopped drinking a while back in our conversation, and I am feeling lonely," Lord Delamere said, raising his glass.

Dutifully, Tanya lifted hers, toasted him silently and sipped listlessly at her drink. She had a premonition that this conversation would leave her despondent.

After watching her drink for several seconds, Lord Delamere allowed, "The Masai know the terrain, but they're no cartographers. This map was not made by Masai."

"Isak made this map," Tanya stated flatly. She'd recognized his hand the instant she'd unfolded the parchment.

"Baroness, you are keen. He finished this map this morning, before you arrived."

"D., why are you telling me this?"

"You will not mind me speaking paternally to you, Baroness. It's only on account of the age difference. And I've had some experience. War is, of course, abominable —"

"— My father was a soldier —"

"— Then he probably told you that war is not as tragic as marriage."

Tanya's eyes flared. After a moment, she jutted out her lower jaw.

"Your husband, so far as I can tell, has three passions. You. Game hunting. And cartography."

"There are others," Tanya said in a tight voice.

"You know him pretty well."

"Well enough." Tanya construed the ensuing silence as a dare. "Gambling," she tossed on the table, raising the stakes.

Lord Delamere nodded, his eyes fixed on Tanya's face.

"I fear he's prone to debt," she said softly. "And drink. And —" Tanya bit her lip. Confessing her husband's vices was shameless, but she wanted to show D. that she trusted him as a way of reinforcing that the reverse should also be true.

"If I was going to carnival in Venice, no man would rank higher on my list of desired companions than Baron Isak von Brantberg. He is made for life's celebrations," Lord Delamere observed.

Tanya winced. Never so clearly had she registered that a celebration husband was not an unmixed blessing.

Lord Delamere rolled on: "But I'm not in Venice, I'm on the Narosera River. I'm not at carnival, I'm at war. And I don't need the good Baron to revel in life's pleasures; I need him to draw maps."

"I beg you, say directly: why are you telling me this?" Tanya entreated.

"Because the only time Isak von Brantberg sobered up long enough for a good stretch of work was yesterday, after that native runner returned announcing that you were on your way." Lord Delamere spoke seriously, but not unkindly, and his watery eyes watched Tanya's face carefully. When he saw that she was able to control the spasm of displeasure that had been disfiguring her features, he continued. "Because I have a proposal for you."

This shift in attention from Isak to herself surprised Tanya. "For me?"

"It will be dangerous." Lord Delamere paused. "It's more danger than any woman should be asked to confront. But you maneuvered four supply wagons across Masailand. You killed a lion. You saved a woman's life. You are the muse that was mid-wife to this map. I am not entirely convinced that you are mere mortal."

"D., don't be daft. I don't know how to do anything on my own."

"Now you're being daft. Some people admire female modesty. I'm not one of them."

Tanya opened her mouth to protest, but her objection remained unspoken. She'd realized before the words escaped that Lord Delamere would neither appreciate nor care if she insisted that she was not being modest, and she didn't know what else to say. She was too confused by the situation. The brandy, the flattery, the map, the disclosure of Isak's drunkenness, the allusions to tragedy and danger – all conspired to leave her unmoored in the conversation.

Before Tanya could close her mouth, Lord Delamere returned to his proposal: "I have absolutely no doubt that you can do what I'm proposing. But you must know that it will be dangerous."

"I'll do it." The answer flew from her mouth before her mind could approve, but her feelings fully supported it. D. had declared his faith in her, and instinctively, instantly she'd known herself worthy of it.

"Baroness, don't be reckless."

"On my word of honor, noblewoman to nobleman, I am not reckless to accept that which you ask of me. I know you wouldn't ask it unless it was necessary."

"I see no other way," Lord Delamere apologized.

"I'll do it. What is it?"

"Carry this map to army headquarters in Nairobi. It's urgent, so take the Magadi branch line from Kajiado. Don't muck with your ox team. Send them back to Kijabe. I'll give you Kalonzo to lead them back – he's a proper soldier, even if he is Kamba. Anyway, your wagons are empty now so there's nothing to steal. You'll have to make something up about why you're sending the team back alone, I can't think what, but material for good lies is all around us – we just need to look. If you succeed in this mission, come for another map when I call you. Your being courier – I think it will keep Isak motivated to work if he knows you'll shortly be arriving."

Tanya looked at the map where it lay on the table. Then she looked at D.

Her expression confirmed for Lord Delamere the correctness of his decision to recruit her, though the sweetness of her determination also caused him some regret at the necessity of endangering her. But he truly saw no other way. Only he, Isak and non-English speaking Masai knew of their unit's undercover mission. Originally, Isak's job had been both to draw the maps and transport them to Nairobi, but Isak had proved himself too unstable to allow out of sight. When Lord Delamere considered sending the map back to Nairobi in Isak's care, his mind jammed on visions of the invaluable map, soaked with grain alcohol and trampled underfoot in some corrugated iron shack in the bush; and Isak, irreplaceable cartographer, passed out with an ox wagon rolling over his hands.

Unfortunately, no substitute courier was readily apparent. Obviously, no black could be trusted with so critical a task, Lord Delamere couldn't leave his unit, and every other white soldier was already overburdened. Lord Delamere had sought assistance from Army headquarters, but the intelligence chief, Colonel Meinertzhagen, had claimed to be too understaffed to supplement the irregular units. (Lord Delamere was almost gratified by this response, since sustained interface with the "regular" British Army invariably entailed unfathomable disorganization, communications breakdowns, and a leadership vacuum. In Lord Delamere's view, the "irregulars" were better left to their own resources.) Confronted with the imperative of taking another person into his confidence, Lord Delamere was now satisfied, as he gazed at Tanya, that the person he'd chosen was adequate to the mission and could also be relied upon to precipitate a highly-efficient, sober state in her husband.

All the same, Lord Delamere was an enthusiast both of strong wills and of strong women; and placing this strong-willed woman at risk of harm from the Germans was painful indeed. "If you are caught by the Germans, you must destroy the map," he said, distinctly pronouncing each word. "Hundreds, maybe thousands, of men will die if the Germans obtain accurate maps of British East Africa. Their maps are even worse than ours. Don't fail the cause: destroy the map. It's more important than," here Lord Delamere lowered his voice respectfully, "your life or . . . your honor."

"They would never dare," Tanya objected.

"They're Germans," Lord Delamere shrugged.

"Rape" was not a word that occurred to Tanya. Rather she dismissed the possibility – unnamed – with the thought of her photograph of von Lettow-Vorbeck. Flashing that picture, she would never even be searched by a German soldier. D. had made a better choice of spy than he'd realized.

But how, Tanya wondered, would D. react if he knew that she had von Lettow-Vorbeck's signed portrait? Tanya shivered. D. might applaud her possession of the ultimate repellant against German harassment. Or he might kill her.

Well, let him, she thought grimly. As Hassan would say, if it is the will of Allah, God is great.

Notwithstanding the reference to Islam, an embrace of fatalism did not account for Tanya's suddenly cavalier attitude about her own life. Rather, ever since he'd said it, Lord Delamere's remark that, "war is not as tragic as marriage," had been rattling around inside her skull.

Tragic? When they'd canvassed Isak's vices, they'd mentioned drinking, gambling and debt. Those behaviors weren't tragic; they were typically the stuff of comedy. Tragedy, as defined by that other emotional Dane, Hamlet, involved sturdier sins: betrayal, murder . . . and forbidden sex.

Tragic? Tanya felt convinced that Lord Delamere was telling her something with his choice of that adjective. Nor could she avoid suspecting, as well, to what sort of betrayal Lord Delamere had been alluding.

How twisted, she thought, that within minutes of feeling herself worthy of Lord Delamere's trust she was to discover herself unworthy of her husband's fidelity.

"You have chosen better than you thought," Tanya announced defiantly. "While I live, I shall never willingly surrender any map you entrust to me."

"Unusual bravery," Lord Delamere reiterated, "for anyone."

"Not bravery," Tanya corrected him. "My life is simply insignificant. To save it in exchange for a map would be an unconscionable bargain."

"Baroness, you speak wrongly."

Tanya stood. "D., are you telling me that you have not counted another woman among my husband's passions?"

Lord Delamere looked up, guiltily. He shook his head.

"No?"

"Baroness, that question has terrible implications, whatever the answer."

"Whatever the answer, I must know."

Lord Delamere shook his head.

"You disappoint me, D. You have the title, but nothing could be less noble than to prefer deceit over honesty to a wronged lady."

Lord Delamere shook his head again.

"It doesn't matter." Tanya lifted her chin. "I know anyway." She paused while Lord Delamere raised his head. "Am I wrong? Not a woman?"

"No," he sighed. "Women."

Though the word thrashed Tanya as thoroughly as a belt, she was proud enough to force herself to remain composed for a final question: "Native women?"

"Baroness, don't ask —"

"— I will carry your map. I will die for your map if need be. As a man of honor, you must recognize that the least I am owed is an answer to my question."

"Mostly Masai."

Lord Delamere admired the deliberation with which she retrieved the map off the table, secreted it in her shirt, turned away from him and walked, one foot in front of the other, towards the tent flap. The way she handled herself suggested that she could stand a lot of liquor. The quality was commendable in a noblewoman. "Tanya," Lord Delamere stopped her with his use of her name, "you must never doubt that you are his great love. He is only Sisyphus, lowering Merope in her own esteem. But not," he wagged a finger at her, "in mine."

Tanya swallowed and nodded faintly. She suspected that Lord Delamere was paying her a compliment, and she tried to be grateful. He had no idea of the inadvertent insult with which he had just complicated her pain. Blast those noblemen with their educations in the classics; she made a mental note to find out who Sisyphus and Merope were.

EIGHT

Sensitive to the awkwardness that could arise from the presence of two women in an otherwise all-male military encampment, Hassan had pitched his Memsahibs' tent at a respectful distance from those of the unit's officers. Although he assumed that both Tanya and Malena would sleep in their husbands' tents, he expected that they would find a need for their own tent; Hassan had observed that the camp had neither toilets nor bathing areas for ladies.

Kamau, for his part, had been profoundly underwhelmed by the lunch he'd consumed in the mess (consisting of flavorless *posho*, a thin gruel made from corn meal), and he'd resolved to cook a proper dinner to celebrate the reunions of Isak and Tanya and Erik and Malena. He was assembling the necessaries for his bush kitchen, and was about to find Tanya and ask her to shoot a guinea fowl or small antelope, when she marched past him and crawled into the tent.

Hassan, who had been adjusting a tie at one of the tent's corners, stood up. He exchanged a look with Kamau, who had also stood, pot-in-hand and face aghast.

From inside the tent came the kind of wailing that might have befit the Trojan women, their men slaughtered, their homeland conquered, their futures confined to slavery and concubinage. The tent literally quivered with Tanya's cries.

As if gaining a sudden awareness that canvas is not sound-proof, Tanya ceased screaming mid-ululation in favor of a more muffled sob. Hassan raised his eyebrows at Kamau, who frowned, dropped his pot and scurried to the tent.

"Memsabu?" Kamau asked, kneeling at the flap and permitting only his head into the privacy of the tent. Tanya was curled in a ball in a corner, pounding her legs with her fists.

Her grief staggered Kamau, who had never before witnessed anyone in the throes of such hellacious emotion. He'd seen Kikuyu women cry before, after their husbands had beaten them, but such tears were typically restrained by their pride and reluctance to reveal their hurt.

Kamau knew that his tribeswomen cried, too, when their children died, but at such times the other women prevented the grieving mother from lapsing into demonic emotional abandon. Kamau was confident, however, that neither situation applied now: Isak never beat Tanya, and they had no children. Although Kamau had no inkling of the true cause for Tanya's despair, had he known, he would have been astonished. Himself the son of his father's second wife, Kamau couldn't understand a man sleeping with another woman as a reason for his wife's emotional breakdown.

"Memsabu?" he whispered, determined not to be frightened, "I know the food here is unworthy of you, but you must not be so upset. Kamau will take care of you. Tonight, I will make a supper for your delight." He paused, wondering how to broach the subject of game. She did not seem to be in a state conducive to hunting; perhaps, Kamau considered, he could ask Bwana Isak to shoot their evening's meal.

But before Kamau could decide how to proceed, Tanya staggered him by rolling into a seated position and demanding, "Kamau, am I ugly?"

Kamau was taken aback, but also relieved. Here was a subject on which he felt competent to expound. "No, Memsabu," he answered with confidence. "You are not 'ugly.' You are 'very ugly.' Your trousers are the costume of Bwanas. Woman can be but very ugly dressed as a man. Looking upon you, a man sees another man, except not a handsome man, because your appearance is too much like a woman."

So certain was Kamau of the correctness of his discourse that he was indifferent to the impact his speech was having on Tanya: every statement caused her physically to shrink back, each conclusion added another crease to her face. In his innocence, Kamau would have continued his dissertation, but for the fact that Hassan at this moment hooked his hands under Kamau's armpits and lifted him away from the tent.

Tanya found the abrupt disappearance of Kamau's head from the tent flap perturbing; but she was also relieved. She heard a scuffle outside that seemed to entail a rather lot of whispered recriminations, including snippets of absurd conversation: "Only a madman makes argument with a stone"; "Obsidian doesn't cry," etc.

Then, after about a minute, Tanya heard Hassan cough outside her tent. "Memsahib?" Hassan asked tentatively.

Tanya returned to a fetal position. Her urge was to tell Hassan to bring her mother, Bess Rungsted. Instead, she moaned: "Hassan, I want a blanket and a pillow."

"I will find them, Memsahib," Hassan promised.

Listening to the sound of Hassan's retreating footsteps, Tanya closed her eyes and gulped thickly. What happens in a marriage is private, she thought, clenching her teeth and squeezing her eyes so tightly shut that she began to feel dizzy. Private, private! How could Isak dishonor her so thoroughly as to – she couldn't name his crime, she realized; "adultery" didn't capture the scandal of his descent to lie with native women, and "fornication" didn't place enough emphasis on his betrayal of her – but she couldn't even focus on her feelings about what Isak had done because she was reeling from having been humiliated in front of an entire unit of men.

All these men – including Lord Delamere, the most important nobleman in British East Africa – knew that she was sexually insufficient for her husband. Indeed, not merely that she was sexually insufficient, but that she was entirely incapable of satisfying his fancy: she was short, while the Masai women were tall; she was compact, while the Masai women were elegant; her skin posed no contrast to that of her husband's, while the Masai women lay against him resplendent in their variation. And their experience! Tanya had heard that even teenage Masai girls had loved many warriors. She was as helpless to compete as a warthog lusting after a lion.

She'd reflexively known that the Masai were danger personified. She'd intuited that their example would weaken her attachment to Isak, although she'd miscalculated how the rift would occur. She'd feared that the Masai would persuade her that "marriage without lovers was impossible" – that Hilary, therefore, was possible. Instead, they'd shown her that marriage *with* lovers is impossible – if the lovers are those of one's husband.

"Oh Tanya, I'm despondent." Malena's whimper exploded like a dynamite blast at close range. So absorbed had Tanya been in her own thoughts that she hadn't registered Malena's entrance into the tent. "Erik isn't here!" Malena dragged out the word "here" as if it was the high note in an aria. Then, sobbing, Malena buried her head in her hands.

Tanya opened one eye and appraised her miserable friend. Plainly, Malena was in no state to comfort anyone else. In a certain respect, Tanya didn't mind. Malena might well be the only person in the camp who didn't know of Isak's betrayal and before whom Tanya was not humiliated. And, as morbidly unhappy as she was, Tanya was willing to delay any act that would put Malena in the know, even if the price of Malena's ignorance was the total absence of womanly commiseration in Tanya's sorrows.

"Lie down here, Malena," Tanya murmured, patting the area on the tent floor next to her. "Did you see the doctor?"

"Useless," Malena whined, rubbing her eyes and lying down. "He says there's nothing for him to do."

"What?" Tanya opened her eyes, concerned. "Didn't he put antiseptic on the wound and bandage it?"

"Oh he did that," Malena affirmed, "but he said that the Masai medicine had already prevented infection, so the iodine and bandages were a needless waste of medical supplies."

"Stitches?"

"No, he says everything's already healed beyond stitches."

"But will the wounds scar?"

"He doesn't think so. He wants to talk to Lekishon about what herbs he used."

"Idiot doctor," Tanya snorted.

"And Erik isn't heeeeere!" Malena began crying again.

Outside the tent, Hassan cleared his throat prominently. "Memsahib," he announced, "the blanket and pillow is come."

Tanya lifted her head in the direction of the tent flap and called, "Bring them in, Hassan." As he did so she added, "And bring a blanket and pillow for Malena, too." As soon as he'd disappeared on this fresh mission, Tanya asked, "Why isn't Erik here?"

"He's been sent to the East African Mounted Rifles. Oh Tanya, I so wanted to see him! I am so disappointed!"

"Where are the East African Mounted Rifles?" Tanya asked to preempt more crying.

"They're protecting the Magadi branch line. Oh, why couldn't we have gone there?"

Tanya stifled an exclamation. Material for good lies was indeed all around her.

"I wanted to see him more than I love my own life," Malena sniffled, "and so the good Lord is punishing me for my sin of overzealous desirousness."

As Malena surrendered to a bout of sobbing, Tanya resisted the sardonic observation that Malena had no experience of overzealous desirousness or the associated punishments.

Outside the tent, Hassan coughed again. Bringing in the second pillow and blanket, Hassan asked if he could be of additional service to his Memsahibs, and Tanya replied that they wished to nap. Hassan departed with a nod, and Tanya urged Malena to rest. "You'll feel better when you wake up."

"I'll never feel better," Malena vowed, "until I am in Erik's arms."

Tanya didn't reply, but as she closed her eyes, she tried not to linger on how differently she felt about her own husband.

* * *

Tanya awoke, famished. Her awareness eventually expanded to take account of her face, which felt puffy from crying, and her throat, which felt scratched and dry. As an experiment, she opened her eyes. The darkness in the tent was absolute.

Curiosity as to what time it was goaded Tanya to shake off her sleep. Stretching, she realized that Malena was no longer in the tent. Feeling anxiously guilty, as if she'd overslept and was missing something, Tanya threw off her blanket and stepped out.

The moon was high and full, and the stars striped the sky as if it was a celestial zebra. Tanya squinted her eyes against the dazzling intensity of the moon's light. It drenched the camp in a cool luminosity, faintly greenish in tinge, and imbued everything with the mystique and romance of a black-and-white photograph.

Kamau looked up from where he was preparing to bed down. "Memsabu," he greeted her, "you are hungry."

"I'm starving," Tanya agreed. "What time is it?"

Kamau leaped to his feet. "Memsabu, Kamau will cook now. You will be very pleased. Very, very pleased. I have saved the livers from the birds Bwana Isak shot for supper, and I will prepare, right now, I will prepare: *omelette à la chasseur*. For you, Memsabu." Excited, Kamau bustled around the campfire as he spoke, gathering various bowls and pans, his tins of salt, pepper and spices, eggs, onions, garlic and oil. "Tea, Memsabu?"

Nodding her assent, Tanya asked, "Bwana Isak shot birds? So he already ate?"

"Yes, Memsabu," Kamau confirmed, rekindling the campfire. "He and the officers ate the fine guinea fowls I roasted for them with the sauce of wild figs. But I saved the livers especially for your omelette."

"Were you going to bed just now?"

"Yes Memsabu. It is time. Past 11."

"I'm sorry, Kamau. You must be sleepy, and I'm making you work."

"Memsabu, you must not worry yourself. You must be very, very happy."

From the tone of his voice, and his manifest eagerness to please, Tanya gathered that her earlier upset had discomfited Kamau. She felt bad: what happens in a marriage is private; her private woes should not be fretting the staff. Unfortunate that safaris afforded no privacy, she thought. "Where is Malena?" she asked, consciously dissuading herself from pursuing her thoughts any further.

"She is at the doctor. Lekishon is showing the doctor the treatment."

Tanya sighed heavily. She never should have slept so long. Her gluttonous sleep had disarranged Kamau's schedule and exposed her friend to unseemly advances, in the guise of medical care, from that cretinous Masai. And, of course, now she wasn't tired. She'd be sitting up all night while Isak . . .

Tanya sighed again, this time collapsing forward, head in hands, chest caved. She did not want to face Isak, but appearances demanded it. Spending the night elsewhere than in his tent would, naturally, compound the hateful gossip and bring more humiliation upon her. No, there was nothing for it: she would have to sleep – or lie awake – beside her husband, docile and obedient and without causing a row that could be overheard by his army mates. It was the only dignified course, the noble option.

Kamau thrust a cup of hot tea into her hands and resumed his cooking. Tanya grunted a demoralized thanks and caved forward again. Inhaling the steam, Tanya was about to capitulate to another crying jag, when the sound of footsteps made her sit up and compose herself.

From the direction in which Tanya turned, Lekishon carried Malena into the sparking firelight. "You can walk," Tanya said, coldly, as Lekishon gently deposited Malena beside Tanya.

"Lekishon is just being a gentleman," Malena smiled, patting the *moran*'s arm.

"A gentleman wouldn't devote such obvious attention to your thighs," Tanya objected.

Lekishon had been standing, smiling, until a combination of the knife-edge in Tanya's voice and a remark in Swahili from Kamau sent him off again into the night. Lekishon found Tanya's hostility curious when he pondered it, but typically he didn't. Unlike Kamau, Lekishon wasn't interested in the Kenya remade by British colonialism, except to the extent that it could be used to reestablish Masai dominance. For this reason, Lekishon reserved his interest and attention for foreigners who were susceptible to an appreciation of Masai superiority. Malena obviously recognized that Masai warriors like himself were creation's most exemplary expression of masculinity. Lord Delamere, as well, was a man appropriately humbled by Masai customs and society. This Tanya, however, was nothing: merely a stunted, cantankerous female, out of place in her own world. Lekishon saw no gain in seeking an understanding of her, and he readily dismissed her obvious dislike of him. Of course, that Kikuyu cook was another matter: Lekishon was annoyed that the boy had had enough arrogance even to address him in Swahili, much less to tell him to go away.

Watching Lekishon retreat, Malena tried placating Tanya, "The doctor was very impressed with his poultices."

Kamau cut short Tanya's riposte by proudly presenting her with the omelette and a fork. Tanya smiled gratefully at Kamau and stared down at her supper. She had felt virtuous in her starving state, nobler for being slimmer. Did she want to sully that achievement with this omelette? Even Isak, who was typically oblivious to her weight fluctuations, had called her "gaunt" – surely a good sign. But then two thoughts collided in her mind. The first was that Isak's opinion was nothing she wanted to consider right now. The second was that she adored *omelette à la chasseur*. Crashing together, these thoughts had the effect of starting Tanya eating in a voracious fashion that, had it been witnessed by anyone of noble birth, would have reminded them of their hounds tearing apart a fox.

"Besides, I am so blessed that the good Lord has seen fit to restore my health through Lekishon's graces," Malena continued. "My only regret is that this injury has been in vain. To have seen Erik, I would have willingly submitted to injury of any severity, but to have suffered without seeing him —"

"— You'll see him," Tanya interrupted curtly.

"The good Lord willing, of course, he will be returned to me," Malena agreed. "But I had wanted to see him now."

"You'll see him now. Three days."

Astonished, Malena looked inquiringly at Tanya, who was licking her fork and eyeing her plate with the plain intent of running her tongue over it. Kamau discreetly handed Tanya a biscuit with which to wipe the plate, and Tanya again smiled her gratitude.

"Tanya, what can you mean? Have you had word that Erik is returning to Lord Delamere?"

"No, Malena. We'll go to him. We'll send the porters back to Kijabe with the ox wagons. This nice soldier Kalonzo will lead them. We're taking the Magadi branch line from Kajiado to Nairobi. We'll go with Hassan and Kamau. And, I guess – we'll need a guide, it's a three-day trek – with Lekishon."

"You're not serious? Tanya, what about your work at Kijabe?"

"Gokal is already running the telegraph machine without me and, anyway, we'll be back at Kijabe before the ox wagons. No, Malena, you need a doctor in Nairobi, and you need one immediately."

"A doctor? But I'm healing —"

"— Malena, you cannot seriously credit the work of that libidinous charlatan. What has he done? Crush plants and mumble spells —"

"— The doctor was impressed with his cures —"

"— Doctor!" Tanya rolled her eyes. "The camp doctor must be a man of puny abilities or miniscule experience if he is not aware of the disposition of wounds in East Africa to knit up on the surface, while remaining a runny mess of puss beneath!"

Malena recoiled at the image.

"Remember Gokal's arm?" Tanya asked. "We cannot take any such risks with your," and here she lowered her voice almost to a whisper, "thighs."

Malena looked down, as if being reminded that she had such sinful parts saddened her.

Tanya crunched the biscuit with satisfaction. The omelette had rejuvenated her, and she felt confident that her next statement would win Malena to her cause: "Malena dearest, cheer up: we'll see Erik on our way to Kajiado."

When Malena raised her head, her eyes were narrowed, but her mouth was repressing a smile. "Tanya, you are scaring me into seeing the doctor in Nairobi so that we can see Erik, aren't you? It's a ruse!" She savored the last word, as her eyes widened and the smile overcame any tendencies to squelch it.

"A ruse," Tanya agreed genially. "So hush up and don't tell anyone. And there's nothing to tell anyway because it's real. You need a doctor, and we'll take you to one in Nairobi."

"Oh Tanya!" Malena clasped her hands together and raised her face heavenward. But momentarily the expression of ecstasy melted into one of turmoil. "You'd not dare mock me, Tanya?"

"Malena, how can you ask such a question?"

"We are really going to see Erik?"

"We're taking you to a doctor in Nairobi. Yes. We depart before dawn."

"Oh Tanya!" Enraptured, Malena threw herself at Tanya. Capturing her friend in a hug, Malena bubbled, "Tanya, no woman has been blessed with a better friend!" Malena kissed Tanya's face exuberantly. "If it were not blasphemous to say so, I'd call you my savior in time of despair!"

"A bit extravagant," Tanya grumbled, squirming to extricate herself from Malena's arms.

"But Tanya," Malena pulled back and gripped her friend's shoulders, "how can we leave before dawn? You've had no time with Isak!"

"Time enough," Tanya assured her with a choked smile, "short though it's been."

"No!"

"Yes."

"No!"

"Malena dearest, Isak agrees that you need a doctor. Earlier today he insisted that I take you immediately. He demands this sacrifice of himself."

"The good Lord has never blessed a woman more graciously than when he made the von Brantbergs my friends," Malena declared. "But Isak's sacrifice will not include tonight," Malena resolved. "Go Tanya! Get with your husband! I'll not be the cause of your present separation."

Finding no argument to rebuff Malena's command, Tanya set off. Groping her way in the darkness, Tanya felt thudding dread in her belly. She was going to see Isak; she did not want to see Isak.

Kamau caught up with Tanya in the dark and handed her a paraffin lamp. She squeezed his shoulder in gratitude, for his service was more meaningful than he knew. His presence emboldened her. She felt that she could not fail him by collapsing emotionally in front of him twice in one day. His eyes upon her back were the crutches that held her upright as she crossed the camp to Isak's tent.

As Tanya opened the flap, Dionysus bounded to the tent's entrance from where he'd been lying at Isak's side. Energetically, he licked Tanya's hands and nuzzled her legs. "Oh," Tanya exclaimed, nonplussed to see Hassan bending over Isak, removing his boots.

"Good evening, Memsahib," Hassan replied. "I was just helping Bwana Isak into bed."

Tanya raised her eyebrows and peered at Isak's face. His visage was handsome, and Tanya felt herself reticent in its seductive power. Even now, with her knowledge of his transgressions – and with the drool dripping down his chin, and with his snores filling the air, and with his perfume of grain alcohol – Tanya felt herself cowed by his magnetism. Perhaps loving Isak was too powerful a habit for her; or maybe she'd gained a fresh understanding of her vow, "for better or for worse." "I appear to have missed the revel," Tanya sighed.

"Bwana Isak played cards with the other officers tonight," Hassan reported.

Tanya frowned to indicate that she knew Isak must have lost money gambling, and Hassan cleared his throat to confirm her suspicion. Tanya knew that Hassan was trying to be helpful, but Tanya couldn't bear yet another instance of a third party knowing intimate details about her married life. "Go to sleep, Hassan," Tanya said, "I'll take care of Isak."

"Yes, Memsahib," Hassan nodded.

As he was leaving the tent, Tanya added, "We depart tomorrow before dawn."

"Yes, Memsahib."

"Kalonzo will take the ox wagons and the porters back to Kijabe."

"Memsahib?"

"We're going to Kajiado, so we can catch the Magadi line back to Nairobi. But first we'll liaise with the East African Mounted Rifles."

"Yes, Memsahib." The statement was one of acquiescence to her order, but from the tone of his voice, Tanya knew that he was asking her a question. Hassan lingered at the tent's entrance, but Tanya purposefully avoided his eyes and, eventually, he left.

Tanya knelt beside Isak. Delighted, Dionysus immediately threw himself on his back, presenting his belly to Tanya for scratching. Absently petting Dionysus, Tanya looked at her husband's prone, passed-out form. His appearance gave all indication of having thoroughly enjoyed a celebration tonight – a celebration in which she had not taken part; a celebration that had coincided with her despair.

What happens in a marriage, she thought, is private. Private. Private.

NINE

Despite having slept for most of the day, Tanya dozed off in Isak's tent, lounging against a pillow, with Dionysus flopped against her. Some time in the night, Isak awoke and, finding his wife in his tent, nestled on top of her, so that by 3:30 a.m., Tanya was suffocating. Awaking short of breath, Tanya wriggled out from under Isak and inadvertently rolled over Dionysus, who squeaked in his sleep and resettled himself on Isak's neck. Experiencing the large dog as an imposition on his windpipe, Isak dislodged Dionysus and readjusted himself around Tanya's body. Frustrated, Tanya whispered, in as noble a manner as she could muster, "Isak!"

To her surprise, he opened his eyes. Other than being bloodshot, they showed no evidence of intoxication and gave every appearance of being alert and comprehending. "My darling *prinsesstårta*," he smiled, kissing her forehead and snuggling closer.

"Isak," Tanya struggled against his crushing weight, "I must, uh, away."

Isak's eyes opened again. He gaped for a moment and then began laughing. Kissing her, he murmured, "I'm drunk. I thought you just said that you're leaving."

"I am leaving."

He looked up abruptly, an anxious expression on his face. "You must be drunk."

"No, I'm not drunk! Our safari departs at 4 a.m. for Magadi."

Isak propped himself on his side. "Why?"

"Malena needs a doctor."

"But there's a doctor here." Isak looped his arm around Tanya's ribcage and drew her towards him. He began to nibble her earlobe.

Tanya craned her neck away from Isak's lips, to no avail. Feeling distinctly like an acacia tree being licked clean of its leaves by a hungry giraffe, Tanya made an effort to control the annoyance in her voice as she argued, "She needs a Nairobi doctor."

"Don't go." Isak sat up. His voice was serious, and the seductive expression had melted off his face, replaced by one of concern. "It's too dangerous."

The transformation startled Tanya. "No more dangerous than here," she retorted softly.

"Much more dangerous than here," Isak insisted, cupping Tanya's face in his hands.

Watching his conflicted expression, Tanya realized the enormity of the information chasm between them. Isak didn't know, she realized, that Lord Delamere had revealed to her his unit's true function. About her own role in the mapmaking mission, she realized, Isak was also ignorant. Nor did Isak know that she knew of his unfaithfulness. Most importantly, Isak didn't know how these events had changed her. He was talking to her like she was still the love-struck wife he'd ordered to Kijabe. "Why do you say it's dangerous?" Tanya asked, swallowing her welter of emotions.

If Isak had confessed that he was thoroughly familiar with the challenges of protecting the Magadi branch line because he'd drawn a map of the relevant territory, and that his consequent knowledge of every skirmish fought between the East African Mounted Rifles and the Germans convinced him that traversing the area was suicidal folly, Tanya would have responded with complete honesty. She would have broken her word to Lord Delamere and admitted her intelligence mission to Isak.

But Isak didn't take her into his confidence. He just shook his head and murmured, "My *prinsesstårta*, you are too precious." He took her hand and nuzzled her fingers. "Stay by my side."

Tanya was not unmoved by Isak's entreaty, but it confused her. If his intentions matched his words, then he ought (in Tanya's opinion) to bring his actions in line and stop humiliating her with native women. But beyond her sense that his words were empty, Tanya found herself increasingly aggravated by Isak's whole approach. Telling her, without explanation, to stay by his side was no longer good enough.

"Isak," Tanya began, laying her hand on his cheek. "I beg you let me go. We both must be brave. We must think of others and sacrifice our happiness for them."

Isak clasped her hand where it lay against his cheek and, partially closing his eyes, turned to inhale the scent of her wrist. "Why?" he whispered.

"Because we are healthy, and our happiness is unbounded, but Malena and Erik may have but a short time together."

"What are you saying?"

"Malena is . . . not well. She may be dying."

"That can't be."

"We were too late. Those Masai medicines caused sepsis."

"That's what the camp doctor said?"

"She cannot wait another day. She must reach Nairobi immediately."

"The poor girl!"

"I must go. I must take the poor dear —"

"— Yes, you must —"

"— I am indebted for your understanding —"

"— I'll go with you! To protect —"

"— NO!" Tanya hadn't intended to yell. Her interjection in the exchange of murmured sweetnesses unnerved them both. "You are too . . . valiant, Isak," she recovered quickly, "but I am not so helpless. I killed a lion."

"Famed lion hunters have been felled by German bullets."

"Lekishon will guide us. He'll keep us away from the Germans."

"You can't trust the Masai!" Isak objected. "I would forswear my duties as husband if I allowed you to go unaccompanied —"

"— Isak, my lord, your place is here. You have important work to do. Critical work. Work upon which lives depend. We must remember the cause. You'll not forswear your duties as husband so long as you maintain my honor as faithfully as you serve the cause." Tanya ceased her speech, worried that she'd said too much. She studied Isak's face for clues. Would he deny the implications of her words? Would he confess?

His response, when it came, surprised her with its tenderness: "You'll come back to me?"

Tanya thought she detected fear in his voice. His response perplexed her, but Tanya opted not to examine her confusion. "I'll return to your side," she assured him.

Isak scooped Tanya in for a passionate kiss, to which she surrendered with the relief of victory.

From outside the tent, Hassan's cough was audible. "Memsahib," his voice floated into the tent, "the time for leaving is come."

With a last kiss, and a squeeze of Isak's hand – and then another kiss, more squeezing and a final extraction – Tanya was out of the tent. She felt unexpectedly exhilarated. She had initially recoiled from the necessity of looking upon Isak with her newfound knowledge of his weakness for native women, but now she had done it and triumphed.

She hadn't wanted to lie to him, but then she was sure he hadn't wanted to betray her.

* * *

Though still hours before dawn, Lord Delamere's camp had a bustling air. The porters who would shortly be returning with the ox wagons to Kijabe were absorbed in various pre-departure tasks: finishing their breakfasts, napping on their feet, haggling over unidentified goods, rifling through everybody else's personal items in search of anything worth stealing. Lekishon and Kamau stood on the sidelines, both wearing the resigned expressions of husbands waiting for their wives to finish their errands. The oxen blew puffs of steam in the chilly air, and the mules stamped their hooves impatiently.

Standing by her mule with one foot in a stirrup and Dionysus seated at her feet, Tanya was sipping tea and watching the porters when Hassan informed her: "Memsahib, Lekishon says the Germans are many in this place we are going."

"I have heard," Tanya nodded wearily.

"But Memsahib Malena," Hassan objected, "is already weakened. Passage through enemy land will overstrain her."

Tanya wanted to say that Malena would crawl ecstatically across enemy territory if doing so would allow her to see Erik. But instead, she said, "We have no choice. Malena must see a doctor in Nairobi."

"Memsahib," Hassan persevered, "without a mule for carrying supplies, we must ourselves carry everything."

"Malena and I will ride the same mule, and you can use the other mule for supplies."

"Lord Delamere's camp has no supplies to spare. What we have taken from the ox wagons is too little."

"But we'll be in Magadi in three days, Hassan. I can shoot game. And Lekishon will find *manyattas* to host us."

"Three days is enough time to die of thirst. Many misfortunes may befall in three days, like perhaps the safari takes six days. Our supplies are too few —"

Hassan's resistance to crossing hostile territory had bewildered Tanya initially. She knew Hassan was no coward. Nor did his objections on Malena's behalf resonate: Malena was at her healthiest since the lioness' attack. But now Tanya felt that Hassan's focus on supplies had exposed his gambit. "Hassan," she interrupted him, "you are reluctant to go on this safari because the opportunities to profiteer are few."

"Memsahib?"

"You were happy to bring supplies to Lord Delamere because you could sell them on the way."

"I never —"

"— Don't deny it, Hassan. Supplies listed on the inventory weren't on the ox wagons when we arrived. Your profits from our Narosera safari could no doubt underwrite our Magadi safari."

"Memsahib?"

"Or you can take a loss on this safari, Hassan, I don't care. This one you'll have to do for the cause."

"What cause, Memsahib?"

"The cause of freedom, Hassan. The British stopped the slave trade that your Swahili cousins were so deeply invested in. We don't condone slavery in the Empire, Hassan, which is why you are so well paid. So take your money and stop your whining."

With that concluding remark, Tanya charged off. She'd caught sight of a black soldier bringing order to the morning bustle. Assuming that he was Kalonzo, Tanya headed over to introduce herself.

Kalonzo politely returned Tanya's attentions. He was a stocky sergeant with a shaved head and a goatee. Trained in the King's African Rifles, Sergeant Kalonzo was the closest thing to a professional soldier in Lord Delamere's unit.

Tanya wished Sergeant Kalonzo luck on his safari, and he replied with reciprocal good wishes. "The Masai are bad," he added, voicing hostility commonplace among Kamba tribesmen. "Your guide is bad."

"Sergeant Kalonzo," Tanya sighed, "You and I are of one mind. I wish you were our guide."

He nodded, acknowledging her compliment. "Your oxen will be safe."

Tanya smiled. "My porters are fortunate."

"Don't allow the Masai to deceive you."

Assuring Sergeant Kalonzo that she'd remain vigilant against Masai deception, Tanya took her leave to assist Malena onto their mule. As Tanya mounted in front of Malena, Sergeant Kalonzo ordered the porters to fall into position for departure.

To Tanya's disbelief, on Sergeant Kalonzo's command, a multitude of the porters climbed onto the supply wagons. A quick glance at the caravan revealed, however, that twenty porters still stood at attention, five to a wagon, beside the four wagons.

"Wait, Lekishon!" Tanya called to the *moran*, who'd already struck out into the early morning gloom. "Stay here, Malena," Tanya said, not wanting to trouble her friend with the pain of dismounting and remounting. "Sergeant Kalonzo!" Tanya called as she jumped off the mule. Racing to him, she missed the glance that Kamau shot at Hassan, who remained deliberately impassive. "Sergeant," Tanya inquired breathlessly as she reached his side, "are you taking Lord Delamere's native runners to Kijabe?"

"Certainly not, Baroness," Sergeant Kalonzo answered.

"Then who are these people?" Tanya asked, ushering him to the back of the first ox wagon, where five men sat, chatting intently in Kikuyu. The men all had a ragged appearance. What clothing they wore was torn; two were shirtless; not one possessed shoes.

Sergeant Kalonzo made an inquiring face at Tanya. "Are these not your porters, Baroness?"

"Definitely not."

On noticing Tanya and Sergeant Kalonzo staring at them, the men abruptly ceased conversation and looked, each of them, in a different direction.

"Kamau!" Tanya shouted. She heard him trudge to her side with a marked absence of his usual eagerness-to-be-of-service. "Your assistance, please, as translator. Ask these men who they are."

"They are Kikuyu, Memsabu," replied Kamau mutedly.

"I know that," snapped Tanya. "That's why I asked you to translate."

"They are *kariakor*, Memsahib," came Hassan's quiet voice behind Tanya.

Tanya jerked around to glare angrily at Hassan. "What did you say, Hassan?"

"*Kariakor*, Memsahib," Hassan repeated without expression.

Kamau, on the other hand, was expressing himself freely: his composure was distraught, on the verge of nervous collapse.

Tanya narrowed her eyes and looked from Hassan to Kamau and back again. After a pause, she said icily, "You mean they are *kariakor* deserters."

"They are men seeking freedom, Memsahib," Hassan said simply.

"How much are they paying you?" Tanya demanded.

"Nothing," Kamau sputtered. "Not much. A fair fee. Kamau and Hassan get a month's salary from each of them."

"How many are there?"

"Twenty-three men, Memsahib," Hassan answered.

"That's two years' salary for both of you," Tanya calculated; then she barked: "Return the money. They're going back."

"No Memsabu!" Kamau exclaimed.

"*Kariakor* will kill them," Hassan said flatly.

"They can't escape *kariakor*!" Tanya huffed. "Even if they go home, they'll just be sent back to *kariakor*. The district commissioners can't allow a single eligible man to remain in their districts – they're all sent to *kariakor*."

"But these are your new employees, Memsahib," Hassan said, introducing the men with a wave of his arm.

"That's what we told them," Kamau added helpfully.

"What?" Tanya's head began to throb.

"The plantation needs workers, Memsahib," Hassan said.

Tanya stared stonily at Hassan. Blast him, she thought. He was right. Labor recruitment, a challenge even at the best of times, had been rendered near impossible by the war. *Kariakor* competed with colonist farmers for the already-thin supply of able-bodied laborers. The coffee plantation had been understaffed since the war's start, and now the short rains and harvesting were only weeks away. Tanya hated to think of the (further) debt into which she and Isak would tumble if they couldn't process their coffee harvest.

But how, Tanya agonized, could she harbor *kariakor* deserters! Those Nairobi busybodies were hungry for any confirmation that she was a German sympathizer: employing *kariakor* deserters would make colorable their malicious lies. And if the British authorities discovered her crime, she'd be imprisoned – or hung. "They are not my employees," she intoned.

Kamau, sensing Tanya's fear of repercussions, assured her, "I will fix it so these workers cannot be discovered."

Kamau couldn't tell, from the withering look that constituted Tanya's response to his remark, whether she didn't believe him or whether she'd intuited his methods and was expressing her contempt for them. His "I will fix it" referred to his intention to purchase a spell from a wizard to blind the British to the presence on the farm of these former *kariakor* enlistees. Kamau had used such spells before and knew that they worked: many times he had seen colonists maintain complete ignorance of the presence, absence or rotating identities of natives around them. But Kamau also knew that Tanya derided "magic." After the dismissive reception that had greeted his earlier offer to procure a spell to enhance Tanya's fertility, Kamau had learned not to mention the magic, even if he planned to use it. Now he suspected that she'd divined the supernatural in the subtext of his reassurance, and that it had failed to reassure.

Hassan was equally condescending of Kamau's methods, but he nonetheless agreed with Kamau that Tanya's anxiety about being caught was misplaced. If Allah wanted her to be caught, she would be caught; and if He didn't, she wouldn't. That matter wasn't worth mulling. Another matter, however, was (in Hassan's view) very much worth threshing out: "*Kariakor* made slaves of these men," he said.

"And the British authorities will make a prisoner of me if they catch me employing them," Tanya countered.

"Impossible, Memsahu, you are beloved by the British —" Kamau began, before he was interrupted.

"— He," Hassan said pointing to a man in the ox wagon behind Tanya, "and he," Hassan pointed again, "and he, and he – all taken from their homes. Forced to serve in *kariakor*. Paid *nothing*," Hassan's eyes flared, "they were never paid, but ordered to walk and walk and walk and carry, before dawn to walk and carry, after sunset to walk and carry. If you were ordered to walk and carry without pay, you would not like it. And what food? These men were forced to walk and carry and starve until they die. And what purpose, Memsahib? A war without a prize is without meaning. It cannot be allowed! Why waste a man's life if you get not a camel for your trouble? To refuse to explain the purpose of the war, it is the British choice. But not to kill men for no reason. Not to lie to say they die for 'principles.' What principles? *Kariakor* is slavery. The British are bigger slavers than the Swahili ever were. The British stopped the Swahili slave trade to remove their competition!"

Kamau was dumbfounded by Hassan's speech. Hassan had always seemed stoic; never had Kamau seen the man's orator side. Moreover, Hassan's passionate discourse didn't seem to square with his advice not to argue with stones and noblewomen. Perhaps, Kamau thought, Hassan had previously neglected to mention a corollary that allowed argument where profits were at stake. In any event, Kamau recoiled a bit with each declamation of Hassan's; however impressive Hassan's argument might be, Kamau felt that distance might be advisable when the opportunity arose for Tanya's rebuttal.

Tanya, for her part, was equally astounded. Hassan's speech seemed uncharacteristically genuine. She was used to Hassan mocking her reliance on concepts like "the cause," but such needling was always (she'd thought) for sport and not sincere. In addition, Tanya knew that Hassan thought the natives of British East Africa to be slave races, inferior to Somalis generally and to himself specifically. The impetus for his inspired argument was, she felt certain, profit, not freedom. Nonetheless, manipulative as he was being, she found both the reason and passion of his remonstrance difficult to refute. She was, after all, a noblewoman, and these men – *kariakor* deserters though they might be – were seeking her protection. "Hassan," she argued, "understand what I risk: *prison* —"

"— You fear for freedom, but these men plead for their lives," Hassan parried.

"I am —"

"— a noblewoman for whom imprisonment for the cause would be an honor," he asserted.

"And if they hang me instead of imprisoning me?"

"A quick death, very good compared with a starving death march in the equatorial sun."

Tanya pivoted to Sergeant Kalonzo. Although she was agitated to the point of apoplexy, Kalonzo's expression was courteously blank. And his features (Tanya noted) were comfortingly native – not British. Straightening her spine, tossing her head and arranging her face in her expression of dignified noble suffering, Tanya said to Sergeant Kalonzo: "I am constrained to admit that I failed to recognize my own farm laborers. These are my employees."

"I understand, Baroness," Kalonzo assented.

Then Tanya turned to Kamau. "Tell my new employees that I will pay for their freedom. They owe you and Hassan nothing."

Hassan gestured as if to protest, but Kamau was already translating Tanya's happy news. The *kariakor* deserters responded effusively, with cheers and whistles. Beaming, Kamau turned to Tanya and reported, "The men are overjoyed by your generosity."

"Your generosity as well," Tanya snapped. "You're giving up your fees."

"Memsabu?"

Hassan closed his eyes and inhaled before reopening them, during which duration he'd prayed that, in the future, Allah would grant Kamau the cunning to perceive a gambit like Tanya's in advance of falling into its trap.

"As Hassan has very movingly explained, these men have suffered enough. Their exploitation ends now. No one will profiteer off them."

"But Memsabu," Kamau protested, "these men offered to pay us —"

"— You must decline their offer. That is the noble course," Tanya said curtly. "And if you disgrace me with low conduct, if you disobey me and collect your fee," Tanya drew herself to her full height and tossed her head, "I will withhold your salary until you have repaid every rupee." Then she barreled between them to return to her mule. Behind her, she heard their muttered "Yes, Memsahib," and "Sorry, Memsabu."

Maybe, Tanya thought grimly, if I'm caught employing *kariakor* deserters, the British will accept my service with Lord Delamere as proof that I'm not a German sympathizer. But as she placed her foot in the stirrup, she felt convinced that clearing her name would not warrant divulging this mission; Lord Delamere would probably deny using her as a courier.

As Tanya mounted in front of her, Malena inquired, "Tanya, what is it? Why was Hassan shouting?"

"Sacrifice for the cause," Tanya replied in a strained voice. "It is but a pleasure." Then, with a noticeably displeased whack of the mule, Tanya followed Lekishon into the budding dawn.

TEN

About the time that Tanya was expecting to reach the territory of the East African Mounted Rifles, Lekishon pointed to men on horseback, advancing across the wooded grassland, scattering a herd of Thomson's gazelle and a pair of jackals stalking them. Tanya peered through her field glasses. She scanned the stands of toothbrush tree, umbrella thorn and African wild olive, skimmed passed a termite mound, and then finally framed the men on horseback, thundering towards them against a backdrop of rising mountain ranges. They looked marvelous.

Tanya was relieved at the sight because, three days of his guidance in the bush notwithstanding, she'd continued to harbor a distrust of the *moran*. Lekishon, Tanya believed, possessed as much potential to lead their party astray as Masai women had to route Isak from the path of fidelity.

Tanya's relief at the presence of the mounted soldiers evaporated, however, when further inspection through the field glasses raised a question about the nationality of the mounted men. She paused, unsure why she thought the soldiers must be German. Of the ten men, only one was white. Their uniforms appeared a mere smudge of khaki. But the very fact of the uniforms and, she realized, the organized way their patrol rode towards her own small party, reinforced her fearful intuition that Germans were approaching.

"Hassan," Tanya said in a controlled voice, "ask Lekishon where we are." While Hassan posed the question in Swahili, Tanya craned behind her to Malena. "Don't be frightened," Tanya murmured, in a remarkably unsuccessful attempt to preempt her friend's fright.

Malena immediately did what Tanya had hoped to prevent: she screamed. Then, her hand at her throat, sweat beading her forehead, Malena cried, "Oh Tanya, no! You don't think they're —"

"— Hush, Malena! If you cry, I shall cry too."

Malena clamped her hand over her mouth and swallowed several times, while the melodrama unfolded on her face. Tanya turned away: Malena's flushed cheeks, hysterical eyes and trembling lips were having a Medusa effect, transforming all who looked upon them into cowards.

"He says we're south of the Magadi branch line, Memsahib," Hassan reported.

Ostensibly, "south of the Magadi branch line" was where they were supposed to be. The Besil River fort, where the East African Mounted Rifles were camped, was south of the Magadi branch line, but a glance at Lekishon left Tanya with the surmise that Lekishon had led them elsewhere than to the Besil River area. Amusement flickered on his face. His focus was concentrated on the approaching riders; he was eager to see the outcome of this confrontation.

Anger swelling her chest and thickening her throat, Tanya looked down at Hassan. Standing beside the mule, he emboldened her with his implacable stance. "Memsahib," he whispered, without looking at her, "the photograph."

Tanya nodded and clenched her teeth. She'd already decided that, should they confront some such circumstance, she was going to confront the Germans alone. She didn't want Malena, Kamau or Lekishon to know that she had a picture of von Lettow-Vorbeck because the more people who knew, the more likely that Tanya's loyalties would be questioned. Also, with every meter that brought the soldiers closer, Malena's sniffling grew more pronounced; Tanya wished to put an immediate end to the suspense that was causing her friend so much suffering. "Hassan," she said, "help Malena down. I'm going to ride out to them."

"No don't!" Malena shrieked.

"Hush Malena!" Tanya snapped. "Dismount quickly. I'll be in no danger. We're none of us in danger," she emphasized, though she didn't believe it.

Hassan was holding his hand out to Malena, who leaned forward and circled her arms around his shoulders. With a frown, Tanya noticed that Lekishon had materialized as well, eager to assist with Malena's hips. Together the men hoisted Malena from the mule. Tanya straightened in the saddle.

Now that the moment for action had arrived, Tanya realized that she needed strength. She thought of Kamau, charging out to meet the attacking *moran* and, again, of Kamau clanging pots and pans in the lioness' face. She wished she could send out her courageous cook as an advance party now. She felt confident that she could ride after him, but the loneliness of rushing into peril, a solitary woman on mule back, suddenly stayed Tanya's resolve.

"A handkerchief, Hassan," Tanya requested, to postpone the inevitable, "or anything I can use as a white flag."

Hassan turned to Kamau, who was holding the supply mule steady. Hassan barked something in Swahili. Moments later, Hassan thrust into Tanya's hands a dirty, but whitish, kitchen towel. Nodding thanks, Tanya asked Kamau to hold Dionysus, so that he wouldn't follow her.

THE CELEBRATION HUSBAND

"Remember, Memsahib," Hassan encouraged her, "your contempt must be like a knife thrust between their ribs."

"Hassan, lend me your contempt."

"Memsahib, you have it."

Wishing that she felt like she had it, Tanya flogged her mule.

"Go with Jesus!" Malena yelped behind her, as Tanya galloped towards the Germans, waving the white towel like a lasso above her head.

Jostling Tanya so that she felt like her pelvis was being smashed upwards into her ribcage, the mule on its charge also kicked up dust that stung her eyes, clogged her nose and deposited grit on her teeth, tongue and throat. Maintaining her balance occupied so much of her concentration that she was within shooting range of the German rifles – indeed, rifles were being pointed at her by men whose facial expressions suggested that their aim from horseback was deadly accurate – when Tanya remembered that she had Lord Delamere's map. Idiot, she castigated herself for having failed to stow it secretly on Malena's person before facing down the enemy.

Slowing her mule sharply enough to jeopardize her hard-won balance, Tanya caught her breath and consoled herself she could not have concealed the map on Malena without alerting Hassan, Kamau and Lekishon – to say nothing of Malena herself – to its existence. Tanya was simply going to have to bluff her way through this confrontation without being searched (or killed, she fleetingly acknowledged) because she was without means to destroy the map if these Germans decided to take her prisoner (or worse).

Tanya held the kitchen towel aloft like it was a heliograph machine, flashing the words "peace" and "brotherly love" in Morse code. Getting the message, the German soldier in command signaled for the others to lower their rifles. Relieved, Tanya found herself waving and smiling at the enemy, calling out, "*Guten tag!*" She continued in German, "I am a friend! I am happy to see you!"

Tanya's German had a curious quality to it: it was flirty. This characteristic was all that remained of Tanya's first suitor, a German speaker, whose interest in Tanya had precipitated Bess Rungsted's willingness to send her daughter to art school in Paris. But although Tanya's German romance came to naught, Tanya's German never lost the tinge of sultry nights and whispered intimacies.

Captain Tafel started at the appearance of this German-speaking, buxom thing. Notwithstanding the many contingencies for which he'd budgeted on this patrol – rhino charges, thirst, enemy fire, casualties, horse theft – this one left Captain Tafel at a loss. A speedy mental review of von Lettow-Vorbeck's procedures for engagement revealed no prescription for dealing with *fräuleins* in the field.

Captain Tafel's surprise deepened – and apprehension gripped him for a moment – when the young woman dismounted and, after casually slinging about her shoulders the filthy rag she'd been waving, began feeling in her shirt. Fearing a concealed weapon, Captain Tafel's hand instantly went to his pistol, but after another moment failed to produce a gun, Captain Tafel panted with the fear that she was disrobing, and his hand fumbled through a couple of adjustments in the area of his saddle. But the woman's shirt remained intact and from it she pulled something small – too small even for a .22 – as she walked, beaming, towards where he'd called an abrupt halt to the patrol.

"Kind noble Sir," said Tanya in German, "thank goodness you have come to our rescue."

"Captain," the soldier replied in German. "Tafel. I'm a Captain, Captain Tafel," he repeated, wondering if he was babbling. Captain Tafel was shy of women in circumstances most conducive to his confidence, and this was not one of them. Everything about this situation baffled him.

The nine mounted *askaris* surrounding Tanya and Captain Tafel observed their commander's fluster with muted amusement. Gruffness, firmness, discipline – even meanness – all were consistent with the leadership and military prowess that Captain Tafel typically displayed. This undignified simpering was a new side of the man and, though humanizing perhaps, not entirely welcome. The *askaris* didn't like to think of themselves as commanded by a man who allowed women to unnerve him.

"I am Tanya." Tanya smiled and lowered her eyes, while she simultaneously raised her hand to show him a slim silver case. "I'm a good friend of your esteemed Lieutenant-Colonel."

Somewhat reluctantly, Captain Tafel accepted the silver case and opened it.

Seeing the look of amazement on his face, his *askaris* jockeyed their horses around Captain Tafel to peek at the object that was causing such astonishment. Upon viewing a black-and-white blot, however, the *askaris* muffled their disappointment. Not one had seen a photograph before, and they didn't realize that they were looking at a two-dimensional depiction of a face.

Captain Tafel, sensitive to some disrespect of the German leader, hissed in Swahili to his troops that this object was a photograph of the legendary von Lettow-Vorbeck. Whereupon the *askaris* besieged him in their attempts to glimpse an image of the great man.

Captain Tafel savaged their hopes by snapping shut the silver case and returning it to Tanya. On command, the *askaris* fell into formation behind Captain Tafel, who addressed Tanya stiffly: "Though we are on enemy land, you are our guest."

"How gracious, I am indebted," Tanya replied, holding Captain Tafel spellbound as her hand again crept within her shirt to return the silver case. "Perhaps you might tell me where we are?"

Had Tanya not been in the predicament of trusting the enemy more than she did her own Masai guide, she would have done well to have skipped this question. Its practicality jarred Captain Tafel into a more professional mode, and he responded with an interrogation of his own: "You're German?" Captain Tafel didn't think she was – her accent sounded foreign – but he wanted to be polite.

"No, but I am a friend," Tanya replied.

"Not English?"

"Indeed not! I am a friend."

"Belgian?"

"Danish. My country is neutral, but I'm a friend."

"You are in the Ingito Hills. What is your purpose here?"

Tanya giggled. Why she hadn't already prepared an answer to this question, she didn't know. Failing to believe that dangers will materialize is, of course, as common a human weakness as believing that every possible danger is imminently about to occur. New spies, also, must be forgiven their inexperience at anticipating necessary cover stories. "We're on safari," she heard herself say, truthfully.

Captain Tafel squinted into the distance and gestured to his *askaris* for a pair of field glasses.

"My girlfriend, Malena, and I," Tanya began, not knowing how she would finish, "love hunting." She smiled, hoping to augment her credibility.

Examining the other members of Tanya's party through the field glasses, Captain Tafel observed, "You have no porters." His voice sounded confused and also, possibly (Tanya feared) suspicious.

"Oh we do," Tanya protested. "Many porters. They are at the camp. We were following a kudu, and I'm afraid we're lost. Ingito Hills you say?"

"Kudu?" Captain Tafel furrowed his eyebrows. He didn't consider himself a first rate sportsman, but he knew that kudu were elusive, extremely difficult to track and were seen, if at all, at dawn. "At this time of day?"

"Maybe it was something else," Tanya suggested, flashing a "what can you expect a girl to know in the way of species identification" smile.

"You are aware of the war, of course?" Captain Tafel inquired hopefully. Painful memories of previous conversations with the fair sex prompted this question. So often he found that women were ignorant of events that he considered to be of the utmost international consequence.

"Captain Tafel," Tanya pouted, fixing him with eyes that conveyed a mixture of hurt and recrimination, "you are not suggesting that we should have postponed our safari because of the war?"

Captain Tafel cleared his throat and looked around helplessly. His *askaris* were barely maintaining stoic bearing; he feared he would soon be subject to open jeering. He cleared his throat again and tried to adopt a scolding tone. "A war occasions some delay in our leisure —" he began.

"— But we'd planned this safari months ago!" Tanya cut in, placing her hands on his saddle.

Captain Tafel looked at the closeness of her hands to his legs and blushed. Immeasurably thankful that his *askaris* were assembled behind him, he tried, "Even plans must change to accommodate —"

"— All my girlfriends have gone on safari now. Wartime is so dreary for us ladies. There are no men around for our amusement. You cannot expect us to remain bored and confined to our homes!"

Remaining bored and confined to their homes was precisely what Captain Tafel envisioned as right and proper for ladies, but he suspected that voicing such a view at present would not result in an outcome that he would welcome. "You have my fullest sympathies," he said with clipped pronunciation, "but this area is dangerous. The enemy is everywhere. Ladies must not venture on safari here." To his great disappointment, this lady didn't seem perturbed by his argument.

"Oh Captain Tafel," she murmured, craning her head up in a position that seemed almost to invite a kiss, "we didn't mean to be lost in enemy territory."

Sweat was making continued occupation of his saddle uncomfortable. Captain Tafel wished he could unbutton his uniform jacket. Truly, he wished he could kick this woman away from his horse. The thought of his *askaris* guffawing at his mangled handling of this female restrained his leg, however. In a compromise, his arm shot out to point south, and he informed her, "German East Africa is that way."

"But our porters are this way," Tanya blinked innocently, pointing north.

"That is entirely the wrong direction."

"But we'll suffer so to leave all our supplies!" Tanya objected.

Captain Tafel yanked on his horse's reins and guided the animal two steps away from Tanya. He was without any idea of the correct response. She was neither soldier, nor British, nor a German subject in need of rescue. She was merely in the way: an amiable idiot who viewed battlefields as a variety of spa retreat. How she came to be an intimate of the great von Lettow-Vorbeck he'd rather not consider. But, floundering as he was in his dealings with her, he wanted to be free from her presence before he lost additional face in front of his men. "Go," he blustered, "and don't get shot."

* * *

"Hassan!" Tanya shouted from mule back, as she galloped within earshot, "beat him!"

The instant Tanya had emerged safely from her trial with Captain Tafel and his *askaris*, she'd been seized with fear, a delayed reaction. She'd experienced a similar emotional deferral once before in British East Africa. On safari with Isak in March, Tanya had been on the verge of settling into a chair with a sundowner, when a charging buffalo had stormed out of the bush, snatched away the chair on his horns and carried it beyond the camp site, where the buffalo proceeded to maul the chair into shreds. Had Tanya been sitting in the chair, she would have died, ruthlessly dismembered and gored.

Only after she'd witnessed the destruction that would have been her fate did she respond: dropping her drink, she'd shrieked. Isak hadn't comprehended her fear: "You are fine! You are not hurt!" he'd repeated, frustrated at her continuing fright. But Tanya had understood that she could only afford to feel the fear once she was safe.

In the same way, Tanya's dread of confronting the German troops manifested in full force only after the threat had subsided. Riding away from Captain Tafel and his *askaris*, she'd been shaking and crying with alarm – and rage.

Rage because, once out of sight of the German troops, she'd stopped beneath a knobwood tree and surreptitiously examined Lord Delamere's map. It had convinced her that Lekishon had betrayed them.

"Beat him!" she shouted at closer range.

Malena looked stupefied to hear such a command issue from Tanya's lips, and Kamau flinched slightly, not confident that Tanya wasn't referring to him.

"Memsahib?" Hassan turned in a circle as Tanya rode around him, raising a trail of dust.

"Lekishon, that traitor," Tanya barked, jumping off her mule. "We're in the bloody Ingito Hills! We are days south of Magadi! But we're within range of the German fort that's sending out raiding parties into British East Africa. He led us into the enemy!" Standing rigid, fists clenched, Tanya had shouted the last sentence. Now she bent over to catch her breath. Dionysus trotted up to her and raised his nose to her face in commiseration.

Hassan turned instantly to Lekishon and began interrogating him harshly in Swahili. Lekishon responded in that same curious, vaguely amused manner with which he'd watched the approach of the German soldiers. Hassan raised the volume of his voice with each question, but no amount of vocal pressure broke Lekishon's façade, even as Malena and Kamau both shrank from the sound of Hassan's voice booming across the grassland, and Dionysus raised his head to bark. Then, abruptly, Hassan stopped shouting and faced Tanya. "He says it was an accident."

"Nonsense! The Masai know every shrub and riverbed on this plain!"

"He says his birthplace is far away."

"He's a liar! Beat him!"

"Tanya, all is well," Malena tried to mediate. "We had a scare, yes, but mercy is the Christian course. How can you —"

"— We're not on a Crusade, we're on a military mission, Malena, and soldiers who are insubordinate get beaten. Traitors get shot. He's lucky I don't shoot him! Beat him, Hassan."

"Beating a Masai warrior in Masailand is not possible, Memsahib."

"The good Lord counsels forgiveness," Malena piped.

"Then banish him! We're better off without him. Send him away!" Tanya waved her arm in the direction of German East Africa. "I told you he wasn't trustworthy," Tanya accused Hassan. "To have lost our medicine box for this traitor!" She clutched her hair miserably.

Hassan paused momentarily before offering, "Memsahib, you said we're days south of Magadi. Our supplies are not enough. We will need Lekishon to find hospitality at *manyattas*."

Tanya glowered at Hassan. Hassan had never before seen a person who bore so remarkable a resemblance to lit dynamite. Although Hassan met her fiery gaze with implacable confidence, Kamau double-checked that Tanya's rifle was actually strapped onto the supply mule.

Lekishon broke the stand-off with a comment in Swahili.

"He promises to try very hard not to get us lost again," Hassan translated.

"Tell him that I'll kill him if he leads us to the enemy again," Tanya instructed through clenched teeth.

Hassan relayed a modified version of her instruction to Lekishon, one that omitted any reference to murder and instead thanked Lekishon for his efforts on their behalf.

Meanwhile, Malena tried to console Tanya. "He did guide us to Lord Delamere's camp. But we must conform our expectations to our circumstances, Tanya. The good Lord made humans fallible. We all lose our way without a map."

* * *

Behind Tanya on the mule, Malena was expanding on her topic of the human propensity for getting lost without a map. "That map," she intoned, urging Hassan to translate for Lekishon, "is Jesus' love."

Tanya closed her eyes and willed herself to adopt the unflappable demeanor of a commander. They had been traveling north for some hours, and yet still she was furious. Now they were at least three days behind in delivering the map to Nairobi. This senseless extension of their safari endangered them all, increasing the risk that harm would befall them from wild beasts, military engagements, sunstroke, thirst, starvation . . . and infection. Tanya was sincere in her determination that Malena must see a doctor in Nairobi, an event that maddeningly would now be delayed as well.

Tanya opened her eyes at the sound of Malena's squeal. "A bicycle!" her friend pointed, interrupting her own sermon.

Kamau joined Malena in her laughter at the peculiar sight of a man riding a bicycle across the bush. Hassan squinted his eyes. Lekishon planted his walking stick in the earth and regarded the bicycle with his unfailing expression of amused interest. Tanya raised her field glasses.

"Erik sometimes rides a bicycle across the bush," Malena gushed. "It's probably Erik come to meet us! And you thought we were so far away from them!"

"I better walk out to meet him," Tanya said softly, lowering the glasses.

"What is it Tanya?" Malena queried, as Tanya climbed down from the mule. "It's not Erik? It's not another German!"

"Another German," Tanya confirmed.

"But Tanya, why must you always go?" Malena cried.

"Because I speak German," Tanya replied.

"But alone?" Malena protested.

"Don't go alone, Memsabu," Kamau agreed.

Tanya gave Kamau a small smile at his concern for her wellbeing. "Come Dionysus," she called. "Let's go for a walk."

Striding through the grasslands, Tanya and Dionysus kicked up locusts that sprang away. A passing herd of bushbuck failed to distract Dionysus from his determined trot towards the bicycle; but the bushbuck, unusually, minced aggressively towards Tanya, rather than fleeing. A rustling from a nearby bitter leaf shrub suggested the presence of a baby bushbuck, deposited by mama with a botanical nanny. Tanya obliged the anxious bushbuck by hurrying away after Dionysus. Well ahead, Dionysus had almost reached the cyclist.

"Ah, Dionysus, you remember the good Lieutenant-Colonel," Tanya commented in German when she caught up. Dionysus was wagging his tail and panting his greeting to the man, now standing beside his bicycle, which he'd leaned against a desert date tree. The man reciprocated by affectionately patting the hound between his ears.

"We made friends aboard the ship, and neither a dog nor a Lieutenant-Colonel forgets a friend." Paul Emil von Lettow-Vorbeck smiled. He was a tall, solidly built man, with a round face, a receding hairline and close-set eyes. In his uniform, with his cap and his mustache, he looked dashing. "Baroness, you are infinitely more beautiful now than when I last saw you."

"I'm not seasick now."

"I am gratified to know that an interaction with Captain Tafel didn't turn your stomach."

Tanya laughed and lowered her eyes. Then she admitted, "He frightened me."

"For that I must apologize," von Lettow-Vorbeck said. "But you have repaid him. He fears he may be seeing specters."

"A German-speaking woman interrupting his raiding party through the African bush was too much of an oddity?" she asked lightly.

"Our entire situation is an oddity," he acceded. "An unfortunate oddity."

"Lieutenant-Colonel —"

"— Paul —"

"— Paul. I, how shall I say." Tanya paused. "I feel bitterly used by the circumstance of finding ourselves divided by this war."

He smiled affably.

"You don't blame me —" she began.

"— Of course not. I am a soldier. Fighting the English is my profession. But we are gentlemen. Our professional duties do not interfere with our personal views."

Tanya exhaled with relief. "You have my gratitude —"

"— I cannot conceive how a woman of your caliber could imagine that I would hold you in any but the highest esteem, or regard you with any but the greatest admiration, whatever the military exigency."

Tanya looked down and nodded, embarrassed by his elaborate praise. Then, looking around, she whistled for Dionysus, who was some distance away, stalking spur fowl.

"May I ask, Baroness —"

"— Tanya —"

"— Tanya, may I ask why you crossed paths with my good Captain Tafel? He came away with the understanding that you were on a leisure trip, which I am afraid contributed to his suspicion that he had seen a wraith."

Tanya covered her mouth and looked down to hide her smile. "My sincere apologies to the Captain," Tanya said, "but we are in fact on a leisure trip."

Von Lettow-Vorbeck raised his eyebrows.

"Our guide got us lost, and we're making our way back to camp." Though repetition of this lie made it sound more plausible to her own ears, Tanya wasn't persuaded that von Lettow-Vorbeck believed her. "Now is a foolish time and place for a hunting safari, it has become apparent," Tanya hurried, "but we thought we were avoiding dangerous territory." She finished speaking and swallowed inadvertently; guiltily, it struck her.

He appraised her face and put one foot on the pedal of his bicycle. In a measured voice, impossible for Tanya to read, he said, "I beg you to show all diligence in avoiding military skirmishes."

"I will," Tanya promised, feeling chastised. She beat a fist nervously against her thigh. "And why," she burst out, "if I may, Paul, why did you ride out after a specter?"

He smiled. "I know of only one woman in British East Africa to whom I've given my autographed picture," he said. "And I wanted to see her."

Tanya blushed, and she was aware that her mouth was uncomfortably dry. She tossed her head, straightened her spine and cleared her throat. "Still ascribing to foolish views about Beethoven?" she asked in a thin voice.

"No more foolish than your views of Faust. Arguing that his pact with the devil was worth it. Absurd." Von Lettow-Vorbeck's playful smile was almost an air kiss.

Tanya looked away to hide her expression; she feared it was adoring. Then, subduing her giddiness, she retorted, "I was being provocative."

"It can be more important to be sincere." He mounted his bicycle. "Baroness," he nodded, as he began to pedal.

"Lieutenant-Colonel," she replied.

ELEVEN

Although Tanya had many times imagined scenes that would humble and break Lekishon – a lacerating kick from an ostrich, castration in the cross-fire of a British-German engagement – nothing in her fantasies approached the effectiveness of Malena's reunion with Erik. Upon sight of one another at the Besil River fort, the tents, the other soldiers, the war – even Africa – dissolved, and the entirety of their existence was concentrated in their embrace.

This demonstration caused Hassan to slink away with the excuse that he would see to Tanya's tent. Dionysus also bounded off, chasing darting dik dik being preferable to watching kissing Swedes.

Kamau, however, stood rooted, appalled. Public affection for a beloved not being a Kikuyu custom, Kamau found such behavior a mark of weakness. But the display that Erik and Malena provided was, not merely evidence of the white man's fundamental unworthiness for the warrior role, but cause for shame: Kamau had never groped a woman with such apparent neediness.

Even Tanya felt off-balance watching the couple's never-ending kiss. Surely, they've had enough by *now*, she thought, noticing that neither member of the couple seemed to tire of the other's lips. But then Tanya saw the stupendous impact that the couple's tet-à-tet was having on Lekishon – and she rejoiced.

Lekishon looked unmanned. He'd dropped his jaw and his walking stick. Tanya realized that she was seeing the *moran* unselfconscious for the first time; his preening and showing-off was gone, replaced by a stunned paralysis.

When he revives, Tanya thought, he's going to put grass in his mouth – the Masai sign of defeat.

When Lekishon did recover, however, his mouth bore, not grass, but African unity: he casually asked Kamau if any of his sisters were marriageable. Kamau, who hated the Masai with the diligence of any Kikuyu warrior, was nonetheless strategic about his sisters' marriage prospects. "My sisters are all famous beauties," Kamau declared, "and their bride prices are very high. They will cost you many goats and cows."

Lekishon doubted that Kamau's sisters could be so beautiful; Kikuyu women, after all, were short and plump. But Kikuyu women could farm, which – now that cattle raiding was illegal – was (to Lekishon's thinking) the future. Lekishon wanted very much for his wife to embrace agriculture, since he wasn't going to muddy his noble hands with manual labor. A useful bride, then, might be worth as much as a beautiful one. "I will see your sisters," Lekishon announced, "and then I will decide their value."

* * *

Ducking away from the Malena-Erik extravaganza, Tanya investigated the Besil River fort. It occupied a clearing on the northern bank of the river. The water was turbid, a state that could not have been improved by the trash pile that Tanya spied downstream.

A troop of baboons was feasting amid the garbage. At a distance from the group – though at insufficient remove from Tanya – a baboon couple was energetically copulating in the underbrush. Tanya averted her gaze in disgust.

Drying on branches overhanging the river were articles of men's clothing, ornamenting the trees as if for a khaki Christmas. Lying impertinently on one such pair of trousers was a black-faced vervet monkey, adding color to the decorations by exposing his blue balls and red penis. Competing with this festivity, a nearby stand of sausage trees flaunted their large, oblong, yellowish fruits.

Feeling that nature was conspiring against her, Tanya turned her back on the river and faced the camp. In the clearing, the men had erected their tents in ragged rows on one side. Tanya noticed that the black soldiers congregating around the tents wore turbans; they were Somalis. One of them looked up from his conversation and eyed Tanya. He was an emaciated figure with a bright orange, hennaed beard. His confident eyes expressed piqued disapproval of a woman in the military camp.

Tanya looked away uncomfortably. The presence of Somali soldiers made her nervous, but she didn't know why. Perhaps she was anxious that Hassan's potential for mischief would be multiplied in the presence of so many of his countrymen.

Hastening away towards the parade grounds on the other side of the camp, Tanya froze at the sight of a gramophone sitting outside one of the tents. It had a mahogany exterior and an opalescent horn that could contend for beauty with any flower in British East Africa.

Tanya stared at the gramophone, transfixed, as if suspicious that it might attack her. Then, advancing with hesitant steps, she peeked at the record on the turntable: Schubert. Inhaling sharply, Tanya tried to calm her racing heart with a willful breath. She lectured herself about jumping to unwarranted conclusions. Then she decided to hide.

Veering away from the parade grounds, she retreated in a wide circle around the fort, keeping alert for Hassan. She needed to instruct him to move their tent to a remote area.

Trudging through long grasses, passing behind the command center and the officers' tent, however, she realized that her urge to hide was a ridiculous impulse. Their arrival had not been secret and, thanks to the marquee attraction of the "Erik and Malena spectacular," the entire fort must be aware of their presence by now. She was on the verge of thinking that she might as well walk openly through the camp, when she tripped over a grand piano next to the officers' tent.

Rubbing her shin, she stared resentfully at the piano. Black lacquered and gleaming, it had obviously been dusted that day. The maker, "Challen," was inscribed in gold lettering over the keyboard. She couldn't imagine why she hadn't seen the piano, but she hadn't been expecting it. A crotchety crocodile, jaws agape, next to the officers' tent she could have managed more expertly than this grand piano.

Still rubbing her shin, Tanya called to a passing officer, "Hello! Sir, please, if I may?"

He was an exceedingly short man, just a smidgeon taller than herself, and he had an angular, boney face. He wore a khaki, cotton button-down shirt, matching trousers and weathered safari boots. "Ah, Baroness, is it?" he asked brightly.

His manner was disarming, and Tanya smiled despite her disquiet. "Yes, I'm afraid I don't know —"

"Lieutenant Miles," he beamed back. "Tich Miles. I've heard about you." Tanya was about to ask from whom, when he continued, "Are you alright? You and our piano seem to have played an unharmonious duet."

Tanya straightened up with an awkward smile. "I don't think amputation will be necessary," she allowed, "I'll hobble through. But what is this piano doing here?"

"It doesn't fit in the officers' tent."

"Yes, but how did it get to the Besil River?"

"Carrier Corps."

Tanya's eyes widened. "They carried it here? On their backs?"

"On their heads, I expect," Lieutenant Miles chortled and continued in comic vein: "Did you know the first time natives were given wheelbarrows to haul dirt, they loaded them up and carried them on their heads?"

"But why?"

"Naturally, they'd never seen a wheelbarrow before, and they weren't up to discerning the mechanism of the wheel."

"No," Tanya shook her head, "I mean, why bring a piano? Supplies are so short – I know, I've been hauling them – shouldn't the Carrier Corps reserve their strength for ammunition and food?"

"My dear Baroness," Lieutenant Miles said amiably, "how can we fight for civilization without music?"

"I see your point, of course, but —"

"— And Hilary would be as depressed as Apollo without his lyre if he couldn't play the piano."

"Hilary?" Tanya's throat constricted after the name escaped her lips. Her fears were vindicated. Forcing breath out, Tanya struggled, "Lieutenant Miles, the Somalis here – they're with Cole's Scouts?"

"That's it exactly. We're camped together with the East African Mounted Rifles."

"And the gramophone and the Schubert?"

"Hilary's, of course. Music may be the food of love, but with Hilary it's just food, you know."

"How would I know?"

"You're his friend from Paris, aren't you?"

An explosion behind them preempted any response Tanya might have made. The sound caused a spasm to shiver up Tanya's spine, and her hands shot out to grip Lieutenant Miles' arm.

"Bloody biscuits and bully beef," he swore genially, "swarming Krauts. We need to get you out of here." The rapid cacophony of machine gun fire confirmed his prescription. Grabbing her wrist, Lieutenant Miles ran dragging Tanya towards the soldiers' tents, from which men were streaming on foot and horseback.

Plunging through the mass of soldiers buckling on holsters and securing weapons, Tanya fought for breath. The combined noise of men shouting and rushing, of horses and mules snorting and neighing, and of gunfire – the sonic embodiment of terror – overran her body. Bumping and banging against shoulders and flanks, Tanya at last came to an abrupt halt against a leg. The leg was slung over the side of a mule. Lieutenant Miles looked up cheerily at the leg's owner. "I caught the piano flirting, Captain."

"I've been meaning to get that piano fixed, Lieutenant. The competition is arousing my jealousy," Hilary Gordon replied jovially, with a wink at Tanya. Then, apropos of the soldiers surging on either side, Hilary added, "Lieutenant, allow me to release you from your chivalrous duties and impose upon you some military ones."

"Ah, only decent in the circumstances."

"If you'll give the Baroness a hand, I'll keep her safe."

Then, before Tanya could fully assimilate what was happening, Lieutenant Miles kneeled and laced his hands together; she placed one foot on his hands and mounted Hilary's mule; and Hilary galloped off into battle with her. She wrapped her arms desperately around his body.

* * *

Her eyes closed, cheek pressed against his back, Tanya felt certain from the stomach-churning noise that they were riding into machine gun fire. Fear tightened her grip around Hilary's abdomen; and then another fear caused her to loosen her hands. She couldn't decide what was more unnerving: the aromas of Hilary's body – Macassar hair oil, bay rum and the musk powder he favored; or the odor of burning gunpowder. Hilary's scent evoked the emotional tumult of her past in Paris; the gunpowder made her sure that death was imminent.

With that conscious acknowledgement of the consequences of allowing Hilary to drag her into battle, Tanya's stomach revolted. Her guts cramped and her throat clenched: she needed to flee.

Her eyes flew open. They were jolting across grassland, pockmarked with treacherous aardvark holes capable of bringing down Hilary's mule with a broken leg. Looking over her shoulder, Tanya could see the fort receding behind her. The last of the soldiers was speeding off in another direction.

Feeling another abdominal convulsion, Tanya knew that she needed to return to the fort. She was not a soldier; she was a woman. She had no duty to be courageous in battle; the panic pounding through her was the natural and proper response of her sex. She needed to flee.

Then a vicious stab of guilt superseded her fear. She realized that, for the second time in four days, she was riding to confront the Germans with Lord Delamere's secret map on her person. Blast Hilary! She'd been bundled onto his mule without warning, and she'd had no opportunity to stash the map. And now the enemy would steal it off her corpse. Tanya's face contorted with dread, and tears hovered at the corners of her eyes.

"Hilary," she whispered.

He didn't hear.

"Hilary," she said, turning her head to direct the sound towards his ear. The air was clogged with dirt and gunpowder, and the wind was streaking her face with sparks. She shouted with pain, "Hilary!"

He turned his head. But before she could explain that she needed to retreat to the camp, he yelled, "We need to dismount!" The mule stopped so precipitously that Tanya would've pitched forward over its ears had Hilary's body not blocked her tumble. She jarred her right temple against Hilary's spine and experienced a knock of such severity that it temporarily conked the fear from her mind.

With a speed and fluidity impressive in a man of his build, Hilary slipped off the mule with his rifle and pulled her after him, passing a hand over the temple she'd been clutching.

Tanya had just time to observe that they were in a huge grassy field, in view of a tree and a lump in the grass, behind which soldiers were battling on horseback. Then she heard shouting in German – she could make out "Behind you!" – and Hilary hissed, "Down!"

His hand between her shoulder blades, she dropped into the long grasses. Bullets exploded from a rifle; she'd seen black smoke in the distance, but her vision was at ground level by the time the bullets flew overhead. A lizard scuttled into the grasses in front, and some impressively large ants resolutely rerouted themselves around the bodies plopped suddenly in their path.

With her right cheek to the ground, Tanya found herself facing Hilary, who'd turned his left cheek downward. His eyes were shiny with intensity, and his mouth abundant with poetry: "To do good for mankind is the chivalrous plan / And is always as nobly requited," he whispered mischievously. "Then battle for freedom wherever you can / And, if not shot or hang'd, you'll get knighted."

Following this recitation, in what seemed from Tanya's vantage point to be a single motion, Hilary popped up and swung the rifle onto his shoulder. He was back, belly-down beside her, before the sound of the gunshot had finished reverberating.

"Shelley?" she asked, oddly invigorated by the action around her.

"Byron," he answered. "'When a Man Hath No Freedom to Fight for at Home.'"

Their conversation was silenced by the emphatic bullets puncturing the air above; however elegant Hilary's shooting, he'd left at least one German capable of volleying gunfire at them. Hilary sneaked forward, crouching and peering over the long grasses; aiming at the black smoke wafting from the German's rifle, Hilary fired again. This time a choked cry could be heard in the aftermath.

Tanya bounded after him excitedly. The words, "Well done," were poised on her lips when, his face alarmed, he cried, "No!" exasperatedly and tackled her.

When his body hit her, Tanya felt certain that even Malena couldn't have known greater force when she was felled by the lioness. As Tanya skidded under him, the razor-edged grasses and the knobs of roots tearing at her skin and clothes, she fleetingly acknowledged surprise. Hilary was large, yes, but in height and build he was smaller than Isak; and yet Isak had never marshaled anything on this scale of physical momentum in her presence. Tanya snorted an insect out of her nose.

Hilary sprang onto his knees so as not to crush her. He placed a hand sympathetically on her cheek and murmured, "My fault. I should have told you to stay down." Then, still kneeling over her, he fired twice and was rewarded with a scream.

Hilary patted her shoulder. "Carefully now," he cautioned, indicating that she could rise. "Are you all right?"

She looked up just as a German solider crashed out of the tree. A broken branch hung with sickly resign over where the man had thudded to earth. Tanya turned quizzically to Hilary. She opened her mouth, but was seized with a spasm of coughs, as her lungs emptied the dirt and noxious powders she'd been inhaling. When she regained her equilibrium, she rubbed tenderly at a grass burn on her arm and asked, "What the devil did you mean when you'd said you'd keep me safe?"

Hilary laughed. Holding out his hand, he helped her to her feet.

Taking account of her numerous bruises and abrasions, Tanya noticed that the cavalry beyond them had dispersed. The Germans appeared to be in retreat. She could hear shouting and gunshots receding in the distance.

Steering her in the direction of the tree, Hilary explained, "I'm afraid the only safe place I could think of was behind me."

"What about the officers' tent?" she retorted.

He shook his head. "Machine gun fire, Titania —"

"— Baroness!"

"— Baroness, is not normal. The German raiding parties target the Magadi branch line. They've come from Mount Longido, which is a considerable safari —"

"— We met a raiding party in the Ingito Hills."

"Did you?" He stopped and eyed her. Then he recommenced his brisk stride. "Over such distances, they travel light. Dynamite, yes, but not machine guns. Too heavy, and carrying machine guns is porters' work —"

"— What do they do? Toss the machine gun on top of the piano?"

Hilary smiled. "Naughty piano. I told it not to tell anyone. And, besides which," he said, returning to the main topic, "a machine gun is useless if the goal is to blow up a train track. No, if they lugged a machine gun here, it was to attack our encampment. So you see, Baroness," he said, stopping again and smiling a plea for understanding, "I couldn't leave you at the very place that was the target. If we hadn't been able to chase them off, and they'd rampaged through the camp, they'd have found you alone in the officers' tent."

He continued walking, leaving Tanya to brood. When she caught up with him again, she asked, "Why would they attack the encampment?"

"I fancy," he said with a waggle of his eyebrows that, she knew from past experience, meant he was joking, "that they were trying to get at you. Now —"

Tanya twisted her mouth into a nervous smile and stilled her hand from reaching inside her shirt to finger the map. She understood that Hilary wasn't serious; but she wondered if he hadn't inadvertently spoken truth in jest.

Hilary had no inkling of her thoughts because he was staring downwards, utterly absorbed, "— let's see how War again did glut himself on a meal of blood."

They were beside the tree, and in the grass before them was a mangled body. The man was a German. From his uniform, he was a Lieutenant. His holster was empty of its pistol, and his rifle had fallen between his body and the tree trunk. He lay face up, eyes and mouth open, blood drenching his upturned hands. Hilary's gunshot had torn open the man's midriff. The black and maroon wound gleamed sinisterly against the khaki cotton of the man's uniform.

"Poor devil," Hilary murmured, squatting beside the corpse to close his eyes. "Hardly sporting. We're shooting 303s – smokeless, you know," he said, glancing at Tanya to emphasize the salient feature of the British firearms, "and their damned 1871 rifles belch black smoke every time they fire. Gives their bloody position away."

Tanya nodded dully, her hands covering her cheeks. She was forcing herself to look upon the corpse in honor of the man who had once been. She wondered if he'd died before he'd fallen from the tree. Dying in a tree struck her as particularly horrifying. "What was he doing in the tree?"

"Directing machine gun fire." Hilary stood and looked over at the lump in the grass. Tanya realized for the first time that the "lump" was a machine gun perched on a mound. The thick instrument balanced on a tripod, its barrel facing in the direction of the soldiers who'd been skirmishing on horseback. Shiny black in the sun, the gun lurked in the tall grasses like a spitting cobra. "The Germans are even worse off than us for supplies," Hilary explained, walking over to the machine gun. "Our Navy commands the Indian Ocean, so the Germans can't reprovision by sea. They have to husband their ammunition very carefully, so they don't go shooting machine guns with abandon. Short, controlled bursts of gunfire on the command of a look-out, usually perched in a tree like that guy." Hilary stopped and put both hands on his hips. He frowned at the sight of the machine gunner's corpse at the base of the mound.

The German machine gunner had taken Hilary's bullet in the face. The right side of his head was an eruption of glistening flesh, shards of bone and foaming brain matter. Tanya covered her mouth and looked away, clutching Hilary's arm for support. She realized that, earlier, in the headiness of battle, she'd been about to congratulate Hilary for his good work on delivering death to the machine gunner. Now she shuddered with shame that she could ever had thought to characterize this outcome as, "well done."

Sighing heavily, Hilary turned to face her back and put his hands gently on her shoulders. He bowed his head and recited,

> The land of honourable death
> Is here: — up to the field, and give
> Away thy breath!
>
> Seek out – less often sought than found –
> a soldier's grave, for thee the best;
> Then look around, and choose thy ground,
> And take thy rest.

Hilary raised his head. "I'll have to tell the men to bury these two."

As he took her arm and guided her away, Tanya followed Hilary's gaze upwards. Vultures were circling.

Hilary whistled for his mule, which was grazing several hundred meters away. The beast ignored him. After Hilary had whistled several more times – and after they'd covered most of the ground separating them from the pack animal – the mule looked up and trotted towards Hilary.

The mule, Tanya noticed for the first time, was discolored with uneven, purplish stripes. Seeing her stupefied reaction to the animal's odd appearance, Hilary clarified: "Iodine. We painted them like zebras for camouflage."

Reeling as she was from the battle, Tanya was still able to grasp the futility of this action. With its outlandish purple fur, the poor animal could blend into a pack of zebras about as effortlessly as Pegasus. And, having just seen the wreckage wrought by rifle fire, Tanya was confident that iodine could be put to better uses in war time. "Bored at camp?" Tanya asked, as Hilary assisted her mounting the painted creature.

"As dull as prison," Hilary nodded grimly, "except prisoners get better food. Today's spot of war is, well, I won't say 'welcome,' but – honestly, any variance in the routine of parading, digging trenches, standing guard, and riding around the bush without food or water is a relief." Hilary whacked the mule, and it lurched into a gallop in the direction of the machine gun.

Stinging from her slide across the grass under Hilary's tackle, and queasy from having glimpsed the corpses, Tanya feared that the mule's jerking would rattle her to the point of vomiting. She tried holding her breath. She knew she could never bear the humiliation if she was sick on Hilary. But holding her breath only heightened her nausea, and her mouth filled with saliva. Swallowing it desperately, she beseeched Hilary to slow down the mule. "I should like to return to the camp," she pleaded feebly.

He shook his head, but he eased the mule's pace. "Not safe yet. We're sweeping the area for any remaining enemy." He swiveled in the saddle to examine her. "Are you unwell, Baroness?"

"No, I'm, I'm," she struggled for a word and eventually settled on, "upset." She breathed deeply. Slowing the mule to a trot had allowed her nausea to pass, and she was grateful, even though now for some reason she felt like crying.

"You've not seen corpses before?" he asked with quiet respect, craning around to meet her eyes.

"Not with gunshot wounds," she admitted.

They'd reached the battlefield beyond the tree, and Hilary now slowed the mule even further so that he could check the ground for the dead and wounded.

Tanya closed her eyes, rested her head against Hilary's back and tried not to cry. Now that the dazzle of seeing him again had worn off, now that the fear of battle and of dying had subsided, now that she had witnessed the travesty that war inflicts on human bodies, now that she was momentarily safe, she wanted to find refuge in his arms.

The thought was unhinging her.

She preferred to be angry at Hilary. Her anger was a shield that protected her from the danger he posed. But she didn't feel angry. The thought that he had humiliated her once, long ago, didn't arouse her fury any more.

Right now, she felt drained and dislocated, as if in a semi-waking state, besieged with dream-like memories: Erik and Malena's passionate kiss, Lord Delamere's face when he'd said, "Mostly Masai"; Lekishon rolling up his *shuka* to show Malena the scars on his thighs, the old Masai woman saying that, "Marriage without lovers was impossible"; Hilary kissing her forehead when he'd saved her from Mr. Baden. The day had seen fighting sufficient to sate her for her lifetime; she wanted to surrender.

She opened her eyes at the sound of Hilary's voice. He was commanding one of his subordinates to bury the two soldiers by the machine gun and to provide medical care to several other wounded men on the field. Looking around, Tanya saw that the British soldiers were trickling back after having given chase to the retreating Germans; the soldier to whom Hilary was speaking was part of a trio of these returning men. Saying that he would ride on to complete his inspection of the vicinity, Hilary left the men to the post-battle let-downs of patching together broken bodies and digging graves.

Hilary brought the mule to a canter and rode, scanning the ground, the trees and the horizon, but he spotted neither additional threats nor casualties. Behind them came a cheer as the British soldiers discovered the abandoned machine gun in the long grasses.

Hilary rode on, away from the reality of war, until they described a wide arc around the fort, and Tanya could hear the river flowing behind the thicket of trees at its banks. Hilary pulled the mule to an easy stop and dismounted. Helping Tanya down, he smiled at the pliancy with which her body responded to his hands.

They walked together along the bank. In the shade of the trees overhanging the Besil River, the air was invigoratingly moist and fragrant with the tang of botanicals. The underbrush yielded readily beneath their feet. Hilary squatted and washed his hands and his face. "Ah," he uttered, the water purging the blood he'd just shed. "That I might . . . leave the world unseen / And with thee fade away into the forest dim," he sighed. Then he reached a hand, chilled by the river, and placed it on the back of Tanya's neck.

Shying away at first, she then submitted with a small smile to his touch.

He smiled in return. He released her neck and clasped her right hand in both of his. He pressed her palm to his lips fervently and, then, holding her hand close, so that his breath teased her fingers, he whispered, "Forgive me, Titania."

The tone of his voice evoked a moment a decade previously, and Tanya experienced a tingling heat sweeping downwards from her blushing cheeks.

The feeling appeared to be mutual. Hilary continued, "I cannot contain myself. Wordsworth wrote of the soldier who, in crisis, "Is happy as a Lover; and attired / With sudden brightness, like a Man inspired." And he was writing only about battle, not about the warrior riding into combat with the woman he loves embracing him, finally, after these many years of yearning. I've never known aliveness like this. Am I attired with a sudden brightness? Because I am a man inspired. I must tell you countless things, I want to unburden everything that has happened since I saw you last, but for this moment let my declaration of love take second place only to my apology for assaulting your honor as a married woman."

His words had been caressing Tanya, enchanting her into an enraptured receptivity, but now she stiffened.

"Dishonorable and shameful to plead my cause too late, I know, unworthy behavior, I know, but you must forgive me. Right now, I cannot restrain myself from at least speaking my desires. From telling you how I want to take you to England, like I should have done ten years ago. How I want to show you the house where I grew up. How I've dreamed of presenting you to my parents as the woman I love."

"Hilary, what are you saying?"

"I'm saying I love you."

"It can't be."

"It is. Ten years of separation have confirmed that you are my match in this world."

"I'm married. I cannot love outside my marriage."

"Nonsense. The Masai do. Oberon and Titania did."

"Savages and fairies!? These examples you suggest to me? Me? I'm a woman of honor and a noblewoman —"

"— Yes, I know," he cut in, assuring her, "I've crushed myself repeatedly with the reminder that my desires can never materialize into flesh. But always the hope endures. Nothing suppresses it. Nothing blunts it. I live in hope, however foolish. Dare I hope that you will someday forgo your title Baroness, and be but the humble Honorable Mrs. Hilary Gordon?"

For all his poetry and inspired, romantic outpourings, Hilary Gordon – with that last question – bungled his chances. Tanya snatched her hand from his clasp and slapped him. She jumped up, shouting, "How can you insinuate that all I care about is a title?! You know I'm a woman of depth and sensitive feeling! You wouldn't love me if I wasn't! And yet you insult me with these base accusations that I could marry for anything other than love!"

Hilary stood, dumbfounded, his face smarting. He'd thought he'd been proposing marriage, and he was unprepared for his question to be received in anything but the spirit with which it was intended. "I —"

"— Ten years haven't changed you at all. You're still mocking me, just as you did in Paris —"

"— Mocking you?"

"You recite all the Romantic poets, but you're not serious about love! You're not serious about anything but frivolity, painting mules purple and hauling pianos into the African bush at the expense of other men's lives!"

"Mocking you? How did I mock you in Paris?"

"That same thing you just said! That I would marry for title! You —"

"— Grigory? You are referring to him? That oaf? That drunk? That boar in a bowtie?"

"That prince. That nobleman who would never display himself to such poor effect as you are doing now."

"Ha! A drunk of more loutish, vile disposition I've never met. Grigory was everything you loathed. He had no taste. He was incapable of conversing about anything other than race horses, whores and vodka. And pickles! You wouldn't have permitted him to breathe in the same room as you had he not been a prince!"

Hilary was not correct. Tanya permitted Grigory within her sphere not because he was a prince, but because he was such an effective instrument for provoking Hilary. So well had she chosen her man that, a decade later, he was still working Hilary into a froth.

"He would have hurt you!" Hilary spluttered. "I pray you have never seen him drunk. Had you married him, you would have passed your days penning sonnets about the virtues of suicide!"

Notwithstanding Hilary's assumptions, Tanya hadn't been pursuing a title *per se* in Paris. She'd been after a sense of worth, and titles are alluring in the appearance of worth that they impart. Hilary was so grandly more than she was in those days; as much as she'd loved him then, he'd made her feel small. She'd latched onto Grigory as a man with whom she could enjoy her newfound worldliness; however little of the aristocratic arts she'd mastered, she was on equitable footing with Grigory.

"And you, you haven't changed in ten years, either!" Hilary charged. "Still after men for their titles! This latest one is an inconstant man! You dare speak to me of depth and sensitive feeling, when your every action in your marriage must be to bury and smother the same? Was that why you rejected me in Paris, Tanya? Because I wasn't boorish enough?"

Hilary didn't have his facts straight. As often happens with the passage of a decade, memory massages the story into a narrative we favor. While his abiding jealousy of Prince Grigory had left this youngest son of an Earl (and therefore only entitled to use "Honorable" in front of his name) with a stubborn sense of rejection, Tanya had not rejected him in Paris. He'd never declared his love for her. Even if he had, she'd been too insecure to accept it; seeing the numerous aristocratic beauties who competed for Hilary's attention, Tanya would've assumed that Hilary was only professing love to make sport of her. Instead, Tanya had pursued Prince Grigory, and Hilary had followed, mocking and belittling her flirtation until he disrupted and humiliated her in an intimate clinch with Grigory. A period of separation between all three parties had thereafter ensued.

"My God!" Hilary exclaimed, falling to his knees in shame. The sudden realization of the offense he was giving first blanched his face and then flushed it crimson. "I am an ass. I cannot hope that you will accept my apology, but I offer it —"

"— Oh shut up."

"I would not have spoken thus if the emotion of the moment —"

"— If boorish is what I liked, I couldn't have done better than to marry you."

"I don't blame you for so saying," Hilary bowed, "but I beseech you to understand the compulsion of my passion! My love's excess, that's all — I was expressing it with words of unmeant bitterness."

"Hilary, I married for love, and I am constant in my love. And I am a woman of honor. I would never disgrace my husband, myself and our families with any vulgar entanglement or breach of fidelities."

"I want no such thing, but only I beg you, reflect upon the preservation of your honor in times of tribulation. I could never desert you in times of woe."

"And what blessing is that if you're so much the cause of my woe?"

"I am sorry," Hilary sympathized, "but could I have been so rude but for the depths of my love and my despair?"

"I care to hear nothing further from you."

"My despair at losing you —"

"— I'm going back to the fort." Tanya turned and stalked off.

"The fort is in the other direction!" Hilary shouted, pointing.

She stopped, glared at him and stomped off in the direction indicated.

"Take the mule!" Hilary jumped to his feet and rushed after her.

Tanya stopped again, shot him another foul look, and elbowed away all his attempts to assist her mounting the mule.

"Tanya, at least consider forgiving me. Please. My life will be worth nothing if you do not."

Tanya steered the mule away from his outstretched hand and rode off without a word.

Watching the dust cloud raised by the mule's hooves, Hilary contemplated shooting himself. Now more than ever seems it rich to die, he thought. Keats. But looking around him, he realized that his rifle was strapped to the mule's saddle.

Resigning himself instead to Byron – More than this I scarce can die – he trudged back to the fort.

TWELVE

"My darling *prinsesstårta!*"

The shock was more than Tanya could absorb in stride. She tumbled off the mule. Lying on the tough, bitten ground of the military camp, she mentally reviewed the scene that had just assailed her: separated from the other tents by a respectable distance, her own tent stood with a small campfire glowing nearby. Over the fire, Kamau had been boiling water for tea. By the fire, Dionysus had been napping. And seated around the fire had been Hassan conversing with . . . Isak.

No, his presence was not possible. She must have imagined him. Seeing Hilary again, witnessing war death for the first time, hearing Hilary's extraordinary declaration of love, rejecting Hilary in favor of Isak – the accumulated stresses had addled her such that she was conjuring her worst fear: her husband's presence.

If given a choice between allowing her husband abundant opportunities to indulge himself with Masai women, and having her husband discover that she and Hilary shared a past (that was attempting to become a present), she would have resoundingly selected the first option. However much Isak might hurt her, she couldn't countenance him knowing that she'd dishonored him: the indignity would be unbearable. Not that Tanya thought she'd dishonored Isak in her dealings with Hilary, but under no circumstances did she want Isak to have enough information to judge for himself.

Yet, she wondered, if Isak was merely a product of her discombobulated mind, who was now calling, "*Prinsesstårta*, are you hurt?"

Within moments, her husband, the eleventh Baron von Brantberg, was shading her from the sun with his prodigious shadow. He stood at her feet, a look of tender concern softening his broad features.

She gurgled a weak smile up at him.

His own face reciprocated with an overjoyed grin. "My battle-weary *prinsesstårta*!" He gathered her in his arms. "I heard that you sampled war today. An acquired taste, no?" Cradling her, he threw her a centimeter in the air. "Oo-pah!" he laughed. "Nothing broken?"

She shook her head, declining to add that, if anything had been broken, throwing her around was not the most sensitive means of diagnosis.

"What happened to your mule?" he inquired, carrying her to the campfire. "Is it sick?"

"It's not mine. It's supposed to look like a zebra."

Isak threw his head back and guffawed. "Whoever painted that mule is a bigger fool than me. I never thought it possible – thank you *prinsesstårta*!" He smothered her neck in an outsized kiss.

Tanya tried to smile, but she felt too confused to share her husband's laughter. "Isak," Tanya ventured, as he was lowering her beside the campfire. "Why are you here?"

"I'm escorting you to the train station."

"We are rejoicing that Allah has returned you safely from battle," Hassan said, rising to restrain the mule, who'd begun to eat Tanya's tent.

"Thank you, Hassan," Tanya replied, adding that she would be gratified if Hassan would stable the mule. As Tanya made herself comfortable on a rock, Dionysus raised his head to sniff happily in her direction. Holding out her hand for Dionysus to lick, and looking shyly away from her husband, she replied softly, "You are very kind to put my own safety above your work."

"What happiness is mine if your welfare is not assured?"

Tanya turned to him and searched his large face. She couldn't listen to such talk without reflexively objecting: why didn't he consider fidelity to be necessary for her welfare? An openness in his expression, however –

his slightly raised eyebrows, his wide eyes, his slack cheeks and jaw devoid of tension – made her feel the force of his sincerity. She struggled to smile. "I can watch over myself."

"Better than I watch over myself," he admitted, "but not," he said, wagging a meaty finger at her, "as well as I watch over you."

Tanya managed to smile at the teasing gleam in his eye. "But the most dangerous part of our safari is passed. We're almost at the train now. And Lord Delamere will be furious with me for having lured you away from your work."

"He'll have all the work he needs once you're on the train," Isak pronounced, sipping the tea that Kamau had just handed him.

Tanya accepted her tea from Kamau with a gracious nod that didn't entirely smooth her troubled expression.

Before Kamau turned away to pluck a spur fowl for dinner, he noted Tanya's distressed air, and inwardly he frowned at this additional evidence of the negative effects of the white man's customs of love. A Kikuyu warrior would never desert his fellow soldiers to trek across the bush for a woman. Discipline would not be necessary to restrain a Kikuyu warrior from such an impetuous act; rather, the impulse would never occur.

These overt demonstrations of love were slack habits that had sapped the white man of his suitability for war, Kamau concluded. Of course, such men could still shoot guns; but shooting guns was not war. *Women* could shoot guns. Guns were like witchcraft: they might diminish (even kill) a warrior, but they didn't change the witch-doctor into a warrior. As the Kikuyu saying held, going near the battlefield doesn't make you a warrior.

"War," as Kamau defined it, wasn't sniping with guns (or magic spells) at a distance, but charging into hand-to-hand combat with a Masai *moran* and vanquishing him with a spear through his guts or a knife in his neck. White men couldn't do it. And Memsabu knew it. Kamau had seen that Memsabu was a more perceptive *mzungu* than most. He was sure that her observations could not have failed to reveal the inherent superiority of the African warrior to his white counterpart. This heavy knowledge explained Memsabu's concerned look: she needed to convey that Bwana

Isak must behave more like a warrior, and less like a child easily distracted by his urges.

Staring at Kamau's back as he plucked the bird, Tanya asked Isak, tentatively, "Does D. know that you followed me?"

"I left in the middle of the night."

"But Isak," Tanya exclaimed incredulously, "You can't travel at night. It's too dangerous. Lions —"

"— But those, my sugared *prinsesstårta*, are the reasonings of a sober mind. Myself, on the other hand, was not in possession of one at the time. I simply rose from the card table and left."

"What do you mean 'left'? With nothing?" She restrained herself from adding, "with nothing save a gambling debt."

"Correct."

"No supplies, no mule?"

"No, I walked here."

"*Drunk?*"

"Not after the first few hours." Then he leaned over and, cupping her head in his enormous hands, kissed her sloppily on the forehead. "Malena has not polluted you with her religion, no?" he asked, pulling back his lips, but continuing to hold her head. His brow hovered closely, and Tanya felt as if she were beneath the overhang of a mountain. "Don't look so disapproving," he chided. "It was the best decision of my life."

Tanya was straining not to cry, and she met his gaze with moist eyes.

"Seeing you now, sheltering you in my arms, protecting you until you board the train – my life needs no other meaning," Isak declared.

Tanya lowered her eyes, swallowed heavily and nodded.

Isak rested his forehead against hers and whispered, "I am a sinner, like all God's creatures, and I ask forgiveness whenever I remember to pray."

"And does God forgive you?" Tanya asked, her voice cracking.

"He has given you to me," Isak murmured in a satisfied tone.

* * *

Tanya lay awake in the tent beside her sleeping husband. She recalled how, earlier that day, Hilary had called Isak an "inconstant man"; now a snippet of Coleridge that Hilary had taught her paraded through her mind: "constancy lives in realms above; / And life is thorny."

Tanya wished she could dispel her thoughts of Hilary with Isak's presence, and her inability to do so disappointed her. A noblewoman should exalt in her duties to her husband, she thought. But her duties to Isak merely made her anxious. Throughout their supper together – which she'd been unable to eat – her contribution to their conversation had been negligible. She'd been too preoccupied watching for Hilary – an ultimately unfounded fear, but one that deprived her of any capacity to support her husband with interjections of, "How fascinating," and, "What a man you are," at the appropriate moments.

Later, Isak's amorous explorations of her torso had terrified her with the possibility that he would find the map concealed in her inner shirt pocket. For the first time since Lord Delamere had entrusted this critical document to her, Tanya had removed her shirt. Her haste in tearing the garment from her body had, unfortunately, conveyed an unintended message to Isak, who was elated by what he took to be his wife's ravenous desire. Tanya comforted herself with the thought that a husband who thinks his wife is so rapturously in need of him is not a husband who thinks his wife is susceptible to the attentions of another man; but she couldn't reciprocate Isak's enthusiasm.

Buzzing away beneath her anxiousness all evening was a single, confounding fact: she could not fathom Isak's sudden appearance at Besil River. If his story was true, then he was committing a military crime – deserting his post or some such. But how could it be true? One of the officers with whom he'd been playing cards would have stopped him from a suicidal trek into the bush during the small hours of the night. Unless they were also nicely plastered, as they probably had been . . .

But wouldn't Lord Delamere have sent a search party out for him? Once Isak's absence had been discovered, D. would've spared no expense to return his precious mapmaker to camp. Wouldn't a team of Masai scouts have been able to track Isak within a matter of hours?

Convinced that Isak could not possibly have escaped such a dragnet, Tanya wondered if Lord Delamere had sent Isak after her. She was, after all, days late in arriving at Nairobi. D. might have expected word of her arrival by now, and he might have worried that she'd been captured or killed.

But if that were the case, why wouldn't Isak tell her? And why, for that matter, would Lord Delamere send Isak? D. had made clear that he loathed for Isak to leave his sight. If D. were willing to let Isak trek across the bush, why wouldn't he have simply sent the map back to Nairobi with Isak, according to the original plan?

No, Tanya decided, D. wouldn't have sent Isak. But what if Isak had gleaned that D. had recruited her to be the map courier? What if, out of anxiety for her safety on this mission, he'd slipped away from camp, careful to cover his tracks or otherwise elude the trackers that D. was sure to have sent after him? Isak might well risk a military reprimand if he knew his wife was undertaking an espionage assignment.

Tanya elbowed Isak in the ribcage. "Isak!" she whispered.

"Mmmmm?" he responded, shaking away a snore.

"Isak, tell me truly, why did you follow me?"

"I missed you." He rolled over to enfold her in a hug.

Tanya felt frustrated. She realized why his presence remained incomprehensible to her. Every reason he gave related, in some way, to his love for her, and yet these professions of love intuitively rang false. An uxorious husband does not cheat on his wife. A man so keen for his wife's company does not lie with native women in her absence.

Or does he?

"What did you mean earlier when you said you were a 'sinner'?" she asked.

"I have sinned," he grunted into her hair.

"How so?"

"Hmmmm?"

"Why tell me, now, that you're a sinner?"

Isak raised his head groggily. Tanya turned towards him and, in the dark, she could see that he seemed to have only one eye open. "Marrying a sinner is no tragedy," he said. "It's a commonplace." Then he lowered his head to nestle again in her hair.

"As much a truism nine months ago as it is today," Tanya conceded. "Why tell me now?"

"War. Heinous sin happens in war."

"What sort of sins?" Tanya persisted.

But Isak was snoring again.

Tanya couldn't summon the gumption to question Isak directly about the Masai women. The words seemed to gather in her mouth – infidelity, adultery, betrayal, fornication – and once there they seemed to strangle her vocal chords. Could she really use these words with her husband? She did not want to: neither to have the conversation, nor to know his answer. And yet she wanted him to confide in her. Confessing to her and asking her forgiveness seemed the only form of the conversation that she could bear.

Gradually, though, a thought coalesced and corralled her other voluble worries into soothing silence: what if Isak's trek after her, his professions of love and his vague admission of sin, what if these actions *were* his confession and request for forgiveness? Perhaps he could not speak his heart openly – and, obviously, he lacked Hilary's facility with language and poetry – but who needs to be like Hilary, Tanya scoffed. Couldn't Isak, out of guilt, to repent, walk under lashing sun through the African bush to shepherd his wife to the train?

Settling on this agreeable conclusion, Tanya finally capitulated to sleep's beckoning.

* * *

Poised for departure from Besil River, Tanya wondered if Hilary had ever returned to the camp; since she'd left him yesterday, he'd not shown himself. Even their leave-taking didn't produce the man. He was not among those gathered to say good-bye.

Tanya supposed that, circumstances being as they were – her refusal even to consider forgiving him, as well as her husband's unexpected presence in the camp – Hilary's absence was understandable. But it irked her. If he really loved me as he claims, he could not resist bidding me farewell, she thought resentfully.

Lekishon, she noticed, hadn't hesitated to offer Malena an oily farewell, despite Erik's presence. Of course, Erik's appearance was unlikely to intimidate the Masai *moran*: Erik was slim and short (for a Swede); he stood at the same height as Malena. He had straight hair, light brown, that hung limply around his head and curled slightly near its ends. His sunburned face was perpetually smiling, and his small brown eyes conveyed delight with everything. Watching Lekishon embrace Malena, Erik didn't seem to mind the *moran*'s familiarity with his wife; indeed, Erik seemed to think it evidence of his wife's Christian charity.

Lekishon announced that he would not be accompanying them to the train station. Ordinarily, this development would've made Tanya sing hosannas, but she simultaneously learned that Lekishon had opted to remain at the fort and work as a scout for the East African Mounted Rifles. That the East African Mounted Rifles would give Lekishon a chance to worm into their operations worried Tanya, and she delayed their departure in order to warn the squadron's commander, Captain O'Brien, that Lekishon was not trustworthy.

She found the Captain sitting outside his tent, shirtless and eating a breakfast of bully beef out of the tin. He was washing it down with beer. A wide, strapping man with salt-and-pepper hair and a peeling sunburn on his face and neck, the Captain listened to Tanya's report, scratched his chest and shrugged. Then he demanded that she leave Hassan and Kamau with him, so that they could serve in the Carrier Corps.

Flabbergasted, Tanya stammered, "Hassan is Somali."

"So give him to Cole's Scouts," Captain O'Brien waved his hand dismissively. "The Kikuyu boy goes to Carrier Corps."

Tanya swallowed, set her jaw and tossed her head. "Captain, I am a Baroness, and a woman of honor. I have given my word to my employees that they shall never serve in Carrier Corps so long as they prefer to remain in my service. My word cannot be broken."

"That's very noble of you Baroness, but we need food carried into the bush more than you need your coffee picked. It's just a cash crop to you." Captain O'Brien swigged his beer. "It's starvation for us."

Tanya wanted to shout that, if food was what needed carrying, then the Carrier Corps shouldn't be used frivolously to haul pianos around the bush. She wanted to shame Captain O'Brien for his limited inclusion of "us" in the group at risk of starvation. In fact, she wanted to remind him, starvation was a reality – not a risk – for the Carrier Corps porters. But Tanya sensed that expressing her anger would beggar her dignity, and she preferred simply to end the interview. "Kamau enlists in Carrier Corps after I do," Tanya declaimed, quivering.

"Hold on, Baroness," Captain O'Brien ordered, putting down his beer. "Don't be a hot head." Then, looking her over, he said, "I'd like a word with your husband before you go."

Tanya was about to retort that "a word with her husband" was something Captain O'Brien could have after he himself enlisted in the Carrier Corps, but she checked herself. Suspected German sympathizers cannot disrespect British military authority, she admonished herself. Nor, she added, do spies carrying vital documents pick fights on their courier routes. Pursing her lips, she nodded her assent.

Immediately upon Isak's conclusion of his conference with Captain O'Brien, their safari departed: Tanya and Malena riding mules; Isak, Erik, Hassan and Kamau on foot. Tanya kept waiting for Isak to broach the subject of the Carrier Corps, but he didn't raise the topic. So Tanya rode silently, glad that the conversation seemed to need no participation from her. Malena and Erik captivated their party with their account of yesterday's battle with the Germans – a battle that turned so critically on Erik's role in the cavalry that any listener would've had the impression that no machine gun had been involved – and Tanya was free to mull.

Principally, she hoped she would see Hilary again, so that she could tell him that she would consider forgiving him. He was, after all, a soldier in war time, and denying him such a small measure of solace was, she felt on reflection, unduly unkind.

Their safari lasted the better part of the day, but they reached the Kajiado station on the Magadi branch line in time for the 4 p.m. train to Nairobi, which was waiting on the track. The station sat on a patch of clear-cut land in the long grasses. In its defining features, the Kajiado station was largely indistinguishable from Kijabe. It had a comparably squat station house and a similarly ramshackle corrugated iron hut for the station master, who – of course – was a Goan: a "Babu" to those colonials who couldn't accord Goan station masters individual identities. (This Goan station master, unsurprisingly, had an individual identity: his name was Dinesh.) Around the station house milled laborers from the

Magadi Soda Works and soldiers, all drinking beers and eating chapattis while they waited for the train to leave. In addition to repairing trains, chopping wood, operating the telegraph machine, selling train tickets, loading cargo, running a small import/export business, and making chapattis, Dinesh was, by all indications, a gifted gardener: both sides of the track were planted with beds of cabbage, lady fingers, carrots, potatoes, maize and tomatoes.

Erik and Malena disappeared like a pair of rabbits into the vegetable beds, while Hassan and Kamau headed for the station house to investigate the chapatti situation and infiltrate the crowd of laborers and soldiers, who were likely to be spreading useful gossip.

Holding onto the mules – now entrusted to his care – Isak looked down sheepishly. Tanya felt a surge of tenderness for him, her ardent, inarticulate husband. "Isak," she said, seeking his eyes, "promise me you'll go back to Lord Delamere's camp now."

He nodded. "I will *prinsesstårta*."

She held his chin in her hands, and he clasped her left hand, pressing his lips to her fingers. "Even if D. punishes you for disappearing without leave, or whatever it is you've done wrong, your work for the cause is important." Tanya hesitated. She wanted to assure Isak that D. couldn't inflict any truly miserable hardship on him because Isak was such a critical a part of D.'s operations; but she didn't think she could offer that comfort without exposing her own knowledge of the mapmaking project. So she said, "I'm relying on you, all the settlers are relying on you, to protect us."

He nodded again.

"Besides, I need you to stay in D.'s good graces so I can prove to the Nairobi busybodies that I'm not a German spy," she said with a lopsided smile. "Would a German spy have a husband serving courageously in Lord Delamere's unit?"

He returned her smile and asked, "Can I have some money?"

Tanya's eyelids fluttered. "Money? Don't you have any?" she murmured, trying – and failing – to achieve an airy tone.

He shook his head.

Remembering that Isak had left Lord Delamere's camp with gambling debts, Tanya straightened her spine, swallowed uncomfortably and tossed her head. "I don't either, dearest," she lied.

"But you must. How will you pay the train fare?"

"Oh yes," Tanya laughed, the sound catching in her throat like an acacia thorn. "Of course, I have train fare. But only just barely enough. Nothing else."

"Then leave Kamau and Hassan with me and give me the money for their train fare."

Tanya stared sullenly at Isak. Inwardly, she castigated herself for her sentimentality in thinking him ardent and inarticulate. He was, if anything, vulgarly calculating. Now she understood why he hadn't mentioned the Carrier Corps for the entirety of the trek from the Besil River fort. He'd been devising a plan to get both Hassan and Kamau *and* money for his gambling debts.

The realization that he was willing to subject Hassan and Kamau to the Carrier Corps mortified her. Just as discomforting, however, was her emerging suspicion that Isak had trekked after her for money.

Her hand twitched, and the memory of slapping Hilary yesterday played itself out in her mind. How easy dealing with men could be if one wasn't married to them! If Isak wasn't her husband, she would slap him. She would tell him that he was conducting himself utterly without dignity and dishonoring his title and his person. She would refuse to acknowledge him until he begged for forgiveness, whereupon she would ignore his pleas.

But the difficulty arose in that he *was* her husband. She could not dishonor him by scornfully refusing his request, nor could she bring shame upon their marriage by rowing with him in public. Nonetheless, she could not grant his request. Taking a step back from him and looking down, she stammered, "Please forgive me, Isak, but I desperately need Hassan and Kamau with me at Kijabe."

"You can watch over yourself," Isak argued softly, but firmly.

"Yes, but I can't cook in a bush kitchen," she protested. She was feeling light-headed, as if blood were leaking from her body. "And Hassan deals with every practical task at Kijabe. I'd be useless without him," she admitted.

"Sending them back to Kijabe by train is too expensive," Isak insisted. "I'll return them on foot from Lord Delamere's camp."

Tanya looked away, trying to control the anguish that was overtaking her face. Her eyes found Erik and Malena kissing between the maize stalks. Tanya looked down and blushed. She and Isak had known such affection for one another: on their safari together in March, they'd been so enamored of one another's touch that dropping hands to shoot their guns had been a burden.

Tanya clenched her jaw with the realization that such "I remember when" reminiscence might be acceptable ten years into their marriage, but seemed pathetic within the first year. The rapid accretion of lies and lacunae that now separated them, in September – only six months later – impressed Tanya. She had obviously underestimated the difficulty of maintaining honest, dignified relations with one's husband.

Nonetheless, such obstacles must be surmounted, as others before her had done. Casting her mind over other noble examples, she settled on King Francis I and Claude, Duchess of Brittany. He was a notorious philanderer, and she . . . predeceased him. Tanya frowned: surely, alternatives to an early death existed for managing marital infidelity; Tanya would have to discover them.

But her immediate concern was that Isak had caught her in a lie, and she was embarrassed. She was also at a loss for strategies to evade the consequences of her dishonesty. Either she would have to break her word and lose Hassan and Kamau, or she would have to confess to deceiving her husband and ransom them.

The blush intensified around Tanya's ears, and she brushed away a tear. Drained of strength, her will eroded and her emotions overtaxed, Tanya could no longer summon the dry-eyed demeanor most befitting a Baroness. She cried. Her sobs were muted at first, but as tears flowed, her sorrow intensified, and she threw her arms around Isak's neck. "Please don't take Hassan and Kamau from me," she begged him.

"Sweet *prinsesstårta*, don't cry," he urged her impatiently, impaired in his ability to quiet her sobs by the two mules whose bridles he was holding in each hand.

"I can't," she sniffled on his shoulder, "I can't manage without you *and* them. Leave them with me, please, I beg you," she moaned.

"They'll come back to you, I promise," Isak assured her gruffly. "But spending train fare on them —"

"— Isak, I just remembered," Tanya coughed. She stepped back from him and wiped her eyes with both hands. "I just remembered I do have a little money extra." She rummaged in her inner shirt pocket. "Please," she said, holding it out to him; and then realizing that he lacked a spare hand with which to accept it, she slipped the money into his trousers pocket. Then she laid both hands on his chest and kissed his cheek. "Don't deny me train fare for Kamau and Hassan," she whispered. "War time luxury is limited enough. Don't ask a Baroness to go without her servants," she pouted.

Isak smiled indulgently. "I didn't know I'd married such a frivolous girl."

Tanya shrugged, as if to say, "I can't help the way I was born."

A light kiss on the lips sealed their parting.

* * *

Kamau loved riding the train. Excitement seized him every time he entered the heavy teakwood cars; he felt important as he ducked to walk between them. The hard-back seats in the non-sleeper cars seemed to Kamau the epitome of beauty. Sliding open the glass window, Kamau laughed when the wind gushed into his face and deposited dust on his teeth. To Kamau's ear, the rumble-rock of the train's enormous engine descended directly from the heights of Mount Kenya, where the Kikuyu god kept his cloud drum that thundered around the mountain's peaks. But, above all else, Kamau appreciated the way the train humbled Hassan, making him stoop to avoid smacking his head.

Over the thirteen years of the railroad's operation, Kamau's understanding of the train had evolved. Initially, like all the Kikuyu in his village, he'd thought the train was a gargantuan snake. Over time, however, Kamau had witnessed the *mzungus* feeding their crops into the snake. Knowing that *mzungus* do not, as a general rule, worship or make crop offerings to snakes, Kamau deemed that the "snake" was actually a pack animal for agricultural goods. Subsequently, Isak had allowed Kamau to accompany him to Mombasa to meet Memsabu's ocean liner, and Kamau had been thrilled to learn that they would be riding the "train" there – and back! On this trip, Kamau finally learned the true nature of the train: neither a snake, nor a pack animal, it was the world's most sensational mode of transport.

Precisely because Kamau thrilled to every train ride, he linked arms with Hassan and drew him to a seat well away from Tanya, who was dampening Kamau's jolly mood with her tears. "*Effendi*," Kamau said, as they sat, "I have now concluded that Memsabu is a woman."

At the opposite end of the train car, Tanya was emoting unabashedly. She'd been crying since the train's wheels first began to turn. On becoming aware of Tanya's tearful collapse, Malena had embraced her friend and cushioned Tanya's head on her bosom. For the remainder of the trip, Malena cradled Tanya, patted her every so often and occasionally murmured, "The good Lord provides solace for all miseries."

In her frenzy, Tanya didn't parse or analyze the many complaints whose jagged edges were needling the tears from her ducts. Instead, Tanya squeezed closed her eyes and imagined that Malena was her mother, and that she herself was again a girl in Denmark, sobbing over a juvenile agony that time and her mother's comfort would assuage. Nearing Nairobi, however, Tanya sat up purposefully. "Malena," she said in a low, intense tone, "you are seeing the doctor immediately upon our arrival, yes?"

"He won't see patients now, dearest. It's too late. We'll need to pass the night in Nairobi."

"We'll stay at the Stanley then?" Tanya asked, naming their regular hotel for overnights in Nairobi.

"I think that's best."

"Grant me peace of mind, and let Hassan and Kamau escort you to the Stanley."

"But where will you be, Tanya?"

"I have to see my solicitor. He is holding some valuables for me. Isak," she sighed. "Gambling." Her eyes welled with fresh tears.

"Oh precious," Malena cooed, wiping her friend's tears with a handkerchief she produced from her pocket. "But will the solicitor see you at this hour?"

"He's expecting me," Tanya hiccupped. "I sent word from the Kajiado station."

"Oh Tanya, I do fear for you in the Nairobi night. You must take Hassan at least to the solicitor's office."

Tanya shook her head and clenched her jaw stubbornly. "The office is just near the train station. And I cannot shame Isak in front of his manservant."

Malena nodded slowly, as she mentally pieced together the cause of her friend's sorrow. Isak – weak man – was bleeding Tanya of financial resources to pay for his drink and games in the bush. Malena knew some extent of her friend's financial limits; if the von Brantberg's coffee harvest failed, they would be bankrupt. No wonder the poor darling had cried all the way from Kajiado. "The good Lord will protect you," Malena pronounced as the train braked to a stop in Nairobi.

"Thank you, Malena," Tanya gushed, kissing her friend on both cheeks. "I will meet you at the Stanley."

Then Tanya detrained and hurried, alone, to deliver Lord Delamere's map to British Army headquarters.

THIRTEEN

Playing Beethoven's *Kriegslied der Österreicher* on the piano, Governor Heinrich Schnee reflected that wars were good source material for poems, plays and music. Without wars, he mused – as without God – art would be deprived of the inspiration for so many of its masterpieces. Remove war and God (which so often equated with war) from the realm of human experience, and artists would be reduced to creating works about love. So, in this respect, war was positive.

But from no other angle could Governor Schnee view *this* war as contributing to the glory of humankind. He wasn't unpatriotic; on the contrary, he was Germany's staunchest advocate of – and proudest participant in – the colonial development ongoing in German East Africa. Agriculture for export, roads, lorries, cars, rail, hospitals, mosquito bed nets, schools, churches, industrial production, ports – all had been non-existent before Germany took a kindly interest in its East African colony. The war was laying waste to Germany's investment and halting (if not regressing) all this commendable development.

Moodily practicing a descending scale sequence in the right hand part, Governor Schnee saw no justification for this martial interruption in Germany's excellent colonial efforts. As he read the 1885 Treaty of Berlin, African colonies were excluded from European wars, absent an election to the contrary. And neither Germany, nor England, had elected to toss their East African colonies into the trenches.

Von Lettow-Vorbeck had made the election.

Governor Schnee brought his hands down petulantly on the piano in a chord resonant with wrong notes. Although he, Governor Schnee, was the supreme military commander in the colony, von Lettow-Vorbeck had proved impossible to restrain. Kaiser Wilhelm II himself, in his communiqué to the colony announcing the war, had indicated that it did not extend to East Africa; but von Lettow-Vorbeck had disagreed. "What have we to lose?" von Lettow-Vorbeck had argued. "If we keep Britain busy here, we stop her from sending her fighters in East Africa to more important theatres."

Governor Schnee had reminded von Lettow-Vorbeck that German East Africa was neutral in the war, and that wars aren't fought simply because Lieutenant-Colonels see nothing to lose in them. But "collaborative" was not an adjective that applied to von Lettow-Vorbeck, and he'd mobilized his troops without consulting the Governor. When Governor Schnee had responded by surrendering Dar-es-Salaam and entering into a truce with the British navy without first notifying von Lettow-Vorbeck, the Lieutenant-Colonel had countered by invading British East Africa and occupying Taveta. Rabid monkeys on a banana plantation would have been easier to control than von Lettow-Vorbeck.

But now – and here the Governor played the song's marching chords with jaunty fingers – the Lieutenant-Colonel had learned what could be lost: eight German officers, eighty *askaris*, eighty-five horses and mules, and forty chickens.

This monument of wasted human and animal resources commemorated von Lettow-Vorbeck's folly at Mount Longido. Two days previously, on 15 September, the British had attacked the German fort on Longido with startling success. The British had somehow managed to descend from the vicinity of the Besil River and traverse the terrain around Longido without being detected by the German look-outs on the mountain. Then a Masai *moran* had ascended Mount Longido, followed at a distance by a detachment of the East African Mounted Rifles. Whenever the Masai had encountered German guards, he'd said he was a scout in the employ of the Germans. The Masai had either been a double-agent, or the German guards had been too ignorant of their own scouts to recognize the lie. The German guards had allowed the Masai to pass, after which the soldiers of the East African Mounted Rifles had seized the German guards. This ruse had continued up the mountain, until the British had captured, injured, killed or (in the case of the horses, mules and chickens) stolen every man and beast in the German fort.

"Lieutenant-Colonel von Lettow-Vorbeck!" Governor Schnee's butler announced at a volume that, if it had been sustained, would have caused the piano strings to spring from their moorings.

Governor Schnee crashed into the opening regimental chords of *Kriegslied der Österreicher* as von Lettow-Vorbeck entered. At first, von Lettow-Vorbeck seemed disoriented in the Governor's music room, as it contained no trenches, no rifles, no heliograph or telegraph machines, nor any subordinate soldiers. In lieu of these usual trappings of the Lieutenant-Colonel's surroundings, the music room featured a handwoven silk rug of Oriental design, a zebra-skin upholstered divan, an oil portrait of Kaiser Wilhelm II, a bust of Beethoven, three Renaissance lutes, a grand piano and von Lettow-Vorbeck's civilian superior. "March to the music, Lieutenant-Colonel! *Eins-zwei-drei-vier!*" Governor Schnee shouted as he continued playing.

Despite the insult in the Governor's greeting, the militarism of being ordered to march relaxed Lieutenant-Colonel von Lettow-Vorbeck. Now, at least, he recognized something in his surroundings. He strode to the piano.

"With the rhythm!" Governor Schnee barked, and then broke off playing, disappointed. "I pity the woman who draws you for a dance partner."

Noting the pique in Governor Schnee's manner, von Lettow-Vorbeck smoothed his mustache defensively. The Lieutenant-Colonel was accustomed to Governor Schnee's abrasiveness, but he magnanimously attributed it to the Governor's frustration at constantly being outmaneuvered on questions of military deployment. Von Lettow-Vorbeck did not approve of cruelty to the defeated enemy, so he accepted the Governor's critique graciously: "I'll convey your sympathies to my wife."

"Lieutenant-Colonel," Governor Schnee said, returning to his piano playing, "you probably think you know why I have called you here."

"Yes, Governor."

"You don't. I am a man of some musical ambition, though – sadly, as you can hear – less talent. I have been practicing this marvelous piece of Beethoven's, *Kriegslied der Österreicher* – do you know it?"

"*War Song of the Austrians*, yes." Though I wouldn't, von Lettow-Vorbeck thought, characterize it as "marvelous."

"Superb. I approve of well-rounded men. Poet-warriors, musician-statesmen – how's your baritone?"

"I'm a tenor."

"Ah well, we'll have to make do. It's too much to hope that you have the song memorized, I suppose?"

Von Lettow-Vorbeck raised his eyebrows. He did not appreciate the direction in which the Governor was taking the conversation.

"The words are there," said the Governor, nodding in the direction of sheet music that lay open on top of the piano.

"Thank you," von Lettow-Vorbeck said stiffly, adding in a low tone, "So what?"

"So sing!" Governor Schnee ordered.

"I am not a singer-soldier."

"Ach!" Governor Schnee pounded a wrong note several times and then tore his hands from the keyboard. "My dear Lieutenant-Colonel, I have summoned you here today to sing."

"Why?" Von Lettow-Vorbeck touched his mustache again. He was beginning to rethink his policy of mild-mannered acceptance of the Governor's antics.

"Haven't you been listening? I am a man of musical ambition, and *Kriegslied der Österreicher* requires a singer. I cannot realize my ambition for this song alone. Therefore, I am grateful to you for accommodating my request that you pick up that sheet music and sing. Now."

Von Lettow-Vorbeck briefly considered protesting, but after the passage of no more than five seconds, he snatched the lyrics from the piano. He was going to conduct his war exactly as he pleased and, in exchange, he was going to allow Governor Schnee to dictate proceedings in his music room. Confident that the Governor's power didn't extend much beyond the music room, von Lettow-Vorbeck counseled himself to indulge this little man. And so von Lettow-Vorbeck sang:

> *Ein großes deutsches Volk sind wir,*
> *Sind mächtig und gerecht.*
> *Ihr Franken das bezweifelt ihr?*
> *Ihr Franken kennt uns schlecht!*
> *Denn unser Fürst ist gut,*
> *Erhaben unser Muth,*
> *Süß uns'rer Trauben Blut,*
> *Und uns're Weiber schön;*
> *Wie kann's uns beßer geh'n?*
> *Wie kann's uns beßer geh'n?*

"Thank you, Lieutenant-Colonel, thank you!" Governor Schnee shouted, taking his hands from the piano keys and clapping loudly, slowly and condescendingly.

Von Lettow-Vorbeck was relieved to end the song after the first verse; too relieved to question the Governor's bizarre and abrupt termination of his stated ambition.

"*Wie kann's uns beßer geh'n?*" Governor Schnee repeated, articulating each word with exaggerated care, as if he were teaching the phrase to an idiot. "'How can we do our best?' Is that not the question?"

"That is the song lyric," von Lettow-Vorbeck agreed.

"No!" Governor Schnee bellowed, bringing his hands clanging discordantly onto the piano. "That is the question for every German in this colony! How can we do our best? Tell me, Lieutenant-Colonel, how could we have done our best on Mount Longido?"

Von Lettow-Vorbeck betrayed no consternation or nervousness. But he reminded himself that scenes like the one unfolding were a principle reason that he preferred life in the bush, however inconvenient. Emerging from the bush always necessitated some variety of unpleasant submission to supposed authority – now being a case in point – before he could return (as he was always permitted to do) to savaging the enemy on his own terms. Behaving respectfully in response to Governor Schnee's interrogation was merely the price of the freedom he enjoyed elsewhere in his job. "We have the best *askaris* of any colonial force in Africa —"

"— What we have done well is a matter we shall reserve for another discussion! How could we have done our best? Answer the question!" Governor Schnee shrieked.

"We could have done our best," von Lettow-Vorbeck answered dutifully, "if we had more carriers. Our soldiers are vulnerable from insufficient supplies."

"Porters provision the front lines, Lieutenant-Colonel. Longido was a fort! A fort, I add, that the British traveled over distance to capture without the assistance of porters! My good Lieutenant-Colonel, your answer is not relevant. Focus please! Answer my question: how could we have done our best on Longido?"

"We could have done our best," von Lettow-Vorbeck persevered, "if we had modern artillery. The 1871 rifles our men carry are killing them. Black smoke from the rifle reveals their position with every shot."

"Lieutenant-Colonel, you try my patience. I ask you how could we have done our best, and you respond by imagining a world different from the one we occupy. If we'd had the budget for new rifles, they'd have been purchased before the war. Now, while our budgetary constraints remain, our needs are overtaken by those in the European theatre. Even if we could pay for modern artillery, the Fatherland cannot divert guns from France. No, you are evading, and I insist that you answer the question: how could we have done our best?"

Von Lettow-Vorbeck sighed inwardly and, outwardly respectful, tried yet again: "We could have done our best if we'd avoided recruiting any Masai scouts and shot the ones we already had."

"Indeed?" Governor Schnee's eyes widened. "And how do you propose to find your way without Masai guides?"

"We were betrayed by our scout, Lekishon. He told us he was going to his native village to bring more scouts, and he came back working for the British."

"You have managed your Masai scouts poorly," Governor Schnee declared.

"On the contrary, the Masai are born liars and inherently untrustworthy. They are the original Jews."

"What?"

"That's correct. Moritz Merker is the world's expert on the tribe. In his book, *Die Masai*, he proves that the Masai and the biblical Israelites were once a single people. I shall loan you my copy. It is too informative to remain unread."

Governor Schnee glowered. "If the original Jews had been Masai, they wouldn't have wandered in the Sinai for forty years," he growled. "Without Masai, you are lost."

"Unless you have an accurate map."

"Accurate maps of East Africa don't exist!" Governor Schnee bellowed.

"I have reason to believe that one exists."

"Oh? Why?" Governor Schnee glibly resumed playing the piano. Von Lettow-Vorbeck was just making excuses now, and Governor Schnee enjoyed the spectacle of the man debasing himself with lies.

"Because our intelligence reports that the British used one in the Longido ambush. That was their advantage, allowing them to advance undetected."

"They had a Masai guide!" Governor Schnee hollered gleefully. "He showed them the paths known only to the native, allowing them to slip around unseen to the detriment of your mis-managed men!"

"The Masai," von Lettow-Vorbeck began after a surreptitious breath, "never take soldiers where they want to go without a detour first to sell them to the enemy. Lekishon was not a guide; he was led. By a soldier with a map."

Governor Schnee turned from the piano in mid-phrase, raising his hands to conduct the air. "Excuses, excuses!" he mocked von Lettow-

Vorbeck. "Here is how we could have done our best: we could have been less aggressive. Diplomacy, Lieutenant-Colonel, is an under-rated weapon in your artillery."

Von Lettow-Vorbeck declined to interject his opinion of Governor Schnee's diplomatic capacities.

"Your army is too small! You cannot beat the British with 230 German officers – excuse me, 222 German officers. The only hope for German East Africa was neutrality, and now that you have condemned that hope to die like your men on Longido, our best hope is diplomacy. You are too aggressive, Lieutenant-Colonel! You provoke attacks that your miniscule force cannot withstand. The war in Europe may last as long as six months, but here in East Africa the war will end with your next defeat. And we will lose German East Africa, this glorious achievement of the Fatherland – we will lose it forever because of your unwise aggressiveness!"

"I believe I can get the map."

"You are not listening!" Governor Schnee played a chord four times – tum-tum, tum-tum. "You will listen to *this*, though: one more failure like Longido, and I'll have you deported to the European theatre of war."

Von Lettow-Vorbeck looked down. He was not frightened, but embarrassed. The British navy controlled the Indian Ocean. German vessels – with the exception of the occasional, lucky blockade runner – were incapable of reaching or departing from German East Africa. Governor Schnee could no more send von Lettow-Vorbeck to Europe than he could become a Masai.

"You are thinking that I can't do it," Governor Schnee laughed, returning cavalierly to his piano. "You are wrong. I will ask the British for a limited truce, for the sole purpose of allowing the ship on which you are a passenger to sail. You cannot deny that the British will be overjoyed to grant my requested truce. If they sink your ship at sea, such are the hazards of war. And, if they don't, more hazards await you in the European trenches."

Von Lettow-Vorbeck looked up. "You hate me that much?" he asked, momentarily forgetting himself.

"No." Governor Schnee ceased tinkling on the piano keys and faced von Lettow-Vorbeck squarely. "I don't hate you at all. I hate seeing the destruction of everything for which I have worked – and paid! I hate seeing Germany's investment squandered. I hate seeing the lives of the natives return to squalor. I hate waste. You, Lieutenant-Colonel, waste people. That is your professional calling. You excel at it. And while I admire talent in any form, I do not admire failure. If you will not heed the restraints of your Kaiser, then I cannot make you obey the orders of your Governor. But I can punish you for your failures. And I will do so if you fail again."

"It will be the downfall of your career," von Lettow-Vorbeck pronounced coldly.

"This war is the downfall of my career, Lieutenant-Colonel, and you are foolish to cross a man with nothing to lose." Returning to the piano, Governor Schnee re-commenced *Kriegslied der Österreicher*. "Dismissed!" he shouted. "March to the music! March! A sprightly, high-stepping march!"

Von Lettow-Vorbeck pivoted neatly and exited with a determined stride that bore no resemblance to a sprightly, high-stepping march.

FOURTEEN

"Memsahib, Tsavo is needing you," announced Gokal, looking up from the telegraph machine.

After glancing over her shoulder to confirm that they were alone, Tanya snatched the telegram from Gokal's hands: "REPORT TSAVO IMMEDIATELY. D." "That's it?" Tanya asked, her eyes beseeching Gokal for more information.

"No more than that, Memsahib," Gokal confirmed.

Tanya pursed her lips and nodded resignedly. Lord Delamere was summoning her to Tsavo; truly, she needed no additional information: he wanted her to courier another map to Nairobi. "Thank you, Gokal," Tanya smiled, attempting to conceal her nervousness. It was 5:40 p.m.; the next train was in twenty minutes, and Tanya knew she had to be on it. Bolting for the door, Tanya stopped sharply, turning to add, "Gokal, please wire back that I'll be on the 18:00 train." Then she ran from the station house.

Tsavo was roughly twelve hours from Kijabe by train. She would arrive early the next morning, and she assumed that D. would want her to return to Nairobi the same day. Still, she'd wished he'd clarified how many days she'd be traveling.

Flushing with shame, Tanya recalled D. telling her that Isak had been incapacitated with drink until he'd heard that she would be arriving within the day. Perhaps, Tanya wondered fretfully, D. was calling her to Tsavo to dry out Isak. She might have to wait for a day or more until Isak finished the map. Tanya decided to pack a bag with minimal provisions.

"Hassan!" she hailed, unable to locate him after scanning the area around the station house. "Hassan!" But her call remained unanswered.

Tanya was kneeling in her tent, stuffing a sack with dried fruit, biscuits, soap, a hand towel, field glasses, and underclothes, when Hassan coughed beside the wood pile to indicate his presence. "Hassan?" Tanya asked, leaning her head out of the tent. "Gokal may need you to assist in my absence. Please do so graciously. Don't extort anything in exchange for your help."

"Your absence, Memsahib?" Hassan raised his eyebrows quizzically.

"I'm taking the next train," Tanya said, emerging from the tent. "Isak," she shook her head – hoping the gesture expressed dismay, when in truth it was masking her face, which she feared would betray that she was groping for an excuse on short notice – "Isak needs me." She sighed heavily. "Dysentery," she improvised, "like Kamau. I think the water they drank on the safari from Besil River to Magadi was bad. One of the water calabashes must have been contaminated."

Kamau had indeed been sick, but he was almost recovered. In Hassan's experience Bwana Isak's constitution was immeasurably stronger than Kamau's. And Kamau was less than half Bwana Isak's weight. Hassan recalled a Somali adage, be a mountain or lean on one. Bwana Isak had always been a mountain. If Kamau was now healing while Bwana Isak was needing support, then only one mountain could serve: "Bwana Isak needs Allah's blessing."

"Thank you, Hassan. Bwana Isak," Tanya closed her eyes and hoped for the best, "wants to see me. In case." Tanya didn't believe that lying about a beloved's health could make manifest the lie, but the mere thought of Isak being so sick that he feared death panicked her.

Hassan bowed his head. He'd developed a strong affection for Bwana Isak. The Baron was a man in whose company Hassan could pass easy, amusing hours. Among white men, Bwana Isak was the rare specimen who had earned Hassan's respect, even if Hassan knew that the Baron was too slack to greet death with contempt. Bwana Isak was more likely to invite the Angel of Death for a game of dice. If Allah was claiming Bwana Isak's soul now, Hassan would grieve him. Hassan looked up, his face grave: "Memsahib, all is in the hands of Allah."

"May He be merciful," Tanya said, grabbing her sack of provisions. "And please remember: it is the will of Allah that you assist Gokal if he needs it."

With this statement, Hassan's face registered surprise. He'd suddenly assembled the disparate pieces of their conversation and realized that Tanya meant to travel to Tsavo without him. "Memsahib," he said, delaying her as she was turning to the station house, "if I remain here, who goes with you to Tsavo?"

"I travel alone," she stated grimly.

"Memsahib, you must not," he pronounced. "A companion is necessary for safety. I go beside you."

Hassan's resolute expression revealed authentic concern that stirred Tanya. All the same, Hassan was not currently on Tanya's list of trustworthy characters. Breakfasting at the Stanley with Malena on the day after they'd returned from Kajiado, Tanya had overheard a conversation at the next table – a discussion plainly intended for her ears:

"I don't suppose Belfield knows that she has a signed picture of the high commander of the German military," a nasally voice brayed. "Belfield" was the Governor of British East Africa.

"Such matters are none of Henry Belfield's concern," a robust alto voice replied. "They're Stewart's business, and Stewart would hang her." Almost two weeks earlier, Brigadier-General Stewart had taken charge of the British Army's operations in the East African theatre.

Fearing that any acknowledgement of the comments would be construed as an admission of their accuracy, Tanya ignored the women at the next table. Doing so required strenuous effort; Tanya could feel the women's accusatory stares boring like ticks into the flesh of her face. She was blushing. But she refused to capitulate to the pressure being applied by the nasal-voiced Mrs. Carberry and the alto, Miss Beckett. Tanya had not weathered three confrontations with German soldiers only to allow herself to be defeated by Nairobi busybodies.

Returning to Kijabe from the Stanley Hotel, Tanya had been as anxious as a *boma*-bound ox watching a lioness circle in search of suitable entry points. After a week had elapsed without military police storming Kijabe and arresting her, however, Tanya's jitters had abated somewhat. Rumors in war time were like maggots on a three-day carcass; an experienced soldier like Brigadier-General Stewart wouldn't act on a mere rumor without evidence, she comforted herself.

Nonetheless, Tanya had lost confidence in Hassan. He was the sole other person who knew of von Lettow-Vorbeck's photograph. Intentionally or inadvertently, he must have been the source of the rumor.

When she'd confronted him with this complaint, he'd denied the charge. Disgusted by his refusal to confess, Tanya had banished Hassan to the coffee plantation, whereupon he'd advocated his innocence so zealously that Tanya had concluded that the information must have escaped carelessly, rather than maliciously. Hassan stayed in Kijabe. Tanya knew she would eventually forgive him; but she couldn't trust him to accompany her on this map courier mission. "Hassan," she said gently, "I rely on you to be me, when I can't be here. Kijabe needs your intelligence and your practical skills."

Hassan scrutinized Tanya's face as she spoke and used the intelligence to which she'd referred to deduce that she didn't want him in Tsavo for some reason that she was unwilling to confide. Perhaps this "illness" of Bwana Isak's was embarrassing. Hassan recalled Tanya rushing him out of the tent, the night Bwana Isak had been passed out at Lord Delamere's camp; Hassan knew Tanya didn't like the servants to see the Baron in a compromised condition. And Hassan was aware that strong drink was not the only vice that could compromise the Baron. Being noble himself, Hassan was sympathetic to Tanya's insistence on preserving the appearance of Bwana Isak's honor. Still, Hassan didn't think Tanya wise to permit pride to preempt safety: "Go then with Memsahib Malena."

Tanya negated his suggestion with a shake of her head. "Have you forgotten? Bwana Erik arrived on two-day furlough yesterday. Extracting Queen Victoria's bloodline from the royal houses of Europe would be easier than prying Malena out of Erik's arms right now."

"Kamau," Hassan proposed, reasoning that Tanya might object to the Baron's humiliation before another noble, like himself, but that no one could feel embarrassed in front of a member of a slave race, like Kamau.

"He's still too frail. He can barely stand!"

"Gokal," Hassan tried. "He travels with you only. He waits outside the tent when you see Bwana Isak."

"Who will run the telegraph machine? You don't know Morse code."

Her last sentence was inaudible beneath the blare of the incoming locomotive's horn. Hassan and Tanya both bowed their heads and shaded their eyes from the airborne dirt loosed by the train. After a moment, Tanya lowered her hand and stared determinedly at Hassan.

He met her gaze with equal stubbornness. "Dionysus."

Tanya relented with a small smile. "You will be satisfied if I take Dionysus?"

"Dionysus," Hassan nodded, "and this." From beneath his tunic he removed something small, hard and sinister. He held it out to her. "For carrying in your sack."

"Hassan," Tanya balked. Then she whispered, "It's illegal for you to have firearms. Where did you get this pistol?"

"Memsahib, I got it."

Frowning to hide her admiration of his resourcefulness, Tanya accepted the gun with a nod of thanks and examined it. The revolver was an 11.6mm caliber Webley Mk IV – a common pistol in the British Army; Hassan could've gotten it anywhere. She stashed it in her sack. Then she hurried towards the idling train.

Before boarding, however, Tanya stopped. The rumble of the British Army's lorry rolling away caught her attention. Tanya turned in the direction of the sound, and she glimpsed a Somali at the wheel.

Pivoting to face Hassan, Tanya widened her eyes and frowned in exasperation.

"The camel who does not drink the sweet water at the oasis is not worth keeping, Memsahib."

Shaking her head and sputtering with frustration, Tanya boarded the train.

* * *

"Baroness, Lord Delamere sent me to take you to Fort Maktau." The soldier was lean, with a horsey face and a thatch of unwashed red hair. He'd pushed his goggles onto his forehead, and he wore leather gaiters over his khaki cotton trousers. "Lieutenant Dudgeon, East African Mechanical Transport Corps," he said, starting to hold out his hand and then, changing his mind, pointing at his chest. Pausing, he shifted awkwardly, and bowed.

Amused and taken aback by the Lieutenant's ungainly formality, Tanya tried to set him at ease with light humor: "Thank you, Lieutenant Dudgeon, but you should be called Lieutenant Psychic."

The joke failed. "Why?" he asked, one eye on Tanya, the other on Dionysus.

"Because you picked me out of a crowd," Tanya said with effortful brightness. Although she'd taken a sleeper car on the train, she'd slept for only limited stretches between Dionysus' whiney, scratchy attempts to exit the car and heed nature's call. Given her less-than-rested state, she wondered if she was overlooking some obvious explanation for Lieutenant Dudgeon's crack skill at identifying her. "Or did Lord Delamere describe me to you?"

"See any other ladies here?" Lieutenant Dudgeon asked.

A survey of the train platform proved the astuteness of Lieutenant Dudgeon's point. Soldiers, train engineers, construction laborers, colonial administrators and mysterious suited men abounded, but amidst this crowd only one woman was apparent.

"Nobody told me you were bringing a dog." Lieutenant Dudgeon spoke as if the fact pained him. "You'll have to hold him in the sidecar."

"Sidecar?"

Lieutenant Dudgeon drove a "Trusty Triumph" motorcycle with a four-stroke engine. Affixed to the handlebars was a squeeze horn. The side-car appeared to have been fashioned from a giant wicker basket, and the tires looked too insubstantial for the rough African bush. Tanya was skeptical of the vehicle; the only people she knew who traveled in baskets were babies, and the tires on their carriages were (in her opinion) more durable than the ones with which this motorcycle had been outfitted.

Dionysus didn't have any such qualms. Sniffing eagerly around the wheels, he detected some pleasing odor and bounded into the basket for a more extensive investigation.

Lieutenant Dudgeon handed Tanya a pair of goggles.

"You didn't happen to bring a nice mule?" Tanya inquired hopefully.

"Tse-tse fly country," Lieutenant Dudgeon replied brusquely. "Mules here die in two weeks. But the damned flies, ah excuse me," he corrected himself, "the blessed flies have yet to figure how to bite a motorcycle."

"How fast does this contraption go?" she asked warily.

"Don't worry. The rocks stop us from going much over forty miles per hour."

Zooming across the bush, however, Tanya decided that she liked traveling by motorcycle. Lieutenant Dudgeon was clearly familiar with the terrain, and he steered them along dirt paths and through open fields. The ride was considerably less irksome than galloping on mule back, even if the engine noise was grating. The wind, thankfully, blew the motorcycle's foul exhaust behind them. Dionysus sat happily on his hind quarters, his front paws resting on the rim of the basket, tongue lolling and ears flying.

They were heading south from the Tsavo train station, towards the border with German East Africa. The landscape was hilly and thick with elephants. The train station had no sooner receded from view than the motorcycle plunged into a corridor lined on either side by pachyderms. Tanya laughed at the sight of an elephant baby showering itself in dust that it scooped from the ground with its little trunk.

But her voyeuristic enjoyment was short-lived. The roar of the motor-cycle provoked a negative reaction. A gargantuan male with tusks that descended almost to the ground before curving forward to encage the base of his trunk glared at the motorcycle and took several belligerent steps in their direction. Tanya rushed to restrain Dionysus, who was barking and threatening to leap from the sidecar to confront this mammoth. But after pausing to flap his ears angrily, the male followed the lead of the majority: where they had been feeding contentedly, the elephants were now legging it. Tanya was astounded both by the speed with which the pachyderms moved and by the effectiveness of their concealment in the bush. She hadn't imagined that an elephant could hide itself anywhere, much less that multiple herds could camouflage themselves in seconds.

Releasing her hold on Dionysus, Tanya scanned the horizon. The sky was cloudless, and Tanya had a clear view of distances she couldn't have glimpsed on an overcast day. Now she could see a hill directly ahead, behind which the field rolled even farther; and beyond, several distinct ranges of mountains. Ringing the horizon, the mountains glowed a muted blue, as if the azure sky above had seeped in and was assimilating the solid bluffs into its ephemeral miasma.

Then Lieutenant Dudgeon banked the motorcycle, and Tanya squinted sharply as a laser of light pierced her frame of vision. Tanya knew that the British used heliograph machines to send coded signals via sunlight reflected off mirrors, and she would have asked Lieutenant Dudgeon if the light bolt came from a heliograph station, but the sound of the motorcycle's engine made conversation impossible. Then she pondered that, if the gleam had been a heliograph signal, it must have been sent from the world's highest heliograph station: the flash could not have originated higher in the sky if God himself had leaned from the heavens holding a torch. Curious, Tanya glanced again in the direction from which the glint had come, and her jaw dropped.

She quickly closed her mouth, however; the dust, grasshoppers and lion flies rising from the terrain made gaping unsustainable. But her sense of incredulity persisted.

Tanya was gazing on the source of the mysterious flash, and it was no heliograph station: it was snow. Allowing her eye to descend beneath this glacier in the sky, Tanya realized that she was confronting Mount Kilimanjaro: the most massive of dormant volcanoes. From Kilimanjaro's snowy crater, the mountain sloped into a valley of arctic desert that rose again into a second snow-capped peak and then descended in a thicket of rainforest.

Tanya had never before seen Mount Kilimanjaro. Although passengers on the Mombasa-Nairobi train often glimpsed the monarch of mountains as they crossed Tsavo, Tanya had made the journey on a day when Kilimanjaro had been cloaked in clouds. Seeing it now, she was baffled how anything of its magnitude could vanish into the sky, as if its heft were a mirage, and its substance no more concrete than heat.

Despite the noise of the motorcycle engine, Tanya shouted ecstatically, "That's Kilimanjaro!" Lieutenant Dudgeon didn't hear her, and Dionysus seemed immune to her exquisite elation. Alone in her intense joy, Tanya smiled and smiled in wide-eyed humility.

* * *

Lieutenant Dudgeon delivered Tanya to a military encampment at the base of the hill that'd stood directly in front of them as they'd motored through the field. "Maktau," he said, turning off the engine.

In the sound vacuum left in the engine's wake, Tanya realized that her ears were ringing.

"Lord Delamere's tent is there, in the officers' row." Lieutenant Dudgeon gestured to a line of tents at the front of the encampment. The hour being eight in the morning, the tents appeared deserted. "He might be in the command center right now," Lieutenant Dudgeon added.

Tanya stepped out of the sidecar and collared Dionysus before he had a chance to tear away. Holding the hound, she surveyed the Maktau camp. It had been freshly clear-cut. Green wood lay scattered around the perimeter. Rolls of barbed wire were heaped hazardously in the clearing. Across from the tents, men were waist-deep in a trench they were digging; a sergeant stood yelling orders at the men wielding shovels. The camp appeared to be in a state of mid-construction.

Behind the tents, a slab of corrugated iron balanced on four poles and served as a makeshift hangar for an aeroplane. Tanya started; she'd heard of aeroplanes, but she'd never before been within walking distance of one. She wanted to examine the machine closely, but recollection of her mission stayed her.

"Where is the command center?" Tanya asked.

THE CELEBRATION HUSBAND

"Up the hill," Lieutenant Dudgeon indicated, pointing.

Following his hand, Tanya saw men traversing footpaths along the hill. "And where – do you know Baron von Brantberg?"

A sly expression – a variety of mocking sneer – stole across Lieutenant Dudgeon's face so quickly that Tanya wondered if she'd presumed it. Then Lieutenant Dudgeon said cordially, "Course I know him. Everyone knows him. Jolliest fellow I ever met."

"A shared sentiment," Tanya replied. "Do you know where he is?"

"Sorry, Baroness," Lieutenant Dudgeon shook his head. "But if you look for Lord Delamere, you'll find your husband."

Tanya smiled her acceptance of this plan. Then, thanking Lieutenant Dudgeon for the ride, and snapping for Dionysus to follow, she shouldered her sack and began trudging up the hill.

She hadn't trekked long before Lord Delamere hailed her. He was threading his way downward. "Excellent timing! I was expecting you right about now," he called, clambering at a pace that Tanya feared would finish him. He looked haggard, and Tanya suspected that he was ill. But upon reaching her a severe energy exuded from his bearing: "Good woman arriving early," he said, clapping her on the upper arms, and then charging down the hill with her in tow. "Let's get you back on the 10 a.m. train. You left Lieutenant Dudgeon waiting for you?"

"Oh, I didn't know," Tanya said, feeling rushed and confused. "He didn't say, that is, we didn't discuss —"

"— No doubt he's waiting. He's a responsible fellow. A drink in the officers' tent?"

With the exception of the tough dates and stale biscuits that she'd choked down on the train for supper, Tanya had had no food for almost a day and a half. The thought of alcohol prompted strong condemnation from her stomach. "Lovely offer, D., but I'm not my husband," Tanya demurred.

"My eyes are infinitely grateful for that fact," D. replied. "But war without drinking is like the virgin birth: inconceivable." D. chuckled at his own pun, and then seized with the realization of his audience, muttered an apology: "I'm accustomed to male company."

"As am I by now," Tanya assured him. "Though not my husband's, sadly. Isak knows I'm here? Lieutenant Dudgeon said you'd know where I could find him."

They'd reached the bottom of the hill, and D. veered sharply to the officers' tent. It was the largest tent in the camp, made from sheets of canvas thrown over a bamboo frame and staked to the ground. "Baroness," said Lord Delamere, holding open the tent flap for her, "how about that drink?"

Ordering Dionysus to wait outside, Tanya was about to decline a second time, but the scene in the officers' tent persuaded her otherwise. A paraffin lamp cast an ashen glare from its perch on a rudimentary bar that tilted on one side of the tent. The bar had been cobbled together from wooden crates that, from their labels, had borne ammunition. Empty brown beer bottles stood on the bar, along with several open, half-empty bottles of Rose's lime juice. Different sized crates served as tables and chairs spread around the bar. A pack of cards had been strewn across one of the crates, aces and spades spilling onto the floor. Behind this pub arrangement, at the far end of the tent, was a grand piano. And seated at the piano, playing Schubert's Sonata No. 16 in A minor, was Hilary Gordon.

"A double, please," Tanya told D.

"Baroness!" Hilary yelped, jumping to his feet, wild-eyed.

Tanya retorted with a stony-faced stare. True, she had wanted to see him again. Yes, she had wanted to tell him that she would consider forgiving him. But not *now*. Timing, of course, was critical for the success of such a reunion, and no time seemed more ideal to Tanya than after the war's end.

"What are you shouting about Gordon?" Lord Delamere demanded from behind the bar, where he was pouring stiff portions of rum that the British Army had confiscated from merchant ships docking in Mombasa.

Lord Delamere's presence disciplined Hilary's emotions. Striding purposefully to Tanya, he said, "When you are at liberty, allow me to take you up in my aeroplane." He spoke casually, as if flying was a hobby for them both, as if his proposal were no more extraordinary than showing a newly-acquired steed to a hunting companion.

"Your aeroplane?" Tanya's surprise shattered her flinty façade, and the question ripped from her lips.

"Yes, she's gorgeous!" Despite his shock at seeing Tanya in the Maktau officers' tent, Hilary smiled exuberantly, so great was his enthusiasm for his toy. "She's a Bleriot XI, with tandem seating. I'd ordered her in England before the war, and thankfully the ship was already at sea when Duke Ferdinand was assassinated. My Bleriot arrived at Mombasa last week, and I flew her down here two days ago."

"You're a pilot?" Tanya asked, still reeling.

"I'm going to make him fly if he doesn't pilot himself out of here," Lord Delamere growled, standing suddenly at Tanya's side and holding out a tin cup. "You've been swishing around that piano all week while your men are slouching into uselessness and criminality. I saw them on parade yesterday. They look like hell. Have you forgotten why you're here?"

Hilary accepted this vicious critique stoically. Except for swallowing, he betrayed no physical reaction to Lord Delamere's assault. "My mission is always foremost," he said, "and I believe we have served you to great effect. If I have given offense, I apologize." Then he turned to Tanya: "Baroness," he bowed. "Lord Delamere," he nodded. Then he exited with a proud, straight-backed gait.

Lord Delamere's rude dismal of Hilary jarred Tanya, but she had no desire to query D. on the issue. The sight of Hilary had already subjected Tanya to more emotional upheaval than she could easily endure; and she had more to bear still.

Silently watching Hilary go, Tanya's eyes widened in sympathy, and she tried to prevent her lips from trembling. She dropped her sack and sipped the rum Lord Delamere handed her. Perhaps, she hoped, the drink would dissipate Hilary from her thoughts. But, the liquor on her tongue, Tanya blurted a question unwise in its persistent relation to Hilary: "Did the Carrier Corps haul that piano all the way from Besil River?"

"No," Lord Delamere shook his head, lifted a ladle and imbibed a generous mouthful.

Turning to him, Tanya saw that D. had placed a bucket of rum on a nearby crate.

The ladle still at his mouth, Lord Delamere glanced up and caught Tanya's judgmental gaze. He lowered the ladle. "There was only one cup," he apologized, "and I don't like to drink from the bucket around ladies." He raised the ladle to his mouth again.

"How did the piano get here?" Her voice was neutral, but she felt completely disarranged. She drank more rum. It was repellently sweet, but extremely strong, and the first sip had numbed her taste buds.

"Carrier Corps took it to Kajiado, transported it via rail to Tsavo, and then carried it from Tsavo to here."

"Does the piano matter so much?" Tanya asked acerbically.

"If you want to hide documents, it comes in useful," Lord Delamere chuckled.

Tanya glanced at him to ascertain if he was kidding.

He raised his eyebrows in the direction of the piano. "Lift up the top," he said, and then clarified, "Not over the strings, over the hammers."

Tanya placed her cup of rum on a nearby crate and walked deliberately over to the piano. She ran her pointer and middle finger over the top. The lacquer caused her fingers to drag slightly on the cool surface. She eyed the keyboard longingly. Hilary's distraught fingers had confided their intimacies to these ivories. Tanya stroked the keys lightly, but if she'd been expecting the action to yield some communion with Hilary, she was disappointed. Sighing, she lifted the piano top with both hands.

The back of the tent was poorly lit and, peering into the cavern of the piano, Tanya's eyes had to adjust. Slowly, she discerned the hammers, as soft, round and still as sleeping sheep – and as smelly. Whatever effort had gone into dusting the exterior of the piano, little thought had been given to freeing the piano's interior of its accreted crud. Now it floated up lazily, and Tanya sneezed several times. Recovering, she glanced along the row of hammers until she saw it: a folded document at the end. Nimbly, she retrieved the map with her left hand and lowered the piano lid.

Her fingers tingling, Tanya carefully unfolded the map. Even in the dim light, she could see that, framed, the map could have held its own on the wall of a museum. In great detail, it depicted an area stretching from north of Tsavo to south of Mount Kilimanjaro. Dense forest, open plain, hills and mountains, areas of elevation, the Bura Hills, watering holes, Lakes Jipe and Challa, rivers, villages, motorcycle routes, railway lines, footpaths, forts, heliograph stations, sites of skirmishes with the enemy – all were rendered in a bold, self-assured line. Tanya lingered over the border between British East Africa and German East Africa. Mount Kilimanjaro was just south of the border, just within enemy territory. Moshi, a town on the slopes of the mountain, caught Tanya's eye. The map indicated a German fort there.

"A thing of beauty it is," Lord Delamere pronounced from across the tent, his voice resonant with pride. "Took almost three weeks to make it," he added, shaking his head to convey displeasure with the exorbitant delay.

Refolding the map, Tanya stowed it in her inner shirt pocket and walked back across the tent. Retrieving her cup of rum from the crate, she marshaled her courage and asked, "Was that length of time because – because of Isak?"

Lord Delamere looked away and coughed. Then he made an aggravated face. "Somalis. Berkley Cole is my brother-in-law, so he won't mind me speaking the truth: he'll never be a bigger jackass than on the day he formed Cole's Scouts – except maybe for the day he took that Somali mistress of his. She colors his judgment! Somalis cannot be integrated into a modern army. They cannot be disciplined. You try to punish them for insubordination, and they spit on you. They're crazy.

"Berkley had some harebrained notion that they'd make good scouts, so we brought them out here to do rough reconnaissance. We needed the information to make this map. Not that we told them what we were using the reconnaissance for, of course. You can't trust the Somalis any more than you can trust the Masai, though I wish we had Masai out here. They rendered fine service to us in Longido! Wouldn't be a lie to say that we won that fight because of our Masai scout. Seeing their fine contribution at Longido, I was proud, I admit, proud to have so long been their patron. It's our loss that Tsavo is out of their range, the buggers. Well, we got the information from the Somalis, but it would've been faster if I'd covered every inch of land on that map myself."

Tanya took a relieved sip of rum and, feeling tipsiness encroaching, returned the cup to the crate. "I'm so glad – I'm sorry – that is, not glad about the Somalis. I am gratified that Isak's service has been satisfactory.

May I see him before I go? It wouldn't compromise my mission, would it? I assume you told him . . ." Tanya's voice trailed off.

D.'s head was bent, and he clasped his ladle in both hands like a candle at a vigil. After a moment, he broke his penitent pose and ladled more rum from the bucket.

"Baroness, may I refill?" he asked considerately, holding the ladle in her direction.

Tanya shook her head. "I can't drink any more, I'm sorry. I'm not like Isak. I'm, ah, obviously, I'm small. And I haven't eaten in a long time."

A crestfallen look draped itself over Lord Delamere's face. Darting eyes suggested that he was grappling for a back-up plan. Then he brightened marginally with the suggestion, "The boys in the mess will feed you."

Tanya waved her hands in protest. "I couldn't. The food is for the soldiers. I'll eat in Kijabe. I'm well as I am, truly." Uncomfortable as hunger pangs made her, Tanya was now at her lightest weight since she'd reached maturity, and she was enjoying her meagerness. "Besides, if I am to make the 10 a.m. train, I should go. I'll just take a moment and see Isak."

"Baroness," Lord Delamere began, and then he stopped. He drank most of the ladleful of rum. After wiping his mouth with his forearm, he began again, "Men are hard to love."

"On the contrary, they're easy to love. Hard to live with."

Lord Delamere smiled appreciatively. "You may recall the powerful effect that knowledge of your arrival had on Isak when we were at the Narosera River."

Tanya nodded. "I do."

"I must admit, Baroness," Lord Delamere cleared his throat, "I was unable to resist exerting that power over your husband, repeatedly, in the course of the last three weeks. I am sorry, but there was no other way. The map's creation would have been delayed still longer otherwise."

"I don't understand, D." Tanya swallowed, picked up her sack and took a step backwards involuntarily. She wondered what she was doing; her body seemed ready to bolt without awaiting a command from her mind.

Lord Delamere threw the ladle into the bucket of rum and faced her squarely. His eyes seemed to be sinking into his skull, and his cheeks were hollow. Tanya renewed her assessment that he must be ill. But, again, when he spoke, his voice bore the authority of a vigorous man: "Most mornings for the past two weeks, I sent Lieutenant Dudgeon to the Tsavo train station. I told Isak that Lieutenant Dudgeon had gone to fetch you. I said that you'd wired that you'd received supplies that you were bringing to Maktau. When Lieutenant Dudgeon returned without you, I explained that you'd wired that you'd be coming the next day. The trick was effective. Isak worked every day. But Isak isn't stupid. He knew my game. And, after finishing the map, he thought he was owed a little celebrating. So when I told him last night that you would be arriving this morning —"

"— He didn't believe you." The saliva in Tanya's mouth seemed to have evaporated, and the words she uttered were husks of sound. "Where is he?"

"Let Lieutenant Dudgeon return you to the Tsavo station."

Tanya caught her breath. D.'s resistance provoked stubborn rebellion in her. She straightened her spine, tossed her head, and was about to argue, when some delicacy in D.'s face stopped her. Wilting visibly, she pleaded, "Don't deny me."

"Allow me to protect you," he entreated. "In return for endangering you with that," he gestured to the map in her shirt, "let me shield you now. Tsavo waits."

Tanya wanted to shout, I don't need your protection! But, instead, she maintained her pleading posture and murmured, "Tell me where he is. Please."

Tanya needn't have begged. When Lord Delamere threw back the flap of the officers' tent and pointed, his finger indicated to where Dionysus was seated outside Isak's tent, panting.

Each step drawing her nearer to the tent felt unaccountably significant. If she'd been walking a plank with the Indian Ocean roiling beneath her, or balancing on a high wire over a bed of spikes, she could not have felt that her life was more at stake with each movement. She could hear the crunch of dry earth beneath her tread. Her hands were sweating, and she shifted the hand in which she was gripping her sack. She felt as if 10,000 eyes were trained on her, judging her a stubborn, childish, foolish woman and awaiting her comeuppance.

Looking around, though, she saw that the significance of her walk (if any) was apparent only to herself. Lieutenant Dudgeon was speaking with the sergeant by the trench, and the men tasked with creating that earthwork were digging; Lord Delamere had retreated back into the officers' tent, Hilary was nowhere visible, and the men scurrying up and down the mountain could hardly see her, much less detain themselves with her petty domestic fears.

Circumstances having so conspired, only Tanya and Dionysus witnessed what happened next: the flap of Isak's tent opened, from which emerged a Swahili woman, adjusting the patterned kanga fabric tied around her waist as a skirt.

Dionysus leaped to his feet and growled menacingly at the woman. She was small and plump, with mocha skin and features that reflected Arab ancestors. Her head was covered with a red scarf. Dionysus' growling didn't faze her; she walked away briskly without turning. Finding a footpath in the surrounding woods, she slipped from view.

Tanya covered her mouth. Then she bit her fingers. When she felt pain, she took her hand from her mouth and ran.

FIFTEEN

Tanya staggered like a frantic sleepwalker. She had no awareness of the direction in which she was heading. Her headlong frenzy sent warthog scurrying and caused a flock of ostriches to sashay in a direction opposite to Tanya's own, but Tanya didn't notice. She was vaguely cognizant of Dionysus, behind her at first, then trotting supportively at her heels; and she knew that she was crying.

Eventually, she became entangled in a wait-a-bit tree, and the necessity of disentangling herself prompted a state of relative calm. A small, thorny, tenacious acacia, the wait-a-bit tree, true to its name, snagged her as she passed within its ambit. Now Tanya dropped her sack so that she could slowly and painfully detach the tree's branches from her clothing. Dionysus sat patiently and panted.

Once freed, Tanya saw that she was at a border of forest and wooded grassland. She'd run northeast from Maktau, in the direction of the Tsavo train station, along the edge of the field across which Lieutenant Dudgeon had driven her. Wiping her face with one hand and picking up her sack, she began walking, away from Maktau at a fast pace. She knew she should turn around; she'd miss the 10 a.m. train from Tsavo if she didn't, but she couldn't bear being seen by Isak's colleagues just yet.

She imagined what her mother would advise. Bess Rungsted never walked any way but upright, but Tanya lacked her mother's imperiousness to the actions and slander of others.

So Tanya tried lecturing herself that the cause must take precedence to her personal matters, which were in any event measly. The lives of thousands of men depended on her delivery of the map. How could she jeopardize their safety because of her own hurt feelings?

The lecture didn't work. Stubbornly, morbidly, she clung to her sense of righteousness and entitlement: any wife who wasn't crushed beyond functionality by what Tanya had just experienced couldn't love her husband. Couldn't have any sense of pride or honor, Tanya elaborated internally, couldn't represent anything greater than herself, couldn't inspire the devotion of others.

Every single man in that camp knew the folly in which Isak was engaged, even while his wife was at Maktau! Lord Delamere knew – that's why he'd been trying to bundle her back to the train station. Lieutenant Dudgeon knew – Tanya was convinced now that his mocking sneer had been real. And Hilary – Hilary had called Isak "inconstant" at Besil River. Hilary had long known. The realization withered Tanya, and she dropped to her knees, sobbing, her hands covering her face, her sack thrown to one side.

Dionysus sniffed around her with concern. He licked her fingers and made soft whining sounds.

But in her shame and grief, Tanya was inconsolable. She keened and keeled forward, emitting a high-pitched wail that trailed off into nothing. Then she snapped up and lunged through the grass for the sack. Ripping it open, she tore out of it the pistol that Hassan had given her.

Once the appalling object was in her hand, she froze.

She'd watched Hilary kill two men; could she kill one woman? Hilary had undertaken the task with an odd mix of insouciance and remorse. He'd quoted Byron before blowing a hole in a man's face; then he'd closed another corpse's eyes and speeded both their souls to rest with more poetry. If Hilary's approach was the secret to discharging a soldier's burden without losing his humanity, Tanya didn't think she could do it. If she fired the pistol Hassan had given her, it would be from despair, not insouciance; and if anyone felt remorse thereafter, it couldn't be her.

Her attention to the weapon befouling her hand was broken by Dionysus' barking. She looked up curiously because Dionysus sounded happy.

He was. He was wagging his tail, leaping jauntily around Lieutenant-Colonel Paul Emil von Lettow-Vorbeck, who had just emerged from the forest and was walking towards Tanya. Imposing and dashing as ever, his face was ruddy, and the sun glinted, fire-like, off the buckle on his holster. Tanya saw the Lieutenant-Colonel's bicycle propped against a fever tree; red billed firefinches hopped on an overhanging branch.

Von Lettow-Vorbeck squatted beside where Tanya was kneeling, pistol in hand, in the tall grasses. "My darling Tanya, if you want to emulate Faust, I can offer you a better deal than the devil." He smiled warmly. "May I?" he asked, removing the gun from her clutches.

Tanya quickly smoothed her face with her fingers and tried to eliminate any puffiness under her eyes with quick rubbing motions. "How," she mumbled, and then tossing her hair, looked directly at him, "Paul, how did you know I was here?"

Von Lettow-Vorbeck turned the revolver over in his hands; the gun seemed insignificant between his palms. "We have Maktau under surveillance."

This statement struck Tanya as ominous.

Reading her thoughts, von Lettow-Vorbeck offered a corrective: "Had we not, this war might have passed dully, taking lives and not saving them."

"I wasn't," Tanya denied, pointlessly.

"I mean no disrespect," he added. "As I've said previously, nothing could diminish the esteem in which I hold you, nor the affection I feel for you. I am a creature of loyalty. And darkness is no stranger to me. I can only admire the courage of those who also know its debilitating beauty."

Tanya looked away and wiped her nose. She felt as if she were being pressured in a vice. She was desperate for human connection, and she was grateful to Paul, whose words affirmed and assuaged the profound agitation within her.

Yet she knew that anything other than hostility to Paul in this moment was wrong. Without a doubt, she was betraying the cause by accepting succor from this man. She was also in extreme danger. The only copy of the world's most accurate map of the Tsavo theatre of war was secreted in her inner shirt pocket, while she sat cross-wise from the high commander of the enemy forces, who was holding a pistol.

"I invite you to turn your eyes on a miracle," he said, gesturing to Mount Kilimanjaro, its towering splendor a rebuke to the vulgarity of the Great War. "That mountain wrests me from depths. Even a chance glimpse transports me. The Chagga tribe claims they fought the Masai on its slopes. They named that battleground 'Shira' – meaning 'war.' Conducting operations in such a setting must be devastating. The enormity of battle and of death must vanish in the bosom of that mountain. Such power I struggle to comprehend. I've been a soldier my whole life, and I have known terror and bravery. I have listened to the wails of wounded, and I have been the wounded. I have witnessed looting, rape, blood and human parts severed from the man, things of such awful weight that I believed I could never be free of them. But to war on Mount Kilimanjaro would be to eclipse all that seems so huge. Kilimanjaro overwhelms our petty human profanities into their place, into," he paused, searching for the word, "insignificance."

His words accelerated the searing conflict Tanya was experiencing, and she suppressed an urge to get up and run away. Steeling herself against flight, she stammered miserably, "Forgive me, Paul, but this situation is too complicated. I am in too difficult a position." She shifted in the grass, but she managed not to rise.

"I am sorry," he nodded, leaning forward to kneel. Standing higher than their heads, the grass formed a herbaceous curtain that screened their conference. "I understand. And I am truly sorry," von Lettow-Vorbeck continued, "because I know you are a noblewoman and a woman of honor, high ideals, morals and rectitude. You, too, are a creature of loyalty. You are not made for betrayal." Not for betrayal of any sort, neither personal nor professional, he thought, but allowed his commentary to remain unspoken. "You understand fairness, and you feel unfairness acutely. Even in war, if you'll allow me to confide concerns that bedevil me, even in war unfairness has its limits. In the bush, for instance, we must all – British and German – rely on the same water sources or our men die of thirst. Poisoning this water is unfair. Respecting this limit is part of what makes us gentlemen soldiers. These limits ensure civilized warfare. We Germans never poison watering holes."

"Have the British?" Tanya asked.

"Yes," he said simply. "Among the British forces is a man, Richard Meinertzhagen, who has no scruples. He has poisoned a pond on which our raiding parties rely. Two of my officers have died."

Tanya was scared to speak. Her impulse was to commiserate and express her condemnation of such behavior, but she felt certain that aligning her sympathies against the British in this situation was treasonous. She could see that responding receptively to Paul's conversation, in the normal flow of social discourse, would have the worst ramifications, and she resolved to remain silent and detached.

"Meinertzhagen is frankly psychotic," von Lettow-Vorbeck opined, "but deviousness, not illness, accounts for the German defeat at Longido."

"Oh?" Tanya let slip, clicking her jaw shut firmly afterwards and doing her utmost to appear uninterested.

"We were the victims of a treacherous Masai guide, named Lekishon—"

"— Lekishon!" Tanya pinched her wrist and inwardly admonished herself to speak no further. But she was as confounded as a weaver bird finding her nest occupied by a green mamba. Lord Delamere's rhapsodic description of the heroism of the Masai scout at Longido had naturally banished Lekishon from Tanya's mind; she didn't associate Lekishon with heroics.

"Lekishon. I believe you know him. He appears to have spread a story that you have a signed portrait of me. Our intelligence sources heard the East African Mounted Rifles discussing it. We don't know how Lekishon learned of the portrait. Perhaps he witnessed your interaction with Captain Tafel?"

Tanya managed to check the exclamation loitering in her throat, straining to dash out of her mouth. But, mentally apologizing to Hassan, she fervently cleared him of her suspicions.

Explaining Lekishon's deceit during the Longido battle, von Lettow-Vorbeck concluded, "An unfair, ungentlemanly trick, you will agree."

Tanya looked away, embarrassed at her inability and unwillingness to respond. Seeking some relief from the awkwardness, she reached out for Dionysus, who was circling them, as if hesitant to intrude. Now Dionysus settled with his head in Tanya's lap.

"I have given much thought to the question of why Lekishon didn't lead the East African Mounted Rifles to us," von Lettow-Vorbeck admitted. "Lekishon usually guides his charges to the enemy."

Scratching Dionysus between the ears, Tanya bit her lip, stifling her longing to confirm Paul's assertion.

"I have concluded," von Lettow-Vorbeck stated, "that the reason Lekishon did not do so was because he was led by the East African Mounted Rifles and not the other way around. The British were capable of this feat," von Lettow-Vorbeck paused and slowed the pace of his revelations, "because they possess an excellent map of the area around Longido." Von Lettow-Vorbeck studied Tanya's downturned face as he spoke. She seemed, he thought, to be holding her breath. Then he delivered the *coup de grace*: "We Germans are at a disadvantage because we lack personnel with the talents of your husband."

Tanya choked in alarm and leveled a glare at him. "Nonsense."

"I believe you know that your husband is the British military's cartographer."

"I know nothing of the kind!" Tanya found firm ground. The bind that had made her scared to speak had released; she felt herself goaded into vehement defense of Isak.

"If you don't know," von Lettow-Vorbeck said softly, "I am telling you now that he is."

"Isak?" Tanya laughed harshly. "Isak can't make maps! He has no sense of direction. He's a man who could set out from Nairobi, trying to get to Mombasa, and wind up in Cairo."

Von Lettow-Vorbeck wished Tanya wasn't resisting him so strenuously. He esteemed her for doing it, but he saw now that he might have to disclose unpleasant facts. She would be hurt, and the thought of hurting her was distasteful. He tried another appeal: "I am confiding in you because of my high respect for your nobility. The values of a noblewoman are unimpeachable. A noblewoman hopes only for the triumph of human dignity and the cause of civilization. A gentleman's war is in a noblewoman's interest. A gentleman's war cannot happen on unfair terms."

"Nothing could be more unfair than your accusations about my husband!"

"I beseech you, Tanya, a fair fight is my most avid wish."

"No fight is mine!"

"The fight cannot be fair if we are denied access to these maps," von Lettow-Vorbeck persisted.

"What maps?" Tanya demanded. "There are no maps!"

Dionysus had looked up curiously as the verbal volleying intensified. Now he growled, seconding Tanya's displeasure. Tanya stroked his head to calm him, and herself.

Von Lettow-Vorbeck's visage bore an expression of sincerity, tenderness and affection. It was a look he saved for his most piercing maneuvers. He spoke gently, so that every indication in his physical person was contrary to the substance of his words: "We have reports of maps made by Isak. Credible reports. Our informants have regular access to Isak."

"Tell me who this traitor is, and I'll show you a liar," Tanya rebuffed.

"Our informants are women. Locals." Seeing the destruction that these words wrought on her face, he added, "I am sorry."

Tanya sat immobile. A visceral terror throttled her, and she feared movement. She couldn't name why the thought of moving paralyzed her. She wasn't scared that she would die if she stirred; on the contrary, death was not nearly as scary as living. Perhaps she had a sense that sitting immobile would cause the onward grind of life to cease, and this idea may have animated her fear: moving would shatter her hope that the scene before her could be made to stop.

Dionysus sensed this tremendous closure in Tanya. He began licking her hands in an effort to coax a reopening from her.

"I am sorry also," von Lettow-Vorbeck proceeded, "to have to ask you to deliver the map to our agent in Tsavo. I must insist that you comply with this request. I am pained to convey this order to you, but I have no choice. The map will be returned," he assured her, "after we have copied it. We claim no unfair advantage. We want only a gentleman's war, on even terrain."

Apparently, the German surveillance of Maktau did not extend to learning that Tanya was already in possession of the map. Tanya recoiled inwardly from speculating how their conversation might have differed if Paul knew that he could take his quarry off her person. She hurried to deflect his demand: "This perfidy you call a 'gentleman's war'?" In a peculiar way, Tanya was grateful for this invitation to double-cross the British; she knew, at least, how to reply. Whereas she had no inkling of the correct response to the evidence of Isak's unfaithfulness with which she was so regularly presented.

"My dear Tanya, have you not read *Les Liaisons Dangereuses*? You must know that intrigue is the way gentlemen war, when ladies are involved."

"You know what you ask is impossible."

"To decline is impossible," von Lettow-Vorbeck stated in his quietest, most respectful, and most profoundly threatening tone. "If you deny us the map, we will take the mapmaker." Confident from the transformation in her face that she understood the score, he said, "My agent will find you at the Tsavo train station." Then he rose and dusted his trousers with his hands. "Baroness," he nodded in farewell. But as he turned to depart, she surprised him.

"Lieutenant-Colonel, I am grateful for the return of the pistol you took from me."

She was still sitting in the grass. Her facial expression was blank, her hands absently stroking Dionysus' head. She looked like a Buddah in her resigned acceptance of the pain intrinsic in the material world. Nothing in her current presentation suggested that she would use the pistol to shoot him, or herself. And, for this reason, von Lettow-Vorbeck was worried. He groped in his jacket pocket, where he had stowed the gun. "Baroness," he requested, "your word of honor as a noblewoman please. When I return this pistol, you will not shoot at me."

"You have my word."

"And you will not shoot yourself," he added, his voice sensitive, his eyes courteous.

"On my word as a noblewoman and a Baroness."

He nodded and removed the revolver from his pocket.

"In the sack there," Tanya gestured with her head.

The Lieutenant-Colonel placed the pistol in the sack and bowed again. Then he turned his back – a sign of trust – and walked to his bicycle, his hand in his jacket pocket, jingling the pistol's bullets.

* * *

Tanya remained seated, watching von Lettow-Vorbeck cycle along a footpath in the woods until he was no longer visible. Dionysus stood, panting in the direction in which the Lieutenant-Colonel had gone. Tanya felt, finally, alone.

Arduously, achingly, she angled herself on her knees so that she faced Mount Kilimanjaro. On the corridor of plain stretching before her, round white butterflies fluttered, their wings beating like nuns' wimples in a breeze. Looking on the mountainous sanctum in the distance, Tanya saw that a cloud mass had swept over the snowy peak. Her view of the colossus now occluded, Tanya remembered von Lettow-Vorbeck's remarks about Kilimanjaro's ability to dwarf an event as monumental as battle. The mountain was so miraculous that it could remove any vastness from her perspective, even itself.

As it is with the mountain, let it be with me, she thought. Let Kilimanjaro be my cathedral, let my perspective be guided by the light it filters onto me. If war itself vanishes into the maw of the mountain, let me cast my pain upon it, and let my sorrows dwindle in its immensity.

Then, still kneeling, Tanya bent her torso forward until her forehead touched the prickly ground. She had seen Hassan bow this way during prayer, and the action had puzzled her. She didn't understand how Hassan could willingly adopt a posture of such abject submission. Now she imitated him intuitively. She'd had no expectations of the movement; she had prostrated herself unthinkingly. And yet, with this motion, she gained a sense of power. Bowing to the mountain, Tanya was blessed with the insight that triumph, too, can emerge from surrender.

SIXTEEN

Maktau was throwing a party. From the sounds that reached Tanya as she trudged back to the camp, sack in hand, the celebration was boisterous: raised voices, occasional shots fired in the air, revving motorcycles, clanging kitchen ware, breaking glass and some discordant abuse of the piano. Indulging in such festivities in the midst of war seemed to Tanya uncouth, but she supposed that no appeal to decency and taste would persuade men in the grips of a booze fever. At one time, even in the recent past, she'd have resented such revelry coinciding with her own despair, but now she felt impassively accustomed to being surrounded in her despondency by merrymaking men.

As she walked, however, she found she had reason to be glad of the uproar. Perhaps D. would be sufficiently distracted that he wouldn't notice that she'd missed the 10 a.m. train. She resolved that she wouldn't give him an opportunity to notice: before he could look up from his drink, she would steal into camp, find Lieutenant Dudgeon, and be on her way back to the Tsavo train station.

Shivering with the knowledge that von Lettow-Vorbeck's "agent" would be waiting for her at the station, she sunk, for the moment, any consideration of how she would handle him. Having been humiliated by the Swahili woman's exit from Isak's tent at 8:45 that morning, and having been ordered to become a double-agent by von Lettow-Vorbeck at 9:30, and now having to convince Lieutenant Dudgeon to spirit her away at 10:15, Tanya was realizing that one crisis per hour was the limit of her capacities.

Reaching the camp, Tanya observed that Dionysus was tense, restless and prone to growl. Tanya thought his behavior curious because she knew that Dionysus (consistent with his name) enjoyed parties.

Surveying the scene at Maktau, however, Tanya empathized with her hound: this bash was so disorganized, so violent and so *male*, that Tanya felt that her mere witnessing it was illicit.

A Somali soldier was racing around the camp ground on a motorcycle that looked identical to the one that belonged to Lieutenant Dudgeon. Lieutenant Dudgeon's whereabouts, however, were not easily discerned.

Near the piles of green wood along the camp perimeter, Somali men were besting white soldiers in what appeared to be a wrestling competition; Tanya thought that Lieutenant Dudgeon might be among the wrestlers. One of the white participants (brown-haired and therefore not Lieutenant Dudgeon, Tanya was relieved to note) had rolled painfully out of range, with the consequence that he was in the process of being impaled on a barbed wire heap. The Somali standing over him didn't seem to be helping to extricate the poor wretch. Meanwhile, in the trench that men had been assiduously digging earlier in the day, Somali soldiers were now engaged in punching the sergeant who had been overseeing their work.

From inside the officers' tent, crashing sounds suggested that someone was attempting to play the piano with a sledgehammer. Beer bottles were flying out of the officers' tent, thrown by hands heedless of where they might land. An unconscious Somali soldier with a bleeding forehead demonstrated the consequences of this recklessness. Broken glass from the bottles was strewn across the parade grounds.

The mess tent, too, seemed to be the site of a sizable ruckus. Utensils and pans were being used to create auditory torment. Tanya found some consolation in the thought that, so long as the kitchen implements were being banged against each other, they weren't being smashed into people. But people were definitely being smashed with something in the mess tent. Discoloration on the tent canvas suggested a food fight, and the many bodies (on the interior) colliding with the tent's walls caused the structure (from the exterior) to appear to be in the throes of a twitching fit.

The hill on which the command center was situated also appeared to be writhing with the many white soldiers scrambling down it; periodically, they fired their guns in the air.

Assessing the intent of others is always a risky proposition, even at close range. At a distance, the task is exponentially more difficult. Nevertheless, watching the white officers tear down the hill, Tanya had the distinct impression that they were not men on their way to a celebration. On the contrary, they resembled firemen dashing to the scene of a conflagration.

And, on reflection, she had to agree that the commotion before her didn't look much like a party. It looked like the Somalis running amok.

"Tanya! You think you're in the pit of the Globe Theatre? You're in danger!" Hilary had materialized from behind her and grabbed her wrist.

She looked down at his hand encircling her own.

His eyes followed her own. "I know you hate me, but it doesn't matter. Fight me now or fight me later, I'm still going to save your life." And he yanked her after him.

Hilary ran, ducking through the rows of soldiers' tents. Tanya stumbled forward and then allowed herself to be dragged along. Alert and defensive, Dionysus guarded their rear.

As they reached the last of the tents, however, Tanya perceived their terminus: the aeroplane hangar. Deciding to fight now, she allowed herself to be dragged no longer. Wrenching herself free from his fist, she shouted, "Stop pulling me where you want to go! I don't want to go with you!"

"Titania —"

"— Baroness!"

"Baroness," he grabbed her shoulders and jerked her into a crouching huddle, "you must trust me. Your life depends on it."

She struggled against his shoulder lock, but his hold remained unimpaired. "You're the only danger to my life," she spat, near tears.

"The Somalis are mutinying." His eyes pleaded with her to comprehend the gravity of his statement.

"If they are, it's your fault! Lord Delamere said so. You're not serious, so why should they respect your orders?"

"Lord Delamere wasn't serious!" Hilary looked away frustrated. "He only yells at me because Berkeley's his brother-in-law, and D.'s wife has forbidden him to be cross with her brother. I'm D'.s scapegoat. He doesn't mean anything by it."

"You didn't spend a week playing the piano, instead of commanding your men?" Tanya felt ignoble arguing this point. Behind her was a mutiny and before her was the urgent need to deliver the map to Nairobi. But Hilary had a way of distracting her, and resisting his diversions had always been a challenge.

"I could have spent a month playing the piano without this sorry consequence!" Hilary shook her shoulders for emphasis. "Understand the circumstances: we ran out of ghee."

"Ghee?"

"It's like butter, it's part of the Somalis' rations. They've been mutinying every day since we got to Maktau. Berkeley finally told them that they could only mutiny on Mondays. That's the only order Berkeley gave that they obeyed whole-heartedly. And it was a tactical error. Daily mutinies were manageable. Now the men have saved up all their mayhem for a week, and they're beyond control. Thank the devil that their rifles are locked up, but that happy condition may not long prevail. Nobody knows how this mutiny is going to end, so I beg you: allow me to take you from here."

Hilary's case left Tanya reeling. "Isak," she stammered.

"You must leave without him," Hilary urged, tightening his clasp on her shoulders.

"I can't," she moaned, bucking against his grasp. As unbearably and as recently as Isak had made her suffer, Tanya had no hesitation about her obligations in an emergency. Both love and nobility – and the cause – demanded that she save him. But, unable to articulate her reasoning to Hilary, she said only, "He's my husband."

"He's a soldier!"

"You said nobody knows how this mutiny will end —"

"— I know that Baron von Brantberg will be untouched by the violence!" Hilary snorted. "Do you know where he is right now? He's passed out in his tent. He's not putting down the mutiny." Hilary's voice had been harsher and more derisive than he'd intended. He saw that Tanya had taken his words like a blow to the gut. She was straining to double over, her head limp on her neck, her eyes watery and regarding him with a silent entreaty for mercy. "Tanya," he relented miserably, "my passion makes me sound cruel, but the cruelty is hardest on me, that when I most desire to be soft, I am hard, and when I most ache to soothe, I am cutting. I cannot mold my expression to my intentions, but I can promise that they are good. Let me take you from here."

Tanya tried to break away from his gaze, but he followed her face until she met his eyes squarely. After a moment, she looked sharply to one side. "I need to go to Tsavo," she mumbled.

His hold on her shoulders relaxed, and he caressed her cheek with his hand. "Thank you," he whispered.

The relief on his face was so palpable that Tanya felt that her rough treatment of him approached heartlessness. "Hilary!" Tanya cried, as he again tugged her to the aeroplane. He turned, an instinct for responsiveness overriding annoyance at this further delay. "I will consider, no, no, I forgive you. I forgive you." She closed her eyes, breathed, swallowed and reopened her eyes. "I forgive you for everything."

Tanya hadn't thought that Hilary could ever look more relieved than he had when she'd said she'd let him to fly her out of Maktau. But now he did. Raw and exposed, his face was flayed by emotion. He clutched Tanya to his chest, seized her head in his hand and touched his lips to the top of her head.

So fiercely did he hold her, and so quickly did he pull away again, that Tanya hadn't had time to breathe in his embrace. But once freed, she felt herself swathed in his bouquet – gentle hints of ylang-ylang and coconut from his hair oil, a whiff of bay rum from his aftershave, a tinge of musk. The sweetness and singularity of these olfactory sensations in the context of the mutiny at Maktau swayed her with a consciousness of dislocation. But she also felt safe.

The feeling was short lived. Up close to the Bleriot XI, she was convinced that the machine had only one destination: Hades. The plane looked like a skeleton. Its wooden frame was covered in places with canvas: at the wings, over the tip of its tail and around the seats of the open-air cockpit. The remainder of the plane's structural ribbing was as exposed as an unfinished building. Cabling along the wings revealed itself to be piano wire; it culminated in an apex over the cockpit. The two-blade wooden propeller at the plane's front was lopsided, and the tires under the cockpit were even slimmer than those on Lieutenant Dudgeon's motorcycle. A third thin tire supported the aeroplane's tail. "We're going to die if we try to fly in this contraption," Tanya balked.

Hilary responded by lifting her into the passenger's seat, behind the pilot's berth. "Banish your fears!" he scoffed. "This beauty can put a girdle round the earth in forty minutes," he boasted. "Well, not really," he relented, "but she flew across the English Channel."

"Are you a very experienced pilot?" Tanya asked nervously, as she dropped her sack on the floor of the passenger's berth and lifted up a brown leather jacket that had been piled on the passenger's seat.

"Put that on," Hilary instructed, handing her goggles. "My enthusiasm for flying outstrips my experience," he admitted, adding with a grin, "But fear not: 'Thou wast not born for death, immortal Bird!'" Whether he was invoking Keats in reference to Tanya or the plane remained ambiguous. Turning to Dionysus, Hilary whistled.

Dionysus sat in a corner of the hangar, blinking. Then he yawned. He seemed to share Tanya's wariness of the aeroplane.

Disagreeing emphatically with Hilary's opinion that his lack of experience was no cause for concern, Tanya signaled surreptitiously for Dionysus to run away. Dionysus rose off his haunches quizzically but, after receiving additional encouragement from Tanya's harried facial expression and hand movements, he trotted away towards the woods.

"Oh don't be a hell hound," Hilary muttered and raced after the dog.

As soon as he'd disappeared from sight, Tanya grasped the sides of the plane and tried to extract herself from the passenger's seat. But the plane was elevated, her legs were short, and no dignified, lady-like means of exit was immediately apparent. Before she'd made any progress beyond this observation, Hilary had returned with Dionysus wriggling in his arms.

Tanya was amazed at Dionysus' docility, until she saw that the faithful beast was chewing some dried meat.

Hilary explained, somewhat morosely, "I gave him my lunch ration." His voice hardening into an order, he continued, "Jacket, Baroness. And goggles." While he waited for her to comply, he struggled to contain Dionysus, whose wiry coat was beginning to irritate Hilary's nose.

Tanya hurried into the gear, murmuring, "Hilary, I'm afraid confidence fails me —"

Hilary ignored her and dropped the hound in her lap. Donning his own leather jacket, flying cap and goggles, Hilary vaulted into the pilot's seat. Turning behind him to address her, he directed, "Hold your dog tight. And don't stand up. The tail on this baby is liable to snap up and pitch us forward if you stand, or if the hound jumps out of the plane. Do either of these things, and we'll die."

With those comforting words, they were off.

The engine's first growl escalated into a metallic grinding that wholly drowned the roar of the mutiny they were leaving. The engine's sound had Tanya cowering before they'd gone anywhere. Gradually, the plane began to roll. Hilary taxied down a makeshift airstrip behind the rows of tents. "Rickety" was the word that leaped to Tanya's mind as the plane bumped along the grassy ground; understanding that she was trapped and about to die, she clenched her teeth to prevent herself from screaming – not that any sound could've escaped the engine's din.

Reaching the airstrip's end, Hilary turned the plane around, paused and then sped forward. Certain that the wings, propeller, canvas and fuselage would disaggregate as the machine's speed increased, Tanya crushed Dionysus to her and buried her head in his back.

Death was either slow in coming or imperceptible on arrival. After another few minutes, a softening of the engine's deafening clamor, and a diminution in the air temperature, made Tanya peek up from Dionysus' fur. The wings were intact; the propeller was pinwheeling so fast that it was almost invisible; the canvas was in place; the fuselage – though trembling – was holding together; and she was not dead. These basics established, Tanya gave herself permission to notice that she was flying.

She discovered that she was exhilarated, though battened by the elements. She was shivering and needed several moments to realize that she could breathe. Inhaling, she imbibed the stench of aeroplane fuel. As much as the wind in the open-air cockpit gave Tanya a fresh appreciation of the aerodynamics of birds – she now understood the benefits of having eyes on either side of the head – the wind couldn't dispel entirely the rank odor of oil.

Feeling destabilized, she hugged Dionysus tightly. He seemed to comprehend that his orientation to the planet had dramatically altered and, not altogether in favor of this upheaval, he submitted willingly to her constraint.

Hilary banked the plane, and Tanya gasped as she tilted downwards. The landscape below was transformed. Tanya felt as if she were gazing on a hitherto undiscovered part of the earth. The perspective from above flattened and shrank some features, like trees and herds of animals, while it expanded others, like rivers. As they soared, Tanya watched flowing water unwind across a panoramic expanse and realized that she'd never before comprehended a river's length.

Only then did she reflect that her aerial view corresponded to the map she was carrying. She apprehended that Isak intuited the aerial perspective in order to draw his maps. Tanya had an insight into von Lettow-Vorbeck's frustration at lacking "personnel with the talents of your husband"; she saw, for the first time, how rare indeed Isak's talent was.

Losing her diffidence, Tanya swiveled around, searching for Kilimanjaro. Craning to see behind her, she eventually found it, winking a snow-capped farewell. It, too, changed its character when she peered at it from her airborne vantage point: she felt eye-to-eye with the mountain; if not its equal, she was at least its challenger.

This acumen made Tanya reflect on the differences between her perch in Kijabe and her current position. In Kijabe, although still physically on the earth, she'd felt the sky beneath her; the escarpment had elevated her into the heavens. Oddly, in the aeroplane, she didn't feel a part of the sky. The sky instead had seemed to recede upwards, as if taunting humanity to reach, in its paltry machines, the same heights to which nature could raise it. The aeroplane gave human interface with the environment a competitive aspect that was lacking when humans were unenhanced by gadgetry.

Ahead of her in the cockpit, Hilary was concentrating intensely; Tanya could discern his effort from the tension in his neck muscles. Last time she'd stared at the back of his head, they'd been riding into battle together; now he was flying her out of danger, saving her yet again, as he'd done when she'd been menaced by Mr. Baden. Resting her chin between Dionysus' ears, Tanya recognized that her most vivid moments of the war had been passed in Hilary's company. As a hero, musician, killer, poet, pilot, and lover, Hilary was a man, Tanya mused, with whom life could be exciting.

Hilary banked again and began a wide circle preparatory to landing. Peeping around his body, Tanya tried to spy where they would reconnect with earth. She struggled to see the Tsavo train station, but she couldn't locate it. With a start, she recollected that she hadn't observed the railroad for the entirety of their flight. Having witnessed the disappearing acts of elephants and mountains, however, Tanya no longer doubted that a creation as significant as the railroad could lurk unseen. She would have to ask Hilary where it was.

As Hilary brought the plane lower, Tanya glimpsed buildings and roads through the foliage. She was impressed: she'd had no idea that Tsavo was that developed. It looked like Nairobi.

As the grounded world drew nearer, Tanya saw that Hilary was landing the plane on a stretch of grass edged on one side with acacia trees. Remembering the flimsy wheels on the vehicle, Tanya squeezed shut her eyes and crouched forward, squashing Dionysus beneath her. Failing to appreciate the imminent risk of disaster, Dionysus whined and squirmed.

When rubber and grass met, however, the union was happy. The plane was stopped and the engine was off before Tanya absorbed the reality that they hadn't crashed.

Dionysus, in fact, was the first passenger to raise his head. Fidgeting his way free from Tanya's clutches, he placed his front paws on the edge of the cockpit and surveyed his new domain. A self-satisfied air infused his manner, due no doubt to his cognizance of his newly-earned title: Africa's First Flying Dog. Look at me, he seemed to bay, here I am, where I landed after a gambol with the clouds. This pronouncement having been issued, he sprang from the cockpit and commenced sniffing the aeroplane's tires. Finding them unsullied, he lifted his hind leg and left an unmistakable message for Africa's subsequent flying dogs.

Hilary offered Tanya his hand. "Baroness, may I have the honor of assisting your dismount?"

Warily unfolding from her crouch, Tanya ran her hands reverently along the cockpit's canvas. "It's just bits of wood and fabric," she marveled.

"And a cracking good Gnome rotary engine," Hilary laughed. He stepped back and regarded Tanya in the Bleriot XI. "You should become a pilot," he suggested.

Tanya shook her head quickly, in a restrained, compact movement. "I don't even know how to drive a car." But she was smiling.

Renewing his offer to assist with her dismount, Hilary first took Tanya's sack and rested it on the ground. Then he lifted Tanya out of the passenger's seat.

As Tanya rejoined the earthbound mortals, she murmured, "Thank you. For this gift. Of my safety. Again." She spoke haltingly. Each word was an effort; she was still overawed by the flight and regaining her voice in the wake of the engine's volume. "And for showing me Africa. From the perspective of this," she gestured, "remarkable machine. The impressions you have given my life are indelible."

Hilary offered a relieved, love-drenched smile.

Tanya reached out for his arm to steady herself. Any lingering now, she feared, would lead inexorably to an embrace and more compromising entwinement. Reminding herself that she had a map to deliver – and that she was married – she hurried, "But I am selfishly detaining you too long. You must go – your fellow soldiers need you. Will you just point me to the train station? And you don't happen to know when's the next train to Nairobi? I missed the 10 a.m.," she concluded ruefully.

His arm extended, Hilary had been about to advise her how to reach the train station, when he heard her say, "Nairobi." He stopped and clarified, "Kijabe, surely?"

Tanya bit her lip. Army headquarters in Nairobi, of course, was her immediate destination, but Tanya couldn't confide this fact to Hilary. She hoped that she hadn't already betrayed a clue to her mission. "Of course," she smiled effortfully, "I meant only the next train from Tsavo in the direction of Kijabe. It stops first in Nairobi," she added, feeling stupid because this point was obvious.

Hilary, smart as he was, didn't seem to be following her explanation. "Next train from Tsavo?" he blinked. "But we're in Nairobi."

Now Tanya strained to make sense of Hilary's words, as if confusion was a set of clouded field glasses they were passing between them. "Nairobi?" she eventually croaked. "Did you say we're in Nairobi?"

"Yes."

Had the aeroplane plummeted from the sky, it couldn't have had a bigger impact on Tanya. She tottered backwards, verging on collapse.

Hilary mistook her wobble for a faint. "It's quite alright," he assured her, catching her and propping her against his chest. "It's normal. Have you eaten today?"

Had Tanya been able to respond, she would have refused food with the tenacity of a proud dieter sticking to her regimen. But she couldn't talk. Her mind was fixated on the conclusion to which it had instantly leaped: Isak's life was in danger.

"I'm a miserable wretch, I have nothing to feed you," Hilary bemoaned, fanning her face with his hand. "I gave my lunch to the dog."

Tanya had no awareness of Hilary; she was concentrating too intently on her analysis: von Lettow-Vorbeck had told her that he'd take the mapmaker if she didn't deliver the map. She was sure that his threat had not been idle. And, while she hadn't decided what she was going to do when she met von Lettow-Vorbeck's agent, she hadn't wanted Hilary to remove the choice from her power. She found voice: "I said I needed to go to Tsavo."

"Did you?" Hilary remarked, pleased that she seemed to be regaining consciousness.

Tanya made an effort to stand on her own. She wanted to be away from Hilary. If von Lettow-Vorbeck executed his hateful threat, it would be Hilary's fault.

No, she shook her head, it would always be her fault: she hadn't given the map to the agent. "Tsavo," she insisted, "not Nairobi. Take me back to Tsavo."

"But darling Tsavo isn't safe," he reasoned, still holding out an arm to support her. "German raiding parties are everywhere. Tsavo is a target. Even if you don't encounter Germans, you'll be endangered by their handiwork. Bombs on the track derail trains regularly. Besides," he added, "you're a mere hour's train ride from Kijabe now. You'll be back there this afternoon."

Tanya raised her hands to her head, as if to rip out her hair. She couldn't dispute him. Under other circumstances, she would have bestowed unremitting gratitude upon him for depositing her in Nairobi. And, of course, she couldn't reveal the true cause for her distress. Covering her face with her hands, she breathed inwards sharply. Thought was failing her; she lapsed into panic. Tearing her hands from her face, she burst out, "Isak's in danger!"

In response to this melodramatic declaration, Hilary could do nothing but look baffled. Tanya couldn't blame him. The non sequitur had been too extreme.

"It's my fault!" Tanya assured him, fighting back tears. "I can't tell you why or how. I can't say anything. Except I'll die if I don't tell you that Isak's in danger. It's my fault, it's on my head. I have to help him. But I can't. What can I do? He needs to escape Maktau now. Immediately. Please," Tanya beseeched Hilary, the tears flowing freely now, "please go and take him. Return to Maktau and rescue him. Fly him to Nairobi. He'll die. I swear he'll die if you don't. And it'll be my fault."

As Tanya unburdened this request, the determination to help her welled within Hilary. He didn't understand the particulars, but he believed her. Tanya's presence at Maktau had been bizarre. To conclude that she was supporting Lord Delamere's unit in some way required no strenuous brain exercise. Of course, if Lord Delamere had in fact recruited Tanya, his choice to involve a woman was non-traditional, but tradition had to yield to exigency. The British Army had botched its coordination and communication with the irregular troops, and Lord Delamere plainly needed to staff his unit however he could. (Berkeley Cole, after all, had done the same in enlisting Somali scouts.) The likely scenario being that Tanya was engaged in military work, she readily could have been privy to some plot against Isak.

All the same, Hilary's most abiding impression of Tanya's appeal had been her guilt. She was obviously distraught about the risk to Isak, but her own complicity in his fate was what had driven her to speak as she had.

Hilary could not countenance Tanya's point of view. From his perspective, Isak had no claim to Tanya's guilt. Isak had dishonored Tanya and their marriage. He was plainly unworthy of her. Hilary harbored no notion that such unworthiness ought to find its reward in death, but he was not going to rescue Isak only to condemn Tanya to a future of continued mistreatment. The price of Isak's life must be freedom for Tanya.

Hilary reached into his jacket pocket and found a handkerchief. Reaching out gently, he began to wipe Tanya's eyes. Sniffling and hiccupping, she accepted the handkerchief. Embarrassed, she turned away, attempting to hide her face.

Hilary gazed sadly at the side of her head before daring to tuck a strand of hair behind her ear. When he spoke, his voice was resonant with confidence of his moral righteousness: "I'll do it."

His pronouncement heightened Tanya's emotional output, adding relief to the swell of emotions provoking her tears. Still hiding her face, she stretched an arm out and threw it about his neck. Through the sobs, he could discern that she was thanking him.

"Cry no more, I'll do as you wish," he soothed her, stroking her head. Her sobs subsided, but he continued brushing her hair with his fingers. "And once Isak is safe, you will wake."

She sniffed and looked up. Blinking rapidly, she released her hold to wipe her eyes. "Wake?" she managed, in a small voice.

"See as thou wast wont to see," he urged. "Now, my Titania, wake you, my sweet queen."

Tanya furrowed her eyebrows. The present relevance of these lines from *Midsummer* escaped her. "You'll save Isak?" she confirmed.

He nodded. "And when I have, you'll marry me."

"What?"

Seeing that he had, once again for all his poetry, misphrased his words, Hilary rushed to explain, "This last decade and everything that's happened – your marriage, my loneliness – can't you see it's a bad dream? You're no different than Queen Titania, under a sleeping spell and enamored of an ass. I am breaking the spell, Titania. A true queen cannot love an ass! You were born to live for love! I'm releasing you from your guilt, your obligations, your duties, and I am taking you back, where you belong, with me. As my wife."

Tanya stepped away rapidly until she collided with the side of the aircraft. She steadied herself against its frame. "Am I deceived?" she asked him. "Are you imposing a condition on Isak's life?"

"A condition on him, yes, if you care to express it in those terms. He must give you up. Otherwise, after saving him, the whole earth would be a wider prison unto you!" Hilary cried, exasperated.

"Prison?"

"Be honest, I beg you!" he exploded. "Reason and love may keep little company nowadays but, in the extremity of unreason, love must wither! You cannot fail to know that marriage to an adulterer is little better than to be cast in a dungeon! This marriage has made you, not a noblewoman, but a captive! I know you, Tanya. You cannot bear being trapped. You cannot withstand being shamed. You cannot expect me to believe that your marriage to Baron von Brantberg is anything more substantial than a peculiar vision flickering beneath the African moon. Awake! I beg you, wake from this nightmare and embrace the man who loves you."

Tanya slapped him. "You ransom another man's life, you filth! I will not be your bloody prize!" she shouted.

"Don't misunderstand me! I am rescuing you as much as I am saving —"

"— Your conditions are repugnant! If you don't rescue Isak, you're no better than a murderer!" She attempted to slap him again, but this time, Hilary dodged the blow. Vocalizing incomprehensibly, Tanya unleashed her fists, punching him around the torso.

The furor brought Dionysus bounding from the acacia trees, under which he had been giving grief to birds. Now he barked angrily and leaped about Hilary's midriff.

Notwithstanding the combined assault of woman and hound, Hilary succeeded – with as much gentleness as he could manage – in catching both of Tanya's wrists, cuffing her hands with his own.

"If you walk straight, Baroness," he convulsed for breath, wavering slightly at the interruption of Dionysus, who – seeing his mistress suddenly silent – sat growling at Hilary, "you'll reach the center of town in fifteen minutes. I presume," he said, breathing heavily, "that you can find the train station from the center of town."

Tanya was quivering, eyes moist, muttering, "Murderer. You're no different than a murderer. A murderer."

Hilary released her hands, an expression of helplessness holding hostage his face. "I will do your bidding, Baroness," he said, pulling himself together to bow slightly.

"Murderer," she repeated.

Shaking his own head in bewilderment and self-disgust, Hilary walked away and hoisted himself into the cockpit. Decade-old experience taught him that Tanya could go deaf with rage. He tried nonetheless: affixing his goggles over his eyes, he turned to Tanya and shouted, "I will do your bidding. Hear me, I will do your bidding!"

"Murderer!" she retorted. Then, before he could start the aeroplane's engine, before he could see that she was sobbing again, she grabbed her sack and ran pell-mell towards Nairobi, Dionysus loping along at her feet.

SEVENTEEN

Landing the Bleriot XI at Maktau required more skill than Hilary, strictly speaking, had. The airstrip was a smidgeon too short for guaranteed-safe landings, and Hilary knew that luck, not talent, would bring his plane down in Maktau without mishap. Now, however, he was too distracted to pay the necessary attention or to concentrate his energies on invoking good fortune. Consequently, on landing in Maktau, Hilary damaged the Bleriot's propeller in a rolling stop that came close to refashioning the plane into an accordion against a baobab tree.

Swearing, Hilary sprang from the cockpit and examined the propeller. Its polished surface was scratched. Relief melted the aggravation off his face: the injury was minor – and more importantly, easily repaired by sanding the surface smooth. Hilary patted the propeller gratefully and relaxed enough to acknowledge that his luck had held.

His own life intact, Hilary turned his attention to Isak's. He began striding through the rows of soldiers' tents in search of the man.

As he walked, Hilary became aware of the stillness. Maktau seemed a ghost fort. In the abnormal quiet of the camp, he noticed the birdsong from the surrounding forest. This tranquility was unexpected; he wasn't surprised that the mutiny had been suppressed, but if the fight was over, the conquered Somalis should be undergoing punishment. But he couldn't see or hear anyone receiving the lash. The administrative tent – where court martials were conducted – appeared devoid of human life. The trenches, parade grounds, mess tent – all were empty.

Taking a pair of field glasses from his jacket pocket, he trained them on the command center at the top of the hill. Spying scurrying human activity, he satisfied himself that Maktau had not been deserted. The absence of humans on the camp ground remained a mystery, but one that – having arrived at Isak's tent – Hilary would postpone solving.

"Captain von Brantberg," Hilary called from outside. He renewed the greeting after receiving no response. His second try brought the sound of rustling from inside the tent. Hilary pulled aside the flap to investigate.

Reclining on bedding laid on the ground, Isak was fumbling for his canteen. He squinted at the incoming light. Clothed only in his trousers, he was several days unshaven, and his hair hung shaggily around his head. He was puffy from over-revelry and under-sleep, and his eyes had a lava hue. After a moment, he raised his eyebrows in recognition: "Captain Gordon."

"Am I intruding?"

"Come in!" Isak gestured a welcome and then winced, the action having aggravated his headache.

Hilary entered the tent and sat on a crate. Once inside, Hilary felt akin to a man closeted with a behemoth. The sensation was strange. Hilary's tent was identical in size to Isak's, and Hilary had never before felt claustrophobic in it – not even during the frequent card games and drinking sessions he'd hosted. Isak had often been in such social gatherings, but the crowd somehow distracted focus from his size. Now Hilary felt the magnitude of the man. "I didn't wake you?"

"Ya no," Isak said ambiguously, retrieving his canteen and sipping water. The fluid spilled down his chin as he drank. "Berkeley was just in here," he said, wiping his mouth.

"Did he tell you why the camp's so quiet?"

"Somalis deserted." Isak dropped the now-empty canteen. "Looted the stores, stole the supplies, rode off on the motorcycles." He laid back on his bedding and covered his eyes with a hefty paw. "Almost everyone else is out looking for them. Pointless. They're halfway to Somaliland by now. Lucky bastard," Isak raised his hand and winked at Hilary, "your job is finished." Isak's hand again flopped over his eyes.

"Lucky bastard you missed it."

"Unlucky devil. It would have been fun."

"Then you'll be ready for some fun now. I'm flying you to Nairobi, so ready yourself. We'll leave as soon as I repair my propeller."

Isak raised his hand again and shifted his eyes in Hilary's direction. Then he guffawed violently, his laughs degenerating into a bout of coughing and head gripping. Brow in hands, Isak rolled onto his side, in a movement that bore comparison with an avalanche. Tentatively, he sat up. "You pox mark." Isak lobbed the insult amiably. "Joking with me in my condition. Laughing hurts."

"I'm not joking." Hilary waited, allowing Isak to absorb the seriousness of his manner. "Your life is in danger. I'll fly you to safety."

Isak rubbed his head and looked confused. Then, concentrating on Hilary, Isak asked, "What's so special about me?"

"Your charms appear irresistible."

Isak snorted. "What sort of danger?"

"I can't say because I don't know." With an inspired flourish, Hilary added, "I just know that my orders are to fly you to Nairobi."

"Lord Delamere told you that?"

"No."

"I'll stay here."

"You'd be wiser to evacuate."

"I'm going to join the others and find these Somalis."

"You said yourself they won't be found. Come with me to Nairobi."

"Lord Delamere couldn't spare me."

"If you're dead, he'll have no choice."

Isak made a dismissive hand gesture and, again, regretted the impact on his head. "I'll get whatever's due me whenever it catches up with me. No sense in running."

Though he lived his life according to a different creed, Hilary couldn't withhold a gruff respect of Isak's easy acceptance of fate. Nonetheless, Tanya's accusation – "Murderer!" – weighed heavily on Hilary, and he knew that she would never believe that Isak had refused to leave Maktau. Hilary had to be more persuasive: "And what of your fellow soldier? Am I to be court martialed because you don't see the sense in me obeying orders?" Hilary smiled, a jocular appeal to Isak to play along.

"I'll give evidence on your behalf." Isak smiled back.

"Why, Isak?" Hilary asked, frustration creeping into his voice. "Your life is in danger. You'll be safe in Nairobi. Why not go?"

"Honestly, Hilary," Isak heaved a sigh, "I don't feel like moving."

"You can't track Somalis without moving."

"Tracking Somalis isn't flying."

"Don't tell me you're scared to fly."

"Nothing I like better, but I'm staying at my post."

"Have you flown before?"

"No."

"Be reasonable, Isak! Think of your loved ones. You are not a man without attachments in the world. Go to Nairobi for their sake."

"I'm sure they'd rather I stayed in the field."

"Preposterous! Your loved ones pray nothing further than for your safe return to them."

"I'm a sinner."

"Who isn't? Sinners' loved ones still wish them safe."

"I don't want to hurt them."

"Then you must fly to Nairobi."

"No."

"You'll die."

"I don't mind."

"You're ill from drink. You will mind."

"I don't believe it."

"You should."

"I don't."

"What can I say that will convince you?"

"Nothing."

"Have a pack of cards?"

"Why?"

"I'll play you for your life. You lose, you come with me."

"And if I win?"

"You stay."

"I'll stay anyway."

"Isak, are you turning down a wager?"

"Yes."

"Then you need a head shrinker. I'll have to fly you to Vienna. That's enemy territory, Isak, but for you I'll risk it."

Isak smiled and collapsed back onto his bedding. "If I could give my headache to the Germans, they'd lose the war," he muttered.

Hilary was at an impasse. Physically moving Isak against his will was not an option. And Hilary was at a loss for further argument. Had he believed the ploy would work, he would have revealed that his "orders" came from Tanya, but Hilary had not received the impression that Isak would leave Maktau because Tanya thought him in danger. If anything, Isak seemed to be suggesting that his death would be to Tanya's benefit. And, of course, disclosing Tanya's hand in this gambit would expose her to uncomfortable scrutiny that Hilary preferred to spare her. He sighed. Tanya would call him a murderer; his only defense was that Isak would give evidence for him. He rose. "I'll take my leave."

"Hilary."

Half out of the tent, Hilary swiveled to face Isak and found him reaching an arm out – whether to extend an olive branch or receive assistance was impossible to ascertain.

Isak dropped his arm. "It's no loss if I die, but my wife won't feel that way."

"I'm sure you're right."

"I want you to care for her if anything happens to me."

"She'll be inconsolable. Think again. Let me fly you to Nairobi."

"You'll be there to console her."

"I'm honored, Isak —"

"— Even if nothing happens to me, take care of her, Hilary. You have my blessing."

Hilary started. Isak appeared to have gone off script. Hilary knew the expected responses to an appeal for support of loved ones after a man's death, but Isak seemed to have invited a wholly different variety of support, and Hilary didn't know what response this cue was supposed to prompt. "Come again?"

Isak went through a chuckle-wince routine, and then coughed. Clearing his throat, he fixed his red-rimmed eyes on Hilary. "I would be proud to introduce you as my wife's lover." Isak was smiling unaffectedly; his whole face was open and sincere. His earnestness transformed his features: the smashed crater look imparted by his hangover seemed to fade, and his countenance took on the glow of an overage, Viking cupid. "I hope I live to do it."

"I hope you do, too."

"That's the attitude," Isak lay back down and covered his face with his hands. "I have your word?" he called up from the bedding.

"You have my word, Baron."

Hilary staggered off on trembling legs, through the silent rows of abandoned tents in which deserters would never again sleep, to fix his aeroplane propeller.

* * *

Tanya had been waiting for hours in Army headquarters.

She'd delivered the map to an intelligence officer before noon. He was of medium build, with a square head and non-descript features. He hadn't introduced himself, but she knew from listening to others address him that his name was Colonel Meinertzhagen. She was certain she'd heard the name before – possibly von Lettow-Vorbeck had mentioned it to her; but then she wondered if she was drawing the association only because "Meinertzhagen" sounded German. She hadn't seen the Colonel on her first map delivery.

In lieu of thanking her for her courier work, Colonel Meinertzhagen had yelled, "Get that dog out of here!"

Tanya had pushed Dionysus away with her leg. She'd wanted to ask Colonel Meinertzhagen to protect Isak, but the Colonel had had no time for her. Upon receipt of the map, he'd set in motion a protocol to examine, log, copy and distribute it. Tanya had been merely a distraction.

Seeking assistance for Isak, she'd wandered the building, which had (in a previous life) belonged to a German import/export business. The British Army had taken over the building at the outbreak of war. A low, one-story structure, it had a large front room and a warren of smaller rooms in the back. Originally for storage, these smaller spaces now boasted a variety of offices that spilled into the hall.

Leaving the intelligence office, Tanya had squeezed through the crowd of soldiers ordering supplies, planning strategy, moving troops, recruiting for *kariakor*, communicating with the Colonial Office, cross-posting communications to the War Office and liaising with the India Office.

As Tanya had navigated this throng, Dionysus had consistently been an unappreciated presence. Beyond eliciting this displeasure, Tanya had been unable to gain anyone's attention.

Stubbornly, she'd refused to leave. Finding the telegraph station in a corner of the large front room, Tanya had felt herself on home turf. Ordering Dionysus to sit at her feet, she'd settled in. She'd interrupted every man who'd stopped to send or retrieve a telegram. She'd explained her situation politely: her husband, Baron von Brantberg, was with Lord Delamere's unit in Maktau; his life was in danger; he needed protection; could they help? Uniformly, the men had replied in the negative.

After three hours, Tanya began to weary. The arbitrariness, rudeness and *ad hoc* nature of headquarters were providing disheartening insights into the general state of disarray of military operations in the field. And the dismissiveness of everyone at British Army headquarters demoralized her. She wanted to yell that she'd undertaken tremendous risks to courier maps from the field; that she'd expended her own resources to bring supplies to troops; that she was also volunteering at the Kijabe railway station; that, for all these sacrifices for the cause, she'd earned the right to demand her husband's safety! She restrained herself because she didn't want to be ordered to leave. Also, she was confident that her sacrifices wouldn't make a difference: the men still wouldn't care about Isak.

After four hours, Tanya was on the verge of weeping, when the telegraph operator forestalled her tears: "Lady, your husband's a Baron?"

This telegraph operator was the first that Tanya had seen who was not of Indian extraction. He was a young, UK-mutt of Scotch-Irish-Welsh-English descent, with a narrow, weasely face, overlapping teeth and eyes that – in contrast to the rest of his appearance – made Tanya think he was an artist. At his question, Tanya sprang to the telegraph counter, followed by Dionysus, who rose to stand beside her with his tail wagging. "Yes, Baron von Brantberg," Tanya answered breathlessly, continuing, "'Isak' is his name. Do you have word from him?"

The telegraph operator looked at the message in his hand. "No," he frowned, "not from him. About him, I think: 'Troops sweeping Maktau caught in rhino charge'," he read. "Baron von Brantberg shot rhino."

Tanya clapped her hands together. "Wonderful! That's Isak. Large game hunter *extraordinaire*. Wire back, please, wire back that he needs to leave Maktau immediately. His life is in danger. Make sure the telegram says that – his life is at risk."

"Aftermath rhino, commotion, BvB missing. Believed captured by enemy. Alert Col M Army Intelligence," the telegraph operator finished reading. He looked up. "It's from Lord Delamere. I shouldn't have read this to you, Baroness," he said, as if just comprehending that he'd breached Army protocol. He made an aggravated face. "Sorry, but Colonel Meinertzhagen needs to decide on the reply."

As he spoke, Tanya saw herself reflected in the telegraph operator's artist eyes. She was drained of vitality, her lips pale and her flesh rigid. Her portrait was indistinguishable from a death mask. When finally she opened her mouth, her cheeks seemed to crack and her voice rang mechanically in her ears: "Quite right, thank you, never mind."

EIGHTEEN

"Why didn't you overthrow the British?!" For twenty days, Tanya had telegraphed Army headquarters in Nairobi, without result. "The British build a railroad across your land, and you just watch?!" Eight times, Tanya had tried to communicate with Colonel Meinertzhagen, but he'd never responded. "The British say, 'You're living on my land,' and you let them?!" Four times, Tanya had tried to contact Lord Delamere, until she'd been told that he was incapacitated with tick-bite fever. "They say, 'Pay taxes to the King,' and you do?!" Tanya had even tried to find Hilary, but no one knew where he was now that Cole's Scouts had disbanded. "They outlaw your dances and appoint a pawn as your leader, and you just accept it?!" Tanya had ached for her mother, but Bess Rungsted's voice – as much as her arms – were inaccessible. "Wear trousers, believe in Jesus, use rupees – whatever they tell you, you do it!" Every day, Tanya had collapsed from lack of nourishment. "If you'd only overthrown the British, the Great War wouldn't be here right now!" She had nothing left to do but berate Kamau for the presence of the Empire.

"Tanya darling, you know the poor lamb had nothing to do with the war." Laying a gentle hand on Tanya's shoulder, Malena attempted to comfort her.

Tanya and Malena had just emerged from the Kijabe train station. Tanya had been telegraphing Army headquarters, and Malena had been her constant companion since Isak's disappearance. Behind them, Gokal hovered in the station house doorway; in front of them, Hassan and Kamau stood, eyebrows raised and mouths agape.

Between them, Kamau and Hassan held a cake. Nine days previously, Gokal and Kamau had sneaked back to the von Brantberg coffee plantation to rifle through Tanya's recipes – Kamau to locate them and Gokal to read them. Upon hearing Gokal read the recipe for a confection of whipped cream, custard, jam and sponge cake iced with marzipan,

Kamau had known instantly that Memsabu couldn't resist it. If he made it, she would finally eat. And once she ate, she would feel better. She would see, at last, that a man – even a husband – is no reason to starve.

The only problem with the cake was the ingredients: they were all scarce and, in Hassan's and Kamau's hands, contraband. After eight days of painstaking efforts, Hassan had "got" all the ingredients, and this morning Kamau had stolen to the coffee plantation's kitchen to bake the Memsabu-saving cake (as Kamau had come to think of it).

After Kamau's return to Kijabe, cake in tow, he and Hassan had waited until Tanya had finished her day's telegraphing, so that she could eat without distraction. Knowing that the cake presentation would be made after he completed wiring Tanya's messages, Gokal had followed Tanya and Malena to the train platform, so that he could share in the cake-giving festivities. On exiting the train station, Tanya and Malena had been greeted by Hassan and Kamau, smiling broadly and holding out a gorgeous, dome-shaped sweet.

"*Prinsesstårta!*" Kamau cried jubilantly, announcing the name of the cake that he'd proudly remembered from when Gokal had read it.

Tanya had responded with a screed blaming Kamau for British colonialism in East Africa. The situation was very confusing.

Attempting to ameliorate the prevailing awkwardness with sensibility, Gokal broke the silence by asking, "Memsahib, how are you thinking the British should be overthrown? Defeating conquerors with guns is taking many years for people without guns. It is needing many hundred years in India, and now still we are requiring a leader. British East Africa is also requiring a leader. We are saying, 'No taxes,' but how is King George listening to a people with no guns and no leader?"

Feeling that Gokal had missed the most important aspect of the issue, Hassan jumped in, "The British are today's conquerors only. We Somalis once conquered the slave races, like the Midgan, and we have now been conquered by the Italians. We will vanquish the Italians someday, and then we will conquer the Bantu slave races, like the Kikuyu. This is only a wheel, turned by Allah, according to His will. The conqueror thinks the civilization he brings is a pearl, and the conquered say it is a curse. But it is just history, according to the will of Allah. If it pains, ignore it. Life in any event will be birth and death, marriage and children, vengeance and faith."

During this exposition, Kamau had been staring peevishly at Hassan: understandably, references to the "Bantu slave races, like the Kikuyu" irked him. Nonetheless, Kamau felt his ultimate opponent was Tanya, since she had begun the conversation with a strong condemnation of him. Now he rejoined: "Memsabu, the Kikuyu elders who ruled when the British came taught that the *mzungus* had superior magic. No Kikuyu likes to live under a sorcerer's spell, but powerful magic must be appeased. This war has made me learn many things. The elders were wrong. *Mzungus* are not sorcerers, they are men. They have no magic, they have machines. They are not a single tribe, they are like the Kikuyu and the Masai. They are not like animals, that kill for food, or Kikuyu, who kill for defense and goats. *Mzungus* kill for no reason. These things are not like powerful magic. They do not have to be appeased."

Malena sighed audibly. "Well, Tanya," she said brightly, "have a piece of cake."

* * *

The cake was delectable. The marzipan had been perfumed with rosewater, and the custard flavored with vanilla. The jam was thick with raspberries, and the sponge cake was moist and light.

Kamau's intention was that Tanya should eat the whole thing, but she'd insisted that everyone share it. With each bite, Tanya felt dignity returning. The cake had tapped into her rooted belief that luxury was the domain of the aristocracy around whom dignity flocked like protective fairies. And the cake – in wartime, in Kijabe – was the greatest luxury she'd ever experienced.

Malena's response was similarly keyed to deprivation, though not from dignity, but from sugar. After two-and-a-half months without, the cake was like opium. Telling herself that the good Lord made gluttony a sin, she restrained herself from shoving the cake into her mouth with both hands. But just barely.

Gokal, too, was sugar-needful, having gone almost a year since he'd last tasted dessert – and the small square of cassava halwa that he'd eaten then had lacked the complexity of this cake. Gokal ate slowly, trying to identify and savor the many flavors and textures that composed the *prinsesstårta*. And although the cake bore no resemblance to any food he had encountered in India, in the way it provoked a multiplicity of sensations, and in its sheer splendidness, it made him homesick.

Hassan obliged Tanya with a mouthful, but he found the cake too sweet and cloying. He gave the remainder of his piece to Dionysus, for whom the cake was an ear-raising departure from his recent diet of vermin caught after an exhausting hunt. His blood sugar levels boosted impressively, Dionysus tore away in pursuit of a serval cat slinking through the underbrush; losing his prey to a tree branch beyond his reach, Dionysus collapsed in an abrupt-onset nap.

Kamau, for his part, ate the cake wondering if it was supposed to taste as it did. From Tanya's and Malena's faces, he couldn't discern approval. Malena looked anxiety-ridden as she eyed the three remaining slices, and Tanya – as she had so often over the past twenty days – was beginning to cry.

The 4 p.m. train disrupted their picnic with its blaring horn, flying dust and detraining soldiers. Thanking Tanya for the cake, Gokal excused himself to attend to his duties in the station house.

Tanya turned her tear-stained face to Kamau and Hassan and murmured her gratitude for their exceptional efforts. "You have done well to permit the British to establish a protectorate," she congratulated Kamau, "if you hadn't, I would've been deprived of your company, your kindness and your cake."

Malena missed Tanya's encomium because she was staring at a man who had moments before leaned over their party. He was clothed in a British Army uniform of khaki cotton, but his real attire seemed to be a pall of grief. The man had arrived on the 4 p.m. train, and Malena had noticed him begin to enter the station house and then divert his route upon catching sight of their picnic. Malena thought that she might have seen the man before, but she couldn't place him. He didn't notice Malena; his attention was devoted entirely to Tanya.

Moments later, Tanya sensed his presence and twisted around to find Hilary Gordon standing over her.

Malena could see that when Tanya and the man locked eyes, the connection seemed to loose a renegade electric charge. Violence was likely.

"Baroness, I must speak with you alone," the man said in a low tone, heavy with responsibility and anguish.

Malena loved Tanya, but she knew that the good Lord had graced Tanya with an overabundance of emotion and a temper quick to see the attractions of slapping. Though Tanya was still seated, Malena needed no psychic powers to know that within the minute, Tanya would be standing and this obviously suffering man would be holding a stinging cheek. Malena's hand shot out to Tanya's shoulder and, bounding upwards, Malena pressured Tanya to stay seated. "Welcome friend," Malena smiled brightly. "Have a piece of cake."

* * *

"Isak's in Moshi. That's the German base at Kilimanjaro. He appears well." Hilary spoke directly, in the sincere manner of one who hopes that his words will forestall an unpleasant row, but who also doubts that such an outcome is likely. He'd waited to begin speaking until they'd reached a secluded bend in the footpath meandering through the juniper and cedar forest that surrounded the train station. Malena's intervention had prevented a scene on the train platform; but, from Tanya's manner as they walked together in the forest, Hilary concluded that Malena had merely succeeded in postponing, rather than obviating, unpleasantness. Now he faced Tanya with the depressed resolution of a man resigned to be singed with fire-hot pokers for a higher cause. "We found Isak when we sent an emissary on a routine prisoner-exchange meeting," Hilary explained.

Whatever Hilary had been expecting, Tanya's response wasn't it: her lips trembled, her breathing grew pronounced, and she brought her fingers to the corner of her mouth. "Is this true?"

"Yes, though I fear my overall report isn't happy." Hilary's entire appearance was grave, his face, voice and physical stance united to reinforce his awful message.

"They won't release him?" Tanya remembered von Lettow-Vorbeck saying that he'd take the mapmaker, and she grimaced. Of course the Germans wouldn't release Isak! They were going to force him to draw maps for them.

"No, that's not it. The Germans have no proper facilities for holding prisoners of war, and they're quite willing to send him home, but Colonel Meinertzhagen won't hear of it."

"What?" The German willingness to release Isak, and the British unwillingness to accept his return, flummoxed Tanya: both were incomprehensible.

"The standard condition of release is that the soldier will not participate any further in the war effort."

"Why that's fine!" Tanya cried. "We can go back to the coffee plantation and save this year's harvest." She checked herself before adding that, with Isak out of the war, the von Brantberg plantation had a chance of avoiding bankruptcy.

"Meinhertzhagen says no. He says Isak's too valuable to lose. Lord Delamere hasn't objected, I'm afraid. Whatever Isak's doing for them, it must be critical."

"But Isak can't do anything for them if he's in enemy custody," protested Tanya.

"Yes, but he won't always be in German hands, and when he's free, Colonel Meinertzhagen wants him back in the fight."

Tanya heaved a frustrated sigh at the density of this argument and looked upwards. The forest canopy admitted only a dappling of late afternoon sunlight. The effect contributed, she knew, to the camouflage of any leopards that might be dozing in the branches above her. Thickets – whether of argument or of foliage – held unseen danger, and she felt frightened when she faced Hilary again. "Why can't Colonel Meinertzhagen accept the condition and then return Isak to service once he's free?"

Hilary half-smiled, conveying – not amusement – but sadness. He looked away. "You're too much of a noblewoman not to know the answer to that question."

"I'm too much of a noblewoman to leave my husband in Moshi!" Tanya bridled. "Isak must go free. You said yourself that they have no facilities for prisoners."

"He'll go free. Colonel Meinertzhagen is betting on it."

"When?"

"When we capture Moshi."

"When will that be?"

"I can't give you a date, but it's inevitable. The Germans are outmanned and outgunned, and we control the Indian Ocean. They can't win."

"The British are outgeneraled and outmaneuvered, and von Lettow-Vorbeck commands the best *askari* troops in Africa. Everyone is saying so. Who's to say the Germans won't hold out for years?"

"The war can't go on long! It can't!" Without warning, Hilary was yelling. The vociferousness in his voice – so different from his tone until now – made Tanya flinch. As she recoiled, she almost thought that his eyes were blurring with tears. "We have to wait!" Hilary shouted. "All of us are waiting for salvation! Do you think you're the only one who suffers because of this war? That your sorrows are the only ones that matter? The war cannot go on without killing us all with misery and grief. Be patient and your grieving will abate. Isak will be freed. He at least *can* be freed. He is not in the grave."

"Not yet!" Tanya retorted, recovering her bravado after her initial surprise at Hilary's outburst. "I'll not wait until he's dead! If the British Army won't free him, I'll find a way myself. I'll not have him imprisoned interminably, suffering illness and hunger, until I am rending my garments because I listened to the advice of men cowardly and malign who are themselves no better than murderers! You," she bellowed, the familiarity of her theme heating her blood to a comfortable boil, "are the cause of this disaster! If you'd flown Isak out of Maktau he would not be a prisoner right now! You dare come to me now with this sorry story of military feebleness, when you know that Isak's safety would have been assured had you not been impotent —"

Her tirade ended in a scream. Tanya was not generally scared of wild animals, but snakes are shy of humans, and she hadn't met one before.

This specimen was long, longer than she could fathom (in fact, it was sixteen feet). It had an exploratory tongue that shot from between its fangs to take measure of the environment. Its head was diamond-shaped, and its markings would have been the envy of any soldier in need of camouflage gear: olive, tan and brown splotches arranged to interact with the play of smattered sunlight so as to render the snake virtually imperceptible. So effective was its disguise that the snake had been slithering between where Tanya and Hilary stood for some time before either had noticed it. Indeed, Tanya only registered it because Hilary had lifted his foot to stroke the snake's back with his sole. Had she not eaten Kamau's cake, Tanya would have fainted at the sight.

"What are you doing?" Tanya squeaked once her scream had faded. She'd jumped back and was considering fleeing. Prodding the snake, as Hilary was doing, seemed a worse strategy than any other she could imagine.

"It's a python," Hilary murmured, looking up. "Not poisonous."

Tanya once again had the idea that Hilary's eyes were tear-filled. Tanya opened and shut her mouth without speaking. Her anger had not so much been spent, as replaced – wholly and precipitously – with uncertainty.

Hilary looked down at the python. It was muscling its way through the underbrush in search of a hare or dik dik, the protagonist of its own hunt, the human drama around it of no interest. Some quality in the snake's indifference emboldened Hilary to speak. "Did you hear about Ypres, Tanya?" he choked.

She swallowed. "Belgium?" she asked in a small voice.

He nodded, eyes fixed python-wards. "It's nothing like the fighting we're doing here," he managed eventually in a strained voice. "In Europe, it's like shoveling men into an exploding volcano. It sucks them in, and they dissolve in the heat and the lava and the ash." Hilary stopped because his voice was trembling; after a pause, he continued in a whisper, almost to himself:

> The many men, so beautiful!
> And they all dead did lie:
> And a thousand thousand slimy things
> Lived on; and so did I.

Unable to see Hilary's face, Tanya reflexively looked where he was gazing as if the focus of his attention might offer clues to his facial expression. Drops of water were now splashing on the snake's back. They glinted as they caught a sprinkle of sunlight, and then dissipated, burnishing the sheen of the python's smooth scales.

"Thomas Gordon was killed last week at Ypres. I received word today. My middle brother."

Tanya's mind was empty of words. Impelled to express her condolences, finding herself without speech, she would have stepped forward to embrace Hilary, but the snake was still operating between them. She jostled her brain to produce a consoling phrase, but no verbiage seemed adequate to the circumstances.

Then her body moved without her conscious control and almost without her awareness. She stepped forward, towards the python. She stepped again, closer. And again, a smaller step this time. Another step, higher than the others, took her over the snake and landed her beneath Hilary's bowed head.

The snake behind her, consciousness restored itself to her actions. Encircling Hilary's chest, her hands on his back, she coaxed him to her. When his arms responded, coming to life constricting her shoulders, she found words. "I love you."

* * *

The sun was setting, and Kamau was readying supper, when Tanya and Hilary emerged from the forest and seated themselves next to Malena around the campfire. Tanya introduced Hilary as her companion from her school days in Paris and explained that he'd missed the last train back to Nairobi. Malena commiserated, saying that she'd pitched her tent next to Tanya's twenty days ago, and that Hilary could use it tonight; she'd sleep in Tanya's tent.

Tanya hadn't eaten dinner for twenty days, but tonight she was hungry. Kamau was unearthing a pot that he'd buried over hot coals, in which a peppercorn-crusted impala fillet had been roasted with potatoes and carrots from Malena's farm. As Tanya had been insufficiently motivated to shoot game for some days, Hassan had taken up the task, using

Tanya's rifle and going out a half hour before dawn to avoid being seen by *mzungus*.

As they ate, Hilary raved about Kamau's cooking skills, and Malena thanked the good Lord for Tanya's resurgent appetite. After these preliminaries, Tanya reported on Isak's situation to the assembled party. Kamau was worried, knowing – as he did – the amounts of food necessary to sate Isak's gargantuan appetite. Hassan, too, expressed concern about Isak's welfare if too long deprived of outlets for certain of his vices. Malena, alone, opined that Isak would triumph, relatively unscathed, because the good Lord was with him.

To Tanya's assertion that she would "do something" to free Isak, the group's reaction was mixed. Malena was skeptical and advised Tanya to leave rescue operations to the British Army. Tanya riposted with some characterizations of the British Army that Malena would have condemned, had she not taken the broad view that the good Lord put such words into the English language for a reason. Hassan and Kamau were guardedly supportive of the idea of a civilian rescue mission, provided that the details were sound. Tanya, however, could provide no details. She admitted that she didn't know what she was going to do – what she could do – except that she trusted the problem would admit an answer after a night's sleep. Hilary didn't comment.

The night's sleep on which Tanya had pinned her expectations was long in coming, however. Tanya lay on her back, staring upwards. Her body was asserting itself in an unusual manner: the arches of her feet contracted achingly and, while shivers girdled her waist, sweat dampened her neck and armpits. The prickles and itches of the blanket were unbearable in her over-sensitized state, and Malena's untroubled breathing beside her heightened Tanya's sense of restlessness. She tried to subdue her physical discomfort with focused strategic thinking about Isak, but every cerebral exertion failed quickly for lack of coherence. She needed the discipline of conversation to marshal her thoughts, she realized. If insomnia was going to deprive her of the benefits of subconscious thinking, then discussion was necessary to spur a consciously-reasoned solution.

"Malena," she whispered. "Malena, darling, are you sleeping?"

The silence that followed this inquiry satisfied Tanya on two points. First, if she wanted a conversation partner, she'd need to look elsewhere. Second, Malena wouldn't know that Tanya had gone to Hilary's tent.

"Hilary, are you awake?" Tanya murmured, outside his tent.

"How could I possibly be asleep?" came his immediate reply.

Tanya heard movement inside the tent. The moon was half-full, but clouds had occupied its territory, leaving the night a suitable veil for stealthy doings. Still, when Hilary pulled aside the tent flap, Tanya had no trouble seeing his face; it shone with the inexplicable light shared by angels and lovers. "Thank God you escaped that Mother Superior," he breathed, drawing her into the tent and onto the bedding beside him.

Once installed under the blanket, with the love of his life nestling against him, Hilary paused. His decade-spanning desire for Tanya, as well as the merciless vicissitudes which he'd endured in the past day, made him hesitant. The intensity of his recent experiences had reduced his thoughts and emotions to the organizational state of bleached bones scattered by industrious hyenas across the savannah. He exerted himself to wiggle his toes to confirm that he was awake, and that Tanya's presence was real. He reminded himself not to make his old mistake of rushing, of leaping vastly ahead of her readiness.

Reaching out his right hand, he touched Tanya's lips and traced their outline carefully. The charge of her flesh blindsided him with a dearth of confidence. His hand began to tremble, and he moved it quickly to the curve of her waist. Her night dress felt thick under his palm. "I see you are guided by Mother Superior in the matter of sleeping garb," he joked anxiously. He himself was wearing a sleeveless, short-legged, cotton one-piece undergarment.

He felt the warmth of her smile and the surge of her breath. "It's cold at night."

"I haven't noticed," he replied softly.

Verifying his remark, his hand on her waist was emitting heat that seemed to have replaced the blood in Tanya's veins; she was sweating again. Her hips shifted in response to his hand, and she stiffened, attempting to hold herself aloof from her desire. She felt sure that if she reached for him, she would embarrass herself. Hilary, no doubt, as appropriate to a man of his handsomeness and vigor, had had the benefit of wide experience in honing his skills as a lover, but in respect of her own competencies in this area, Tanya possessed mostly misgivings. The strident oppositional tuggings of brain and body that she currently experienced made Tanya flush: she didn't know what to do and was rapidly panicking over the prospect of losing any semblance of dignity. "Hilary," she stammered, "tell me what you want from me."

Feeling her recede, he experienced a flash of compassion for them both: so much at stake, so nervous. Reminding himself again to restrain his impulse for speed, he transferred his right hand from her waist to her mid-back. Gently, he eased her closer. Caressing her back to relax her, he rested his right calf over her lower leg. "I want you to tell me again what you said in the forest," he whispered.

Taking his tenderness as an assurance against embarrassment, she breathed, and her body softened under his touch. This next step was one she knew how to take. "You mean when I accused you of complicity in Isak's capture?" Her humor was very dry.

"Not that part."

"I love you."

He inhaled prominently, more audibly than he'd intended. He realized that he hadn't trusted that she'd say it again. He hadn't entirely believed that she'd said it the first time. Heedless of his precautions about pacing, unable to parse the social protocols relating to this important question, Hilary exhaled, "Will you marry me, Tanya?" Her significant delay caused a spasm of anxiety to choke him and, when it passed, he whispered, "I'm sorry, I'm so sorry. I'm always moving too fast. Please don't – don't," he raised himself a little on his left forearm and moved his right hand from her back to her shoulder, "hate me because I answered your question like an honest man. I want you to be my wife, that's what I want from you. Do you want that, too?" He regretted the question as soon as it had shot from his mouth, polluting the air between them as if with black smoke. He did not believe he could survive if she said no.

"Yes."

"What?"

"Yes. I love you, and I want . . . to . . . marry you."

She hadn't said, "and I want to marry you, *but*," but the caveat was present. Hilary studied her face with frantic energy. Given the dim optics and the angle of Tanya's head, however, he saw mainly her hair. She reached out her left hand and laid it on his chest, but he was so agitated with his conviction of impending rejection that the gesture felt like the eagle ripping open Prometheus. He squeezed his eyes shut. "What do you want from me?" he gasped.

"I want you to help me free Isak," she said. A timbre of confidence in her voice made him open his eyes. She continued, "I can't leave him when he's a prisoner of war. It's not noble. I am his wife, and I owe him loyalty, and I cannot abandon him in his time of need. You'd despise me if I did. You wouldn't want a wife who could do that to her husband. I'm not at liberty to marry you while he's at the mercy of the enemy. And I can't," here her voice cracked, "he's my husband." Her voice became progressively more muffled, but Hilary could discern, "I love him. I can't stop loving him tonight any more than I could empty a watering hole in a single visit. It takes time for a well to evaporate." Her body was shaking now, and his chest was wet with her tears. Automatically, he pulled her closer, embracing her and moving his right leg higher so that it covered her hip. "Can you understand that?" she sobbed.

"Yes."

"I don't want to hurt you or lose you, but I can't hide that I still . . . ," she faded out, bereft of courage; then, steeling herself, she finished, "love him. I can't abandon a man I love to the enemy. It wouldn't be noble to lie to you about that."

"I understand."

"It's not a sham marriage!" she cried with newly-emergent indignation, uncovered in the course of her crying jag. "You're always mocking me about my intentions towards men with titles!"

"I'm sorry, forgive me, Titania," he murmured, kissing her forehead. "I understand. I'm sorry I doubted your marriage. I know you better than that, you're too staunch in love to be anything but true."

"Are you angry? About what I said? About Isak?"

"No." He stroked her hair. "No, you are right to say it." Though Hilary had nurtured his yearning for Tanya over a ten-year span, he had not during that duration been without his own amorous adventures, and he'd loved some of those women. Had Tanya returned to his life during any of those affairs, he would have found himself in the self-same position that was now causing her agony. He could not fault her for her love of her husband, nor doubt that her love for himself was genuine and abiding. The ability to love anew and afresh was one of humanity's most redeeming characteristics, and he could only muse that its emergence in wartime was a blessing. Drying her tears with his fingertips, he whispered soothing comforts until her sobs subsided.

She asked, meekly, "You'll help me free him?"

"Yes. Yes, I'll do whatever I can. I tried to fly him out of Maktau, you know. He refused to go. But I tried, I tried everything I could think of, save disclosing your confidence."

"I was wrong to blame you, Hilary. I'm sorry. I owe you many thanks for your kindnesses." Relief and exhaustion flooded her simultaneously, and she rested her head against his chest.

Sternly, she reminded herself that she couldn't fall asleep. She needed to wake up next to Malena; never mind the consequences if Hassan or Kamau trundled by to wake Hilary and discovered her in his tent. Besides, one critical question for Hilary remained.

Lifting her head, she asked, "Before I marry you, Hilary, tell me why you love me. You could have anyone. That's why I was with Grigory in Paris. It was unbearable that every woman wanted you, and only Grigory wanted me —"

"— Not only Grigory, Titania —"

"— and I can't see why it should be that I'm your enduring love. I'm so short, and I gain too much weight, and I burst into tears too often, like now, and I have a bad temper —"

"— Oh Tanya, be quiet."

"But why love me?"

Hilary paused before asking her gently, "Have you ever questioned your place in history? Here you are, doing man's work in the Great War. Risking your life, shooting guns, escaping the enemy, commanding men, *rescuing* men. Have you ever said, how did this happen, I'm unworthy of this? Have you ever said, I'm unfit for the burdens of history?"

Tanya sniffled. She wasn't sure she understood Hilary's point. "I say it all the time."

"Alright, but you do what's necessary anyway. You don't let those questions stop you."

"I cry a lot," she mumbled.

Hilary laughed softly and pulled Tanya to him. "Did Queen Margot cry? Joan of Arc? Queen Victoria?"

"No, I don't think so."

Hilary laughed a little louder and rubbed her nose with his own. "Crying doesn't exclude you from greatness. And, that, Tanya is what you are. You are noble in the purest, most ideal, most Platonic sense. You were born for greatness every bit as much as a queen is. Some people find themselves caught in the machinery of history, and they fail its demands. They treat the whole situation like an accident. They think history can't envelop them because they're just ordinary people. You have never felt this way, but many people do. Me, for example."

"Oh Hilary, you mock me."

"No, I don't, it's true. I am not a great man. I like to think I'm a good man and a competent man, but in the end I'm ordinary. Left to myself, I'd be only too happy if history never knew my name. But I haven't been left to myself. You riled my heart ten years ago, and I've never forgotten the experience, and you renew it every time I meet you. It's like a calling, and answering the call makes me more and better and worthier. You can't understand this, this effect you have on me, but believe me: how can I not love you? It's all I can do not to worship you."

Silence governed Tanya for several moments. Regaining possession of her speech faculties, she demurred, "Hilary Gordon, you are trying to make love with me."

He laughed, shook his head admiringly, and then inhaled seriously. "Swear you'll marry me, Tanya. Once Isak is free."

"I swear," she whispered. "You have my word. I will marry you."

Then he kissed her.

* * *

The sun was rising over Kijabe, its beams cajoling the still night-heavy clouds into a more frolicsome disposition, when Tanya, Malena, Hilary and Hassan sat around the campfire, eating eggs and drinking tea.

Kamau joined them with a calabash of porridge. "You have slept well, Memsabu?" he asked.

"Very well thank you," she replied without looking up from her eggs.

"That is very, very good. What is the plan then?" he inquired, wiping his mouth.

"Plan?"

"Freeing Bwana Isak from the German foes," Kamau said, puzzled that she would need him to explain his meaning.

Now Tanya looked up and couldn't wholly suppress her guilty expression. She'd expended much effort enlisting Hilary's support for rescuing Isak, but they'd exhausted their energies before discussing concrete steps. "My sleep wasn't what I'd expected. I wasn't rewarded with a plan," Tanya mumbled, resuming her absorbing focus on her eggs.

Kamau and Hassan exchanged a look. Hilary caught their non-verbal communication and frowned. He was frustrated by the amount of discretion necessary to keep secrets from native servants; they seemed to discover everything, no matter how stringent the precautions taken.

But then Hassan cleared his throat and spoke, and Hilary wondered if he'd misconstrued the glance he'd witnessed: "I, and Kamau, have a plan to propose, Memsahib," Hassan said.

"Is it like your plan to extort money from the Carrier Corps deserters and get me hanged?" Tanya asked.

"No, it is different from that plan, but it is related," Hassan answered.

Tanya almost replied that the plan sounded rotten already, but instead she relented, "What's the plan?"

"We were discussing this difficulty of bringing liberation to Bwana Isak," Kamau began, "and we think the example of Lekishon is excellent."

"How promising!" Malena bubbled. "Lekishon is such a dear soul, a true lamb of God."

Tanya restrained herself again, this time from saying that lambs like Lekishon were well sacrificed to Yahweh. "What's the plan? Is it going to get me hanged?" she asked, reiterating her main concern.

"No, Memsahib," Hassan assured her.

"Imprisoned?"

"Not by the British," Hassan answered.

Before Tanya could ascertain by whom she could be imprisoned, should this still-unrevealed plan be implemented, Kamau cut in: "This plan cannot fail because it is like our work to kill the lioness, the bad lioness that marked Memsabu Malena," he clarified. "Memsabu Malena struck the lioness with the whip, I with the pot, Hassan with the paraffin lamp, and you with the bullet, Memsabu. Like the lioness, the German enemy cannot withstand our united attack."

"That's fine," Tanya remarked, "but what's the plan?"

"The great Somali chiefs say, people united can repair even a rip in the sky," Hassan advised.

"Exactly!" Kamau agreed. "This plan will repair the rip in our lives, the absence of Bwana Isak, because we will all be united, Memsabu, Hassan, me, Memsabu Malena, Dionysus, even you, Bwana Hilary," Kamau added, turning. "You will help in this plan?"

"Of course," Hilary assented gamely.

"Wait a moment!" Tanya insisted. "Before Bwana Hilary agrees to anything, tell us, Hassan, Kamau: what is this plan?"

* * *

Hilary and Kamau departed on the 9:30 a.m. train. Their destination was the von Brantberg coffee plantation. After attending to his business there, Hilary would return to Maktau, where the Bleriot XI was parked. They would all meet again when he landed the aeroplane at the rendezvous point, six days hence, on All Hallow's Eve.

Tanya and Hassan watched the train's disappearance from the platform. His eyes fixed on the rapidly shrinking caboose, Hassan offered another pearl from the vast supply of the great Somali chiefs: "For every good man, there is a better man."

Mentally scrutinizing this proverb and finding it displeasing, Tanya set her jaw. "Very true," she conceded, "but remember that the camel thinking it walks on a dune, may still fall in quicksand."

Tanya's adage lacked the lineage of Hassan's, since she'd made it up only moments before and, in truth, she wasn't sure what it meant. Nonetheless, this questionable provenance did not appear to diminish the respect with which Hassan viewed the phrase. He raised his eyebrows and remarked, "It is so. This business of deciding who is the better man is a road with many pitfalls."

Tanya turned away, mildly annoyed. "Come, Hassan, we have much work."

NINETEEN

The mountain reared above them. The Moshi fort hunched on the south-eastern slopes of Mount Kilimanjaro, and they huddled beyond the sight-lines of the fort's guards. They'd been traveling since 4 a.m., but now – a half hour after dawn – the colobus monkeys were waking, crowding the air with trilling vocalizations. They sat beneath the monkey sounds, beneath the volcano, waiting.

"They" included Tanya and Malena, who had stoutly refused to stay home. Their raid on the Moshi fort was going to be dangerous, Tanya had warned, and Malena must not imperil herself needlessly. Malena had rejected Tanya's arguments peremptorily. Malena was not a woman to abandon her friends in distress. Anyway, she pointed out, the more women in their group, the more likely the Germans would be to believe their ruse.

Malena's point had merit, especially in light of the way she and Tanya were costumed. For the first time since the war's outbreak, Tanya and Malena were both wearing dresses. Tanya's was pink, with a white lace collar, cap sleeves, and a fitted bodice that laced up the back. She wore a yellow straw hat tied with a pink ribbon and white kid boots with low heels. As much as Tanya loved finery for concerts, balls and banquets, her outfit was currently causing her incessant worry. What if the upcoming ordeal demanded that she run, fight, shoot or ride a mule? More importantly, would anyone believe her in this get-up? After three months spent practically in the same safari suit and pair of boots, she wasn't sure she looked credible in a dress anymore. (Tanya needn't have worried; to everyone else, she looked like a belle.)

Malena wore a sober grey dress with a high neck, long sleeves, buttons down the fitted bodice, and a wide skirt. She wore a white straw hat and flat-heeled black boots. Far from entertaining anxieties of the sort bedeviling Tanya, Malena experienced a boost of courage from her attire. Her dress made her feel like she was in church, and she had complete faith that nothing untoward could happen in church.

Rounding out the "they" were Hassan, Kamau, and the twenty-three Carrier Corps deserters who Tanya had agreed to employ when she'd left Lord Delamere's camp on the Narosera River. All were outfitted in the most expensive clothes they'd ever worn. Hassan had on a maroon tunic brocaded with gold and silver thread and a matching turban decorated with a cockade of iridescent green feathers. As for the others, Tanya, Malena and Hassan had worked ceaselessly, taking up hems, taking in waistlines, shortening sleeves and adding darts to shirts and trousers that had belonged to Erik and Isak. Tanya and Malena had appropriated the clothing and tailored it to fit Kamau and the ex-Carrier Corps porters. Shoes, too, had been commandeered for the mission, again courtesy of the wardrobes of Isak and Erik (with the exception of Hassan, who was never without his camel-hide sandals). Even Dionysus was festooned in a red leather collar with a smart silver buckle.

The new clothing and shoes were essential, both to convey an impression of respectability, and to give the men pockets in which to hide guns. All the men – natives though they were – were armed. (Hassan was wrong when he'd claimed that the plan couldn't get Tanya hanged.)

Tanya had been astounded that Hassan could "get" twenty-five pistols, but he assured her that marzipan, whipping cream and raspberry jam were about the only items he would need more than a day to "get" in Kijabe.

Tanya had been equally impressed by the former Carrier Corps porters' participation in Hassan's and Kamau's plan. Contrary to her willingness in August to staff the supply caravan with her farm workers, Tanya in

October could not spare twenty-three of her staff: they were all harvesting coffee. In fact, Tanya needed the ex-Carrier Corps porters for the harvest, too; but, as Isak's rescue mission required personnel, Tanya agreed that the porters were the best recruits: they knew nothing about harvesting coffee, but they'd had exposure to warfare.

Still, knowing something of their trauma in the Carrier Corps, Tanya hadn't expected the porters to volunteer to return to the martial fray. Especially as the porters had never met Isak, staking their lives for the sake of an unknown *mzungu* prisoner hardly struck Tanya as the sort of proposition that would appeal.

But Hassan and Kamau had rightly supposed that three aspects of the adventure would sway the porters. First, the opportunity to do the *mzungu* a bit of no good – even if he was German, and not British – could not be let pass. Second, Tanya had risked her life for the porters (and saved them the fees for their freedom), and they were honor bound to return the service. Finally, none of the porters was going to decline the chance to shoot a gun.

Despite her sense of genuine awe and gratitude to the ex-Carrier Corps porters, Tanya had been skeptical about arming them. When Hassan and Kamau had described their plan at Kijabe, Tanya had objected that a man with a gun is only as useful as his ability to shoot, and a platoon of men with guns is only as effective as their ability to operate as a unit. The British Army's attempts to coordinate with "irregulars" was enough evidence of the debilitating disorder that untrained volunteers (herself included) could foment. Tanya was wary of ignoring this lesson.

Hilary had assuaged her concerns by proposing that he go to the von Brantberg plantation and train the men for three days – intensively and rudimentarily to be sure, but sufficiently to allow them to function for purposes of their rescue operation. Though still doubtful, Tanya had assented to Hilary's suggestion, and she'd been relieved when he'd found that most of the men already knew how to shoot, having learned on the sly.

Thus had they spent the relentless, sleepless six days since Hassan and Kamau had disclosed their plan: gathering and sewing costumes, smuggling guns, training to be soldiers, traveling by train from Nairobi to Tsavo, and journeying by foot to Moshi, avoiding by means of skill and prayer Germans and British alike. Upon arriving at their rendezvous, they'd stashed their safari supplies in the underbrush and changed into their costumes. Now they sat, with the thicket of Kilimanjaro's rainforest on the slopes above, and the 7 a.m. sun wearing a halo to remind them that gazing upon a new day is a glorious gift.

They were waiting, taking their last deep breaths before diving off a cliff. They were waiting for Hilary.

Kamau nervously counted the bird calls as they waited. He reminded himself that their safari had begun at 4 a.m., before the birds had awakened. He reasoned that their group was now resting on a safari already begun, rather than about to commence a new safari. But the bird chirps nonetheless aroused his anxiety. Persistently, Kamau's instincts agitated for aborting their enterprise. Even clutching the charm he'd purchased from the witch doctor – for success and protection on their mission – didn't placate his qualms.

But Hilary's arrival distracted him. The buzz of the Bleriot XI out-trilled the colobus monkeys before any in their party spied it. Then, low in the sky, the aeroplane emerged from the north-east. The porters, discipline forgotten, were on their feet, shouting, smiling and waving at the mechanical locust-bird. Even Kamau and Hassan were enthralled by the plane, Kamau joining the porters in their reverie, and Hassan rising to peer inquisitively at the Bleriot XI. As Hilary brought the machine to a bumpy landing a hundred meters from them, Kamau and the porters surged forward, thronging the plane to touch its curious frame and to clasp their hands around its intrepid pilot.

"How miraculous that after so many years of human existence, the good Lord has seen fit to grace us with the power of flight," Malena exclaimed, almost to herself.

Hassan and Kamau had deemed the plane necessary to fly Bwana Isak to safety as soon as he was pried from German claws. Although neither Hassan nor Kamau knew Bwana Isak's exact role in the British Army, they – like Hilary – had inferred that it must be extremely special, and they didn't want to allow any chance that German troops could recapture Isak as he fled Moshi.

Tanya had thought this aspect of the plan especially praiseworthy. So had the remainder of their "liberate Isak" party – except for Hilary. The idea that Hilary and Isak would make an airborne escape, while the remainder of the team – including two women (one of whom was his future wife) – would have to scramble on foot across open plain – possibly with Germans in pursuit – struck Hilary as monstrous. He'd been outvoted.

Now, surrounded by jubilant men, Hilary advanced towards where Tanya and Malena sat. His hair was raffishly disarranged from having pulled off his flying cap, and he wore black knee-high boots, white riding trousers, and a navy riding jacket. Notwithstanding the civilian garb, he looked to Tanya like a triumphant conqueror in a victory procession. Dionysus raced forward, tail wagging, to welcome Hilary, and Tanya longed to follow. She'd had not a moment alone with Hilary since their night in his tent. Preventing herself from rushing now into his arms required effort that caused her physical pain.

As he drew near, Hassan called out, "Bwana Hilary, have you flown just now over the great mountain?"

Hilary smiled broadly. "I wish I could, Hassan. But I don't dare take my baby above 8,500 feet, and Mount Kilimanjaro's a good deal higher than that. You can't fly near a crater, anyway. Craters have their own air current systems that can suck a plane in and crash it. Someday, though, maybe in my lifetime even, planes will be powerful enough, and humans will finally know the grandeur of looking down on Kilimanjaro." Hilary shifted his gaze from the mountain to his lady. "Well, shall we storm the barricades?"

Tanya hesitated. "You've received the good word?"

"Yes. This morning's intelligence bulletin reports that von Lettow-Vorbeck is in Dar-es-Salaam with Governor Schnee," Hilary related. "Mind you, the intelligence bulletins are as inaccurate as the old Army map of Tsavo. Brigadier-General Stewart typically ignores them, says Meinertzhagen's an ass. But that's the word – good, if it's right. Onward then?"

* * *

His tongue lapped between her lips, her moan charred him with lust, his hands pawed her bodice, her breasts swelled against his jacket buttons, his pelvis pinned her against the mountain's slope, her breathe ransacked his heart, and their minds pulsed, if I never kiss you again, if I never kiss you again . . .

It lasted twenty seconds. But of course I will kiss you again, Tanya and Hilary consoled themselves, as they spent another two seconds dusting themselves off. Before they could be missed, they reattached themselves to the tail end of their brave band setting out for its mission at Moshi.

Casting a glance over his shoulder, Hassan saw Bwana Hilary supporting Memsahib with a hand to her elbow, as she attempted the challenging task of walking across the bush in her heeled kid boots.

* * *

Although the Germans had clear cut land for the Moshi fort, the encircling forest largely concealed it. Further masking the German base was a barbed wire fence that effectively hid from view the interior. As their rescue party strode within the fort's limited sight-lines, a metallic clanging thrummed from the fence. The foul noise was produced by running a stick along garlands of empty tins that had been strung on the fence like dissonant wind chimes. Dionysus, especially, seemed to find the cacophony grating, and he growled threateningly.

"The *askaris* have sent up the alarm," Hilary observed grimly.

"Hassan, the white flag," Tanya ordered. Remembering her interaction with Captain Tafel and his men, and deeming a dirty dish towel insufficient for their purposes, Tanya had torn up her bed linen to make their flag of surrender.

Hassan produced the banner, and Tanya and Malena unfurled it between them, as they hurried in front of their group, Tanya stumbling repeatedly because of her heels. Although the white flag prevented the Germans from sending out the cavalry to trounce the oncoming visitors, rifle barrels jutted through the barbed wire fence.

Malena seemed to sag at the wall of guns aimed at them, but she bucked herself by muttering prayers under her breath. Sensing her need, Dionysus trotted protectively beside her, the white flag fluttering occasionally across his muzzle.

Tanya squinted at the ground. She couldn't allow her concentration to waver. At the slightest widening of her tunnel vision, she knew she would collapse in a mélange of terror and desire, roused by the good-luck kiss she'd shared with Hilary. Behind Tanya, Hassan murmured, "Your contempt must be like a blow that shatters their teeth." Tanya nodded almost imperceptibly.

And they were at the gate of the fort.

Tanya called out greetings in German until a square-shaped peephole in the gate creaked open. Tanya could see the eyes and nose of a German soldier who returned her salutation with an angry demand in German that she state her purpose. He paused when Tanya shimmied the white flag under her chin and asked for Lieutenant-Colonel Paul Emil von Lettow-Vorbeck.

"He's not here," the soldier barked. "Who are you?"

Tanya hoped that her relief – palpable to her – was invisible to the soldier. The intelligence bulletin hadn't failed them. Of course, Tanya cautioned herself, the soldier could always be lying. But his denial of von Lettow-Vorbeck's presence was a promising start.

"Is Captain Tafel here then?" Tanya inquired politely.

The soldier's eyes widened. "Who are you? Captain Tafel is dead!"

Tanya emitted a mortified exclamation and covered her mouth. She realized that Captain Tafel must have been killed during the British raid on Longido. "My condolences, kind sir," Tanya said, "Captain Tafel was a friend and a fine soldier. The Fatherland has lost a devoted servant." And, however much Tanya genuinely regretted the passing of a man who, for whatever his human failings, had permitted her safe passage through the Ingito Hills, and who, after all, had died in a mindless slaughter orgy that was none of his making, she was buoyed by the news that Captain Tafel wasn't at Moshi. With von Lettow-Vorbeck away and Captain Tafel dead, no one at Moshi knew her true identity. With growing confidence, Tanya unholstered the smile that had done so much to unhinge Captain Tafel and continued in a seductive voice, "But I haven't yet gratified you with an answer to your question. I'm Frau Kermit Roosevelt, but please call me Tanya. This is my husband, Herr Roosevelt." As she spoke, Tanya pulled Hilary into view of the German soldier.

"How do you do," said Hilary stiffly, leaning into the peephole and speaking English with what he imagined was an American accent, but which (to the tutored ear) sounded merely theatrical.

In response to the German soldier's blinking confusion, Tanya explained in German, "He's American and sadly their educational system is too pathetic to teach them foreign languages. Not that German is a foreign language to me! I grew up in Schleswig-Holstein. We both did. Me and my sister, Fräulein Malena." And here Tanya gave Hilary a push and tugged Malena into view.

Malena waved emphatically and beamed energetically.

Tanya rambled on, "That's her way of saying hello, poor thing. She practically died of scarlet fever in her childhood and is mute, which is why we – me and Herr Roosevelt, of course – have to take care of her. And these," Tanya hurried Malena to one side and gestured to the twenty-five African men, "are our dear, loyal, hard-working and dedicated farm workers."

The German soldier hadn't ceased blinking since Tanya's charm offensive had commenced, and now he continued blinking for some moments. When he finally spoke, he made clear his preference for review: "You are Frau Roosevelt."

"Yes."

"From Schleswig-Holstein?"

"Yes. Naturally we fought with the Germans in the Schleswig-Holstein wars."

"But you married an American."

"You mustn't fault a man for the place of his birth, especially since he and his countrymen elect such good leaders that keep them neutral in European wars."

"And you and your husband have brought your farm workers to Fort Moshi."

"Yes, me, Herr Roosevelt, and my sister, Fräulein Malena."

"Why?" the soldier inquired, honing in on the source of his confusion.

"To contribute to the cause, of course! Our farm workers want nothing more than to serve as porters for the German Army, and we – as the

Fatherland's most faithful friends – want nothing more than to support our farm workers, whatever the sacrifice to our farm."

The solider squinted suspiciously. "We know all the German plantation owners around Kilimanjaro. I've never seen any of you before."

"But we're not German plantation owners," she smiled, "we're friends of the Fatherland. And our farm is in British East Africa. Please don't hold that against us. You must know there's a community of Germans and supporters of the Fatherland in British East Africa. Sometimes it happens: the land you cultivate isn't under the political regime you favor. Having grown up in Schleswig-Holstein, I'm used to it. But we've come such a long and arduous way to help the cause. Don't turn us away now."

"Wait here," he snapped, and the square door of the peephole slammed shut.

During the ensuing wait, none of Tanya's rescuing marauders spoke, but the air was far from silent. One either side, and above them, they heard the sound of rifles being cocked, of *askaris* clearing their throats, and of shouts echoing throughout the camp in search of a Major Kraut.

Dionysus, who'd seated himself during Tanya's discourse with the German soldier, perceived the danger and whimpered. Malena slipped her hand into Tanya's, a silent plea for courage. Tanya squeezed her hand.

When the small square door-within-a-door opened again, two ice blue eyes appraised Tanya with skeptical curiosity. Tanya smiled accommodatingly.

"Frau Roosevelt?"

"You may call me Tanya," she said, reaching into her skirt pocket. "Your esteemed Lieutenant-Colonel does." Through the peephole door, Tanya handed the man her signed portrait of von Lettow-Vorbeck.

He took it and read the inscription in a mumble-whisper: "Dearest Tanya, Your charm, wit, intelligence and social graces have rescued me from many a restless hour, and for that noble service I remain, Your faithful servant, Paul." He looked up. The ice had melted. "Major Kraut," the soldier introduced himself.

"Most enchanted."

"Lieutenant Merensky says that you've brought porters."

"We have. May we entrust them to your care?"

"Kindly allow me a moment." The little square door closed softly and, after the rusty thumps of bolts being thrown, the gate wobbled open on loud, old hinges.

Two *askaris* held the gate. Next to them stood Major Kraut, identifiable by his eyes, and Lieutenant Merensky, recognizable by his sullen expression. Behind them stood a platoon of *askaris*, rifles at the ready. All gazed with surprise at the assembled party before them.

Appealingly dressed Frau Roosevelt stood front and center, with her cute, mute sister behind her on her left, and her abominably-accented husband behind her on her right. Behind them was a chap out of *Arabian Nights*, with a fancy maroon turban and tunic. And behind him was a goldmine of porter labor. The group's overall formation took the shape of a pyramid, with Frau Roosevelt at its apex, and ranks of porters composing its base. The effect made Major Kraut feel like a Pharoh.

While the porters represented a splendid bounty, the real good fortune (to Major Kraut's mind) was the occasion of visitors. Life at the Moshi fort was boring. Waking dozing *askaris* on guard duty, seeing off the daily raiding parties, keeping *askaris* busy with earthworks construction, participating in the same tiresome conversations about telecommunications failures and supply line inadequacies, updating the war diary and filling in the necessary administrative forms – these activities dominated Major Kraut's day. The job was unendurable for a man of Major Kraut's disposition.

Fundamentally, Major Kraut saw himself as a ladies' man. A tall, lanky blonde, roughly mangled by his life lived outdoors, Major Kraut's one complaint about army life in general and war in particular was the paucity of ladies. Oh he tried to find satisfaction in the social pleasures of male company, but the effect of a man gazing worshipfully up at him provoked a wholly different response than when a woman adopted the same stance. Frau Roosevelt and Fräulein Malena were gazing upon him that way now.

"*Willkommen*," he breathed, sweeping his arms out.

* * *

"Our chef works miracles with zebra," Major Kraut confided, as they all stood respectfully in the kitchen, watching a frazzled German cook hack a zebra carcass with a meat cleaver. They'd passed the zebra's skin drying on a line outside the mess when they'd entered.

To reward Tanya and her party for their noble actions, Major Kraut was giving them a tour of Moshi fort. Accompanying them were Lieutenant Merensky and a dozen *askaris*, who stood respectfully at the back of the group with an air of forced tolerance, acquired through experience: justly proud of the Fatherland's military achievement in conditions of extreme scarcity, Major Kraut rarely missed an opportunity to play tour guide to visitors.

Major Kraut continued: "And the sweet potato bread that emerges from this kitchen makes one ask: is wheat necessary? The porters will be most invigorated by the food we serve. We treat our porters like humans, not like the British," Major Kraut boasted. "Look, hippo fat!" he gestured to jars lining the kitchen shelves. "We extract it ourselves."

Tanya murmured breathily, inwardly glad that Kamau knew no German and couldn't engage Major Kraut on any food-related inquiries. Malena smiled mutely, and Dionysus panted enthusiastically at the smell of meat. Hilary faded into the group to make less conspicuous his struggle to keep from laughing. Hassan, Kamau and the porters stood around bored; Major Kraut's German-language tour was of no use to them.

But on it went regardless: "We process coconuts to make benzol," Major Kraut declared with a level of pride suggesting that he personally had invented the procedure. They were clustered around von Lettow-Vorbeck's Chevrolet Classic Six, a blue vehicle with a black convertible roof, four doors and a six-cylinder engine. It was parked between four poles over which a thatched roof had been thrown to provide shade. The metal canisters containing the coconut bio-fuel were assembled in the corners of the structure. Gesturing to them, Major Kraut said, "Without benzol, the Lieutenant-Colonel's car might as well be a sofa. As you know, our petrol supplies are interfered with."

"The British embargo is a mere bagatelle in the face of German ingenuity," Tanya cooed. Malena goggled reverently. Behind Major Kraut's back, Dionysus urinated on the wheels of von Lettow-Vorbeck's car. Hassan eyed the car strategically, as if totaling the sums he could make from "renting" it, and Hilary seemed mentally to be comparing the Chevy with his Bleriot XI – to the Chevy's disadvantage. The remainder of the group wore a glazed look.

And: "The fabric for these bandages is woven from tree bark," Major Kraut crowed, as they packed into the infirmary tent. At a desk in the tent, a bearded German doctor was sleeping, face down on his hands, gentle snores drifting upwards. The tent had two beds for invalids, both empty. "Iodine and quinine we make from plants," Major Kraut added, puffing out his chest.

"This infirmary is so excellent that it positively tempts soldiers to be ill," Tanya declared. Malena fluttered her eyelashes appreciatively. Dionysus yawned, Hilary scuffed his boots on the infirmary floor, and everyone else attempted to suppress their antsiness.

And: "The men sleep under mosquito nets!" They were funneled into a row of soldier's tents on the camp grounds. Major Kraut had thrown back a tent flap to reveal mosquito nets slung from the tent's crossbar. "Thanks to these nets, I've had only eight bouts of malaria since I arrived in German East Africa, five years ago," Major Kraut revealed.

"These resources devoted to soldiers' health are extraordinary," Tanya applauded.

"The Kaiser cares!" Major Kraut beamed.

Malena shyly shook Major Kraut's hand, and Major Kraut suggestively raised a debonair eyebrow.

Dionysus began to feel cramped, squeezed among humans crammed into an aisle between rows of tents. Looking for some breathing room, he wended his way underfoot. Simultaneously, Hilary – who was genuinely interested, mosquito nets for troops being a necessary that the British Army neglected to provide – weaved his way forward through the crowd. The resulting dog-trips-man collision sent Hilary sailing into Tanya's back. He caught himself by gripping both her shoulders, a position that allowed him to whisper unobtrusively in her ear.

"Major Kraut," Tanya asked brightly, interrupting him in what seemed to be an eyebrow aria, serenading the silent Malena, "I am most interested to see the defeated enemy. Have you any prisoners of war here?"

* * *

But Isak wasn't among them. As the British had recently completed a prisoner exchange, the population of captured enemy at Moshi had been dramatically culled. Only four prisoners of war remained. Tanya watched them miserably digging a ditch, with one *askari* training a rifle on them and another pacing back and forth with a hippopotamus-hide whip. The prisoners were of average build, thin, shirtless and sun scorched. One bore a whip scar on his back, a jagged, scabrous, violet welt. The prisoners glanced up at Major Kraut and his tour group, but their ghoulish gazes didn't linger, and Tanya saw that their morale had collapsed.

Her own esprit was rapidly deflating. Isak didn't appear to be at Moshi. Hassan's and Kamau's plan had not budgeted for this contingency. Staving off panic, Tanya raced through scenarios. She could ask after her "neighboring plantation owner," Baron von Brantberg, who she'd heard had been taken captive. She could tell Hilary to take Major Kraut hostage until he disclosed Isak's whereabouts. She could inquire whether the fort had mapmaking facilities. Each of these possibilities she dismissed as too risky and impractical. They might have to leave without accomplishing their goal.

Then Tanya staggered. Major Kraut dashed forward to support her arm and, when she leaned against him for support, he commenced his suggestive eyebrow routine.

Tanya didn't notice. She was too absorbed in her thoughts. She had just realized that their company could not depart without accomplishing its goal: Major Kraut was expecting her to leave her twenty-five plantation employees with him; her band of would-be liberators wouldn't be able to leave without a fight.

"Prisoners oppress the joyous heart," Major Kraut pronounced, misdiagnosing the cause of Tanya's malaise. "Allow me to remove you to a happier ground. Even here, even in war, we soldiers must have our celebrations." Major Kraut caught Lieutenant Merensky's eye across their little crowd of tourists: "The officers' tent," he ordered.

* * *

At the entrance to the officers' tent, Lieutenant Merensky attempted to bar the Africans from entry. They were not officers, he objected, and German military rules must be respected.

Tanya hurried to their defense, pleading with Major Kraut to allow her farm workers to glimpse the insides of this exclusive sanctum just once. They had, after all, she reminded Major Kraut, journeyed far and endured hardships to volunteer their services, and they'd earned the reward of seeing what would – for the rest of their time serving the German military – be forbidden them.

"For this moment still," Major Kraut pronounced, "they are not porters, but guests. Allow them pass, Lieutenant."

Lieutenant Merensky relented, but drew the line at Dionysus. "The hound stays here!" he snarled.

Picking her battles, Tanya smiled graciously and bade Dionysus to sit outside the tent.

Filing inside, the group confronted a well-appointed lounge. German plantation owners had donated furniture for the tent's decor. A leopard skin rug adorned the floor between two antelope-hide easy chairs. A yellow silk upholstered sofa looked worse for its wear in the officers' tent, but not by much. Next to the sofa was a basket filled with piles of neatly folded old newspapers – obtained by ambushing British mail carriers.

The generosity of the plantation owners was not limited solely to furniture. On a low bamboo coffee table, Frau Haun's freshly-baked lemon cake stood, missing several wedges. Across from it sat a plate of sliced sausages, donated by Master-butcher Grabow. Between the two food items was a stack of linen napkins.

Nor were the plantation owners merely concerned with their soldiers' diets. Bottles of cordials, spirits and wines crowded a shelf rising above a glossy hardwood bar that lined the back of the tent.

In front of the bar, handmade tables and chairs were tastefully arranged. At one of these tables sat the only occupants of the officers' tent. They comprised a foursome who gave the appearance of having played cards all night and carried on despite the dawn. Now, at 8:30 a.m., they looked haggard, but otherwise seemed to lack no enthusiasm for gaming still longer. A casual once-over of the table revealed that they were sustaining themselves through this marathon on bottled beer, roasted pumpkin seeds and sporting spirit.

Major Kraut hailed his colleagues: "Gentlemen, see here these noble friends of the Fatherland who have come to deliver their farm laborers for use as carriers by our Army," he gushed and eagerly introduced his subordinates. "Captain Adler," he gestured, and the man nodded a greeting. "Captain Baumstark," Major Kraut continued, and the officer rose slightly in a half-bow. "Captain von Kornatzki," Major Kraut pointed, and the gentleman looked the group over with a small smile. "And our guest, Captain von Brantberg, British Army," Major Kraut finished.

Beaming ecstatically, Isak threw back his chair in his haste to stand and, once on his feet, brushed his head on the tent's top. His voice sent the earth rolling under Tanya's feet as he boomed, "*Prinsesstårta!*"

TWENTY

On signal from Hilary, twenty-six revolvers cocked in a display of near-synchronicity that was broken only by Kamau fumbling with his pistol, juggling and almost dropping it, before gaining a firm grip on the weapon and aiming it at Major Kraut. Hilary and Hassan had their pistols trained on the German captains still seated at the card table, while the twenty-three porters – in an array of outstretched arms that bore comparison to an agitated porcupine – split their targets between Lieutenant Merensky, the German *askaris* and Major Kraut.

Taking advantage of the Major's compromised situation, Malena dashed forward and snatched the Luger 9mm from his hip holster. Whether Major Kraut or Tanya was more taken aback was impossible to determine. With a triumphant cry, Malena brandished the weapon, waving it at the ceiling until her better judgment prevailed, and she picked a target: Major Kraut. His facial expression was unmistakably hurt.

"Step over here, Captain Brantberg," Hilary ordered. "Men, shoot anyone who moves besides Captain Brantberg!"

"Captain Brantberg comes with us!" Tanya shouted in German. "Don't move, let him go, and no one will be hurt!"

Following Hilary's command, Isak breezed towards his rescue party, arms wide and face alight. *"Prinsesstårta,"* he cried, clapping Tanya's cheeks between his hands and kissing her loudly on the lips. "Allow me to introduce you to my friends."

"We've been introduced, Isak," Tanya replied, her voice quivering at Isak's unflappable cheerfulness. "Now we must say good-bye."

"No, you haven't been introduced," Isak objected. "Gentleman," he said, turning to his German playmates and speaking in broken German, "this is my wife. Her friend," he said pointing to Malena.

"For God's sake, Isak!" Hilary snorted. "We need to go!"

"Another time, Isak," Tanya pleaded. "After the war."

Following Hilary's obvious preference for departing, the porters moved towards the tent flap. Lieutenant Merensky and the *askaris* gave the porters a wide berth.

A conversational remark from the card table, however, held up the exodus. "I see," said Captain Baumstark in English. "A Trojan horse without the horse. Very nice." He repeated the comment in German, meriting the murmured approvals and nods of admiration from the other German officers.

At this obvious approbation from the Germans, Tanya's plantation workers exchanged questioning glances, and Tanya glimpsed their confusion. That the Trojan horse reference reinforced a bond across the warring sides – and created divisions in Tanya's own team – was, Tanya reflected, peculiarly unfortunate.

"But why the necessity for the guns?" Captain Adler asked in English. "This operation is a fine bit of work. You must know that we applaud your devotion as a wife. You didn't think we'd be stuffy about it, did you?"

Although everyone participating in the rescue mission did think the Germans would be "stuffy" about releasing Isak, when actually confronted with the question, a sense of sheepishness prevailed. The porters, though still careful to point their weapons at the enemy, stole increasingly searching glances at Hilary, who looked to Tanya for guidance. Malena, too, sought Tanya's judgment. Tanya, meanwhile, was focused on the German speakers, trying to gauge whether they were opening negotiations, or stalling for time to mount a counter-operation.

"Fine, yes," Captain von Kornatzki said in German. (He understood English, but didn't care to speak it poorly in front of others, who might mock him.) "Better than our horse-stealing gambit with the East African Mounted Rifles near Magadi. Remember when we ambushed them as they watered their horses?"

Chatter erupted among the German speakers, and Lieutenant Merensky – dropping, for the first time, his sullen expression – called out in German, "Fifty-seven horses we stole!"

"Don't forget the time," Major Kraut burst out, caught up in the conversational tide and speaking German, "when we infiltrated the Tsavo train station, hollowed out the logs in the firewood pile and filled them with dynamite. To have seen the face of the train engineer when his engine blew up!"

"Baroness von Brantberg has the fighting spirit of this war," Captain Adler pronounced in English.

"A very noble woman she is," Captain Baumstark agreed in English, "mounting an operation like this to save her husband."

"Consider Merensky's wife," Captain von Kornatzki suggested in German, "she's hoping the British kill him."

The German speakers bubbled over in teasing laughter, while frustrated Lieutenant Merensky shouted in German, "I haven't got a wife."

"He meant your mother," Major Kraut quipped in German, and the laughter intensified.

"Such noble conduct shows our enemy to great advantage," Captain Adler said, steering the conversation away from topics that stirred young Merensky's hot blood.

Isak, who had been absorbing this praise of Tanya with molten pride, slapped Tanya's back and smiled, "Adler, I forgive debt you owe me."

"What debt?" Captain Adler retorted, also smiling. "Before you go, Brantberg, pay up!"

"Order!" Hilary shouted, impatient for a cue from Tanya and convinced that the German attempts at camaraderie would lead nowhere pleasant. "Isak, let's go."

"With Major Kraut's permission," Captain von Kornatzki began in German, "in recognition of the nobility of this little wife, who we hold as a model and representative for all wives, allow us to escort von Brantberg's party to the border."

"What's he saying?" Hilary hissed in Tanya's direction.

"He's saying they should escort us to the border to honor our noble rescue mission," she translated.

From his facial expression, Hassan seemed to view this proposition with suspicion, a sentiment plainly shared by Kamau and the porters. Hilary, however, seemed willing to explore the sincerity of the offer, and Malena was exuding so much good will in Major Kraut's direction that she seemed almost ready to return his Luger.

Major Kraut nodded, looking from Captain von Kornatzki to Malena (at whom he couldn't resist raising an eyebrow), and solemnly rubbing his chin. "Baron von Brantburg, we have all grown fond of your company these past weeks," Major Kraut said in German. "We have told you before, and I repeat now: we want you on our side."

"I'm honored," Isak replied in German. "But what you ask is impossible. I am loyal to my side."

"A noble couple, it seems. You must go then, Baron von Brantberg," Major Kraut decided, issuing his edict in German. "You eat too much to keep around in the hope that you'll change your mind. But only you may go – and your wife, and her sister and her hus —" Major Kraut was about to refer to Hilary as Tanya's "husband," but then he realized that the designation had been part of the ploy. "That white gentleman," Major Kraut concluded. "The blacks stay. They will serve us as porters."

"*Nein*!" Tanya cried.

"What's he saying?!" Hilary demanded.

"He wants to keep the blacks as porters," Tanya explained in an anguished voice.

Kamau's gun went off. The bullet was fated to bury itself in a tree branch, but not before it burned a hole in the tent's top and skimmed so close to Major Kraut that he felt its inflamed breeze on his cheek.

Major Kraut ducked, his hands over his head. Peering up resentfully, and then – aware that he was tarnishing his prestige in this cowardly posture – straightening up rapidly, Major Kraut demanded in German, "Might you not disarm that incompetent?"

"No I couldn't," Tanya declined in German. "I am very sorry, Major Kraut, but I have given my word as a noblewoman that none of my farm staff would ever serve as military porters, and I cannot break my word. I will carry military supplies before they do. These men have acted today with enormous bravery and loyalty, and I would be an unworthy mistress if I repaid their exemplary service by depositing them into military bondage. You need not fear that, by releasing my farm workers, the British gain any advantage. As I said, I have given my word, and they shall not serve as carriers – for the British or the Germans. You have consented to free Isak. His freedom cannot condemn his rescuers to bondage. You have no alternative but to provide us all with safe passage."

"What are you saying?!" Hilary demanded.

The porters seconded his exhortation with emphatic facial expressions.

"I am explaining that my employees will never serve as carriers for any *mzungu* army," Tanya clarified. "I have told him that he must escort our entire party to the border. None of us remains here."

Tanya's words impressed the porters. They didn't exactly smile, but they exhibited something of a swagger as they trained their pistols on their German targets with renewed vim. Kamau glared at Major Kraut with the haughtiness of a colonist, and Hassan nodded respectfully at Tanya's stand. Malena reached out to squeeze Tanya's pinky finger in support. Hilary, agreeing with Tanya's demands – but recognizing, as well, that obtaining a German escort to the border was vastly preferable to fighting their way out of German East Africa – held his breath expectantly for Major Kraut's response.

Alone among their group in betraying any anxiety, Isak patted Tanya's shoulders, as if she needed calming down.

THE CELEBRATION HUSBAND

Captain Adler broke the silence. "An impressive display of noble integrity," he said in English. "With more like her, our gentlemen's wars wouldn't involve any war."

"We ourselves strive for gentlemen *askaris*," agreed Captain Baumstark in English. "The savage, too, can acquire traits of nobility, if given an example like Frau von Brantberg's."

"I renew my suggestion," Captain von Kornatzki said in German. "With your permission, Major Kraut, allow us to provide an escort to these worthy adversaries."

Perhaps Major Kraut would have been swayed by these arguments. Certainly, had he taken his cue from Malena's encouraging facial expression, little doubt can exist that a truce of sorts would have prevailed, and Tanya's rescuers would have completed their mission in peace and with the blessings of their ostensible enemy. But Major Kraut had no chance to take a decision.

Before he could speak (indeed, before he'd formulated what to say), from outside the officers' tent came the sound of Dionysus barking. Tanya recognized the communication as a cheerful one; Dionysus was greeting someone he knew. With a churning stomach, Tanya had just begun to compile a mental list of candidates for the role of Dionysus' current companion – a list that contained only one plausible name – when Dionysus' happy yaps changed dramatically into a strangled whine. "Dionysus," Tanya whispered, his name catching in her throat.

The tent flap flew open, and Lieutenant-Colonel Paul Emil von Lettow-Vorbeck strode in, appearing taller, thinner and considerably angrier than when Tanya had seen him last. A man of generous temper and, as Governor Schnee had correctly diagnosed, aggressive impulses, von Lettow-Vorbeck had thrown free the shackles of noble bearing that had bound him in his previous interactions with Tanya. The glittering daylight streaming through the tent flap seemed to ring him with a fiery aura, and his whole aspect was calculated to put one in mind of the apocalypse.

From von Lettow-Vorbeck's right hand, Dionysus dangled, legs peddling, tongue drooping grotesquely from the side of his mouth. Von Lettow-Vorbeck was choking Dionysus with his collar. Holding him aloft, von Lettow-Vorbeck was hanging Dionysus before their eyes.

Von Lettow-Vorbeck's dramatic entrance prompted a flurry of simultaneous activity. Tanya screamed. Then, while Isak restrained her from rushing forward, she begged, "Drop him! Paul, I beg you, don't kill Dionysus!"

As she pleaded, all the German officers in the tent stood at attention.

The *askaris*, however, neglected to salute because they were preparing to fire. Awed by von Lettow-Vorbeck, the porters had swiveled to point their pistols at him. In so doing, they'd left the *askaris* unimpaired, and now the *askaris* raised and cocked their rifles at the porters.

Hilary sized up the situation with an inward frown. Twenty-three porter guns were trained on von Lettow-Vorbeck; a dozen *askari* rifles surrounded the porters on all sides; Kamau and Malena – bless them – were still covering Major Kraut, but he was unarmed; Hassan and himself were still targeting the Captains at the card table, but if they dropped their salute and grabbed their Lugers, they'd be three against two; and no one was covering Lieutenant Merensky. In the middle of this cat's cradle of bullet trajectories, Tanya and Isak stood unarmed.

Hilary had never been in such a compact standoff. Bullets were unlikely to miss their marks. One shot would trigger a firestorm. The officers' tent would be flooded with blood. If that happened, Tanya didn't have a prayer of surviving.

"Silence," von Lettow-Vorbeck ordered in German, as Dionysus gagged and twisted. "I've been listening to this treasonous dialogue, until I could bear no longer the exposure of my men as cowards and collaborators. Major Kraut!"

Major Kraut stamped his feet and saluted.

"On my return here from Taveta, I found an aeroplane parked on the field beyond the fort," von Lettow-Vorbeck barked.

Taveta? Tanya thought miserably. Taveta was barely twenty-five miles from Moshi. The intelligence report had placed von Lettow-Vorbeck in Dar-es-Salaam, more than two hundred and fifty miles distant. Tanya spared a caustic thought for Colonel Meinertzhagen and his bunk intelligence reports.

"The aeroplane belongs to Captain Gordon." Von Lettow-Vorbeck's eyes indicated in Hilary's direction. "Confiscate it."

"Yes sir!" Major Kraut shouted.

During the course of this exchange, the porters had grasped the precariousness of their situation as astutely as Hilary had. None of the porters fired on von Lettow-Vorbeck because to do so would be to kill them all. As the rapid-fire German-language volley between von Lettow-Vorbeck and Major Kraut progressed, the porters glanced stealthily behind them at Hilary.

"Paul, I beg you!" Tanya entreated, watching Dionysus' eyes glaze. "Drop Dionysus, please." Then Tanya switched to English. "Hilary, von Lettow-Vorbeck knows about the plane. He saw it on his return from Taveta. Tell them they can have it if he drops Dionysus."

Hilary read her eyes and perceived that she wasn't actually asking him to offer the plane as a trade for the dog.

Von Lettow-Vorbeck, like Captain von Kornatzki, understood English, but he preferred not to speak it imperfectly in situations that required respect for his authority. "Quiet, Tanya," von Lettow-Vorbeck ordered in steely German, shaking Dionysus, who emitted a ghastly, dry croaking sound. "We are taking the plane, we don't need permission. Like we took the mapmaker. We are not giving him up."

"Paul please," Tanya cried in English, switching her priority from convincing von Lettow-Vorbeck to speaking so that her team could understand the score. "Don't confiscate the plane! Don't refuse to release Isak! Be reasonable! Your officers have shown themselves noble gentlemen and credits to your leadership. They have already assured our freedom. Be honorable! Their word is a nobleman's bond!"

Tanya's words caused a ripple of anxiety to run through the porters. The chances of leaving the tent without shots being fired seemed increasingly slim. Malena gulped anxiously, and Kamau held her hand. Hassan remained stoic, but he turned slightly in Hilary's direction. Hilary met his eyes.

"We are all friends here," Isak called out in ungrammatical German. "Friends," he repeated the word in English. "Let's all put down our guns!" he suggested in both languages. "And let's put down the dogs, too," he added jovially, in German.

All the gun barrels remained raised.

"Tanya," von Lettow-Vorbeck said neutrally in German. As he spoke, he lowered his arm so that Dionysus' feet scraped the ground, and he could breathe raspingly. "You told me that you admired Faust for selling his soul to the devil. I gave you a chance to make the same choice, and you refused me, unwisely. Now you will go through with the sale, but I'm afraid you're going to get a very poor price for that soul of yours. You are in German custody, and you will remain in German custody until your husband produces the maps we demand. As for your blacks, they will serve as our Army porters, or my *askaris* will kill them now."

"He's holding all of us hostage," Tanya breathed to Hilary.

"We are through befriending you," von Lettow-Vorbeck decreed. And now he spoke English. He declaimed the one sentence that was so central to his profession that he could issue it fluidly, without hesitation, in eleven languages: "Any resistance to our demands will be met with this." Von Lettow-Vorbeck hauled Dionysus high off the ground, grabbed the hound by the throat, and twisted his hands so as to snap Dionysus' neck.

Hilary fired.

TWENTY-ONE

Carrier Corps porters are well-practiced in collapsing, and this group of ex-*kariakor* hadn't lost the skill despite their time off the job. On a non-verbal signal from Hilary, the porters hit the floor as Hilary's bullet exploded from the revolver's chamber. Simultaneously, Kamau pulled Malena down, and Hassan barreled Tanya onto the floor.

Several satisfactory results flowed from this maneuver:

Hilary's bullet hit its mark: it blew off von Lettow-Vorbeck's right thumb. The Lieutenant-Colonel consequently dropped Dionysus, who wheezed and staggered on rubber legs.

Of course, when Hilary fired, the *askaris* fired, and their bullets also hit targets, though ones which were disagreeable to themselves. The *askaris* had been aiming at the upright porters. But the *askaris*' bullets were airborne – and the air was choked with black smoke – before they could adjust for the newly-prone position of their prey. Nonetheless, this sudden disappearance of enemy porters didn't prevent the *askaris* from being good shots: each managed to wound another. One lost ear, two shoulders scraped of flesh, three arms enhanced by shrapnel, two serious cases of internal hemorrhaging, one bloody wrist, one shattered collarbone, one shot-off nose, one chin heretofore known as "bullet stopper," one neck bubbling like a spring and twelve *askaris* temporarily out of commission was their reward for lightning reflexes.

The black smoke screen resulting from the *askaris'* rifle round impaired visibility for Captains Adler, Baumstark and von Kornatzki, but the gunpowder cloud proved no restraint to Hassan. After having ensured Tanya's safety on the ground, Hassan moved across the floor, between the flattened porters, with a kind of roll-slither-crawl that isn't taught in the British Army and can only be learned through exposure from a young age to Somali desert warfare and hand-to-hand combat. When Hassan surfaced, Lieutenant Merensky was dying on the blade of Hassan's dagger, inserted expertly beneath Lieutenant Merensky's sternum. Hassan was, of course, carrying a revolver, but shooting men from a distance struck him as unrefined. Hassan had certain standards of etiquette that applied to killing, and one of them was that he had to bare his teeth at the dying man so that Hassan's contempt would be eternally impressed on the man's eyes.

Dionysus by now had recovered his breath sufficiently to bare his own teeth, snarl, crouch and spring on von Lettow-Vorbeck, who succumbed under the hound and flailed his bloodied hand to keep the furious beast away from his neck. Dionysus' ferocious roars and growls mingled with von Lettow-Vorbeck's shrieks as the hound assailed the Lieutenant-Colonel's face and hands.

Major Kraut attempted to assist his commander by grabbing a newspaper from the basket beside the yellow silk sofa and swatting Dionysus. "Bad dog!" Major Kraut reprimanded in German. Dionysus wasn't in the mood to be interrupted but, showing cunning in advancing his goals, he stepped away from von Lettow-Vorbeck's body long enough for the Lieutenant-Colonel to whisper, "The aeroplane!" Whereupon Major Kraut tore out of the officers' tent, and Dionysus fell again upon von Lettow-Vorbeck. Rolling, wrestling, snarling and wrangling, the pair dragged each other just outside the tent's entrance.

Hilary had dropped onto Tanya's body immediately upon Hassan's vacating it. Hearing the ringing echo of the *askaris'* rifle shots, the surprised exclamation of dying Lieutenant Merensky, the hideously moist sounds of Dionysus' teeth tearing flesh, and the pounding of Major Kraut's feet racing away from the officers' tent, Hilary determined that the time for cuddling had come to an end. "Kraut's gone for the plane," Hilary whispered in Tanya's ear. "I'm going to stop him. Follow me now with Isak." Then he kissed her ear, said, "I love you," and – before she could reply – bounded through the black smoke and out of the tent.

I love you, thought Tanya, fighting to maintain her composure. God speed.

Hassan was rousing their team – the porters, Kamau and Malena – and ordering them to evacuate the fort. Porters were streaming out of the tent when Tanya jumped to her feet and found her monumental husband standing, unharmed and – in all ways – untouched by the dramatic doings around him. Like the invisible elephant in the room, Isak was exactly the sort of man who could lounge in the middle of a shoot-out and emerge unscathed. "To the plane, Isak," Tanya urged.

But now Tanya saw that Captains Adler, Baumstark and von Kornatzki had their Lugers pointed at her and Isak. The Captains had been standing, pistols at the ready, since the firefight had commenced, but the rifle smoke had occluded their view of everything but Isak's towering form. None of the Captains had seen the point in shooting Isak; he was, after all, unarmed and had been – until a half hour previously – their card mate. As the smoke had inevitably cleared, however, these three Captains realized that they were the only remaining German soldiers capable of stopping the enemy escape. And as Tanya exhorted Isak to flee, the Captains stowed their distaste for shooting unarmed civilians; occasionally, they resigned themselves, the unpleasant task was necessary in wartime.

Tanya caught her breath at the fatal, flinty determination evident in Captain Adler's eyes.

Isak looked upon his three former gaming comrades sadly. "There was no need for this," he shook his head. "Everyone should lower their guns."

Isak's words summarized the personal feelings of all three Captains. But in their professional lives, the only perspective with weight was von

Lettow-Vorbeck's. A superb military strategist, and an unfailing advocate of his troops, von Lettow-Vorbeck was immensely popular with the German officers and *askaris*. His fury – and his characterization of the proposal to escort the von Brantbergs to the border as "treasonous" – had made the Captains feel their failings, and they hastened to remedy them.

"We lower our guns after we defeat the enemy," Captain Baumstark replied in a proud voice, effulgent with the confidence of patriotism.

The confidence was misplaced. From behind Tanya, something slid across the floor and, when it surfaced, Captain von Kornatzki was dying on the blade of Hassan's dagger, with the sight of Hassan's bared teeth his last earthly vision before judgment. In this act of war, Hassan was showing off, as he'd not merely stabbed Captain von Kornatzki with his right hand, but had taken his Luger and was pointing it at Captain Baumstark's chest with his left. Now Hassan turned his bared teeth to Captain Baumstark's aghast face and pulled the trigger.

The shot alone would have made Tanya shrink, but it was amplified by the synchronized shot from another pistol. Tanya threw an arm in front of Isak in a lame attempt to protect him, while she covered her own chest with her other hand. She expected to feel blood somewhere. Looking herself over, and then casting a frantic eye on Isak, Tanya finally looked in the direction of the card table. All three of the Captains were on the floor, bleeding. In addition to Captains von Kornatzki and Baumstark, of whom Hassan had made short work, someone had shot Captain Adler. Her ears ringing, her breathing flustered, Tanya snapped her head around.

Standing in front of Malena to protect her with his body, Kamau was lowering his pistol.

"And Major Kraut called you an incompetent," Tanya congratulated him.

"We go now, Memsahib," Hassan said.

"I'll take Isak to the plane," Tanya agreed. "Malena, come with us. But what about —"

"— Those poor prisoners of war?" Malena chimed in. "The good Lord surely didn't intend for us to leave —"

"— Not now, Malena. This is urgent: we need to do something to stop the Germans from giving chase," Tanya interrupted. "Hilary will fly Isak to safety, but we'll be running for the border, and there's nothing stopping the Germans from rounding us up again."

"You go, Memsahib," Hassan instructed her. "We fix it."

As much as Tanya wanted to believe Hassan – felt, actually, that she had no choice but to take his word as the deed accomplished – she considered fleeing ahead of him without additional information to be a gross violation of the code of nobility. "What do you mean 'fix it'?" she demanded. "Do you have a plan?"

"Memsahib," he assured her, "I got it."

* * *

Dionysus had the upper paw in his combat with von Lettow-Vorbeck and, no doubt, the spectacle of dog-man gladiators locked in vicious battle on the ground just outside the officers' tent would have drawn an audience under certain circumstances. Those circumstances did not prevail.

Hilary sprinted past the Dionysus-von Lettow-Vorbeck match in his haste to catch up with Major Kraut. The porters paid the pair no mind as they rushed out of the tent. Tanya stopped only long enough to say, "Get him Dionysus!" before hustling Isak after Hilary and Major Kraut. Hassan, Kamau and Malena (who had stubbornly refused to accompany Tanya for fear that she'd slow them down and jeopardize Isak's escape) swept past without pause, even though Malena asked, breathless from running, "Will Dionysus follow us?" and Kamau assured her that the hound could take care of himself.

After a pause of some minutes, during which von Lettow-Vorbeck failed to extricate himself from Dionysus' emphatic revenge, the *askaris* began to hobble out of the officers' tent in the direction of the infirmary. Some – like the internal hemorrhaging cases – were too racked with pain to notice von Lettow-Vorbeck's struggle with Dionysus; others, like the missing ear fellow, were already engaged in assisting their more severely injured colleagues and lacked a spare hand. For these and other reasons, all twelve managed to pass without drawing the hound away, although one or two had decided to double back and assist their commander once they'd delivered their charges to the infirmary.

Only four people remained in the tent: Lieutenant Merensky and Captains Adler, Baumstark and von Kornatzki. And they weren't alive.

Dionysus and von Lettow-Vorbeck wrestled on.

* * *

Confronted with Major Kraut hurtling at them like a crazed warthog, the two *askaris* at the gate opened it. Major Kraut should have stopped to give them some instructions. Close the gate after me, for example. Or: the strangers I admitted into the fort were actually undercover enemy, and there's a battle raging in the officers' tent.

For a variety of reasons, however, he declined to provide this – or any manner – of guidance. Von Lettow-Vorbeck's command to confiscate the aeroplane was obviously one explanation. Major Kraut was sensitive to the fact that a certain amount of culpability could rightly be attributed to him in this imbroglio, and he wanted to ensure that he executed the aeroplane-confiscation order expediently.

Major Kraut's embarrassment at having facilitated the entry of the enemy into the fort was another motivating factor. Major Kraut wasn't accustomed to having *askaris* snicker at him, and he didn't intend to acquire such conditioning by giving the *askaris* at the gate a précis of the events at the officers' tent.

Finally, Major Kraut didn't harbor any hope that he could reach the aeroplane without a pursuer. Any moment allotted to instructing the *askaris* was a gift to the enemy giving chase. Von Lettow-Vorbeck had said that the aeroplane was on the field beyond the fort. At a minimum, Major Kraut would have to run a mile to reach the machine, over treacherously uneven wooded grassland. His head start notwithstanding, his general health and fitness aside, he didn't believe that he could survive any serious challenge to his bid for the plane; his lungs were already bursting and his intestines in revolt.

So Major Kraut sailed through the gate without a sideways glance at the *askaris*, who left the gate open and stood, raising their eyebrows inquisitively at each other. After their eyebrow inquiry raised more questions than answers, the two gazed through the open gate at the receding figure of Major Kraut, who seemed to be making good time with an expansive gait. Some sort of *mzungu* sport or initiation ceremony, the *askaris* thought.

While the *askaris* were absorbed thus, Hilary charged towards the gate. The pounding of Hilary's feet along the dry ground did not immediately cause the *askaris* to turn. That sound, after all, was equally appropriate to the image of Major Kraut, running away before them. Only after a critical lapse of seconds did the *askaris* process the footfalls behind them as being incompatible with the scene in front of them. They turned and were picked off by Hilary's bullets before he flew through the open gate and out into the expansive bush.

Although Hilary was now in range for assassination by sharp-shooting *askaris* posted along the fence of the Moshi fort, fortune spared him this death. At the sound of gunfire in the area of the officers' tent, half of the fence's *askaris* had gone to investigate. Now, with shots fired at the gate, the other half of the fence's *askaris* left their posts. Ideally, of course, some *askaris* would have remained at their posts while others responded to the various shootings erupting throughout the fort, but Moshi didn't enjoy the luxury of this kind of staffing. The whole purpose of the tin-can garlands, in fact, was to allow a skeleton crew of *askaris* to raise an alarm worthy of a team ten times its size.

Arriving at the gate, however, the *askaris* found themselves in a shoot-out with the porters. Since the *askaris* had been summoned from different distances, depending on the location of their posts on the fence, they dribbled into the firefight in twos and threes, proving easy targets for the twenty-three porters, who assembled themselves into a block formation, each man facing outwards. Seeing in all directions, calling warnings and commands to each other, firing and reloading with impressive efficiency, the porters disabled eighteen *askaris* in five batches.

For the duration of the shoot-out, Tanya and Isak had been cowering behind barrels of sauerkraut lined up near the gate. Isak had clutched Tanya to his chest, and Tanya had squeezed her eyes shut. She was overdosing on gunfire. The noise of it was making her teeth throb and her elbows ache. The smell of it was coating her nasal passages, throat and tongue. The absence of gunfire, when it came, was as sweet to Tanya as a Beethoven violin sonata.

Hearing the porters begin to run, Isak pulled Tanya up, and the two burst forward. Once through the gate, they ran, still hand-in-hand, after the porters, who were fanning out across the bush and running in zig zags – like fleeing Thomson's gazelle – to make themselves more challenging targets for any remaining *askaris* poised to shoot them.

But no *askaris* remained to man the fence.

Around the gate lay the still-stirring, contorted bodies of twenty *askaris*, seriously or mortally wounded. Most of these men were of the Chagga tribe. They'd grown up at the base of Mount Kilimanjaro, in the same villages where their families had lived for many generations. They would not have been surprised to die at the base of the mountain. But just as no person anticipates a sordid death, they'd never conceived that they would be slain in a *mzungu* war by Kikuyu warriors who were just as clueless about why they were fighting as the Chagga were about why they were dying.

Beside the dying men, the open gate stood unguarded.

* * *

Hassan, Kamau and Malena were a long way from the gate. At Malena's insistence, they had doubled back to the trench where the prisoners of war were digging.

Malena's ability to direct their course away from the gate and immediate freedom struck her as natural. She believed that the rectitude of her cause and its correctness in the good Lord's eyes had enabled her to sway Hassan and Kamau to her will.

Kamau, however, saw no Christian angle in her persuasiveness. Rather, a remarkable sensation had overtaken him as he'd lain atop Malena in the officers' tent during the firefight. He'd felt light-headed and strong together, like a vertiginous eagle. Lekishon might have commiserated but, in the intensity of the moment, Kamau believed that no one before him had ever experienced a like condition. In its thrall, Kamau would have gone anywhere Malena suggested.

Hassan, meanwhile, had consented to this detour because he thought the prisoners of war might be able to help with his plan.

At the approach of these three, the two *askaris* guarding the four prisoners jerked their heads up. The return of Major Kraut's guests was unexpected, especially since the guests were now unchaperoned, but the *askaris* weren't concerned. These visitors had been introduced as friends, and the *askaris* had no reason to suppose that the designation had been revoked.

The *askaris* had heard, of course, the shooting at the officers' tent and at the gate, but in their location they couldn't identify the gunfire's proximity. It sounded merely "distant." Many causes of "distant" gunfire were legitimate; they couldn't become alarmed every time the kitchen staff went out to shoot lunch. In addition, these *askaris* were under strict orders not to abandon their prisoner-guarding posts unless ordered to do so by a German officer; and no German officer had so ordered.

Neither these *askaris*, nor Hassan, Kamau and Malena, could know that, across the fort, German troops were amassing. The sound of gunfire had led Moshi's remaining German officers to conclude that the fort was under attack, and the wounded *askaris* in the infirmary had confirmed that dreadful suspicion. Even now, Captain von Hammerstein was sending platoons to sweep the area. Not knowing these developments, however, neither these *askaris* guarding the prisoners, nor Hassan, Kamau and Malena, had reason yet to fear.

"*Jambo*! *Habari*!" Hassan called out the Swahili greeting.

"*Mzuri*," came the reply from the *askari* holding the rifle.

Kamau shot the *askari* in the thigh. Hassan darted forward and wrenched the rifle from the man's hand as he fell.

The whole operation was completed so quickly that the prisoners didn't look up until it was finished. Raising their eyes, they then experienced the terror of being within close range of Malena firing wildly in the air.

Since the second *askari* was armed only with a hippopotamus-hide whip, Malena had thought that shooting directly at him would be unfair. That said, Malena's greatest chances of hitting the man probably lay in shooting skywards. The whip-bearing *askari* and the four prisoners of war all ducked miserably as a hail of bullets ricocheted off the overhanging acacia branches and rained down on them.

Approaching Malena from behind, Hassan grabbed her wrist and, with an expert twist, disarmed her. "Stop that," he commanded.

Malena was too exuberant about their victory to mind Hassan's rebuke. "Gentlemen, rise and make your way to freedom like the Israelites!" she trilled.

The now-former prisoners of war peeked over the edge of the ditch, confused.

"Come with us please, Bwanas," Kamau clarified. "We come from British East Africa. We will take you back there."

One of the former prisoners – the one with the whip scar on his back – needed no further coaxing. He leaped from the ditch and grabbed the whip away from the *askari*, like a wild dog ripping meat from the mouth of a bat-eared fox. Raising the whip, he brought it down punishingly across the *askari*'s shoulders.

Hassan was on the Englishman instantly. Using the same deft technique that he'd employed to commandeer Malena's pistol, Hassan removed the whip from the former prisoner's hand. "Stop that," Hassan repeated. Then Hassan handed the former prisoner Captain von Kornatzki's Luger (wisely, Hassan had disarmed all the corpses of the German soldiers before he'd fled the officers' tent). "Be useful," Hassan suggested. "Follow me."

Kamau and Malena were assisting the other three former prisoners out of the ditch. Kamau handed them a pistol each.

At Malena's pout, Hassan returned her pistol to her, while silently offering a prayer to Allah that she might do no harm with the weapon.

Hassan gestured for everyone to follow his lead, but one of the former prisoners stopped him. "Oy!" he objected. "What about him?" He gestured to the *askari* who'd previously held the whip; he was presently doubled over, suffering from his shoulder lashing. "We don't want him running around camp, siccing the Germans on us."

"Shoot his foot," Hassan ordered Kamau.

Kamau stepped over to the *askari*. "*Pole sana*," he said. Very sorry. Kamau looked away as he shot the man through his Achilles tendon.

Hassan shook his head, a silent judgment that Kamau's action lacked the necessary contempt.

* * *

Major Kraut heard his own breathing like massive bellows stoking a fire. He had a stitch across his abdomen that would have been crippling had his will to carry out von Lettow-Vorbeck's order not overridden the pain. His knees were complaining, and he'd twice twisted his ankle in a minor way, but he'd kept running. The aeroplane was in sight now, and he couldn't stop. Looking behind him, he'd seen that white man – Roosevelt – in pursuit, and Major Kraut knew that he'd need to have the aeroplane off the ground before Roosevelt reached it.

Roosevelt, Major Kraut had gathered from the dialogue exchanged in the officers' tent, was the plane's pilot. Major Kraut would have preferred another pursuer, someone who – finding himself in the cockpit – wouldn't fight for the controls because he wouldn't know what to do. Major Kraut himself wasn't sure he'd know what to do. He'd flown a Bleriot XI before, among other planes; because of his experience as an aviator, von Lettow-Vorbeck had tasked him with seizing the plane. But he could see that this Bleriot XI was a two-seater, and Major Kraut had only flown a one-seater. He wasn't sure if the controls, behavior or balance of the plane would be the same. He would have to learn quickly, though, because he felt confident that this Roosevelt character would tear him out of the cockpit if Major Kraut wasn't off the ground fast enough.

Fifty meters from the plane, Major Kraut twisted his ankle again, and this time he fell. He rolled onto the ground and bounded up again, limping slightly as he urged himself through the homestretch. He didn't dare look behind him now. He needed to install himself in the cockpit and take off in the plane, regardless of how close Roosevelt might be.

Finally rounding the tail of the plane, Major Kraut ran his hand along its wooden and canvas fuselage. Major Kraut rested his hands on its body appreciatively, panted to recapture his breath and assessed how to climb into the cockpit.

Lacking ready means of ingress – like steps – the pilot's seat was typically accessed by a ladder laid against the plane. In the absence of such an aid, Major Kraut saw that he would have to launch himself from the ground. He groaned. His twisted ankle, already swelling, wouldn't serve him well as a springboard.

Castigating himself for wasting time, Major Kraut gritted his teeth, jumped up and pulled himself awkwardly into the cockpit. He tumbled in head-and-shoulders first, feet bicycling towards the clouds, but he quickly righted himself and sorted out the gear on the pilot's seat.

He was delighted to find a pilot's hat, goggles and leather jacket. He quickly donned them, experiencing a transformation as he did so: like the horse wearing blinders, Major Kraut in flying gear ceased to have full awareness of his environs. His breathing stabilized, his ankle pain faded and his focus narrowed to the mechanisms in the cockpit.

Surveying the plane controls, Major Kraut was relieved to see foot pedals, a control column with the throttle and ignition switch, fuel gauge, compass, portable barometer and tachometer, for measuring the revolutions of the propeller. The set-up looked familiar enough. Major Kraut flipped the ignition switch.

The engine clatter eliminated any remaining awareness Major Kraut might have had of the world beyond the plane. He was part of the machine now, sharing its fate and its triumphs. Guiding the plane away from Mount Kilimanjaro, Major Kraut taxied the plane down the grass strip on which it had landed. The plane jerked along, while Major Kraut experimented with the throttle and the foot pedals to control the tail rudder.

Reaching the end of the strip, he turned the plane around and commenced his take off. He was relaxed now. He was racing down the grassy air strip. The plane's movement was much smoother, and Major Kraut warmed with confidence at the plane's responsiveness to his hand. No obstacle remained to bringing the plane aloft, after which he would be safe, untouchable.

Just before the wheels lifted from the ground, Hilary Gordon vaulted into the passenger seat.

* * *

A loose formation bound the porters as they ran. Their strides weren't synchronized, but they paced themselves against one another, all being relative, evenly matched in their capacities for speed.

Opportunities to run like this had been few in their adult lives. On the Kikuyu reserve, they'd tended goats and cattle – more exciting exploits having been banned since the colonists outlawed tribal fighting. In the *kariakor*, they'd plodded interminably, laden down with loads that might break a donkey. On the von Brantberg plantation, they'd weeded the coffee trees, plowed the fields and taken the oxen to the dip.

Racing across the wide-open expanse of the African bush, therefore, was a luxury. While all twenty-three of the porters shared this sense of reward, more than a few also reflected on its cost: this freedom had been purchased with the blood of Chagga men who were neither enemies nor oppressors, and from whom no cattle had been extracted, as befitted an honorable fight. The killings had been waste.

Hearing the aeroplane bellowing in the distance, seeing it begin to roll, yet knowing that Isak was behind them, the porters wondered what waste was still to come.

* * *

Tanya and Isak were midway across the distance between the Moshi fort and the aeroplane, when Tanya heard the plane's voluminous engine awake.

To her dismay, she'd been slowing their progress considerably by tripping constantly in her kid boots. The porters had offered to help – even by carrying her – but Tanya had waved them on, and they now lead Tanya and Isak by four hundred meters.

Isak had tried to piggy-back Tanya in the hopes that it would speed their pace, but that arrangement had proved even slower. Tanya had wanted to remove her boots, but Isak had sharply forbidden her to do so, reminding her of the myriad ticks, snakes and thorns that lay in wait to punish the bare sole.

Now she panicked at their measly progress. "The plane's leaving!" she cried. "Why isn't Hilary waiting for you?"

Isak, who'd been observing the progress of Major Kraut and Hilary, shared her concern, but in a less fevered pitch. "I don't think Hilary's in control of the plane."

In her many stumbles, and with her own podiatric woes taking priority, Tanya had lost sight of Major Kraut and Hilary ahead of them. She didn't think her lack of vision problematic. Any outcome other than Hilary trouncing Major Kraut was impossible for Tanya; she'd reflexively assumed that Hilary had dispatched Major Kraut and started the plane. "You must be wrong," she argued. "Hilary's driving the plane over here to pick you up."

"I think Major Kraut is in the pilot's seat," Isak disputed.

Tanya fell again. Isak caught her arm and hauled her up.

Resuming their brisk trot, now hand-in-hand, Tanya wheezed, "Hilary would never let anyone steal that plane."

"He may not have a choice," Isak grunted.

* * *

Assembled beneath the thatched roof structure that served as the garage for von Lettow-Vorbeck's Chevrolet, Hassan pointed at the canisters of coconut benzol. "Two-two-two-two," he said, assigning carrier duties to the four former prisoners of war.

"I'll carry one!" Malena volunteered.

"I'll help her," Kamau assured Hassan.

Hassan assented, giving one canister to Malena for her to carry with Kamau. Hassan then handed another canister to Kamau for him to carry in his free hand, before Hassan picked up the two remaining canisters himself.

Thus loaded, the members of the sabotage party stared at each other.

"Where are we going?" one of the former prisoners asked, seeing from Hassan's face that, behind his eyes, gears were turning without necessarily clicking.

"I consider that you might know this fort best," said Hassan. "It has a munitions dump?"

* * *

To some extent, Captain von Hammerstein could be said to have done the wrong thing. Based on the sounds of gunfire and the reports from the wounded *askaris* in the infirmary, he'd sent platoons to the areas where the fighting had been.

This strategy, of course, lost him valuable time. His goal was to intercept and capture the enemy, and few plans were less likely to further this objective than rushing to locations from which the enemy had just departed. Captain von Hammerstein should have sent half his platoons careening out of the fort in pursuit of the fleeing enemy, and commanded the other half of his *askaris* to comb the areas of the fort where the enemy might be hiding.

In fairness to Captain von Hammerstein, however, undertaking to do what he should have done required that he know certain information that he didn't know, *viz* that the enemy was both fleeing the fort and hiding within it, conspiring to do harm. His ability to gather this necessary intelligence was impaired by his reluctance to credit the reports of the wounded *askaris*, whose accounts were too fantastic (*two* women in the fort? Lieutenant-Colonel von Lettow-Vorbeck strangling a *dog*?). Being, therefore, ignorant of the true situation, Captain von Hammerstein sent *askaris* to the shooting sites to investigate, preparatory to formulating a plan of response.

And, in another sense, Captain von Hammerstein did do the right thing. Arriving at the officers' tent, the *askaris* were able to render a service that was to earn them a military decoration: they rescued their high commander.

By this time, von Lettow-Vorbeck was covered in flesh wounds. Dionysus had worked him over fairly comprehensively, sparing no major muscle group and expending significant energies to chew through the Lieutenant-Colonel's shoes in order to gash his toes and heels. Von Lettow-Vorbeck's uniform was dripping blood, the loss of which had weakened the Lieutenant-Colonel as an opponent. Despite the burning pain of the dog bites, von Lettow-Vorbeck had largely stopped yelling to conserve his energy. He knew that the moment he was drained of strength to resist, the hound would rip open his neck.

But as the *askaris* approached, von Lettow-Vorbeck was screaming. Dionysus was tearing into the Lieutenant-Colonel's hand, and von Lettow-Vorbeck howled unabashedly, feeling that nothing remained to preserve: if the dog killed him at this point, von Lettow-Vorbeck would be relieved.

But Dionysus did not kill him. Hearing the *askaris* advance (the soldiers dared not shoot the dog for fear of hitting the Lieutenant-Colonel), Dionysus looked up. He, too, was coated in clotting blood, a garb that rendered him unrecognizable as man's best friend. In his mouth, Dionysus secreted a trophy, but it wasn't visible for the gore.

Abruptly, Dionysus turned and trotted away, tail wagging.

The oncoming *askari* platoon won voluptuous thanks for their bravery and effectiveness in ridding their high commander of the rabid dog that had menaced his life. And, while in general the *askaris* in World War I were unquestionably under-appreciated and deserved every recognition they received (and more), in fact these *askaris* had had nothing to do with Dionysus' retreat. What drove Dionysus off was his perception of a stimulus that would take many more minutes to manifest itself to the *askaris*.

Dionysus scooted because he smelled fire.

* * *

Hilary prevented the plane from lifting off for two reasons. First, his extra weight destabilized the trajectory that Major Kraut had set, and the plane strained against take-off. Second, Hilary's sudden appearance had gone far towards causing Major Kraut to lose control of his bowels. Major Kraut had never experienced a worse scare and, in his fright, he'd left the aeroplane temporarily unmanned.

The plane motored rapidly towards the slopes of Mount Kilimanjaro, and the looming danger spurred Major Kraut into active recovery from his shock. He lunged forward over the throttle and turned the plane sharply, returning it to another lap along the grassy strip.

Behind him Hilary was on his feet in the passenger's berth, leaning forward towards the cockpit. Crouching over the throttle, Major Kraut hoped he was beyond Hilary's reach. But then Major Kraut felt the blood-draining sensation of the hard barrel of Hilary's pistol against the back of his head.

"Stop the plane!" Hilary shouted.

"What?" Major Kraut crouched even lower and felt the barrel slip momentarily.

"Stop the plane!" Hilary forced the barrel against Major Kraut's head again.

"What?" Major Kraut didn't know how long he could pretend not to hear Hilary over the engine roar, but the gambit was buying him time.

Hilary pitched himself onto the fuselage between the passenger's and the pilot's seats. He was precariously poised, his left hand gripping the edge of the pilot's berth, his legs in the passenger seat straining to keep him steady. With his right hand, Hilary jammed the revolver into Major Kraut's neck. The barrel was warm from having recently been fired.

Hilary lowered his mouth as close to Major Kraut's ear as he could without upsetting his balance. "Stop the plane," Hilary shouted.

"I'm stopping the plane," Major Kraut agreed immediately, adding, "if you shoot me, the bullet's going to hit the fuel tank."

Hilary paused to appreciate the correctness of Major Kraut's assessment. The aeroplane's two fuel tanks occupied the front of the plane and fitted over the pilot's feet. Major Kraut's crouch ensured that any bullet sent into his head was likely to emerge and continue its journey into one of the fuel tanks. Hilary couldn't hope that Major Kraut's brain was thick enough to stop the bullet. And even if the bullet didn't blow up the fuel tank, the cockpit was compact. Hilary could hardly fire shots without destroying something critical.

Hilary's conflict was soon resolved by Major Kraut's upwards elbow thrust into Hilary's armpit. The blow torqued Hilary's right shoulder up, jerking his arm skywards and causing him accidentally to fire a shot through the overhead cabling. As his arm descended, Major Kraut struck again, this time slamming his elbow into Hilary's chin.

With Hilary momentarily dazed, Major Kraut pounced on the pistol, but Hilary still clenched it firmly. Rolling violently to the right and then pulling back forcefully to the left, Hilary tried to dislodge Major Kraut from his arm. Beyond banging the German against the sides of the cockpit, however, Hilary achieved little.

Now Hilary shrank back towards the passenger seat, his arm beginning to slip from Major Kraut's hold. Panicking, Major Kraut heaved forward, grabbing Hilary's arm in both hands and hauling it over his shoulder like a fire hose. Hilary thought he heard a pop and a snap, and a bolt of pain shot through his right side that seemed to travel from his lower back through his trapezoid and shoulder, up his neck, and coming to fullest expression in his eye, which Hilary feared might burst from its socket. The gun rocketed out of Hilary's hand. It sailed forward with a sickening sound that signaled its scraping against the propeller. Encountering the revolver in its airspace didn't stop the propeller's revolutions, however.

Freed from the threat of the gun, Major Kraut dropped Hilary's arm and fell on the throttle.

Hilary tumbled backwards into the passenger's seat like a building collapsing after a dynamite blast; he conked his head on the fuselage as he landed.

Without attention to its steering, the plane had rambled. Now straightening the machine's course, Major Kraut threw a glance behind him at Roosevelt. The man gave the appearance of taking a momentary breather. His face looked groggy, and his left arm was gripping his right shoulder.

Satisfied that he wasn't imminently to be thrown from the cockpit by his American foe, Major Kraut eyed the traffic oncoming from the Moshi fort. The porters were fast approaching the grassy strip, with Captain von Brantberg and his wife not far behind. Major Kraut estimated that he had just enough time to take-off, if the brawny American didn't cause further trouble.

The prospect struck Major Kraut as unappealing. Being airborne with the American brute entailed a high risk of failure for his plane-confiscation mission, but Major Kraut felt that the other option portended even more certain failure. If he delayed take-off to eject his unwanted passenger, the (armed) porters would storm the plane. His best chance, Major Kraut decided, was to take refuge in flight. Once airborne, he could contrive to fly erratically so as to send the American spiraling to his death.

The plane had now reached the end of the grassy strip, and Major Kraut brought it around once more for take-off.

In the passenger's seat, Hilary had, indeed, needed ten seconds in the recuperation corner. But, groggy as he'd appeared to Major Kraut, Hilary hadn't lost consciousness, and he was cognizant that Major Kraut intended another attempt at lift-off. Hilary knew that he had to prevent the plane from leaving the ground.

As the engine revved and the plane sped down the grassy strip, Hilary slid forward and flattened his torso against the fuselage between the pilot's and passenger's seats. The pummeling wind near blinded him in its attempts to corral him backwards. Patiently, determinedly, Hilary gritted his teeth, clenched his abdominal muscles and inched forward.

Focusing on take-off, Major Kraut was sitting upright. Hilary stretched his arms out and clawed Major Kraut's shoulders.

Major Kraut shook off Hilary's hands and hunched closer to the throttle. The blare of the engine threatened to shake Hilary off the plane with its vibrations. The passing landscape was indistinct, like a smeared watercolor. Choking back wind and grit, Hilary muscled onward, closer to the cockpit, and swiped again. His hands passed cleanly through air. Hilary had hoped to grip Major Kraut's upper body and yank him from the plane's controls.

But they were already airborne.

* * *

Another sense in which Captain von Hammerstein may be applauded for having done the right thing relates to the gate of Moshi fort. Before having sent out his platoons, the gate lay open, like bait for a wild animal. With the arrival of Captain von Hammerstein's *askaris*, however, the gate closed as resolutely as a trap ensnaring its prey.

Of course, the *askaris* would have done better to survey the area visible from the fort's gate before closing it. Though the porters were already out of view, Tanya and Isak could still be perceived in the distance, and Dionysus ran briskly behind them. Had the *askaris* taken this simple precaution of examining the landscape from which they were sealing themselves off before slamming the door, they could have sent troops in pursuit of the enemy.

But at the crucial moment the *askaris* were looking inward, not outward. Specifically, they were distracted by the massacred bodies of their fellow *askaris* strewn around the gate area.

Then, before they had a chance to formulate a response to this horror, they were distracted again, by the arrival of Hassan, Kamau, Malena and the four former prisoners of war, who – not unreasonably – were desirous of exiting through the just-closed gates.

In this face-off, the *askaris* might have been thought to have had the advantage, as their count numbered ten, while the enemy's strength was only six (seven if you included the blonde who couldn't shoot). Nonetheless, the *askaris* were actually at a disadvantage. Trauma from witnessing their colleagues' fates, as well as surprise at the sudden appearance of the enemy, had dulled their reflexes.

Team Sabotage, on the other hand, was enjoying the adrenaline rush that accompanies the knowledge that a munitions dump in the near vicinity will shortly explode. Though they had created a fuse of sorts by liberally splashing the coconut benzol in a line leading into the munitions dump, they knew that they had three minutes – at most – to get past the *askaris* if they were to avoid an Armageddon barbeque.

The minutes were put to good use. Fascinated by the coconut benzol, one of the former prisoners had siphoned a little into a discarded beer bottle that he'd found in the waste heap on the way to the munitions dump. He'd intended to donate the sample to the British Army for reverse engineering purposes. But now he saw that he'd have to divert some of the benzol for a more urgent function. Like all bored males exposed to sufficient quantities of alcohol, this gentleman knew a good number of idiotic and dangerous tricks. Now, as the *askaris* raised their rifles, he did one of them.

He swigged a tiny amount of the coconut benzol from the beer bottle, rolling it to the front of his mouth on his tongue. Then he lit a safety match from the box that Hassan had given him to light the fuse to the munitions dump, and he held the match in front of his mouth. Puckering his lips as if to whistle, he blew a transparent stream of the coconut benzol over the flame.

The benzol ignited in a thunderous ball of flame that rolled across the *askaris* like an ocean tide that had traded its water for fire. In its aftermath, the *askaris* appeared suspended in a stunned trance. Taking advantage of the *askaris*' temporary immobility, the four former prisoners raised their guns and shot four of the *askaris*.

While the former prisoner's fire-breathing stunt was in progress, Kamau grabbed Malena's hand and dived. A cook even when he functioned as a soldier, Kamau had noticed the barrels of sauerkraut. Together, he and Malena pushed over a barrel and rolled it towards the *askaris*. Flustered by the pyrotechnics, two *askaris* delayed in firing, managing only three bullets into the barrel before Kamau and Malena, their hands wet with sauerkraut juice leaking from the fatally cracked barrel, deposited fifty kilograms of fermented cabbage on the *askaris*' feet. The *askaris* looked down. When they looked up, Kamau and Malena shot them.

Kamau deposited his bullet into the rifle-bearing arm of the *askari* across from him. Malena, at a distance of two-and-half feet, put three holes in the gate behind the other *askari*. Kamau then shot the man in his rifle-bearing arm.

Simultaneous to these flaming and culinary approaches, Hassan stuck with his tried-and-true method. Diving away from the sauerkraut barrels, Hassan traversed the distance between himself and the enemy with his unclassifiable roll-slither-crawl. Given the time constraints, Hassan wasn't interested in showing off, and he considered that he could bend an ethical point. He shelved the bared teeth maneuver, opting instead to shoot the remaining four *askaris* in the stomach in quick succession.

The *askaris* thus dispatched, Team Sabotage reopened the gate and tore out of Moshi fort like hares with fire-breathing jackals on their heels. Their impressive sprint exceeded no more than four hundred meters before the munitions dump exploded with a tremor that flattened them face-down in the bush, as a cloud of gunpowder and dirt flowed over them.

* * *

Isak pulled Tanya, heaving and wobbling, into the knot of porters who stood on the grassy strip, eyes fixed upward, mouths agape. Isak, who'd embraced the thrill of being pursued, traded upbeat greetings with the porters.

Tanya couldn't share his enjoyment of the action. At her arrival, a number of the porters pointed at the aeroplane. One said, "Memsabu, Bwana Hilary fights Germany in the sky." The notion was so chilling that

Tanya instinctively deflected it. Instead, she impulsively thought to command the porters to keep running – at any moment, the Germans might come spewing out of Moshi fort in pursuit, and here they were loitering. But, bending over to regain her breath, she postponed her command and tried to order her thoughts.

The porters, she decided, had done well to stop. The grassy strip was their group's rendezvous point. Having reached it, they needed to take a head count and recalibrate their plan before proceeding. She herself needed to change out of her kid boots and into her safari clothing, stashed with the rest of their supplies in the surrounding foliage.

Most pressingly, however, she needed to take a decision about the plane. Tanya looked up, despairing. She could accept that Isak would need to risk recapture with the rest of them, as they fled on foot to the border and then across open bush to the Tsavo train station. Tanya had hoped for greater security for Isak, but if they were to suffer falling into enemy clutches, Tanya felt certain that Isak would weather the ordeal better than any of them.

No, the decision she had to take was whether to abandon the aeroplane . . . and Hilary. By now, the porter's statement, "Bwana Hilary fights Germany in the sky," had penetrated her defenses. Hilary was beyond her reach.

She couldn't allow her thoughts to elaborate on the consequences of that fact. She couldn't watch. Again, the impulse to flee seized her. Hilary, she rationalized, would want them all to flee. The next instant, she stiffened with the conviction that she could never leave Hilary. Everyone else must flee across the border, but she must follow the plane.

A sonic rupture blasted through her thoughts. Tanya couldn't imagine that the sound accompanied anything less dramatic that a fissure cracking the earth and spilling its guts in magmatic fury. Tanya saw a blaze erupt from within Moshi fort.

"Hassan's plan," Isak remarked, a smile playing around his lips.

* * *

The air became wondrously cold. Hilary's clenched hands were stinging with a sweaty, freezing sensation. Major Kraut seemed to be flying directly up into the atmosphere. With the plane at this angle, Hilary was stuck clutching the fuselage. He couldn't safely slide back into the passenger's seat. No doubt Major Kraut was trying to pitch him from the plane.

The wind was too powerful, and the air too chilled, for Hilary to breathe through his mouth, but he could barely pull enough oxygen into his lungs through his nose. Taking short, labored breaths, he squeezed his eyes against what felt like snow whirling in the wind. His biceps ached, and his cheek and ear felt ill-used by the fuselage, trembling abrasively beneath him in time with the thrumming of the engine.

Then the plane leveled off its climb. Hilary risked raising his head in the icy wind, and he almost toppled at the vision before him. Major Kraut had flown the plane along the ascent of Mount Kilimanjaro. Below them was a lush tangle of rain forest which yielded abruptly – almost in a line circling the mountain – to an evergreen-studded grassland. Ahead, two snow-capped peaks glinted like sharpened daggers. Hilary was gazing on a pristine sanctuary, untouched by humans. Amazement and terror gripped him, and his head bulged with the idea that God alone had seen earth as he was seeing it now. His guts were tormented with dread of such a precedent.

Summoning his strength, Hilary dragged himself forward on the plane's fuselage so that he could catch sight of the barometer over Major Kraut's shoulder. They were at 9,000 feet. Hilary goggled. Four years earlier a Peruvian had taken a Bleriot XI through the Peruvian Alps at roughly 8,500 feet, and now Major Kraut had casually broken that record. Hilary didn't know whether to slap Major Kraut on the back in congratulations, or hurl him to his death below and pilot the plane to a safer altitude.

Lurching forward with the sudden awareness of Hilary's nearness, Major Kraut piloted the plane still farther upwards. The air cut away before and closed behind, calling to Hilary's mind the demon's voice in *The Rime of the Ancient Mariner*: "Fly, brother, fly! more high, more high!" He means to kill me, Hilary thought. All consideration of comradely back-slapping vanished. Hilary resigned himself to the reality that, if he wanted to live, he was going to have to kill Major Kraut.

Notwithstanding the arduous hardship of adhering to the fuselage during the plane's ascent, Hilary saw that the plane's angle gave him one advantage. As he'd told Tanya, the Bleriot XI two-seater had balance issues; if a passenger or the pilot stood during flight, the tail would swing upwards, jerking the plane into a vertical position with the propeller facing downwards, spilling passenger and pilot. This problem had cost Hilary substantial thought during their ascent: he didn't see how he could dislodge Major Kraut from the pilot's seat without tipping himself in the process.

When the plane was climbing, however, Hilary realized that this risk was ameliorated. In any event, risk or no risk, if he didn't do something soon, he had no risk of living.

Hilary opened his mouth and filled his lungs with frozen air. Then, powering himself with a spring from his biceps – almost a leaping push-up – he propelled himself upward and forward so that the bottom of his ribcage caught on the edge of the pilot's berth. His head knocked against Major Kraut's; his left arms clenched across Major Kraut's chest, and his right arm locked around Major Kraut's neck. Major Kraut thrashed, but he remained firmly fixed in the cockpit; Hilary dangled off Major Kraut's body like a coat on a peg.

The aeroplane now began showing signs of strain. A fearful clanging noise filled the cockpit, and the propeller seemed to be emitting a high-pitched whine. Still, choking under Hilary's violent embrace, Major Kraut attempted to stabilize the plane. Accepting that killing Major Kraut would gain him no victory if the plane was destroyed, Hilary allowed Major Kraut to level the aircraft, all the while maintaining an unrelenting grip on the German's body.

Like a ghost ship passing across a parched land, they were sailing across a vast arctic desert, sandy where it wasn't snowy. Mount Kilimanjaro's double peaks loomed on either side of them like icebergs. Looking down, Hilary witnessed his first stretch of African earth completely devoid of animals. Despite the cold, the absence of living beings seemed wrong to Hilary – lonely – "So lonely 'twas, that God himself / Scarce seemed there to be." Frightened, Hilary was overcome with the sensation that the desolate land-drift beneath him was a manifestation of Coleridge's horrified imagination: "Nor shapes of men nor beasts we ken— / The ice was all between."

The barometer showed them nearing 15,000 feet. Hilary might have expired from the awesomeness of the landscape had he not been convinced that he was about to expire from mechanical failure: they were too high.

But Hilary couldn't expire. With Thomas' death only the week previously, Hilary's parents had already suffered beyond endurance. He knew he must survive.

Briefly, he considered appealing to his and Major Kraut's common humanity and shouting, Descend, descend! But with the plane stabilized, Hilary saw that the advantage was his. Girding his abdominal muscles, he pushed himself still farther into the cockpit, locking his feet against the rim of the passenger berth behind him. Then he tightened his hold around Major Kraut's neck.

His hands on the throttle, losing breath with every second, Major Kraut couldn't muster a defense. The environment, moreover, was against him: the air was thin and contained so little oxygen relative to sea level that strangling men lost much of its challenge. "If you kill me," Major Kraut choked in a cracking whisper, "we both die." His words were eaten by the wind, just before he passed out.

When Major Kraut's head slumped to one side and his hands slipped from the throttle like expired insects falling to the floor, Hilary released his grip. He elbowed the Major's unconscious body to the left and reached forward to manage the throttle.

Lying with his belly on the fuselage, his feet steadying him against the passenger's seat, and his hands controlling the throttle in the cockpit, he could fly for some time, if he wanted to fly straight. But Hilary knew that, before long, he'd need to turn. To do that, he'd need to control the tail rudder with the foot pedals, and Major Kraut's body was in the way.

Potentially more urgent, however, were the mechanical issues. Stabilizing the plane hadn't fixed the ghastly clanging sound or stopped the propeller's high-pitched keening. Indeed, the propeller seemed to have begun to hiccup as well.

Incredibly, despite these mechanical failings, Hilary felt the plane turning. Craning painfully against the wind to peer over his shoulder, he saw the tail rudder moving. Snapping his head around to peer into the cockpit, he examined Major Kraut's feet. They were limp and still. Hilary glared at the Major's face; but the unconscious man was not stirring. Whoever – or whatever – was turning the plane, it wasn't Major Kraut.

Reflexively, as unbidden as breath and as automatic as struggling against death, Hilary whispered to himself:

> Slowly and smoothly went the ship,
> Moved onward from beneath.
>
> Under the keel nine fathom deep,
> From the land of mist and snow,
> The spirit slid: and it was he
> That made the ship to go.

Hilary had his answer: the plane was being dragged in one of the mountain's powerful air currents.

* * *

When the aeroplane had disappeared from view, Isak had cast a disgruntled look in the direction of Tsavo. Then he'd turned around and stared in the direction of the Moshi fort. Seeing Hassan, Kamau, Malena and the four former prisoners of war running towards them, with Dionysus sometimes racing back to accompany them and sometimes loping ahead, Isak sighed. "When they reach us," Isak proposed, "we should go."

Tanya couldn't accept this suggestion, but she decided to wait to voice her objections. Hilary, after all, might land the plane on the grassy strip before the others arrived. Tanya closed her eyes and swallowed repeatedly. Her throat was swelling, constraining her breathing.

Then, high above, a sound filtered down. It was a buzzing, mechanical sound. Though she had abhorred the sound when she'd been near it, now, when it was drifting from above, Tanya considered it the finest aural experience of her life. Hilary was alive and safe! Her face was broken open in a smile, the tears streaming from her eyes, before she opened them heavenward.

There, circling Mount Kilimanjaro's lower peak, was the aeroplane. It seemed to be gliding in a duet with the mountain, an invisible synchronicity determining their movements. Leaning back against Isak's massive bulk, Tanya admired the spectacle of humanity's humane victory: it had reduced nature not to a slave, but to a dance partner. Tanya had just time to think that this aeroplane-mountain minuet must mimic angels frolicking in the clouds before the aeroplane crashed into the mountainside.

The auditory result of the crash was as nothing compared to the munitions dump explosion. No one heard the crash. The aeroplane had splintered into the snow. Rather, the void signified the crash: the void of sound, for the engine buzz abruptly ceased; and the void of sight, because the aeroplane suddenly dipped from view, enshrouded hereinafter in the mountain's arctic grave.

Tanya's lips began trembling. She seemed to be mouthing words soundlessly. Her teeth began to chatter.

Isak, puzzled and not even sure what had happened, rubbed Tanya's torso comfortingly.

A warm nuzzle on Tanya's palm drew her eyes downwards. Loyal Dionysus met her gaze with eager eyes and a blood-splotched coat, now dried to a burgundy black. Into her hand, Dionysus proudly deposited his trophy.

It was von Lettow-Vorbeck's other thumb.

Tanya fainted.

Epilogue

Hassan and Kamau were both supposed to be elsewhere. Hassan had a private customer waiting to take possession of the von Brantberg tractor, which Hassan had rented to him for the week. Kamau had rising bread dough that needed his attention. But both were too excited to postpone presentation of the item that the Indian had delivered that morning to the servants' entrance of the von Brantberg plantation house.

They'd waited impatiently at the French windows, while Tanya had attended to the multitude of farm employees and other natives – vagrants, reservation dwellers – who sought her medical care each morning, between 9 and 10 a.m., on the patio. This morning's assembly had included two malarial cases (who had received quinine), one throbbing toothache (to which Tanya had applied clove oil), and an extremely hurting boo-boo (onto which Tanya had swabbed iodine, notwithstanding the child's screams).

This last patient was Tanya's final client of the morning. Hassan and Kamau itched to hurry Tanya, as she carefully tied the fabric bandage onto the little girl's thumb, so that it formed a perfect bow.

Watching the little girl toddle off to her mamma, who sat under a baobab tree on the lawn, Tanya was shown to flattering effect in the mid-morning sun. In her blue and yellow dress, with a fitted bodice and a striped skirt, Tanya was the vision of the noble country lady. The casual observer couldn't tell that the dress was years old and well-mended, more suitable as a costume for a character in an Edwardian-era light comedy than for a real live Baroness.

Her morning's work complete, Tanya turned towards the house. Very recently, Tanya had managed to regain some weight. In the opinion of the entire farm staff, the new look suited her: Tanya had recovered her vitality and banished the haggard appearance to which they'd become accustomed. Strangely (in Kamau's opinion), three more years – hard years of physical toil, financial bitterness, marital disappointment and always gnawing grief – had enhanced Tanya's attractiveness. Her facial and physical features seemed more defined, her expressions more concentrated. Kamau had come to see that Tanya was beautiful. Even Hassan agreed that she was more lovely than obsidian.

At the French windows, Hassan stopped her. "Memsahib, you have heard the news of Lord Delamere?"

A worried look wrinkled Tanya's brow, and she shook her head slightly.

"King George is giving him the British Empire Medal!" Kamau burst out.

Tanya exhaled and relaxed her features into a small smile. She'd feared that the news would be of some incurable illness that had overcome the great man's poor constitution. "I'll send him congratulations this afternoon," Tanya murmured. "Thank you for giving me such uplifting news."

"We think it's unfair," Kamau objected.

"Unfair?"

"We do not think King George gives such honor to ladies," Hassan explained.

"But ladies aren't in the army, Hassan," Tanya placated him.

"You were."

"Well, yes, but no. Not officially. No one knows about that. Not King George anyway."

"That's why it's unfair, Memsabu," Kamau insisted. "You deserve honor."

"That's very kind of you —"

Hassan interrupted her by bringing a cardboard box from behind his back and holding it out to her. The perimeter of the box was just larger than a sheet of typing paper, and the box was about four inches thick. "This honor is for you," Hassan began.

"Even though not from the King," Kamau finished.

Tanya looked back and forth between them. "An honor from you is worth more than from a king," she murmured finally. "What is it?"

"Open it."

Tanya took the box, but her hands were trembling, so she carried it through the French windows into the drawing room, where she placed it on an inlaid table. Carefully, she removed the top. Inside was a sheaf of papers.

Tanya reached into the box and ran her finger along the edge of the pages. "What is this?" she asked again, looking at Hassan and Kamau.

"It's history in a book," Kamau boasted.

"We wrote it," Hassan said simply.

"But neither of you can read," Tanya reminded them, flustered.

"We dictated it to the Indian scribe," Hassan clarified.

"But he only typed it, Memsabu," Kamau added. "We are the authors!"

Tanya looked again at the pile of pages. "You dictated all this? It's too expensive. It must have cost you a year's salary."

"No Memsahib," Hassan corrected her. "Two years' salaries. One for me, and one for Kamau. But we are lucky to not need reliance on our salaries."

"On that point, Hassan," Tanya narrowed her eyes, "did your brother-cousin return our tractor yesterday?"

"Yes, Memsahib," Hassan affirmed, neglecting to mention that he was renting it out again today.

Tanya nodded and turned again to the unbound book. She lifted the sheaf out of the box and fanned its pages. She paused occasionally, skimming passages, lingering over descriptions.

Hassan and Kamau eyed her expectantly, nervously.

Tanya, who'd always been shy of praise, knew that Hassan and Kamau never considered her bursting into tears to be a positive sign, so she endeavored to maintain her composure. "This honor is the finest I shall ever receive," she said softly. She could barely look at them for fear of crying. "I must beg your leave to excuse me," she said, in an even quieter tone that still, for all its near imperceptibility, didn't hide the quaver in her voice. "I want to read this, this honor, this history, immediately."

Hassan and Kamau understood. Her response was only to be expected. No doubt, Tanya's reaction – and the myriads like it exhibited by all women accorded honors – was the motivating factor behind denying women honors in the first place: crying was tiresome. Presenting women with honors was too teary and too wearing on the handkerchiefs.

Hassan and Kamau both extended a handkerchief to Tanya now. She accepted them gratefully, after which the men withdrew to attend to the matters they'd been forestalling.

Once alone, Tanya sobbed until one handkerchief was soaked. Then she blew her nose in the other. Wiping her eyes with her fingers, patting her cheeks and sniffling, she settled the sheaf of papers on her lap. With a final clearing of her throat, she examined the title page – which, though she'd glanced at it earlier, she hadn't absorbed, having been so surprised and flattered by the fact of the gift.

Now she smiled. Her smile was complicated and enticing, the smile of a woman who – by thirty – had already lived enough misery and ecstasy, terror and transcendence, to be worthy of a history called, *Being the Entirely True and Complete Account of the Noble and Heroic Baroness von Brantberg and her Husband Who She Honored in Word and Deed and Sacrifice in Celebration of the Glory and Magnificence of Marriage and the Mysterious British Cause, Which Marvels Were Accomplished with the Assistance and Support of Hassan the Wealthy and Kamau the Philosopher and Gokal the Indian and Malena the Christian and Hilary the Knight and Dionysus the Dog, Who Would Never Have Met and Collaborated and Loved and Served and Mourned One Another If Not for the Empire, Which Is UnJust in Governance and Taxation and Worldview and in Denial of Certain Universal Human Liberties, but Out of Which Emerges Some Excellent Histories ["The Celebration Husband"].*

The song of a strange woman is answered after she is gone.

— Kikuyu proverb

Author's Note

The Celebration Husband is fiction. Although I have worked to ensure historical accuracy (or, where not possible, historical plausibility), I have also taken some liberties for plot purposes. The most extreme instance is that I moved around the order of battles on the East African front during World War I. The attack on Longido happened in November 1914, not in September. Other liberties: the Somalis in Cole's Scouts did mutiny, but not at the time or in the way I described. Lord Delamere did lead an irregular unit tasked with border defense, but his unit did not secretly develop maps. (Indeed, both sides lacked accurate maps for the duration of the war, a failing that cost many lives.) Lieutenant-Colonel Paul Emil von Lettow-Vorbeck was in no way a villain (and he finished the war with all digits on both hands intact): hailed equally for his treatment of his troops and his genius for military strategy, at the close of World War I, von Lettow-Vorbeck was Germany's only undefeated general, widely revered both by the Germans and the British, and in subsequent years he earned a place on Hitler's blacklist.

Despite my manipulations of the facts, I hope readers will consult historical accounts of World War I's East African front. Men and women from Europe, India and Africa collaborated and opposed one another in circumstances of extreme hardship, and more than 100,000 lives were sacrificed in this overlooked and under-studied aspect of the Great War. More widespread knowledge of this episode enriches our present and prepares us for the future, as much as it commemorates the many lives lost.

Acknowledgements

I benefited from the support, knowledge, time, hospitality, and generosity of countless people in the course of writing *The Celebration Husband*, including (in alphabetical order) Fanina Kodre Alexander, Ron Alexandri, Marion Amber, Tom Armstrong, Allan Aywak, Tim Banda, Don Becker, Richard Brecher, Robby Bresson, Lesley-Ann Brown, Timothy Challen, Sharon Chavaka, Tom Cholmondeley, Anne-Sofie Dal, Elli D'Olier, John D'Olier, Shaffiq Essajee, Margaret Gichuhi, Julian Grant, Gillion Grantsaan, Mary Hayley, Kurt Rodahl Hoppe, Susan Jakes, Madeira James, Esther Kingori, Mike R. Klein, Arjun Kohli, Catherine Lefebvre, Peter Lighte, Ladif "Moti" Lone, Nazir Lone, Sabeeya Lone, Talat Lone, Beth Magistad, Gabrielle "Gabi" Menczes, Janice Mitnik, Mark Joel Kiama Mutahi, Angela Karuga Mutinda, Charles Mutinda, Helen Thornton Mutiso, Kenya Mutiso, Grace Mwaura, Nella Nencini, Stephen Rain Okoth Ngala, Joel Bitange Ngero, Jonas Olsarara, Daniel Perry, Judy Pitt, Roman Rollnick, Anne Samson, Hedwig Schmitz, Frances Simpson, Anna Sommerville-Large, Sharad Shankardass, Liza Karuga Snider, Phil M. Snyder, Christian Strebel, D.M. Thomas, Angela Thomas, Wampe de Veer, and James G. Willson. To these kind people I express my deepest appreciation and gratitude.

I am also tremendously grateful to the staff of the following institutions (again, listed in alphabetical order): African Forest Ltd, Karen Blixen Museum, Kenya National Archives, Kenya National Museum Archives, Kilimanjaro Initiative, MacMillan Library, Olepolos Country Club, Rosslyn River Café, Siana Springs, University of Nairobi History Department and Library, Xuni.com, and Yellow Wings.

As inevitably happens, I fear names deserving of mention may have been inadvertently omitted from this list, for which I apologize in advance. All errors of fact or judgment in *The Celebration Husband* are my own.

Suggested Further Reading

Among the books I consulted in researching *The Celebration Husband* are the following, which may be of interest:

Best, Nicholas, *Happy Valley* (1979)

Dinesen, Isak, *Letters from Africa: 1914-1931* (Anne Born, trans. 1981)

Dinesen, Isak, *Out of Africa* (1937)

Dinesen, Isak, *Seven Gothic Tales* (1934)

Dinesen, Isak, *Shadows on the Grass* (1960)

Dinesen, Isak, *Winter's Tales* (1942)

Fox, James, *White Mischief* (1982)

Hill, M.F., *Permanent Way: The Story of the Kenya & Uganda Railway*, vol. 1 (1949)

Hodges, Geoffrey, *Kariakor: The Carrier Corps* (1999)

Hordern, Lieut.-Col. Charles, *Military Operations East Africa*, vol. 1 (1941)

Huxley, Elspeth, *Forks and Hope: An African Notebook* (1964)

Huxley, Elspeth, *Red Strangers* (1939)

Leakey, Lewis S.B., *Kenya: Contrasts and Problems* (1936)

Markham, Beryl, *West with the Night* (1942)

Meinertzhagen, Colonel Richard, *Army Diary: 1899-1926* (1960)

Meinertzhagen, Colonel Richard, *Kenya Diary: 1902-1906* (1957)

Miller, Charles, *The Lunatic Express* (1971)

Mitchel, Sir Philip, *African Afterthoughts* (1954)

Mungeam, G.H., *Kenya Select Historical Documents 1884-1923* (1978)

Oyono, Ferdinand, *Houseboy* (1960)

Rosberg, Jr., Carl G. and Nottingham, John, *The Myth of "Mau Mau": Nationalism in Kenya* (1966)

Thomson, Joseph, *Through Maasailand* (1885)

Thurman, Judith, *Isak Dinesen: The Life of a Storyteller* (1982)

Trzebinski, Errol, *Silence Will Speak: A study of the life of Denys Finch Hatton and his relationship with Karen Blixen* (1977)

von Lettow-Vorbeck, General Paul Emil, *My Reminiscences in East Africa* (1920, 1957 English trans.)

von Mitzlaff, Ulrike, *Maasai Women: Life in a Patriarchal Society, Field Research Among the Parakuyo, Tanzania* (1988)

wa Thiong'o, Ngugi, *A Grain of Wheat* (1967)

Willson, James G., *Guerrillas of Tsavo* (2012)

Wheeler, Sara, *Too Close to the Sun: The Life and Times of Denys Finch-Hatton* (2007)

About the Author

Maya Alexandri lived many years in China and Kenya, and has traveled widely. Trained in acting, and then as a lawyer, she has worked in many capacities, including as a professor, and as a consultant to humanitarian and development organizations. She has been writing novels since 2006.

Made in the USA
Middletown, DE
16 February 2022